I0831936

THE FATAL VOW

Also by Francis Lathom

THE CASTLE OF OLLADA

THE MIDNIGHT BELL

ASTONISHMENT!!!

THE IMPENTRABLE SECRET, FIND IT OUT!

THE MYSTERIOUS FREEBOOTER

ITALIAN MYSTERIES; OR, MORE SECRETS THAN ONE

Also Available from Valancourt Books

GASTON DE BLONDEVILLE
Ann Radcliffe
Edited by Frances A. Chiu

CLERMONT
Regina Maria Roche
Edited by Natalie Schroeder

CASTLE OF WOLFENBACH
Eliza Parsons
Introduction by Diane Long Hoeveler

THE VEILED PICTURE
Ann Radcliffe
Edited by Jack G. Voller

THE ITALIAN
Ann Radcliffe
Edited by Allen W. Grove

GLENARVON
Lady Caroline Lamb
Edited by Deborah Lutz

Gothic Classics

THE

FATAL VOW;

OR,

ST. MICHAEL'S MONASTERY,

A Romance.

BY FRANCIS LATHOM.

Edited with an introduction and notes by
Max Fincher

——————————The fatal vow
Has pass'd my lips! methought in those sad moments,
The tombs around, the saints, the darken'd altar,
And all the trembling shrines with horror shook.

THOMSON.

Kansas City:
VALANCOURT BOOKS
2011

The Fatal Vow by Francis Lathom
First published London: Richard Crosby, 1807
First Valancourt Books edition 2011

ISBN 978-1-934555-88-0

Published by Valancourt Books
Kansas City, Missouri

Composition by James D. Jenkins
Set in Dante MT

10 9 8 7 6 5 4 3 2 1

CONTENTS

INTRODUCTION

UNTIL recently, Francis Lathom was remembered primarily as one of the authors of the 'horrid' novels that the fashionable Isabella Thorpe gives to her young naive friend, Catherine Morland, to read in Jane Austen's *Northanger Abbey*.[1] *The Castle of Ollada* (1795), *The Midnight Bell* (1798), *Astonishment!!!* (1802), *The Impenetrable Secret* (1805) and *Italian Mysteries* (1820) have all been republished by Valancourt Books, and show that Lathom was particularly successful in writing Gothic fiction, showing a strong vein of Ann Radcliffe's influence.[2] However, with *The Fatal Vow* (1807), Lathom helps to shape three inter-related literary and cultural changes. Firstly, he helps to break the influence of Radcliffean Gothic on popular fiction that predominated post-1800, with many writers slavishly imitating Radcliffe, by reinvigorating the genre of 'historical Gothic'. Secondly, Lathom's use of the conventions of the fiction of Sensibility complicates Romantic representations of the figure of Richard the Lionheart as embodying a distinctly British, brave, valorous chivalry. And thirdly, Lathom's novel provides further evidence that popular writers at the turn of the nineteenth century were experimenting with the genre of historical fiction long before the rise of Sir Walter Scott in the Regency period.

Certainly, Lathom was by no means the first to write historical-Gothic. Horace Walpole, in his first preface to *The Castle of Otranto* (1765) had claimed that his story was a 'translation' based on real events, 'between 1095, the era of the first crusade, and 1243, the date of the last, or not long afterwards'.[3] Sophia Lee's novel, *The Recess* (1783-85), set during the reign of Elizabeth I, is widely considered to be one of the earliest and most influential English novels of historical fiction, one which contains many Gothic elements in its tale of two imprisoned heroines.[4] Lee's novel was a direct influence upon many writers, at home and abroad, including Lathom's first attempt at historical fiction, *The Mysterious Freebooter; or, The Days of Queen Bess* (1806).[5] Both Lee and Lathom had a background in the theatre and wrote plays. Possibly, Lee's novel with its suspense, drama and cross-dressing encouraged Lathom to take her work as a model for his own historical-gothic fiction. Furthermore, Lathom may or may not have been aware of Richard White's novel, *The Adventures of King Richard, Coeur de Lion*, published in 1791, which we might consider as the first novel to represent Richard I.

Similar to Walpole's novel, *The Fatal Vow* is set in the era of the Crusades. Yet in contrast to Walpole, Lathom draws upon and exploits real characters and events from medieval English history for dramatic purposes. Walpole's characters are from a rather nebulous Neapolitan aristocracy, which is revealed to be fictitious in the second preface to the novel. *The Fatal Vow* features Richard I (Richard the Lionheart, 1157-1199), during the Third Crusade in 1189, and when he was imprisoned in Trivallis Castle by Duke Leopold of Austria on his journey home. The novel also includes Richard's mother, Eleanor of Aquitaine and her nemesis, Rosamond de Clifford, who was one of the many lovers of Richard's father, Henry II. Initially however, the story starts some time earlier, and has all the hallmarks of two of the most popular fictional genres of mid-to-late eighteenth century fiction: the novel of Sensibility and the Gothic novel.

Christabelle Glencowell, a recluse, lives in Rousseauistic isolation with her father, Glencowell, in a cottage on the coast of Cornwall. A lover of music, she is a young woman of exceptional 'rareness' and like Radcliffe's heroines possesses 'the most sweetly expressive voice' (4). Singing to herself sitting on the cliffs one day, she attracts the attention of an enigmatic young man, Reginald de Brune, a mysterious stranger. Reginald is staying on retreat in the local monastery of St. Michael's, 'to forget' his 'misfortunes' (8). Subsequently, we discover that Reginald is Richard I. Charmed by Christabelle, Reginald falls in love with her. Father Benedict, the abbot of St. Michael's, tells Reginald that Christabelle has been sworn to secrecy by her father over their real identities. Concerned that Reginald is becoming too enamoured of his daughter, Glencowell sends her to a convent. Wandering on the cliffs at night, a 'prey to torturing sensations' (35), Glencowell slips and falls over a cliff, his secret dying with him. Prior to his death, Christabelle promises him that she will 'never make an attempt at tracing out my mother, by her resemblance to the lineaments of her portrait' (40), setting up an expectation for the reader that Christabelle is perhaps an illegitimate child. The device of the miniature, revealing a lost or hidden history, is one that Radcliffe employs in her novel *The Italian* (1797) when the nefarious monk, Father Schedoni, is about to murder Ellena di Rosalba at night in her bedchamber, discovers that she is in fact his daughter.[6]

At this point in the novel Lathom's admiration for Radcliffe and Lewis also emerges in the stock setting of a repressive convent. Christabelle, prevented from communicating with Reginald, is confined to the subterranean dungeons of the convent in the manner of the character of Agnes in *The Monk*, accompanied by tombs and dark passageways.[7] Her friend, Sister Corally, promises to aid her escape with the help of Corally's secret lover, Ranulph de Barthe, a soldier in the army of Prince John, stationed in the forest outside the convent. While escaping from the convent, Christabelle meets Reginald, who is discovered to be Prince Richard.

Lathom then backtracks considerably for several chapters to the period of Henry II, specifically to that of Richard and John's parents, Henry II and Eleanor of Aquitaine. The narrator describes Eleanor of Aquitaine as suffering from 'disquietude of mind', possibly meaning mental instability and that 'jealousy had crept with its destructive poison into her breast' (70). In line with eighteenth-century historiographies of Eleanor, she is also painted as an ambitious woman who favours Richard, and sows the seeds of discontent between her sons. This family history describes how the spurned son, (Richard) whom the father (Henry) feels no affection for, becomes the object of a possessive love of the mother (Eleanor). Walpole had established this familial triangle in *The Castle of Otranto* where Manfred despises his 'sickly son' Conrad, the idol of his mother. The main purpose of this backstory is to enable Lathom to explore his characteristic themes of secrecy, by leading us to a dramatic scene of confrontation in the maze at Woodstock Bower between Eleanor and Rosamond de Clifford.

However, deferring us this narrative pleasure, we are taken temporarily back to Reginald and Christabelle in the monastery of St. Michael's. On the advice of Eleanor, Richard is on retreat in the monastery of St. Michael to cool down, after discovering that his father Henry has cheated on him with a prospective bride-to-be, Adelais, one of the daughters of Louis IV of France. Richard tells Christabelle that he will take her from the monastery and that she will be under the protection of Eleanor at Beaumont palace in Oxfordshire, where Christabelle duly goes. Learning of Henry's affair with Rosamond, Eleanor and Christabelle, in disguise as itinerant minstrels, visit the gardens and maze at Woodstock Bower. Here, Eleanor confronts her rival, Rosamond, and stabs her in front of Christabelle. Christabelle has discovered, via the miniature portrait her father has given to her, that Rosamond is in fact her mother, and that she is her daughter, Matilda. Again, a lengthy explanatory chapter follows to explain to us this mystery. We discover that Glencowell is Walter de Clifford, Rosamond's husband, and that Christabelle is their daughter, who will now be known as Matilda. Matilda now laments that she can never be Richard's wife after learning that Richard's father, Henry II, seduced her mother, Rosamond, and that Richard's mother, Eleanor, has now murdered Rosamond. In true Gothic mode, Eleanor goes into a convent to atone for her crime and slowly expires.

The second volume of the novel is taken up with Richard and Philip of France's involvement with the Third Crusade against the Emir, Saladin of Palestine, but specifically with Richard's return through Austria. Richard is imprisoned by Duke Leopold of Austria who takes revenge on him for taking down the Austrian flag from the battlefield at the Siege of Acre and putting up the English standard. Nevertheless, the novel fails to really exploit the full Gothic potential of Richard's imprisonment in Trivallis. Instead, the novel explores Richard's emotional state. Like one of Radcliffe's heroines, alone and imprisoned in the Gothic fortress of Trivallis, Richard weeps over his fate: 'the tear stole down his cheek, and he sat for some moments with his face buried in his hands' (176). One evening, he is approached by Zulima, a native of Palestine who has followed him from Acre. Zulima is in love with him after he took pity on her dying father on the battlefield. Cross-dressed as a soldier, Zulima offers to help Richard gain his liberty if he will agree to marry her. Richard refuses, protesting that he has already pledged his love and hand to Matilda and will not break his vow. In reality, by all accounts, Richard was extremely reluctant to marry. Meanwhile, back in England, Matilda (Christabelle) hears news of Richard's capture. She resolves to rescue him and bring him back to England. Cross-dressing as a male minstrel, she travels to Austria and manages to effect his escape disguised as a soldier. Richard is proclaimed by her to be the true heir to the crown. However, he does not marry Matilda, who dies of a brain fever.

The extended summary of the story I have provided above gives an idea of how the narrative shifts between different times and locations, (confusing chronological accuracy) and its labyrinthine complexity, which is common to all Lathom's novels. The story of *The Fatal Vow*, broadly speaking, falls into that story type which Richard Maxwell describes as found in the historical novel of the dethroned or absentee monarch, who is usually imprisoned, who attempts to reclaim the throne, epitomized of course by Sir Walter Scott's *Waverley* (1814).[8] A recurrent theme running through the story is that of disguising one's real identity, often by reversing one's class and gender positions, which I comment on below.

Contemporary critical reaction to the novel was mixed. Both the *Monthly Review* and the *Annual Review* objected to the novel on the grounds of factual inaccuracy, and that Lathom is, in contemporary terms, wearing his research on his sleeve.[9] In particular, the reviewer for *The Monthly Review* noted: 'Even in works of this nature, the facts which are disputable, yet generally received, should not be altered on slight grounds; and those which have been handed down to us by respectable historians as undoubted truths should not by any means be perverted.' Importantly, Lathom's 'perversions' (a significant adjective that I explore below in a different context) include the legend that Eleanor of Aquitaine may have possibly murdered Rosamond de Clifford in the maze at Woodstock Bower and the 'invention' of Richard's retreat to a remote Cornish monastery in disguise. However, others praised Lathom's 'invention', his capacity to 'please the mind of sensibility' and his ability to develop a renewed interest in the age of chivalry epitomized by Richard the Lionheart. In his preface to the novel, Lathom unashamedly pre-empts critical objection to the charge of factual inaccuracy. 'Respectable historians', such as the eighteenth-century historian and philosopher David Hume, are themselves, as Lathom says, not entirely certain as to many of the facts of this period: 'as their [events] ever having existed is by no means ascertained, I cannot be accused of having violated truth by having dressed them in the colours of my own fancy'.[10] The legends and inventions around the historical figures in this period, Henry II, Eleanor of Aquitaine, Richard I, and Robin Hood, continue to proliferate in fictional narratives today and testify to a continuing romantic (and some might argue, nationalistic) interest in this period.[11]

One can find support for Lathom's defence of the novelist's right to employ his own fancy in some observations that William Godwin makes on the historical novel. Godwin's argument suggests that Lathom's use of his 'fancy', or in modern parlance, his creative imagination, is to be commended: '. . . the noblest and most excellent species of history, may be decided to be a composition in which, with a scanty substratum of facts and dates, the writer interweaves a number of happy, ingenious and instructive *inventions*, blending them into one continuous and indiscernible mass' [my emphasis].[12] If, as Godwin argues, the writer of romance (i.e. the novel) is able to 'impress the heart', a circumstance that the contemporary reviewers felt Lathom's novels did achieve, then as Godwin argues 'in this point of view, we should be apt to pronounce that romance was a nobler species of composition than history'.[13]

Godwin's defence of the historical novelist's artistic license is also echoed by Sir Walter Scott in his first English historical novel, *Ivanhoe* (1820).[14] With the rediscovery of *The Fatal Vow*, we might ask whether we can reclaim Lathom as another historical writer who redefines the genealogical scope of the historical novel for us, especially in perhaps helping to establish a groundwork for later writers like Scott.[15] As Anne Stevens argues, eighteenth-century historical novelists before Walter Scott have been categorized in three limiting ways: (1) 'gothic', (2) 'national tales', and (3) 'inferior forerunners to Scott'. In his 'dedicatory epistle' to *Ivanhoe*, Scott, under the guise of Laurence Templeton, writes to his imaginary antiquarian friend, the Reverend Jonas Dryasdust, in a vindication of writing a historical novel whose subject is Old England. Like *The Fatal Vow*, *Ivanhoe* is set during the time of Richard's captivity in Austria, and the expectation of when he would return home to reclaim the throne from his brother John. Scott observes: 'I cannot but think it strange that no attempt has been made to excite an interest for the traditions and manners of Old England, similar to that which has been obtained in behalf of those of our poorer and less celebrated neighbours [i.e. Scotland, referring to the *Waverley* novels]'. I have been able to find no evidence in Scott's correspondence or diaries that Scott knew of *The Fatal Vow* or of Lathom's work generally. But, clearly, both Richard White's *The Adventures of King Richard* and Lathom's *The Fatal Vow* force us to revise Scott's assertion that he is the first novelist to be interested in the subject of Richard I and the 'manners of Old England'.[16] Moreover, in both eighteenth century and Romantic poetry and drama, there are precedents for some of the legends and inventions that Lathom exploits, especially around Rosamond de Clifford.[17]

Nevertheless, Scott's epistle or preface to *Ivanhoe* outlines a set of creative paradigms with which we can reassess Lathom's effort at historical-Gothic as a positive contribution to the development of both the Gothic and historical modes in the early nineteenth century. In this preface, Scott defends the principles of writing historical fiction, light mocking the figure of the antiquarian scholar, Jonas Dryasdust, and his reservations about the limited factual knowledge romance writers possess about the period of 'Old England', especially the psychology of its characters. To a certain degree, Lathom fulfils many of Scott's observations on how *not* to write historical fiction, as he outlines them in his introductory preface, particularly in how Scott advocates that the subject of the writer's imagination needs to be 'translated into the manners, as well as the language of the age we live in' (18), and an appeal to universal human emotions. However, unlike Scott, Maria Edgeworth and Lady Sydney Morgan, Lathom's literary project is not to depict the manners of a nation in an ambitious, socio-political narrative; the *zeitgeist* of late twelfth-century England is not high on Lathom's agenda. There is no mention of Robin Hood for instance, and there are no epic tournaments or lengthy descriptions of Saxon-Norman relations and battle scenes as we find in *Ivanhoe*. Instead, drama, mystery and the passionate emotions of his leading characters are where Lathom's interests reside.[18] In fact, forgiving the rather routinized conventions of Sensibility that are employed, one could argue that Lathom breathes a degree of emotional life into Richard I that Scott later takes up in *Ivanhoe* and *The Talisman* (1825). In contrast to the bold, proud, fearless, even brutal man of action (if we are to believe Hume), Richard is presented as very much an eighteenth-century man of feeling.

Why was Lathom particularly interested in the character of Richard the Lionheart? The reasons may of course be varied. But, to return to the reviewer's objection in *The Monthly Review*, to Lathom's 'perversions' of the facts of history, one possible idea is that Lathom may or may not have been aware of the belief that Richard was 'homosexual' or to describe it even more accurately, queer.[19] However, this is slippery territory to negotiate. Any evidence to 'prove' that both Richard and Lathom were queer, would have been in the most negative of terms, e.g. a conviction of sodomy. Instead, we have to read between the lines of their biographies, and in Lathom's case, his fiction. The themes of social mobility, secrecy and the instability of class and gender positions are found everywhere in Lathom's novels. These themes may possibly reflect Lathom's own preoccupation with his uncertain origins and his love for other men. There is a strong possibility that Lathom was queer as we would describe it today. Socially gregarious, immersed in the world of the Norwich theatre, he left a successful career as a writer and actor to live on a farm in rural Aberdeenshire. Here, he established a home with another man, possibly his lover, and set up a drama school for the locals, and travelled extensively in Europe.[20]

To justify the theory that Lathom may have been interested in Richard as queer, we might refer again to Scott. Reflecting on the problem the historical novelist faces in (re)constructing the private faces and voices of real historical personages, Templeton observes:

> The scantiness of materials is indeed a formidable difficulty; but no one knows better than Dr. Dryasdust, that to those deeply read in antiquity, *hints* [my emphasis] concerning the private life of our ancestors lie scattered through the pages of our various historians, bearing, indeed, a slender proportion to the other matters of which they treat, but still, when collected together,

> sufficient to thrown considerable light upon the *vie privée* of our forefathers.[21]

Perhaps some of these 'hints' Scott mentions, those that illuminate the 'vie privée', might point to a subject's sexual preferences? Could David Hume's description of Richard's 'voluptuousness', a term associated with the idea of luxury and moral degeneration in the eighteenth century, be marking Richard as queer?[22] In short, could Lathom be one of the earliest writers to be queering history through fiction by portraying Richard as, simultaneously, both resolutely heterosexual, but also attracted to women who cross-dress as men? It is a fascinating possibility, but such a suspicion only remains a possibility.

Contemporary historians have drawn attention to Richard's possible erotic relations with men, particularly Philip IV of France, his travelling companion on the journey to Palestine for the Third Crusade.[23] What characterizes twelfth-century chroniclers' accounts of Richard's queerness is its unspeakability; any sexual relations between Philip and Richard can only be hinted at by being described in terms of 'love'. However, as Robert Mills asks: 'why assume that if we do not have proof positive of Richard's homoerotic inclinations that he must, therefore, by a process of elimination, be stably 'heterosexual'?[24] For much of the time, Richard lived in France, and in the masculine, homosocial environment of the battlefield, where the boundaries between male bonding and sexual desire become readily exchangeable. It is impossible to know whether Lathom could have been aware of Roger of Hovenden's accounts of Richard. Certainly, there is no exploration of the relationship between Philip and Richard in *The Fatal Vow*. But it can be argued that Richard is portrayed in the novel as less than 'stably heterosexual', even if he cannot be shown to be an outright queer.

Certainly, both historical and fictional accounts of Richard in the Romantic period play up an image of Richard as a fearless, brave, proud English knight, defender of the Christian faith and an emblem of soldierly masculinity. School children were brought up to believe that Richard the Lionheart was a model of male heroism: 'of all the real histories of wars, that of the war between

Richard and Saladin is the most heroical: Richard performed feats of personal valour that are almost miraculous'. In Thomas Dibdin's *A Metrical History of England* (1813) Richard is addressed as 'a gallant Prince' renowned for his hand-to-hand combat: 'who in each battle did the work, | Of cleaving Saracen and Turk, | And kept the Infidels at bay, | While jealous Philip walk'd away!' (lines 13-16, p.179). The comparison of Richard's physical courage to Philip of France's cowardice suggests that there was a degree of nationalistic investment in representing Richard as a Englishman unafraid to get his hands bloody, at a time when the English were fighting Napoleon's troops.

However, one way that Lathom's novel signals the instability of Richard's masculinity is through the motif of cross-dressing that occurs throughout the story. In late eighteenth and early nineteenth-century culture, the practice of cross-dressing was much more closely linked to being queer, such as at masquerade balls and in secret places of rendezvous for men, such as the eighteenth-century molly houses in London.[25] When Richard is imprisoned in the castle of Trivallis, Zulima, a woman who has followed him from the siege of Acre, gains access to his apartments in disguise as a male soldier. The narrator suggests that Richard is attracted to the masculine quality of bravery in Zulima, an otherwise 'strikingly beautiful' woman: 'Richard listened with astonishment to her narrative. There was a peculiar energy of mind in the character of Zulima, which charmed him' (XXX). The reversal of gender expectations, and the consequent and baffling attraction to one's own sex, continues when Richard is 'charmed' by a male minstrel singing in the courtyard below his window. The song he/she sings is a ballad that was sung to him by Christabelle (Matilda), and Richard feels unaccountably 'charmed' by the minstrel:

> The voice too by which it was now singing appeared to him not less similar to hers than was the resemblance of the song itself. He could scarcely believe that the effect at this moment produced on his senses owed its being to any other cause than that of magic. (192)

Later on, Matilda adopts Zulima's disguise as a sentinel, guarding Richard's door to gain access to him. When she manages to rescue Richard and bring him home, she appears on horseback in full battle armour at the camp of 'King' John at Wallingford to proclaim Richard as the rightful king of England. Transformed from Christabelle, the weeping heroine of Sensibility to the cross-dressing, intrepid Matilda, there is the suggestion that Richard is attracted to her ambiguous gender.

Despite the conventional, moralistic tone of the conclusion warning the reader against 'the uncounted miseries which flow from an infringement on the sacred honours of the marriage bed' (240) the novel destabilizes the chivalrous warrior and heterosexual Richard through the reversal of these gender positions. Richard is portrayed via the conventions of the Gothic, as an effeminized, powerless victim rescued through the agency of his cross-dressing lover whom Lathom causes to die from a brain fever so he cannot marry after all. There is just one possible hint in the novel that may refer to Richard's sexuality, and which is worth commenting on. Adrian Thelk, a character in Duke Leopold's army, is joking about Richard's character with his fellow soldiers in a tavern. Unaware that Richard is present in disguise, Thelk concedes: 'although the noble Duke and I have a quarrel against him, I must not belie him. Good soldiers ever speak the truth. And I do not believe that Richard's honour was ever tarnished by *a wound in his back*' (169). Significantly, the meaning of Thelk's observation is not immediately transparent to his audience, suggesting that a 'wound' may signify something more than just a physical injury. Thelk explains that 'a wound in the back' is a metaphor for cowardice, suggesting that a soldier has run from the enemy, while a wound in the front is 'deemed creditable and glorious', signifying bravery (169). Could there be another layer of meaning to this seemingly innocent and comic dialogue? Could the wound in the back also be a metaphor for sexual relations between men? While a wound in the front signifies heterosexual prowess? Such an interpretation may be wildly arbitrary, another 'invention' that relies on the very framework of suspicion that still circulates around both Lathom's and Richard's sexual biographies. Nevertheless, with the rediscovery of *The Fatal Vow*, we have now another portrait of

Richard I to add to the gallery, one which complicates our image of Richard the lion-hearted as an emblem of masculinity. We also have a novel that helps to steer the direction of Gothic fiction back towards its roots in medieval history, and suggests a counterpoint to the vision of Richard that has been enshrined through Scott's novels.

MAX FINCHER

MAX FINCHER is an independent scholar and author of *Queering Gothic in the Romantic Age: The Penetrating Eye* (Palgrave, 2007). He has written a screen adaptation of Matthew Lewis's novel *The Monk*, entitled *Ambrosio*, and is currently finishing his first novel, *The Pretty Gentleman*, a queer historical thriller set in the early nineteenth-century London art world.

NOTES

1 Jane Austen, *Northanger Abbey, Lady Susan, The Watsons and Sanditon*, edited by John Davie, introduction by Terry Castle (Oxford: Oxford University Press, 1990).

2 Ann Radcliffe was the most popular and influential female Gothic novelist of the 1790s and wrote *The Castles of Athlin and Dunbayne* (1789), *A Sicilian Romance* (1790), *The Romance of the Forest* (1791), *The Mysteries of Udolpho* (1794), *The Italian* (1797), and *Gaston de Blondeville* (published posthumously in 1826).

3 Horace Walpole, *The Castle of Otranto and The Mysterious Mother*, edited by Frederick S. Frank (Peterborough, Ont.: Broadview Press, 2003), p.59. Walpole is considered to be the first Gothic novelist.

4 Sophia Lee, *The Recess*, edited by April Alliston (Lexington: The University Press of Kentucky, 2000). Alliston, arguably, claims that Lee 'ushered in the great vogue of Gothic fiction in England', p.xii.

5 Alliston documents the novel's international influence and success. She notes that 'the novels that seem closely and specifically to follow *The Recess*' include Lathom's *The Mysterious Freebooter* (1806) as well as Sir Walter Scott's *Kenilworth* (1821).

6 Ann Radcliffe, *The Italian*, edited by Robert Miles (London: Penguin, 2000). See Vol. II, ch.ix.

7 Matthew Lewis, *The Monk*, edited by Christopher Maclachan (London: Penguin, 1998).
8 Richard Maxwell, *The Historical Novel in Europe 1650-1950* (Cambridge: Cambridge University Press, 2004), p.5.
9 See Appendix.
10 David Hume, *The History of England, from the Invasion of Julius Caesar to the Revolution in 1688*. Hume's history was reprinted several times throughout the late eighteenth and early nineteenth centuries.
11 The question of whether Eleanor of Aquitaine murdered Rosamond de Clifford continues to interest contemporary writers, as shown most recently by the publication of Ariana Franklin's novel, *The Death Maze* (in the United States, *The Serpent's Tale*) published in 2008. The legend of Robin Hood has been endlessly retold, its most recent incarnation being by the film director Ridley Scott, *Robin Hood* (2010).
12 William Godwin, 'Of History and Romance' in *Political and Philosophical Writings of William Godwin*, edited by Mark Philip (London: Pickering & Chatto, 1993). See Vol. 5, 'Educational and Literary Writings', edited by Pamela Clement.
13 Ibid., p.299.
14 Sir Walter Scott, *Ivanhoe*, edited by Ian Duncan (Oxford: Oxford University Press, 1998).
15 Both Richard Maxwell and Anne Stevens have reassessed the scope and range of historical fiction before Sir Walter Scott. Richard Maxwell, *The Historical Novel in Europe, 1650-1950* (Cambridge: Cambridge University Press, 2009) and Anne H. Stevens, *British Historical Fiction before Scott* (Basingstoke: Palgrave Macmillan, 2010).
16 Thomas McLean has recently drawn attention to Scott's friendship with the historical novelist Jane Porter, and Jane Porter's later conviction that 'her novels had influenced Scott's subsequent work'. While I am not suggesting that Scott knew of Lathom's novel and deliberately ransacked his ideas, I am correcting Scott's assertion that he is the first novelist to represent Richard I. Thomas McLean, 'Nobody's Argument: Jane Porter and the Historical Novel', *Journal for Early Modern Cultural Studies* 7:2 (2007) 88-103.
17 Joseph Addison wrote an opera *Rosamond* in 1707, and the story of Eleanor of Aquitaine murdering Rosamond in the maze at Woodstock Bower occurs in a ballad by Deloney in Thomas Percy's *Reliques of Ancient English Poetry* (1765), which Lathom may well have read. Renewed interest in the character of Richard the Lionheart is also evident in Romantic poetry. Sir James Bland Burgess (1752-1824) published his epic poem about Richard, *Richard the First*, in 1801.

Thomas Dibdin includes Richard in his *A Metrical History of England* (1813). And Felicia Hemans wrote two poems about Richard I, 'The Troubador, and Richard Coeur de Lion' and 'Coeur de Lion at the Bier of his Father', published in her collection *Tales and Historic Scenes* (1819), a year before *Ivanhoe.*

18 In her introduction to *The Recess*, Alliston observes that 'it must be remembered that, toward the end of the eighteenth century, the only "realism" aimed at by, or expected from, such fiction, was located in the reality of the emotions evoked through readers' sympathetic identification with characters, not in any verisimilitude of plot or situation', pp.x-xi.

19 Both terms may seem anachronistic to describe same-sex relationships in both early nineteenth century and late twelfth century England. 'Queer', as I use it, describes those relations between men or women who experience or express desire for one another in a variety of ways that elude pre-existing, often imposed identity categories (often with negative connotations) like 'homosexual', 'sodomite' or 'tommy'. See my *Queering Gothic in the Romantic Age: The Penetrating Eye* (Basingstoke: Palgrave Macmillan, 2007) pp. 12-16 and Anne-Marie Jagose, *Queer Theory: An Introduction* (New York: New York University Press, 1996) for further discussion.

20 For a full account of Lathom's biography, see both James D. Jenkins's edition of *The Castle of Ollada* (Chicago: Valancourt Books, 2006) and David Punter's introduction to his edition of *The Midnight Bell* (Kansas City: Valancourt Books, 2007).

21 Scott, *Ivanhoe*, p.16.

22 Hume notes that Richard 'carried so little the appearance of sanctity in his conduct' and that the curate of Neuilly 'advised him to rid himself of his notorious vices, particularly his pride, avarice and voluptuousness'. Hume, *The History of England*, Vol. II, ch. X, p.6.

23 John H. Harvey in his book, *The Plantagenets: 1148-1485* (Batsford, 1948) was the first historian to draw attention to the contemporary chronicler, Roger of Hovenden, who recorded that Philip and Richard had shared sleeping arrangements while travelling to Palestine. Hovenden records that 'they loved each other so much that the king of England was absolutely astonished at the vehement love between them and marvelled at what it could mean'. See also Marion Meade, *Eleanor of Aquitaine: A Biography* (London: Phoenix, 2002). However, John Gillingham interprets Richard's relations with Philip as simply political and Platonic. See John Gillingham, *Richard I* (New Haven, London: Yale University Press, 1999).

24 Robert Mills, 'Male-male love and sex in the Middle Ages, 1000-1500' in Matt Cook, *A Gay History of Britain: Love and Sex Between Men Since the Middle Ages* (Oxford: Greenwood Publishing, 2007).

25 See Terry Castle, *Masquerade and Civilization: The Carnivalesque in Eighteenth Century English Culture and Fiction* (London: Methuen, 1986) and Rictor Norton, *Mother Clap's Molly House: The Gay Subculture in England 1700-1830* (Stroud: The Chalford Press, 2006).

NOTE ON THE TEXT

The text of the current edition is taken from the two-volume first edition held by the British Library, and published in London in 1807 by B. Crosby & Co.

In general, the novel's original spelling, punctuation, and capitalisation have been retained, including any errors. However, I have glossed any unfamiliar words, and where Lathom's spelling of proper nouns differs from modern conventions e.g. 'Acquitaine' for 'Aquitaine', 'Guynath' for 'Gwynedd', I have indicated these differences in the notes. A couple of obvious printer's errors have been silently corrected.

THE

FATAL VOW;

OR,

ST. MICHAEL'S MONASTERY,

A Romance,

IN TWO VOLUMES.

BY FRANCIS LATHOM.

AUTHOR OF THE MYSTERIOUS FREEBOOTER—MEN AND MANNERS—HUMAN BEINGS—MYSTERY—THE IMPENETRABLE SECRET—THE MIDNIGHT BELL, &C. &C.

VOL. I.

——————————The fatal vow
Has pass'd my lips! methought in those sad moments,
The tombs around, the saints, the darken'd altar,
And all the trembling shrines with horror shook.

THOMSON.

LONDON:
PRINTED FOR B. CROSBY AND CO. STATIONERS' COURT,
By C. Stover, Paternoster Row.
1807.

PREFACE.

Historical romances are the taste of the times; and I think it a sufficient sanction for an author whose remuneration is to arise from gratifying the public taste, to apply his pen to such subjects as interest the feelings of the majority. The critics frown upon a too free use being made by novel-writers of historical facts; but surely the most rigid cannot object to their laying claim to such events as, although mentioned in history, are doubted even by historians themselves; of this nature will be found many of the characters and circumstances interwoven in the subsequent tale: as their ever having existed is by no means ascertained, I cannot be accused of having violated truth by having dressed them in the colours of my own fancy; and I am equally certain that the cause of morality will not be a sufferer by the contents of my pages—the first and perhaps only important point for an author to consider, who writes only for the amusement of his readers.

THE

FATAL VOW;

OR,

ST. MICHAEL'S MONASTERY.

CHAP. I.

If music be the food of love, play on,
Give me excess of it.
That strain again: it had a dying fall:
O, it came o'er my ear like the sweet South,
That breathes upon a bank of violets,
Stealing, and giving odour.

SHAKESPEARE.*

I.

WHO knocks at the door of this cottage so slowly,
Who asks for the remnant of poverty's meal?
'Tis a poor female pilgrim, all sun-burnt and weary,
For whose fate all the sons of humanity feel.
Gentle pilgrim, prithee say,
Whither lies thy weary way?
I've strayed o'er the wold, and I've strayed o'er the wild,
In hopes to find him whom my presence might save;
O, ye saints lead me to him, O, tell him I'm true!
And preserve him from sinking in youth to the grave.

II.

My father's a yeoman, and wealth is his idol,
For truth and for love, he forbade me to wed

And far from his door drove the faithful young Ferrand
Who a bride to the altar my footsteps had led.
Seeking him, I've bent my way
Many a long and weary day.
I've stray'd o'er the wold, and I've stray'd o'er the wild,
In hopes to find him whom my presence might save;
O, ye saints lead me to him, O, tell him I'm true!
And preserve him from sinking in youth to the grave.

III.

Wide open the door of the cottage flew quickly,
And the pilgrim sunk down on the earth as it mov'd,
For the latch had been lifted by that very Ferrand,
For whom her affection so fully she'd prov'd.
Gentle pilgrim, swift he cries,
'Tis your true love bids you rise.
You have stray'd over wold, and you've stray'd over wild,
Love has led you to him whom your presence can save;
O, ye saints take our thanks, O, ye saints grant our pray'r,
And preserve us from sinking in youth to the grave.

These words sung by the most sweetly expressive voice, and accompanied by the soft tones of a lute, arrested the attention of a young man, who was with slow steps ascending a winding path that led from the sea-shore to the brow of the over-hanging cliffs.

The time was evening; the golden rays of a departing sun were glittering on the bosom of the deep, and the calmness of the atmosphere was such, that the expanded sail gave no celerity to the vessel floating on the glassy surface of the waves—and when the voice of the songstress ceased its melodious warblings, universal silence prevailed.

The young man entranced with the sounds which he had heard, stood fixed to the spot where they had first struck his ear, hoping that they would quickly return; and as his wish was not accomplished, he felt inspired with curiosity to learn who had been the songstress.

Neither the words of the song, nor the manner in which they had been sung, had been at all similar to what he could have expected from the wives or daughters of the fishermen who inhabited the coast; and from this conviction, he felt the more eager to learn what being of a superior order, there could be residing in such a spot such as this was, at the extremity of the county of Cornwall.

The period at which our history opens, was in the thirty-fourth year of the reign of Henry the second of England;* a time at which females only of the first rank had any skill in the science of music; and these were so seldom, except on holidays, to be encountered without the walls of their father's castles; or of the convents, to the superiors of which the training of their minds to religion, the almost single branch of education bestowed on them, was entrusted; that the surprise excited in the breast of the auditor of the unknown songstress, was naturally great, in proportion to the rareness of the instance.

The only habitation near to him, was a small cottage upon the margin of the cliffs, of which the thatched roof peeped over some full leaved elms, which formed a circular defence round the lonely dwelling. The young man advanced towards it, and as he approached, he discovered an archway formed by the twined branches of the trees, in the centre of which was a small gate that formed the entrance—moving on a few steps, he perceived near the door of the cottage, two figures of the most interesting nature: the first was a man whose appearance denoted him to have seen at least fifty summers; his countenance was handsome, its expression was manly and stern; his dress was neat, without ornament; it bespoke neither courtier nor the peasant, but a happy mean between both—he was seated on a sod of green turf; his eyes were raised to heaven, and his hands were clasped together upon his breast.

By his side upon a wicker chair, on the back of which hung a lute, sat a female of the most blooming beauty; her eyes were fixed upon the man with an expression of that nature, which most eloquently bespoke her to be in the performance of a filial duty; and one of her hands was placed upon his shoulder, as if desirous that her touch should arouse him from his trance of thought. Her age appeared at most eighteen; the richness of her charms was heightened by the simplicity of her dress, which was composed of a loose grey robe that flowed to her feet; the fairness of her skin was not less dazzling than the lustre of her dark brown eyes, with the hue of which corresponded the luxuriant tresses that flowed down unrestrained upon her shoulders. If the sound of her voice had inspired him with pleasure, what was the delight which he experienced in the contemplation of her lovely person; he stood fixed on the spot, and probably, had he not been interrupted in his admiration, his trance would have continued till the descending shades of night had closed the interesting picture from his view; but a spaniel, which had been sleeping at the feet of his master, chancing to awake, instantly ran towards the little gate, and by his barking, announced a stranger to be at hand.

The man immediately started up, and perceiving our young enthusiast, stepped forward, and with a voice of displeasure said, "What is your business here, Sir? Have you any with me?"

He paused a moment, as if awaiting the reply of him whom he had addressed, and perceiving him at a loss how to answer, he continued, "I judged you could not have any business with me; I beg therefore that you will leave this spot; the only boon I ask in life is solitude; and I will not suffer its negative charm to be broken in upon by intruders."

"Grant me your pardon, Sir, for my offence," replied the young man, "I was passing this way, and"——

"Pass on then, Sir, I entreat you," rejoined the former with emphasis, and going to the female, took her hand, and leading her into the cottage, he closed the door.

The youth towards whom this inhospitality was exercised, was a stranger to that part of the kingdom in which the occurrence had taken place. About three months before the opening of our tale, he had arrived at the monastery of St. Michael, which was situated upon the coast, about half a league eastward of the cottage, from the gate of which we have just described his dismissal; and was introduced to the brothers of the holy mansion by their abbot, as a youth named Reginald de Brune, who was come to reside for some time under his protection, in the quality of a boarder of the house.

Father Benedict, the abbot of whom we have just spoken, was a man greatly beloved and valued by the community of which he was the superior; whose will it was a satisfaction to them to make their law; and as he forbore to give any account of the family of Reginald, or of his motives for seeking a temporary asylum within their walls, no attempt was made to dive into his history. The young man was in his twenty-sixth year, of a handsome person, engaging countenance, and athletic form; he was possessed of a strong and manly understanding, which had enjoyed the advantages of the ablest cultivation that the advancement then made in knowledge could afford him; and in the polite acquirements he was equally pre-eminent, as in the more valuable ones of the mind.

These endowments alone could have bespoken him of superior birth, had not his attire, though plain, been marked by an elegance unknown to the common degrees of life; the idea which he endeavoured to convey of himself was that he was the son of a gentleman, who wished to pass some time in solitude and study, and who had for that purpose chosen the monastery of St. Michael for the scene of his retirement from the world; which story was propagated by one only attendant whom he had brought with him, and who was called Arnold.

This Arnold it was easily to be perceived, was not less the friend and confident of Reginald de Brune, than his attendant; and till the present evening had always accompanied him in his walks since his arrival at the monastery, but he was then otherwise employed in the service of his master; he had set out on horseback in the morning from St. Michael's, and was expected to return to it again in the evening; no one but himself, Reginald, and their friend the abbot, knew whither he was gone; and our readers must submit to be kept in the same ignorance; we shall, however, give them one piece of information which was not known to the brothers of the monastery: that Arnold brought back with him letters which were of great satisfaction to his master.

Having read these letters, and given some time to reflection upon them, Reginald imparted to his confident his adventure of that evening; and requested him to make some inquiry who the pair he had seen were.

Arnold listened with pleasure to Reginald's account of the young girl, and said, "It gives me happiness to hear you thus ardent in your description of her charms; may she possess the power to efface from your mind, that impression which"——

"Arnold, my friend," interrupted Reginald, "have we not agreed never to speak upon that subject again?"

"Pardon me," rejoined Arnold, "I was not about to speak of its existence; I hoped for your permission to congratulate you on its being utterly vanquished by the brilliancy of her charms whom you have this evening beheld."

"Pray do not revive the theme of my misfortunes," answered Reginald, "recollect that I am come hither to forget them." And having given this admonition to his friend, he retired to one of the cloisters of the monastery, where he continued to wander alone till the hour of retiring to rest.

CHAP. II.

> I could a tale unfold, whose lightest word
> Would harrow up thy soul.*
>
> Shakespeare.

Reginald de Brune had been so entirely lost in thought, as to have been totally insensible to the progress of the night; for the illumination of a resplendent moon rendered it almost a rival of the day; till the voices of the monks bursting upon his ear, united in the hymn which concluded their midnight devotions, recalled his attention to outward objects, and he immediately returned towards the door from which he had entered the cloisters.

He found it locked; the porter of the monastery, had, he concluded, been ignorant of his absence, and closed it at the usual hour. He was on the point of knocking at the door in order to demand admittance, when he recollected that the entrance was so far removed from all the inhabitants of the place, as to render it almost impossible that his knock should be heard; near a door in the opposite cloister he had understood that the porter slept, and thither therefore he resolved to go, as the most likely place for him to gain admittance to his chamber.

In his way to this second door, he was obliged to pass through the northern cloister, which ran parallel with one side of the church; and as he moved along, a ray of light which fell obliquely on his eye, arrested his attention; and he perceived that it was occasioned by the reflection of the moon beaming through a spiral window,* upon the light grey stone which formed the pavement of the church; and which a small door opening upon one of the side aisles, was thrown just sufficiently back upon its hinges, to give him a partial sight of.

He instantly resolved to profit by this inlet for entering the monastery without disturbing any of its inhabitants; he went in, and found that the monks were already retired, and the lamps extinguished. That window only which was placed above the door through which he had gained admission, was so situated as to convey any light into the church from the brilliancy of the moon; and when Reginald had proceeded a few paces towards that part of the building, which was to lead him to the passage from whence a flight of steps conducted to his chamber, the darkness became almost totally unrelieved.

It was that week of the year in which the passion of him who died for the salvation of man, was solemnized with a due observance of mourning pomp; and every saint, every altar which the church contained, were covered with a black drapery appropriate to the season; which concealed every lucid metal, every slab of polished marble, and left no resting place for the floating beams of the planet of night.*

As he cautiously passed a massive pillar upon which the hand that he had extended for the purpose of his preservation from the projecting tombs and shrines which crowded the place had fallen, and which led him into the nave of the church, the faint glimmering of a lamp caught his eye. It was placed upon the table within the railing of the altar, and upon the second step knelt a form, corresponding in dress with that of the female, whom he had that evening beheld at the cottage on the margin of the cliff.

He stood fixed in surprise, and almost ceased to breathe. As he continued to gaze, objects became more perfect to his view, and he beheld a dusky figure standing by her side, whose head was bent down towards her; and in slow and solemn accents he heard him addressing her; but he was too far removed from the altar to be able to distinguish what his words were.

Impelled by that curiosity, which, although natural to the mind of man, is excusable in its gratification only in proportion to the unpremeditated licence which we allow ourselves in that gratification; he approached a few paces nearer to the spot where they were stationed, and scarcely had he ascertained that the male figure was the same which had that evening so inhospitably treated him in his ramble near the shore, than the solemn tone in which he heard him say, "Swear this, I charge thee, swear!" caused him involuntarily to shudder, and to cast a look of awe upon the funereal appearance of every object by which he was encompassed, and of which the mournful hue seemed to increase the solemnity of the stranger's injunction.

The female spoke, but in accents so faint, that they did not reach the ear of Reginald.

The man again addressed her, but his words were breathed with an impressive stillness into her ear, which rendered them only partially audible at the distance at which Reginald was stationed from them—the words which he heard were, "*never to search out for lineaments of face resembling these; never to address or acknowledge that being who——even though it were possible that——never,* UNLESS IN THE DYING MOMENTS OF REPENTANCE, *when——the hand of God should interfere to——so unlooked for a re-union——swear to these terms in the oath which I——and thy wish shall be accomplished.*"

Supporting herself from sinking to the earth, by placing one of her hands upon the arm of the man, the female after a short pause, raised her eyes towards heaven, and having whispered forth some words, which in all probability constituted the oath which her companion had exacted from her, she in louder accents concluded her sentence with, "*I swear!*"

As soon as she had pronounced these words, the man drew from his pocket a small black case, and opening the lid, he held it before the eyes of the female, accompanying his action with the words, "Behold, then, the portrait!"

The lovely girl snatched it into her own hands, and having gazed upon it for some moments, she pressed it fervently to her lips, and repeatedly kissed it; again she fixed upon it her eyes—again she raised it to her lips—a third, a fourth, and a fifth time she repeated these actions, and with every repetition the earnestness of her feelings seemed to increase; while the man clasped together his hands, and stood with his face buried in them. At length, he placed his hand upon the portrait in order to take it again into his own possession. "One minute longer, I entreat," said the female.

This request was granted; and when, at the expiration of the sued-for time, he again extended his hand towards it, her supplication was renewed, "O, consider," she exclaimed, "that this is all I have of a"——the remainder of the sentence died away upon her tongue.

"I promise you, that you shall behold it again," returned the man; and upon this promised, although with evident reluctance on her part, she restored to him the portrait, and he placed it again in his pocket.

Having done this, he knelt down by her side, and they applied themselves to silent prayer.

While they were thus employed, Reginald unable to tear himself from the spot, stood wondering, not less how they had gained admittance within the walls of the monastery, than at the mysterious business in which he had seen them engaged. At the expiration of an hour, the man rose from his knees, "Come Christabelle,"* he said, "let us return." The female directly complied with his request, and her conductor having placed the lamp in a lanthorn which had been deposited at the foot of the altar; drew her arm through his, and carrying the light in his other hand, they left the church by the door at which Reginald had entered it; and he heard the key move in the wards of the lock, from which he concluded that they had fastened it on the outside.

CHAP. III.

> I see men's judgments are
> A parcel of their fortunes, and things outward
> Do draw the inward quality after them,
> To suffer all alike.
>
> SHAKESPEARE.*

No sooner had Christabelle and her mysterious conductor left the church, than Reginald retired to his chamber, where a great part of the night was past by him in reflection on the occurrence of which he had been a witness; and on the following morning, he seized the first opportunity which was given him, for conversing apart with his friend, the abbot, to inquire who the pair were that he had seen, and what could have been the occasion of their midnight visit to the church of St. Michael's monastery.

Father Benedict heard his account of what related to the portrait with evident marks of surprise, and when he ceased speaking, the father said, "Of the occurrence which you last night witnessed, I can give you no explanation, my son; all I am acquainted with concerning those personages who have excited your curiosity, I may freely impart to you; first, because I know too little of them to give you any insight into their real history; and next, because I have never received from them any injunction to keep that little secret."

"You are then acquainted with them?" returned Reginald.

"Whence else should they have procured the key which admits them nightly into the church attached to this building?" replied the abbot, "but you shall hear:—it is now nearly eighteen years since the close of a stormy evening in the month of November, the brothers of this house were disturbed by a loud and unusual knocking at the outward gate of the monastery. The porter proceeded to the grate, and returning almost immediately into the refectory, brought information that there was without, a venerable looking female, accompanied by a fisherman, well known to us upon the coast, at whose cottage, she said, lay dying, a gentleman, in the fate of whom she felt the most lively interest, and entreated, that one of the brothers of the monastery would come and administer to him the last sacraments, ere he quitted life.

"Our former abbot was at that time alive, and I only a brother of the order; and it so chanced, that I was commissioned to attend the sick man. In my way to the cottage, I inquired of the female, whether it was a son of her's to whom she was conducting me? 'No,' she replied, 'no relation, merely a friend, a most valued friend;' and after a short pause, she added, 'but he has a relation with him, for whom, I implore God, and the virgin to prolong his existence.' Who is that relation? I asked. 'An only child,' she answered.

"On arriving at the cottage, I found him for whom my assistance had been entreated, in bed. It is needless for me to describe to you his person, for you have already beheld it; suffice it to remark, that to have judged from his countenance at that time, you would scarcely have supposed him to have lived a third of those years with the appearance of which corroding grief has now marked his features; I approached the bed, and as I stood gazing upon him, I beheld the wildness of phrensy in his eye, and on taking his hand, which was extended on the outside of the bed, into mine, the heat of a burning fever met my touch.

"Another brother of our monastery, named Austin, who was skilled in the art of physic, had accompanied me; he examined the symptoms of the sick man, and declared to me, that his patient was more ill in mind than in body. After a time he fixed his eyes upon us, and sent forth a groan of the most afflicting nature. 'Where is your pain?' asked Austin. 'In my heart, and in my head,' replied the stranger; by which answer he confirmed the opinion that father Austin had formed of his case.

"I knelt by the side of his bed at the request of the female who had summoned us to the cottage, and began to pray; he heard me with attention through one prayer, and then said, '*I* have not offended heaven; *I* have no forgiveness to pray for; I am nevertheless ever ready to pay it my devotion.—Go on, go on, if you please,' he added, after a pause.

"I continued reading to him for nearly half an hour; he appeared to gain composure from my words, and, as I rose from my knees, with a second groan he sunk back upon his pillow, and closed his eyes.

"'Oh mercy, mercy, holy Jesus!' cried the old dame, 'he is expiring!'

"Father Austin explained to her, that no evil of that nature was to be apprehended; that his malady was upon his mind; and that sorrow was a disorder, which although it wear the spirit of life to its extremity, is still slow in the progress of the devastation which it makes.

"'His griefs are of a mighty, of an unparalleled nature,' she returned.

"Who is the gentleman? I asked.

"'His name,' she replied, 'is Glencowell.'

"A Welsh name, I returned.

"'I believe it is,' she said.

"'And his history?' rejoined father Austin.

"'That you will never know from me,' she answered, 'nor from him, I dare venture to affirm; however from me, I am certain you never will: he has sworn me to secrecy; he need not have done that to ensure him the fidelity of old dame Frances; but I have lived to see that men may be driven by the weight of calamity, to distrust even their firmest friends.'

"I understood that your friend had an only child with him, said I, but I suppose I was mistaken.

"'No, you were not,' she replied, 'sweet babe! in yonder crib sleeps a little angel, who has never yet seen a Christmas morn.'

"Glencowell had overheard our conversation, and exclaimed, 'Protect, protect her heaven; shield her from vice; remove her from the evil of temptation!'

"'Amen, amen,' sighed out dame Frances, and went and placed herself upon a stool by the side of the crib.

"Having passed nearly two hours at the cottage, and finding that repose was the only beneficial medicine which could be administered to him whom we had been called to visit, father Austin promised to provide him with some drops, for the purpose of composing his mind; and learning that he did not wish us to prolong our stay, we departed, taking with us the fisherman to bring back the medicine to his lodger.

"In our way to the monastery, he related to us such particulars as he was acquainted with concerning his guests; he said, That having been on the preceding day to a market town in the neighbourhood, to sell some fish, as he was returning home towards evening, along a solitary road which led away from the hamlet of St. Michael, to a sequestered spot where his cottage stood at some distance from the margin of the cliffs, he overtook a man who was leading a horse, upon which sat a woman, supporting in her arms an infant.

"The light was just sufficient for him to distinguish objects, but not features; and he would have passed by them without speaking, had not the man called out to him inquiring, Whether there were any house near at hand, where he could procure refreshment, and a lodging?

"'I replied to this inquiry in the negative,' continued the fisherman. 'Great God! what will become of us?' exclaimed the man, on receiving this information. 'I am myself too ill to be able to proceed further to-night; my aged companion is sinking under fatigue, and my poor babe'—— his utterance became suddenly checked, at it appeared, by his tears.

"'The wind was blowing sharply from the North, the rain and sleet were falling mingled from the sky, and driving in large sheets along the air; the infant was shrieking with the smart which it experienced from the cold; it was a scene that went to my very heart; and explaining to the man that my dwelling was one of the humblest of lowly roofs, I added, that if it would be any relief to him to pass the night in such shelter as it was capable of affording him, he should receive at it a humane reception.'

"'What are the great,' he exclaimed, 'in comparison to thee? How much nearer art thou allied to heaven in that feeling which thou displayest for my wretched situation?'

"'I conducted them to my cot,* and no sooner had they entered it, than it appeared as if the strength of the man had been measured to the journey he had been destined to perform, for he sunk upon a bed, and lay gasping for breath, while the tears rolled down his quivering cheeks.

"'They had with them no change of garments, and whilst my wife furnished the old woman and child with a change of apparel from her coarse wardrobe; I bestowed the gentleman's steed in a hut adjoining to my cottage, and immediately returned to administer to the relief of its master.

"'As comfortable a meal as it was in our power to provide, we served up to them; but repose was the refreshment of which they stood most in need; and having insisted on their occupying the only two beds of which we were possessed, we made up a straw pallet for ourselves in the outer room of our dwelling.

"'This morning we found the gentleman by far the least amended of the three, by the repose of the night; the whole day he has refused all substantial nourishment; and towards the evening, his fever ran so high, that dame Frances judged it necessary to entreat from the brotherhood of your monastery, assistance both for his body and his soul; on which errand to your holy mansion she insisted on accompanying me, fearful as it seemed, of her request not being attended to, if she did not make it in person.'

"This was all that the benevolent fisherman knew of his guests. Father Austin detained him but a few minutes at the monastery, and dispatched him back with the medicine, and instructions in what manner to administer it to his patient.

"In the course of the following day, Father Austin and myself again visited the stranger, we found him sitting up in bed, and contemplating his infant daughter, whom he held in his arms. He did not appear to notice us on our first entrance, and we heard him say, 'For thy sake, sweet bud of innocence, I have made a vow to heaven to live out the portion of life which it hath allotted to me; my vow is therefore incomplete if I do not exert myself to fight against this destroying grief which swells my heart.'

"He paused, and we addressed him, inquiring after his health.

"'It is as well as it probably ever will be,' he replied. 'I am glad you are come, fathers—I thank you for your attendance last night; for I think I recognise in your persons the same holy men who then visited me; I beseech you, let me have your prayers for the endowment of my mind with patient suffering.'

"We immediately complied with his request, and dame Frances joined fervently in our devotions.

"We continued regularly to visit him twice every day, and perceived that he struggled effectually, according to the promise which we had overheard him make to his unconscious child, to subdue that poignancy of sorrow, which, if indulged, must have led to a hasty termination of his existence.

"On the sixth day we found him risen from his bed, and his countenance less distorted by the writhings of affliction than we had yet beheld it; having conversed with him, he requested us to join with him in a prayer which he had been composing; we complied with his petition, and the lines on which he laid the greatest stress, contained these words, and were thrice repeated in the course of the prayer:—'Lead the guilty to repentance, and preserve the innocent from temptation.'"

"Those very words I heard him last night pronounce at the altar," said Reginald, interrupting father Benedict in his narrative, "have you ever discovered to whom they refer?"

"Never," replied the father, "he has so closely concealed from every one his history, just as dame Frances informed us that he would do, that I have not been able to form any idea, who are the guilty for whose repentance he never omits to pray; it appears most likely that it is for the preservation of his daughter from temptation, that he petitions heaven; indeed, I have little doubt of it, from the tender regard with which he viewed her the first time I ever heard him repeat the prayer of which these words form a part."

"I beg your pardon for having interrupted you in your relation," said Reginald, "pray proceed."

"It is nearly concluded," returned the abbot. "On the seventh day after Glencowell's arrival at the fisherman's cot, he requested to walk with us near the sea for the refreshment of the air; and in the course of our stroll, he informed us, that having experienced a misfortune of a very severe and domestic nature, it had once been his intention to quit England for ever; and for this purpose he had been approaching towards the coast, when encountered by the poor fisherman to whose humanity he considered his child to owe the preservation of her existence; but that judging it possible for him to live as much retired from observation on the spot where he now was, as he could do in any foreign country, he had changed his intention; and wished to procure some small, but comfortable dwelling in the vicinity of our monastery. 'My wish,' said he, 'of being able to settle my residence at a short distance from your holy mansion, arises, not from any desire of maintaining an intercourse with your brotherhood; for my powers of companionship are all dead within me, and I am but as a vegetable in the society of men; but because I shall derive a satisfaction from attending divine service in your chapel; for which indulgence I shall crave permission of your abbot; and it is almost the only request of which a refusal could give me pain.'

"Before we parted from him, he commissioned us to make application for him to this effect to our abbot; who judged it becoming in him to grant his request; and from that time he has been a constant attendant upon the morning and evening service of our house. Some difficulty for a length of time attended the procuring him a habitation of the nature he wished to find; but at last we placed him in the one before which you yesterday evening beheld him, and his daughter sitting. He rewarded the humanity of the fisherman in the most liberal manner; and he appears to be possessed of the means of procuring for himself and his child every comfort; although it is equally a secret whence these means proceed, as is the cause which drove him from the world to the retirement he now lives in. I have however been able to gather one most satisfactory conclusion from the general tenor of his conduct, which is, that the pangs of grief with which he is even now not unfrequently racked almost to phrensy, proceed not from the remorse of any guilty action which he has himself committed, but from the recollection of some cruel injustice which he has received at the hands of others. Who they are, heaven and himself alone know. I have accidentally heard him drop expressions which have appeared to hint that his wrongs have flowed from those either high in power or affluence; for with the possessors of these qualities, with the severity natural to those who have been sufferers at their hands, he constantly couples the epithets of tyrants and oppressors."

"O, why will not the great display themselves truly pre-eminent in their pursuit of virtue!" exclaimed Reginald; "but we need not an afflicted Glencowell to tell us that they use their power to shield their vicious inclinations from punishment; and to lash those actions as crimes in their inferiors, which it is an offence against their dignity for others to consider even as errors in themselves."

"Cease, cease my son, revert not to that which you must for your own happiness endeavour to obliterate from your memory; for the wounds which injustice inflicts, heaven has always a balm in store; no more, no more of this; you feed discontent by dwelling on the causes from whence it arises," answered father Benedict.

"Had I endured my wrongs from any man but a father!"—— said Reginald—the signal for dinner was now sounded, which constrained them to break off their conversation and enter the refectory.

CHAP. IV.

I might call him
A thing divine; for nothing natural
I ever saw so noble.

SHAKESPEARE.*

WHEN a second opportunity presented itself to Reginald de Brune for conversing in private with his friend the abbot, he said, "But as I have before told you, on the night that I observed Glencowell in devotion at the altar of St. Michael, his daughter was with him; is it customary for her to attend him to the church of this monastery?"

"For the last five years," replied the abbot, "he has frequently brought her hither to attend matins;* but I am not acquainted with her ever having visited the church at the hour of midnight prayer, till the night on which you beheld her there: our midnight devotions," he continued, "are those at which it affords her father the greatest satisfaction to be present; it is even frequently an indescribable relief to his mind to continue in the chapel in reflection, some hours after the monks have left it, and every light is extinguished; and in order to gratify him in this respect, that he might not be obliged to retire from it at any stated hour, on my becoming the abbot of St. Michael's, I presented him with the key of that door, by which you saw him depart. Nor are his nightly wanderings confined to the chapel of our monastery; sometimes upon the margin of the cliffs, at others upon the lonely beach, will he wander the greater part of the night, and mingle his sighs and groans with the roaring of the waves."

"And has the fair Christabelle no companion in her father's absence, but the old dame Frances whom you told me of?" asked Reginald.

"She has not even her," replied father Benedict; "the good old Frances has been many years numbered with the dead. Poor Christabelle wept for her, as for a mother. Her father dislikes the intrusion of servants, and therefore with some occasional assistance from the widow of that fisherman who so humanely received them into his cottage on the first night of their arrival in this neighbourhood, she contrives to obviate the necessity of domestics—contented most, when she can content her father."

"Exquisite, angelic Christabelle!" exclaimed Reginald.

"One day when I chanced to pass the cottage, and she was alone in it," rejoined the abbot, "I inquired of her if she did not feel the want of a companion? 'I have my father,' she replied. But in his absence from home? I continued. 'Then I have my lute,' she answered, 'and I am generally employed when he is abroad in some little business or other, which shall give him pleasure at his return; and the anticipation of a smile from him for my reward, is a reflection which makes my time pass much more happily than any conversation could do.' But are you never alarmed when left by him in the night? I rejoined. 'Oh no,' she returned, 'the night you know, holy father, is the same as the day to those who have an easy conscience; I have done no wrong, and therefore I fear no injury.'"

"How I envy you the delight of conversing frequently with a being of so preeminent a nature!" said Reginald.

"Not frequently," replied the abbot, "it is very seldom indeed that I have any intercourse with her; whenever I encounter Glencowell in my walks, about the hamlet, I never speak first to him; as he has told me that there are moments at which it occasions him the most acute agony to have his reflections broken in upon; and his eyes are so usually fixed upon the ground that he repeatedly passes without observing me; and it is not once in a year that I see Christabelle, either at home or abroad without him; so my opportunities for conversation with her are very few indeed."

Reginald continued to express his admiration of the lovely and virtuous Christabelle, and the abbot listened to him with attention and adjunction in the justice of those praises which he bestowed on her; but although he, as seriously as Arnold, wished a former impression to be chased from the mind of his young friend, still he did not, like Arnold, desire the daughter of his solitary neighbour Glencowell, to take the place of that image which now filled his heart; as he judged her to be one whose unfortunate situation in life, would but breed fresh cause of anxiety for Reginald. Glencowell had repeatedly said, "My name and history shall die with me. I will not permit a knowledge of either, even to my child. It will be her greatest bliss to die unknown in spotless purity." A declaration of this nature was sufficient to place an irremoveable obstacle between Reginald and his affections, if his affections fell on her in the person of his father, at whom Reginald has already hinted, as having been the destroyer of a plan of happiness which he had sketched out for himself; and on this account father Benedict hoped that love would not succeed the admiration which he now professed himself to entertain for her beauteous person, and her perfect mind.

The reception which Reginald had met with from Glencowell on the evening of his first beholding him and his daughter, determined him from again wandering near the cottage which they inhabited, either alone or in company with Arnold; he therefore pressed the abbot to stroll with him towards it, as he judged him to be the only person, in whose society it might be possible for him to enjoy a momentary gaze at the charms of the fair Christabelle.

From the cause which we have already stated, father Benedict felt averse to procuring his young friend any opportunity of adding fuel to the flame which he feared he saw kindling in his breast; and therefore threw every impediment he could devise in the way of their meeting. For a length of time he succeeded in keeping them asunder to his wish; for Reginald by constant reflection with his own mind having analyzed the nature of the admiration which he felt for the daughter of the mysterious Glencowell; and decided that she was the woman with whom it would constitute his felicity to pass his future days in the rosy fetters of marriage, had forbore an attempt even at beholding her when she visited the church of St. Michael, to be present with her father at the performance of the midnight prayers; if she ever did again visit it with him at that solitary hour at which he had once seen her there; lest, should he be discovered in the meanness of being a spy upon their actions, it might determine Glencowell never to permit his daughter to receive his addresses; and having once resolved upon an honourable profession of his passion, he was become as careful of offending those objects from whom the accomplishment of his desires was to proceed, as true love ever displays itself.

He had himself constantly attended the midnight prayers, and likewise the matins in the church of St. Michael's monastery; but that part of it appropriated to the use of Glencowell and his daughter, was at his particular desire skreened by a curtain from the view of the monks, and other devotees assembled in the church; and to have watched the arrival and departure of Glencowell at the door by which he entered, would have been an infringement on those observations of respect which he had laid down to himself to maintain towards the silent sufferer and his daughter.

Arnold was by accident acquainted that Christabelle had twice been her father's companion to matins since the evening Reginald had beheld her in rapture bending over the portrait which she had received from the hand of her parent, at the altar of St. Michael; but whether she had ever been present at the midnight solemnities of the place, he had not been able to learn without overstepping those rules of caution which his master had enjoined him not to overstep, and therefore had forborne to seek information upon that point.

Nearly a month had elapsed since Reginald's first sight of the songstress of the cliffs, when having been invited by father Benedict to an evening walk upon the beach, they descended the cliffs, after the hour of vespers,* and lighted equally by the last rays of day, and the silver splendour of a rising moon, they pursued their way along the sands. As they moved onwards, they observed two figures advancing towards them, which on nearer approach they discovered to be Glencowell and his daughter; the light was not sufficiently strong for them to recognise each other's persons till they had arrived within a few paces of one another; and just at the moment that Reginald and his companion had discovered who they were, Glencowell and Christabelle suddenly stopped, and father Benedict and his young friend by a momentary observation, saw that they were prevented from proceeding by a creek across the beach which the flowing tide had filled with water.

This was a moment which appeared to Reginald to admit of an offer of service on his part to Christabelle without the possibility of incurring the displeasure of her father, and running hastily through the water, he begged permission to carry her across it.

"I thank you, Sir," said Glencowell, "she would I *dare say* be safe in your arms, but in mine I *am sure* she is so;" and whilst speaking he snatched her up, and bore her to the other side.

When Reginald and the abbot had first beheld Christabelle and her father stop, it was evident that they were hesitating in what manner to pass the run of water which it was necessary for them to cross in their way home; and the hastiness with which Glencowell had since determined on carrying her through it, plainly indicated that he had seized the first method which had presented itself to him, to prevent her being held in the arms of him who had offered to lend her his assistance.

"I am sorry you have wetted your feet to no purpose," said Christabelle, with the utmost modesty and respect, when Reginald had repassed the water. Reginald assured her how happy he should have been, if he had been permitted to have been of the service to her which he had desired to be.

Reginald was at the instant he thus expressed himself by her side; Glencowell pressed himself between them, and drawing Christabelle's arm through his, he said, "Such slender inconveniences are thought lightly of by us; we can ford creeks, and climb cliffs to escape worse dangers;" and having said this, he turned away from Reginald and the abbot, and led Christabelle up a cliff, amidst the rugged knots of which, no path had probably ever been attempted before.

This conduct on the part of Glencowell could want no explanation to Reginald and his holy friend; he had evidently obliged his daughter to climb the rugged rock in order the more hastily to remove her from the presence of Reginald; the abbot suffered the incident to pass unremarked; after a silence of some moments the disappointed Reginald said, "I am still so unfortunate as to be an object of Glencowell's dislike."

"Any stranger would be equally so," returned the abbot.

"And it seems alike his wish," returned Reginald, "to preserve his daughter from all intercourse with her fellow beings."

"It is undoubtedly his intention, that she should never form any connexions in life," answered father Benedict, who judged it becoming in him to prevent by every means in his power the growth of a passion in the heart of his young friend, of which he foresaw that the consequences could not be of a nature conducive to his happiness.

"If he wishes her to live an isolated being in society," said

Reginald, "why does he not place her in the retirement of a convent? Why permit her to be a spectatress of those happy bonds of union which are enjoyed by other beings like herself; and of which she is never to taste the felicity? If it is to her that those words of his prayer refer, which entreat for the preservation of the innocent from temptation, it is the demand of a weak mind, which can for an instant suppose, that the regular course of nature will be changed at the petition of an individual."

Father Benedict could scarcely forbear a smile at the warmth of his young friend, although he was sorry to behold that warmth in the cause of the mysterious Glencowell's daughter. He continued silent, and Reginald sunk into dissatisfied reflection.

If from the hints which our readers have received of the heart of Reginald having been subject to another impression, at the time of his first becoming an inhabitant of the monastery of St. Michael, they should now be condemning the fickleness of his love, for having in the course of one short month transferred itself to another object; let them be lenient in their judgment, till the secrets of his history are disclosed to them.

CHAP. V.

> He, wrapt in clouds of mystery and silence,
> Broods o'er his passions.
>
> WALPOLE.*

ON reaching the monastery, Reginald found his friend Arnold just returned with letters, which he had as usual been to some unknown distance to receive. One of these letters contained matter which he wished to lay before his friend the abbot, and accordingly on the following morning after matins, he followed father Benedict for that purpose into his private apartment. Scarcely had they entered it, ere one of the monks came to the door, and said, "That Glencowell was waiting in the hall of the monastery, and requesting to see the abbot."

Father Benedict remarked that this was a very unusual demand on his part; and apologizing to Reginald for the necessity which he said he felt himself under of not returning a refusal to his request, Reginald withdrew till their conversation should be at an end.

During his absence from the abbot's apartment, Reginald thought only of what might be the business of Glencowell with the superior; he could not divest himself of the idea that this visit bore some relation to himself; he considered it probable that Glencowell might be come to make such inquiries concerning him, as if satisfactorily answered might induce him to permit his acquaintance with his daughter; equally probable was it that he might have visited father Benedict in order to demand of him to interdict all attempts at intercourse between himself and the fair Christabelle.

Glencowell entered the apartment of the abbot with a countenance more than usually indicative of a mind ill at ease; he approached the father, and standing opposite to him whilst he addressed him, for he regularly refused the accommodation of a seat, or the relief of throwing aside his hat, when chance brought him to the monastery at any hour but that of devotion; probably supposing that a compliance with these forms carried with it an air of ease, or comfort, of which he felt himself incapable; he said, "You are the only man in whose friendship I confide; the only one whose counsel I would deign to ask; acquaint me where in this county there is a convent of gentle rules and ordinances, in which I may place my daughter for life."

"Is it then your intention, my son," asked father Benedict, "to part with your only companion?"

"Do not render me dissatisfied with having asked advice of you," replied Glencowell, "by comments on my resolutions; it is impossible that you can form a correct judgment of them, because you know not the motives from which I act." After a pause, he added, "Where is there a convent of the nature I wish to find?"

"I know no one more answerable to the comforts which you appear to wish your daughter to enjoy in a conventual life, than that dedicated to St. Ursula."

"At what distance from hence?" asked Glencowell.

"Not a day's journey towards the east," replied the abbot.

"And you can undoubtedly furnish me with an introduction to the abbess?" inquired Glencowell.

"We are not personally acquainted," returned father Benedict, "but my name is well known to her, and my recommendation will not fail to procure you your desired end."

"Prepare me a letter which shall procure us admission, against to-morrow's dawn," returned Glencowell; "to the protection of St. Ursula, and the holy mother of her house, I will deliver up my daughter, although the last fibre of my heart snap at the moment of our separation. Farewell—I thank thee!" and he was departing.

"Stay yet an instant," said the abbot, recalling him, "permit me to ask, nor deem it an impertinent curiosity, whether any sudden cause has driven you to this determination of committing your daughter to a religious solitude for life; or, whether it has ever been the"——

"Must I repeat to you twice," answered Glencowell, "within so short a space of time—search not into my motives, they are impenetrable!" He paused a moment, then added with a tremulous voice, "Could'st thou be a father in my situation, thou would'st feel that it is a father's first duty to preserve the innocence of his daughter from temptation;" and having uttered these words, he darted out of the apartment.

When Glencowell had left the monastery, Reginald was again admitted to the presence of the abbot; the youth had entirely forgotten the letter of which he had before been about to impart the contents to his holy protector, and remembered only Glencowell's unexpected visit; of which he directly inquired the motive.

The abbot did not attempt to conceal from him the intention of the mysterious inhabitant of the cottage on the margin of the cliffs relative to his daughter; nor was it in the power of Reginald, had it been his inclination, to confine to his own breast, the despondency which this intelligence communicated to his heart.

Father Benedict besought him to listen to the arguments of reason, and in the most eloquent and impressive manner set before his view, the insurmountable obstacles which would be opposed by his family to his union with one whose origin was maintained so inviolable a secret: and besought him to reflect on the fresh source of anxiety which his perseverance in forming an alliance of this nature, would create for himself, and those who were desirous of his real happiness.

In reply to these arguments the youth could only appeal to the force of excessive love, and advance that all happiness was founded in opinion, and that therefore the most interested in his fate could not act towards the felicity of his future life with the same certainty of its accomplishment, as he must be able to do for himself.

His feelings rose almost to madness when informed that Glencowell intended to set out with his daughter for the convent of St. Ursula on the following morning; and nothing but the strict injunctions of the abbot to the contrary, would have withheld him from seeking the father of his adored Christabelle, and with the confession of his love for his daughter, making him acquainted with his real name, and rank, and imploring him to favour his passion.

"Could every objection which I have stated to your union with Christabelle be obviated," remarked the abbot, "you are not acquainted that her sentiments with regard to you are similar to those which you entertain for her!"

There is a language of the eyes which even at first sight of an object which inspires passion, gives the lover some faint acquaintance with the ideas which are passing in the heart; and from those of Christabelle on the first evening of Reginald's beholding her, he had been led to believe that her opinion of him was not an unfavourable one; of her sentiments concerning him, he had no other criterion by which to judge.

"Besides," rejoined the abbot, "although she enters the convent to-morrow, a year must elapse after her admission into it, ere she can be permitted to pronounce those vows which will impose on her the restraint of never again emerging into the world."

"In that reflection there is at least a shadow of hope, a ray of comfort!" sighed forth Reginald, and sunk into thought.

CHAP. VI.

Why speaks my father so ungently? This
Is the third man that I e'er saw; the first,
That e'er I sigh'd for: pity move my father
To be inclined my way.

SHAKESPEARE.*

THE sway of nature is omnipotent, and universal; it matters not whether the sons and daughters of mortality be nursed on the cheerful bosom of society, or in the barren lap of a desert—those passions, those inclinations which are the inheritance of human beings, still exist in their hearts, and will at some period of their lives cause their influence to be felt—those passions which are made a necessary part of our nature, it would be contrary to the principles of our existence, were any local situation permitted to eradicate them from the heart.

Thus the gentle Christabelle, although reared in the solitary cot of the gloomy Glencowell; although taught by his impressive, and constantly repeated doctrine to shun, and to suspect all human beings of the opposite sex to her own, of evil designs upon her peace, and her innocence; although satisfied with the society of her father, while he was alone known to her, and unconscious of the existence of any bliss which it was not in the power of his affection to bestow on her; no sooner beheld the gaze of Reginald fixed in admiration on herself, than a sentiment, of which the origin was perhaps gratitude, for the good opinion which his eyes betrayed his heart to entertain of her, gradually strengthened into a feeling of a more tender, more fervent nature, and led her oft to wish that she could behold him again; aware however that to express that wish to her father, would be a certain method of preventing its accomplishment, she confined her feelings within her own breast; but there were moments at which she would sink into reflection, and during which, an expression of disappointment would steal over her features; no turn of her countenance escaped the penetrating eye of her father; and dating his observations from the time at which the young stranger had appeared at the little gate leading to their cottage, he began to suspect what he feared and dreaded; he however forbore to question her, lest his inquiries might remind her of what it was possible that her memory did not retain that vivid recollection of, which his apprehensions led him to fear it did.

Thus with their thoughts fixed on the same subject, no communication of their ideas escaped the lips either of Glencowell or his daughter, which proves that whenever a parent wishes to inflict an injustice upon his child, all confidence between them must be immediately at an end: Glencowell had resolved that his daughter should never marry; never, if it were possible for him to prevent it, even have the liberty of conversing with a being of the opposite sex to her own; except the abbot of St. Michael's monastery, whom on account of his years, and holy function, he felt little reluctance in making an exception to his general rule—This resolution he had frequently imparted to her, and added to it many doctrines in order to convince her that an entire separation from the male sex, was for the benefit of her present, and future peace; and Christabelle had listened to his arguments without murmuring till, in her view of Reginald, nature had in one instant pointed out to her the fallacy, and inefficacy of those reasonings to which she had listened with patience, rather than conviction, ever since she had been possessed of the powers of understanding:—she began to consider her father as unjust, and cruel in debarring her from that happy intercourse with her fellow beings, by which the law of nature had assigned bliss to every individual of the creation; and without a friend in whose bosom to repose her sorrows, she sunk suddenly from an even gaiety of temper into an agitated despondency. With that anxiety of mind which Glencowell perceived his daughter to be enduring, increased the unpleasant sensation of his own breast. He knew his conduct with regard to her to be such as would in a general practice be conceived culpable; still he believed it to be in his own case, and in hers, individually right; and what alone perplexed him, was, the proof which he had now received of his inability to win her over to his opinion; except by disclosing to her facts in his own history, which he had pledged a vow to heaven, never to communicate to her; lest her breast should, like his own, be wrung with pangs of agony for the guilt of the irreclaimable.

A prey to their silent reflections, were Glencowell and his daughter wandering along the beach when they were stopped in their progress by the rill which had been formed by the hasty influx of the tide; just as they arrived at it, Glencowell felt the arm of Christabelle which was drawn through his, tremble; and when one of the first objects on which his eyes fell as he raised them from the ground, was the youth Reginald, his apprehensions were confirmed; and regarding him as the destroyer of her peace, whose touch would prove contamination to her innocence, he led her hastily up the rugged cliff, as has already been related.

If Christabelle trembled at the sight of Reginald, she trembled infinitely more, and from a far different cause, on her way to the cottage, when she parted from him. The conduct of her father had plainly informed her of his ideas relative to herself and the young man; and the unbroken silence in which he led her home, increased her apprehensions of his displeasure, as every protracted ill wears the more formidable appearance. When they reached the cottage, the shades of night were falling upon the earth. Christabelle went in and sunk down upon the first seat which offered itself to her tottering frame. Glencowell turned into a flower garden on one side of the cottage—in a few minutes he joined her; "Light me a lamp," he said. Christabelle obeyed, and placed it upon the table. "Come hither Christabelle," he rejoined, taking a seat before the table, and beckoning to his daughter to place herself on another by his side.

As she sat down, he regarded her with a look expressive of the utmost tenderness mingled with regret, and spoke thus: "Behold, my child, these two flowers!"

Christabelle cast her eyes towards them, and perceived a full blown rose falling to decay, and a beautiful bud just opening into bloom.

Having suffered her to observe them for a few instants, he said, "When this morning's light burst from the heavens, these flowers were equally beautiful to the sight; equally sweet to the senses. They were as twin sisters entering into life with all the enchanting simplicity of graceful innocence—and how unlike each other has twelve short hours made them! this bud grew beneath the covert of a hawthorn hedge, where in the shelter and obscurity afforded it by the surrounding foliage, it preserved its charms in loveliness, and purity—its sister flower was mounted on the top of a flaunting bush, where exposed to the rays of the sun, its charms soon burst into maturity; its gaudy appearance attracted the eye of the traveller, who snapped it from his stem, and placed it in his breast; where he kept it for the short period that its beauty lasted, and then threw it neglected from him. Just emblems are these flowers of two females placed in similar situations in life. This withering rose resembles the wretched state of her, who sailing headlong down the giddy stream of pleasure, ere yet her noon of life is past, wears out her charms, and sinks like one polluted into disregard. Whilst this fair bud presents a picture of the modest maid, who in seclusion dwells content with innocence, and all train of quiet joys that flow from its possession—still lovely in the evening of her days, sweet and engaging even at the close of life."

Upon these words he paused; and Christabelle heaved a lengthened sigh.

"Now, my child, in which of these two situations must it be the duty of a father to desire to see his daughter? Can there hang a doubt upon the choice? Impossible! Then must it not be still more the duty of a father to ensure his daughter that felicity of which he sees the advantage? It must, it must! and for the happiness of thee, my child, I will sacrifice the only comfort that remains to me on earth—we will part!"

"Part!" echoed Christabelle.

"Aye, and immediately too," returned Glencowell; "whatever is once decided right to be done, cannot be accomplished too quickly. Thou shalt retire to the security of a convent—its walls shall become the sheltering foliage to protect thine innocence from violation, and thou shalt descend to the grave in all the loveliness and purity of this rose-bud. For the solace of my own hours, that I might not be bereft of my only companion, I have too long withheld thee from becoming an inhabitant of those holy walls which can alone protect thee from the bane of thy sex's felicity—*temptation*—but I now resolve to resign thee to the arms of heaven; and for thy loss, I shall joy to accept the consolatory assurance, that I have preserved thee from being plucked by the hand of sensuality; and cast despised away when thy charms begin to fade."

The sensation of being about to be separated from the only parent whom she had ever known, from the only being, who, with the exception of dame Frances, she had ever considered as a friend, or a protector, produced an effect upon her mind, which entirely drove all recollection of Reginald from it, and bursting into tears she fell upon her father's neck, and besought him only to name the terms upon which she might continue to reside with him, and share his converse; and she would with delight submit to the conditions, whatever they were.

"It cannot be," replied Glencowell, "there are no bonds, no conditions, which can secure to a female her innocence, and peace except those by which their lives are devoted to the offices of religion."

"Never to behold you again!" exclaimed Christabelle, "Oh it will be an affliction that I cannot live under."

"Cheer thee, cheer thee," replied her father, "thou shrinkest at a distant apprehension. During the period of thy probation I will often visit thee."

"And when that period is expired?" said Christabelle.

"Thy thoughts will be entirely resigned to him, through whom thy spirit will rise to bliss immortal," answered Glencowell.

Unable to move her father from his purpose by her tears, or her entreaties, Christabelle retired at his command to bed, and passed a night of wretchedness before unknown to her. Now did she for the first time feel the privation of a maternal parent. O! how exquisite to youth are the name, and endearments of mother! mother and child, are the tenderest links of the creation; the affection borne to a mother by her offspring, is of all human passions the most tender, and at the same time the most forcible; it is a feeling of gratitude which nature has implanted in the breast of all, as the most acceptable reward which can be returned to the mother, for the sufferings by which she has given life, and the toils by which she has reared to maturity.

CHAP. VII.

> Oh, if thou teach me to believe this sorrow,
> Teach thou this sorrow how to make me die.
>
> SHAKESPEARE.*

In the visit of Glencowell to the superior of the monastery, and the service he required of him, we have already seen that he continued firm in his intention of immuring the fair Christabelle for life within the walls of a convent.

Father Benedict prepared the letter of introduction which he had promised him to the abbess of St. Ursula, and rose before his accustomed hour, as Glencowell had said that he should fetch it at thc dawn of morning; and the abbot judged that he might have some farther questions to ask relative to the convent.

The dawn had a considerable time been superseded by the rising sun, and still to the surprise of the abbot, Glencowell did not appear at the monastery.—The hour of matins came, and as soon as the monks had concluded their devotions, father Benedict went to the seat appropriated to his use in the church, and found that he had not visited it that morning; his book lay open at the page where the midnight devotions had ended. From these circumstances he knew not what opinion to draw; he judged that there must be some other cause, than his having postponed his purposed time of proceeding to the convent of St. Ursula with his daughter, for his having infringed upon his regular custom of attending matins; and resolved that if he should not arrive at the monastery by the time he had finished his own breakfast, to walk to his cottage.

The father began his morning repast, and having concluded it without the arrival of Glencowell, he set out on his walk.

The distance of St. Michael's monastery from the dwelling of Glencowell was scarcely half a league,* and the road lay along the edge of the cliffs. The abbot moved on at his usual pace, and when he had proceeded nearly two-thirds of the way, he perceived a female figure, which he instantly recognised to be Christabelle, running to meet him. The moment he observed her, he judged from her pace, that some misfortune had befallen her father, and quickened his steps toward her.

When arrived sufficiently near to the abbot, for her inquiries to be heard by him, she exclaimed, "Is my father at the monastery?"

Had the abbot not spoken, his countenance would have furnished her with a negative to her demand; "Great God, where can he be?" she cried, and a fresh flood of tears rolled down her cheeks; for her swoln eyes indicated that she had already been weeping—her knees trembled under her; and it was with difficulty that she could uphold herself from sinking to the earth; the abbot observed it, and supported her on his arm.

In as composed a manner as she was able, she informed him that her father had on the preceding evening appeared more than usually ill at ease in his mind, which she had attributed to the solitude that he was anticipating in her removal from him. "At his accustomed time," she said, "he had taken his lanthorn, and left the cottage in order to be present at the midnight devotions in the church of St. Michael; anxiety for her own future fate had kept her waking during the whole of the night, but although conscious of his absence, she had not been surprised at his not returning till the fifth hour of the morning; as it was by no means unfrequent with him to wander abroad, a prey to his own reflections, till the rising of the day, when he would enter his cottage, and throw himself for a few hours upon his bed. She recollected, that he had spoken to her of fetching a letter at the dawn of day from the monastery, and she endeavoured to compose herself with the idea of his being gone upon that errand. Hence she concluded it probable that he might not quit the monastery till after the celebration of mass; and upon this probability, she had again endeavoured to lull her apprehensions; but when two hours after that time had elapsed, and still he did not return, the anxiety of her mind had become too painful to be endured, and she had set out in order to make inquiries concerning him."

On finding that the abbot could not give her any intelligence of her father, her apprehensions for his safety rose to an extreme height, and she called alternately upon the abbot to instruct her where to seek him with the greatest probability of success; and upon heaven to restore him to her arms.

Father Benedict endeavoured to persuade her to suffer him to re-conduct her to her cottage, promising to remain with her till some tidings should be gained of Glencowell; but Christabelle conceived that there was a possibility of his having reached the monastery during the abbot's absence from it, and she prevailed on him to accompany her thither.

Leaning for support to her tottering frame upon the arm of the abbot, she moved on by his side without the appearance of any object to arrest their steps, till they had reached a turn in the path, which presented them with the view of a range of cliffs, before obscured from their sight; and these they perceived two persons ascending whom father Benedict instantly recognised to be Reginald de Brune and Arnold; and between them they carried the body of a man, whose pendant arms bespoke him to be in a state of inanination.

On him fell the eyes of Christabelle, "Oh God! see there, my father!" she exclaimed, and darted towards the spot; but ere she had proceeded many paces, with a piercing shriek she sunk senseless to the earth.

And happy was it for the wretched Christabelle, that insensibility closed her eyes to a nearer view of the body of her more wretched father—for that spirit which had endeared the outer clay to her heart, was fled—the worthless part of man alone remained of Glencowell.

When on the preceding night after the hour of midnight devotion, he had quitted the monastery of St. Michael; impelled by those restless anxieties of mind which frequently drove him to wander in the air, till the dawn of morning began to chase the shades of night from the heavens; he had continued lingering upon the cliffs, a prey to torturing sensations, which were increased by the idea of his approaching separation from his daughter; till entirely abstracted from the world; unconscious that he raved aloud his grief of heart; and heedless where he placed his quickening steps; he fell from the height of the precipice upon a point of the rock, which received him only to bound him with greater force to the bottom; where his body fell, mangled by its encounters with the knotty prominences of the cliffs; and overpowering agony put a hasty period to his existence.

In this dreadful state was Glencowell found by Reginald and his companion in their walk upon the beach; and by the former he was recognised notwithstanding the disfigured state of his countenance.

The first idea which entered the imagination of Reginald, was the anguish which Christabelle would experience on receiving the intelligence of her father's death; and judging that the pangs with which it would be accompanied to her heart, would be greatly increased by beholding him dyed* with the blood of his wounds; which must unavoidably be the case if he were carried to his own residence; he directed Arnold to assist him in bearing the body to the monastery; and they had just reached the top of the cliffs, at the moment that they became visible to Christabelle and the abbot.

Reginald's eye caught the form of Christabelle, at the same instant that her's fell upon the dead body of her father—he overheard part of her exclamation, and almost immediately after, he saw her sink to the earth. This was a call upon his active services which he lost not a moment in replying to; having commanded Arnold to get assistance to carry the corpse to the monastery, he flew towards Christabelle; and the abbot and himself, profiting by the insensibility into which she had fallen, to remove her from the scene of horror, conveyed her between them to the cottage.

Having already described the tender and dutiful affection of Christabelle's heart, it must be unnecessary to expatiate on the pangs with which it was rent, at being thus torn from the only being whom she had ever known in the character of a natural protector. For the first two days she appeared deprived of all sensation; and sunk into that despairing calmness, of which the effects are infinitely more to be dreaded than those of a frantic grief which vents itself in tears and bewailings.

The abbot and Reginald were unremitting in their attentions to her; and they called to their assistance the good old Esther, the widow of the humane fisherman who had received Christabelle and her father into his cot on the first evening of their arrival in the hamlet; and who had been the only person ever admitted in the residence of Glencowell in the character of a servant.

On the third day after her father's death, Christabelle awoke as it were from a dream, and with a despairing hope that the facts registered upon her memory were but the impressions of a dream, she asked for her father.—This was a moment of too trying a nature for the adoring heart of Reginald, and he rushed from her presence, unable to be present at the confirmation of her fears. His violent emotion spared the abbot a reply;—"Yes, yes, he is dead, he is dead!" shrieked forth Christabelle, "Oh say, who was his murderer?"

In the most soothing accents which religion and humanity combined could dictate to the tongue, father Benedict began the difficult task of reconciling the mind of the sufferer to its fate; he remarked "that those whose society we were for certain periods of our lives blessed with on earth, were but lent to us, as partial cheerers of our pilgrimage through this world; and that by repining at their transportation to a state of bliss, we displayed an ingratitude to the Deity for the benefits which we had derived from our past intercourse with them. The blessings of this world," he continued, "are but as reflections seen upon a glass, which pass away as soon as we behold them; the Christian's hope, is a second state; thither is thy father summoned to prepare for thee a seat of bliss, to which the purity of thy life will eventually lead thee; and thou wilt then be re-united with him in heaven."

"Lend me your kind support," replied Christabelle, "and I will prove myself a worthy Christian; but I cannot also forbear to feel that I am a forlorn, deserted orphan." At this moment Reginald re-entered the cottage.

"Deserted you shall never be!" he exclaimed, sinking upon one knee before her, and pressing her hand to his lips as he spoke; "never while the pulses of this heart continue to beat, shall it heave a throb unladen with anxiety for your welfare and happiness!"

"I accept your friendship, kind stranger," returned Christabelle, "may you never know the situation of a being like myself, who stands alone in life; who has no kindred eye that sympathy can wet in its cause; and therefore hails the tear which trembles on a stranger's cheek, as if it were the gift of heaven!"

"You have made it heaven's gift to me," exclaimed Reginald, "by declaring that it is acceptable to your own feelings."

CHAP. VIII.

What satisfaction can'st thou have?
The exchange of thy love's faithful vow for mine.
SHAKESPEARE.*

WITH the tenderest sympathy, the abbot of St. Michael, and Reginald de Brune continued to watch over the afflicted Christabelle, and to administer balm to the anguish of her heart; with unutterable gratitude she regarded them as sustaining towards her the characters of an affectionate parent and brother; in one only point did she feel herself dissatisfied with her conduct, and that was in a particular where the harassed state of her mind prevented her from perceiving that they were most tender to her feelings.

On the fourth day after her father's death, she expressed to them an ardent desire to be permitted to go to the monastery, and take a last farewell of his corpse; the gratification of this wish, they were both strenuous in denying her, from the consideration of the pain she must experience at beholding the body of a parent in that dreadful state of laceration which even his funeral garments were not capable of hiding from observation; she was therefore in this instance rather compelled to act under their direction, than convinced by their arguments of the impropriety which would have attended the indulgence of her inclination.

At length finding them resolute in not permitting her to behold a spectacle which must have been a shock of the severest nature to her feelings, she requested that the clothes in which her father had died, might be brought to her, without suffering them to be examined by any other person; "she had," she said, "a most particular motive for urging this request." And no sooner had she advanced it, than Reginald repaired to the monastery, and gave orders for the garments of the late Glencowell to be immediately conveyed to the cottage of his daughter.

At the direction of Reginald, much pains had been taken to wipe out from them the blood with which they had been stained; but the marks of it were still visible; and he dreaded that a paroxysm of grief should seize Christabelle the moment she beheld them; but with a fortitude which he had not expected from her, she approached the table upon which they had been placed, and with an expression of the greatest anxiety she began to search a pocket on one side of the vest, from which she drew out, what appeared merely shivers of wood.

"Is it then lost to me for ever!" she exclaimed, "is even the blessing of that portrait denied me?"

The thoughts of Reginald immediately reverted to the portrait, of her first sight of which he had been an unobserved witness in the church of St. Michael; and they were indeed the fragments of the ivory upon which it had been painted, and of the ebony case in which it had been inclosed, that Christabelle had now drawn from the pocket of her deceased father's vest. In his fall down the precipice, one of those blows against the rock which had contributed to his death, had dashed to atoms, the valued portrait, and its case; there was not even a piece of sufficient size remaining to assist Reginald with a conjecture as to the sex of the person whom it had represented.

When the last duties of this world had been paid to the remains of the unfortunate Glencowell, the venerable abbot of St. Michael, took an opportunity of thus addressing his fair charge. "The impropriety, my daughter, of your continuing to live alone in this cottage, must be obvious to you; your youth, and your sex, render it alike unsafe and unbecoming. It is therefore necessary that we should hold counsel together upon what plan promises most security to your future peace and happiness—I must to this end propose to you a question, to which idle curiosity should never have impelled me—Have you any relations, any friends, to whom I may make application for advice in your present emergency?"

"None, none," replied Christabelle; "whether my father has any in existence, I am utterly unacquainted; I have never known more of his history, than that Glencowell was an assumed name, and that a domestic calamity of a most unfortunate nature had driven him from the world."

"That portrait of which you regret the loss, was then doubtless a representation of your father?" said the abbot.

"No, it was not," Christabelle answered.

"You must then at some time have been acquainted with another being in whose fate you were interested, or you could not regret the power which that picture possessed of recalling the recollection of the person which it represented to your memory."

"It represented one whom I never saw, but yet love, and revere," returned Christabelle.

"And you will not explain who that person was?" said father Benedict.

The tears burst into the eyes of Christabelle, and she faintly pronounced, "My mother, my mother!"

A pause ensued—Christabelle broke it by exclaiming, "Oh my mother! thou art unconscious that thy child is at this moment fatherless, and unprotected; if it were known to thee, if some guardian angel could whisper in thine ear, with how unceasing a devotion"——she met the eye of father Benedict, as she was raising her own towards heaven, and immediately ceased to speak.

"Does thy mother then live?" asked the abbot.

"*Not to me*," replied Christabelle with emphasis; "I have pledged an oath to my father, breathed on heaven's attentive ear, never to make an attempt at tracing out my mother, by her resemblance to the lineaments of her portrait; she therefore never *can* live to me—I stand alone in the world; upon the bosom of none of its members, can I claim a resting place for my aching head; consign me therefore, good father, to some holy mansion, where on the breast of religion I may find that repose, which I cannot elsewhere expect."

With a due eulogy on the placidity of mind with which those are in this life blessed, who devote themselves to the service of their Maker; and with a representation of the glorious felicity which must inevitably be theirs in a state of future reward; the abbot left Christabelle, and retired to his monastery in order to dispatch a messenger to the convent of St. Ursula to acquaint its abbess with the circumstances of Christabelle's situation, and to request that she might, with as little delay as possible, be admitted a member of the sisterhood.

Reginald de Brune had also his plans for the happiness of Christabelle, as well as the abbot of St. Michael; his affections were irrevocably placed upon her, and he had resolved never to give his hand to any other woman, whilst she lived unmarried; he had not at the present moment the power of offering her such protection as it would have been his pride to have afforded her; he therefore regarded the convent of St. Ursula, as a desirable temporary asylum for her friendless state; and applauded the steps taken by father Benedict for procuring her a reception within its walls.

Christabelle, we have seen, beheld Reginald with sentiments of a no less tender nature than those with which she had inspired him, but she confined them to the most secret recesses of her heart. The natural humility of her unassuming disposition, led her to consider it as impossible, that a young man of family and prosperous circumstances, which she had discovered Reginald to be, should connect himself with one, who was, like her, unknown and dowerless; and therefore with a sensation of composed melancholy, almost amounting to despair, she looked forward towards the hour at which she should bid him farewell at her departure for the convent, as the last happy one which she should ever experience.

In answer to the letter of father Benedict, the abbess of St. Ursula returned a gracious invitation to the deserted Christabelle to take refuge from the cruelties of the world within her holy mansion; which had been erected for charitable purposes by William Rufus,* and a sum of money set apart by him for its support.

On the last evening that Christabelle was to pass in her cottage by the sea side, notwithstanding the vigilance of father Benedict to prevent any private opportunities for conversation between his young friend and the daughter of the deceased Glencowell, Reginald had the good fortune to obtain a short interview, unwitnessed by him.

The efforts of Christabelle to conceal the depression of her spirits were ineffectual; and as she observed that those of Reginald were even more animated than usual, her heart sunk heavier in her breast, from the idea that she had been mistaken in having supposed that he had ever regarded her in a more tender light than that of friendship; and that she should by this conviction be deprived of carrying with her to the convent, the only consolatory reflection with which she had anticipated to enter it, that of possessing the love of him, on whom her own affections were placed.

"By to-morrow evening at this time," said Reginald, "you will have become an inhabitant of the holy walls of St. Ursula."

"For life," added Christabelle, mournfully.

"Is that decided?" rejoined Reginald, with a tone of mingled doubt and apprehension, "can it be possible that you have resolved to bury your charms for ever in seclusion? To withdraw yourself for ever from the society of your fellow beings? Surely you cannot have formed this determination."

"What alternative have I?" replied Christabelle, "to the acceptance of such an asylum as the walls of a convent will afford me; am I not deserted, fatherless, friendless?"

"You forget that you have accepted *my* friendship," said Reginald.

"Oh, no," returned Christabelle, "it is my chief solace to remember the kind interest which you have taken in my afflictions."

"If these are indeed your sentiments," rejoined Reginald, "if you think me worthy of a place in your memory, transplant me thence to your heart; let the blossoms of friendship grow into the fruit of love; bless me by saying that you will at some future period, which I hope is not far distant, for my sake return to the world; and accept, as a declaration of the most religious sincerity, my promise to dedicate my future days to your happiness."

The crimson hue of modesty stole over the countenance of Christabelle; her head dropped down upon her heaving bosom, and she was unable to reply.

"Blessed silence!" exclaimed Reginald, "I accept thee as an affirmative to the most exalted wish of my soul! my beloved Christabelle consents to share the fate of the man who adores her."

In a few moments Christabelle spoke, she confessed the tender esteem which she felt for him, and gave him the most convincing proof of her affection, by imploring him not to entertain an idea of uniting himself with one whose history was of the equivocal nature of her own.

"If mystery be a crime," replied Reginald, "I am a voluntary sinner towards you; for I confess to you, that you behold me not as what I am, but as what it is necessary to my present circumstances to appear—my name is not Reginald; my fortunes are not what they seem; I therefore ask you to accept only my heart, unconnected with all other considerations; in the same manner that I wish to receive the bequest of yours, for the love which I bear yourself alone."

During the short space of time that father Benedict remained absent from the apartment, Reginald continued to urge his welcome suit, and Christabelle promised not to take the veil whilst the fidelity which he had sworn to her, remained unshaken.

CHAP. IX.

> They are but beggars that can count their worth;
> But my true love is grown to such excess,
> I cannot sum up half my sum of wealth.
>
> SHAKESPEARE.*

AT the hour of the following morning appointed for the departure of Christabelle, father Benedict who had promised to conduct her in person to the convent, arrived at the cottage; Reginald accompanied him; but as he was aware that the abbot would be displeased at any attempt on his part to become the companion of their journey, he contented himself with bidding Christabelle a tender farewell, and whispering in her ear, "that he would in a few days visit her at her new abode."

To part from her beloved cottage, appeared to Christabelle a second separation from her lamented father; with the tears streaming down her cheeks she was lifted upon her horse which had been provided for her; and attended by the good abbot, and two of the lay brothers of the monastery of St. Michael, she began her journey.

Their road lay principally along the coast, the sea being never hid from their sight above a quarter of a league together. Having stopt two or three different times in the course of the day for refreshment, towards the decline of the sun, they arrived upon the precincts of a forest, which it was necessary for them to pass through; and before they entered it, they alighted from their horses, and implored the protection of their tutelar saints in their passage through it from robbers and disasters of every kind, at the foot of a cross which had been erected for that purpose at the entrance of the principal pathway.

After the performance of this act of devotion, they again proceeded, and crossed the forest in safety; and as soon as they emerged from its shade, the convent of St. Ursula, erected on a gentle eminence at the distance of nearly half a league from its precincts, met their sight.

When they reached the gate of the holy mansion, the abbess attended by some of the boarders of the house, appeared within ready to receive them, and by these Christabelle was conducted into an apartment, where the united effects of stifled sorrow, and the fatigue of travelling, to which she was unaccustomed, threw her into a swoon. The sisters rendered her every attention in their power, and having effected her return to sense, they placed before her some refreshments, of which when she had slightly partaken, they attended her to bed; her presence at vespers having been dispensed with by the abbess on account of the feeble state of her health.

After a night of restless slumbers by which she felt herself little refreshed, Christabelle arose, and after she had attended mass in the chapel of the convent, she was invited to breakfast with the abbess and father Benedict, in the private apartment of the former. The meal being concluded, the abbot arose to depart; this was a fresh trial of Christabelle's fortitude. He bestowed on her his blessing, and added to it these consolatory words, "Although we shall live further from each other than we have been accustomed to do; consider me not on that account as less your friend; your happiness will always be dear to me; if you should ever stand in need of advice, or service beyond what the mother of this house has it in her ability, or her inclination to afford you, make application in such an emergency to me, without reserve." He repeated his blessing, impressed a kiss on her cheek, and departed. Christabelle sighing out to him a farewell through her tears.

The closing of the gate of the convent upon the good father Benedict, struck to the heart of Christabelle; at his departure she was separated from every friend, every acquaintance, without one consolatory reflection but the tender love of her Reginald; and she sought the solitude of the garden to indulge in retracing the past scenes of her life, in which he had been concerned.

She had not long wandered through its stately walks of uniform yews, ere the abbess joined her; this female was of a common character; an enthusiast for a monastic life, unpossessed of any arguments by which to win others to her opinion, and considering those who did not prefer to the busy scenes of the world that seclusion from them to which she had retired, as profligates of the most determined kind.

The society of such a woman could not be pleasing to Christabelle, and she therefore only constrained herself to behave towards her in a complacent and civil manner, for the sake of procuring to herself peace and tranquillity in her new retreat—she had been accustomed in the life time of her father to pass much of her time alone; her own reflections she considered as far more pleasant than the conversation of the nuns, and therefore to the solitude of her cell, she almost regularly confined herself.

On the seventh day of her residence at the convent, she was informed that a stranger who had requested to see her, was awaiting her coming in the apartment of the abbess; she immediately obeyed the summons, and found it to be Reginald de Brune. He received her with rapture; and it was in vain that she attempted to conceal the satisfaction with which his presence inspired her.

The abbess remained in the apartment with them during the whole time of Reginald's visit; his hints for a few moments private conversation with Christabelle, were unheeded by her; and he was obliged to depart dissatisfied, after the short stay of half an hour; which the abbess informed him was the period of time allotted to each novice for the reception of a visitor.

Her presence however did not prevent him from telling Christabelle that he should soon see her again; nor did Christabelle hesitate to reply, that his promise gave her pleasure.

"Who is that youth?" inquired the abbess, immediately after the departure of Reginald. "The abbot of St. Michael informed me that you had no relations."

"But I am not entirely without friends," returned Christabelle, "although the number is few."

"My daughter," rejoined the superior, "it is a sin to confess one of his sex a friend, now you are become an inhabitant of these walls."

Christabelle heaved a faint sigh.

"And a sigh at his recollection too?" proceeded the abbess, "I tremble for the purity of your heart—surely it is not possible that you can be guilty of the heinous crime of loving a man! Who is this youth? Whence comes he? What is his name?"

The innocent Christabelle returned no question upon the justice of the authority exercised by the mother of St. Ursula, but ingenuously informed her all she knew of Reginald.

"You must pray for your release from this delusion of the heart," said the abbess, "*I* too will pray for you myself—and I will do more for your happiness—I will guard against the flame which now burns in your breast receiving additional fuel from the sight of him who kindled it; I shall prevent you ever beholding each other again; a service for which you will some ten years hence praise my name, and acknowledge me the instrument of your eternal salvation."

Upon these words the abbess left her; and Christabelle suffered no immediate depression of spirits, for she believed her to have threatened more than she had it in her power to execute; but on the second application of Reginald at the convent for admittance to her presence, the portress refused to open to him the gate; and his request to be permitted to see the abbess was likewise attended with a negative.

Reginald returned home to the monastery of St. Michael disappointed and offended; late as the hour was when he reached it, he sent to inform the abbot that he wished that night to be admitted to his apartment; a request which in compliance with the promise of friendship he had made to the youth who urged it, the superior granted.

Reginald related to the abbot what had occurred to him at the convent of St. Ursula, and besought him to give him his advice how to act under the present circumstance.

"My advice," replied father Benedict, "is such as I have before given you, and such as I wish I could prevail upon you to take;" and he then repeated those arguments which he had before advanced to Reginald, in the hope of persuading him to desist from the pursuit of a passion which seemed to promise him only infelicity, in the additional displeasure which it would create for him in the breast of some of his nearest relatives—but the father might with as great a chance of success, have addressed his calm and gentle reasonings to the raging winds, and have expected them to subside at his entreaty, as to have turned the heart of Reginald from his passion for his beloved Christabelle. "Tell me, father, only tell me," he exclaimed, "whether it is an acknowledged authority, or an usurped one, that the mother of St. Ursula exercises in refusing to admit me to the presence of Christabelle Glencowell?"

The abbot was obliged to confess, "That the abbess had extended her authority beyond the limits which her situation permitted her; as every novice had free permission from the rules of the order, to receive the visits of her friends, once in each week."

With exultation Reginald heard his right of visiting Christabelle in her present seclusion from the world; and vowed revenge against the mother of the community for having deprived him of the enjoyment of that half hour of bliss which he had been entitled to pass in her society that morning.

The abbot besought him, if he were determined to persist in his affection for Christabelle, to be satisfied with the mandate for admission into her presence with which he would furnish him the next time of his visiting the convent; and not to exercise his revenge against an aged woman who believed herself to be rendering acceptable services to her God in restraining those females committed to her care from such worldly connexions as she had herself abjured.

Reginald could not immediately cool the spirit of wrath which was excited in his breast, against the abbess, "The time must come," he said, "when my rank will be known, and my power acknowledged, and it will be well for the mother of St. Ursula, if she is then no longer in existence!" and upon these words he retired to his chamber, but not to repose, for the soul of Reginald was haughty and impetuous; his passions were strong and of that sensitive nature which is most easily roused into anger; love was the only sensation which could melt his heart into softness, and therefore a transgression against the favourite passion of his soul, was one which he found it least easy to forget. At length the heaviness of sleep closed his eyes, but ere the sun was yet scarcely risen, he was awakened from his slumbers, by the entrance of his friend Arnold into his chamber, who put into his hand, a letter which had been brought for him to the monastery by a courier just arrived at its gate.

"Oh, my friend," exclaimed Reginald, after he had perused the epistle, "I am called hence instantly; let horses be prepared for my departure; and announce to father Benedict that I wish to see him, in order to bid him farewell—the hour of retribution is at hand!"

With an expression of joy at this intelligence, Arnold left him to obey his orders, and Reginald as soon as he had dressed himself, repaired to the abbot's apartment, who had already been apprized of his approaching departure; as soon as Reginald entered it, he gave father Benedict the letter which called him away from the monastery, to read.

Having read its contents, the good old monk gave Reginald some friendly admonitions for his conduct amidst those circumstances under which he was now called upon to act; and the youth having returned to him courteous acknowledgements for the hospitable entertainment he had received during his residence at the monastery, they partook together of a hasty breakfast; after which Reginald de Brune attended by his friend Arnold and the courier, set out on his journey.

CHAP. X.

I, under fair pretence of friendly ends,
And well-placed words of glazing courtesy,
Wind me into the easy-hearted man,
And hug him into snares.

MILTON.*

In her seclusion from the world in the convent of St. Ursula, Christabelle had no friend in whose breast to repose the secrets of her own; almost every sister was already provided with a confident to whom long acquaintance had allied her; and no one of the community sought her society, except a female whose mind and whose manners, were so entirely opposite to her own, as to give her no pleasure in the preference which she displayed for her.

Sister Gunilda, for such was her name, was arrived at the age of thirty-five; an age, at which, as the life of every woman is probably more than half run out, it appears but consistent, in every situation in life, much more within the walls of a religious mansion, that she should go down hill with infinitely more sobriety of conduct, than she has mounted the ascent. The sister was short and fat, with a countenance the very reverse of beauty and feminine softness, but entirely unconscious that it was not the seat of every grace and attraction; a strict observer of religious rites, and yet so fond of the world, from which she had been compelled by her relatives to retire, that she always attached herself to all the new comers in regular succession, in the hope of hearing from them some intelligence concerning those scenes of wicked vanity, for which in her heart she still languished.

Christabelle being the last, by three years, who had entered the walls of this holy mansion, at present engaged all the attentions of Gunilda, but the sister was ill repaid for her attendance upon our novice; for the life of Christabelle had been marked with no vicissitudes, no events, and she had no information with which to gratify her inquisitive companion, if even she had been inclined to make her her *confidante;* still Gunilda forced herself upon her for a companion, she considered that although Christabelle had not yet been communicative of the events of her past life, a little better acquaintance might make her so; and upon this hope she continued her endeavours to insinuate herself into her favour; the glimpse which she had caught of Reginald de Brune on his visit to the convent, had immediately conveyed to her mind an idea that there was some romance connected with her history, and gave a keener edge than usual to her passion for gaining intelligence.

The sister Gunilda during her intercourse with the world had believed herself to have made many conquests, and was steady in asserting that she might have been the wife of many a knight, but for the ill nature of her family, who had from her birth destined her to take the veil; thus like all those who have met with disappointments of the heart, love was her favourite topic; and whilst she sat with Christabelle, the varieties of her character were sometimes amusing in spite of her unpleasant manners; she would tell a story of her adventures with some valorous knight; then fall on her knees and read a prayer; rise and question Christabelle whether there were not some amorous prepossession lurking in her breast and then chaunt a hymn; thus between reflection on the joys which were for ever denied to her in this state, and the preparation for a future one, which was to repair to her all her curtailments of happiness on earth; the poor sister Gunilda, in a middle state between what she had lost, and what she anticipated, had no joy in existence; except there were any to be found in suspense; and with this sentence she would often console herself, "Well, well, though I confess I should have had much delight in being a wife and a mother, yet I reconcile myself to my present state of celibacy, by reflecting how infinitely more acceptable to my Creator is the life of seclusion from worldly duties, which I now lead!"

Intelligence hunters are always equally upon the watch with their eyes, as their ears; and as fond of relating news, as they are of hearing it—Gunilda having seen Reginald de Brune visit the convent on the first Thursday after Christabelle had been introduced to it, kept eagerly upon the watch on the second Thursday, the day set apart for the novices to receive the visits of their friends, in order to learn whether he would come again. Reginald did come, as our readers are already acquainted, and was refused admission by the portress in the name of the abbess.

Gunilda having gained a knowledge of this unfair authority usurped by the mother of the convent, it may readily be imagined that Christabelle did not long remain in ignorance of it. As she had not been permitted to see Reginald herself, she doubted not that on the following day she should be consoled with a letter from him; but there tedious days laden with anxious expectation passed on, and no letter cheered her sorrowing heart. She now judged that as the stern and unfeeling abbess had taken upon her to refuse her being seen by her friend, she might also exert an unwarrantable authority for withholding from her such letters as might arrive for her at the convent. The idea almost drove her to despair—she recollected only one consolatory hope, and that was the promise of his friendship which the good father Benedict had given her at parting. If it were possible for her, she considered, to convey to him intelligence of the mother's unjust conduct, he would doubtless enforce her enjoyment of such privileges as the rules of the house allowed her; perhaps remove her to some other community; where if even the regulations of the place were more severe, they might be in the hands of a more lenient superior; and true it is in almost every station of life, that it is the enforcer of law which renders all law either lenient or severe.

In the present crisis of her affairs, Christabelle felt happy in the attachment which sister Gunilda had shewn for her, and entreated her to put her into some way of conveying a letter to the superior of St. Michael's monastery. This office Gunilda readily undertook, and Christabelle having composed her epistle, gave it into the hands of her pretended friend, who would probably have proved a true one, had she been suffered to have perused the contents, or had them read to her before it had been folded up; but as this had not been the case, and Christabelle had not attended to any of her hints for being made acquainted with the matter it contained; curiosity got the better of friendship in the heart of the old virgin; and as she dared not venture herself to break the seal, she determined to make a show of her zeal for the good of the community by carrying the letter to the abbess, which she considered as her only chance of learning what were its contents.

Christabelle continued sitting in her cell wrapt in reflection upon what steps the good father would take for her happiness on the receipt of her letter; and little imagining that it was not already on its way to him, when the abbess, with all the expression of resentment which her unmeaning features were capable of assuming, depicted on her countenance, burst into her presence, with the open letter in her hand. The highest crime which it was in the opinion of the mother abbess, possible for any member of the community of which she was the superior, to commit, was that of making an appeal from her authority to any other power; of this heinous offence against her dignity, the unfortunate Christabelle had been guilty, and the abbess now presented herself before her prepared to revenge the insult that had been offered to her dignity.

We shall not repeat the invectives with which the mother loaded her innocent victim; it is sufficiently grating to the feelings to be condemned in life to hear the coarse arguments of the ignorant, in whose hands circumstances have placed authority, in favour of such unwarrantable procedures as are gratifying to their own spleen, and vanity; without sullying the page with a repetition of them; we shall therefore content ourselves with saying that

Christabelle was by her command immediately conducted to a subterraneous cell, which received the only light admitted into it from the faint gleam of a lamp suspended from the roof; a few handfuls of straw scattered in one corner, presented to her the only bed it was intended she should press till the days of penance were spent; and a jug of water, and a loaf of coarse bread having been placed near a low stool which was the only furniture of the place, the door was closed upon her.

Remonstrance in the case of Christabelle, would doubtless have been in vain, but she did not even make experiment of its powers; the treachery of sister Gunilda, and the severity with which the discovery of her fault, if fault it could be named, was about to be treated, filled her mind with so great a degree of astonishment, as to deprive her entirely of the faculty of speech, and almost the power of reasoning.

Left to the solitude of her prison, a flood of tears relieved her over-burdened heart, and cleared her faculties for reflection—sinking upon her knees, with her hands and eyes upraised to heaven, to which no walls of stone can prevent the suppliant's voice from ascending, "Almighty God," she exclaimed, "can acts like these, be acceptable to thy divinity? Impossible! there is a sense within my heart which teaches me that an injustice exercised against an innocent being in thy name, is a two-fold injury on the part of those who commit it. Impious falsehood! to call this a house dedicated to thy service, and the superior of it the representative of thy benevolence, when ignorance, fraud, and cruelty are the characteristics of her nature; and acts of treachery to their fellow beings, the services by which her disciples ingratiate themselves into her favour; rather than a house of religious offices, should it be named a seminary for the protection of crimes; the residers in which blaspheme thy name, by making it the unlawful sanction of their injuries. Oh Father of heaven! thou only parent now left me, desert not thy child; shield me beneath the wing of thy protection; grant to my sinking heart, strength to encounter the calamities that may await it in life; and vouchsafe me a pious resignation to my fate, a patient suffering, by which I may display to my persecutors a proof of the soothing reflections with which the hearts of those are cheered who tread the paths of religion in humility, and benevolence to their fellow beings."

CHAP. XI.

Shrines! where their vigils pale-ey'd virgins keep
And pitying saints, whose statues learn to weep!
Tho' cold like you, unmov'd and silent grown,
I have not yet forgot myself to stone.

Pope.*

Thus passed on five melancholy days and nights to the unfortunate Christabelle, without any cheering prospect of enlargement from her dungeon presenting itself to her view. Such provisions as she was allowed, were regularly brought to her cell every evening by Corally, a sister of the house, whom Christabelle had ever considered as a female of the most interesting kind; indeed, the only one, whom if her choice of a friend amongst the nuns had been permitted her, she would have selected her to have filled that station; but Corally had retired from every advance of intimacy which Christabelle had made towards her; a dejection of the most melancholy nature was depicted on her countenance, her voice was never heard except in sighs, nor did she ever raise her eyes from the ground except in prayer; and then with a wildness of expression which although it conveyed no terror to the observer, was extremely expressive of the wretchedness of her own mind; in age, she appeared about thirty, her countenance was pale and wan, and her eyes were sunk into their hollow sockets.

Exhausted by despondency of soul, Christabelle would sometimes offer up to her a prayer for her liberty, or her intercession for her with the mother of the house; and the only reply which she received from the sister was, "I dare not; if I durst plead, I have cause enough to plead for myself."

On the sixth evening of her confinement, about the hour that sister Corally usually appeared with her daily meal, Christabelle's attention was awakened by sounds which appeared to her senses like distant music. In a short space of time they approached as she conjectured from their increasing loudness, close to the convent walls. Suddenly they ceased, and a few minutes after they had become silent, the shrill blast of a trumpet was blown through the air. Again silence prevailed, but it was of short duration, for in the space of a few minutes, so great a confusion of sounds became at once audible, that Christabelle felt some difficulty in distinguishing from what causes they proceeded.

After some time she discovered that they arose from hasty and numerous footsteps, treading along the different parts of the building, and the loud clashes which were intermixed with these, she conjectured to be caused by heavy masses of armour falling upon each other, and resounding in hollow echoes through the vaulted passages. For about two hours, as nearly as she was able to calculate the time, these noises were continued, and a gradual return of silence then took place.

Considerably later than her usual hour of attending Christabelle, the sister Corally entered the cell, she placed the provisions upon the stool with a perturbed air that bespoke her mind to be even more than usually disturbed; and retired again precipitately. Christabelle partook of the coarse and scanty meal which had been brought to her; and having addressed herself to that Power from whom she considered that she could expect no relief in misfortune, if she omitted to return him her thanks for the preservation she had hitherto experienced at his hands, she threw herself upon her straw bed;—how long she slept she was uncertain, but on awakening again, she found the lamp which was suspended from the roof of her cell, extinguished; and recollected that she had not on the preceding evening seen the sister Corally replenish the oil as she had always heretofore been in the habit of doing. This she considered as an additional proof that something had occurred in the convent to distract her ideas from her simple routine of employments, and as she joined with this conviction, the recollection of the sounds she had heard, she again wondered what could have occasioned them. She felt herself shivering with cold, which sensation had been produced by her having slept, divided from the stone floor of the cell only by a thin partition of straw, and covered from the damp air of the night only by a stuff cloak.* She rose from her recumbent posture, and began to traverse her cell in order to produce some warmth in her limbs by exercise, and she had not long paced the floor of her prison, ere her eyes were attracted by a faint gleam of light which she perceived playing upon the wall. To her great surprise, she found that the door of her cell was not quite closed, and that the light shone in at a narrow crevice formed by its having started back upon its hinges. It could not be by design, she conceived, that it had been left thus; the agitation which had been so visible in the sister Corally the last time of her visiting the cell, must have caused her to have deceived herself when she supposed that she had fastened the door upon the helpless sufferer within. Christabelle believed it to be the dead hour of the night; universal silence appeared to prevail throughout the building; and she judged that it might be possible for her to effect her escape.

With this idea, a thousand plans entered her head; could she reach the garden and make her escape from thence to the forest which lay at the foot of the easy acclivity upon the summit of which stood the convent, she might, she hoped, be able to retrace her way back to the monastery of St. Michael; inform the worthy abbot of her misfortunes; and throw herself upon his protection. This hope communicated joy to her heart, and considering that if she omitted this opportunity of making an attempt at flying from the present tyrannical directress of her fate, a second might never present itself to her acceptance—with cautious steps she ventured to pass the door of her cell.

It opened upon a narrow passage, against one side of which hung a lanthorn from whence proceeded the gleam of light which she had observed reflected upon the wall of her cell. She proceeded along in that direction which she was acquainted would lead her through various apartments and passages to the refectory, from whence there was an easy communication with the garden; at every step, she dreaded lest the next should involve her in darkness, and render her no longer able to pursue her way; but at every turn another lanthorn served to make her path barely visible; at length she reached a short passage which led into the refectory, but alas! the entrance into it was rendered impervious by an iron grating which was locked, and bolted on the contrary side to that on which she stood.

All her flattering dreams of hope faded under this conviction; the sickness of disappointment filled her heart, and the tears burst into her eyes; the first consolatory thought which entered her mind, was the possibility of discovering some friendly outlet from the building by pursuing the passage which passed the door of her cell in the opposite direction to that in which she had now proceeded. Fearful lest the hollow echo of her footsteps should give notice of her enlargement, she durst move only with caution, and having regained the door of her cell, she proceeded towards her new hope; having passed the first angle, she found herself in total darkness and with difficulty prevented herself from falling down a flight of steps upon the top of which she discovered herself to be standing, by no resting place presenting itself for her foot, when she extended it in order to move forward.

Here she paused, uncertain what course to pursue; she reflected, however, that were she discovered in her attempts at flight, her treatment could not be much worse than it already had been; and that upon her escape in this clandestine manner from the convent, appeared to rest her only chance of ever beholding her Reginald again; as she could never hope for such an indulgence from the cruel abbess, after what had already passed upon his account; she further concluded, that if deprived of all intercourse with him, it was indifferent to her what were her fate; and therefore she resolved to return to the lanthorn which was hanging opposite to the door of her cell, and having taken from it the lamp which it contained, to pursue her way boldly by its light.

Having gained the lamp, she returned with it to the spot where her progress had just before been impeded by the darkness, and descended a flight of steps of considerable length; arrived at the bottom of these, she found a door which was fastened by a couple of bolts on the inside, she withdrew them, and having pushed back the door upon its hinges, she entered a square apartment of stone, from which branched off a passage to the right, and one to the left; uncertain towards which to bend her steps, she stood for some moments considering which of the two appeared the more likely to lead her towards the extremity of the building; having determined on pursuing the one to the right, she again moved on; a second heavy door put a momentary stop to her progress, and as she was in the act of placing her hand upon a rusty bolt, which passed along its centre, she believed that she heard a footstep on the other side; this idea rendered her fearful of pursuing her way; unconscious whither she was wandering, she might burst upon the presence of those who would frustrate the high-raised hopes of her soul—she continued listening anxiously for some time, and as the sound did not return, she at length ventured to undraw the bolt; the descent of a single step from the threshold of the door, which she did not perceive, caused her to stumble, and in saving herself, from falling, the door slipt from her hand, and the current of air which was occasioned by the hasty manner in which it closed itself, blew out her lamp.

Whilst she stood equally lamenting her privation of light, and dreading lest the heavy clap of the door should give intelligence of her movements, her eyes fell upon a long and spiral window through which played a brilliant, and vivid light, that cast a sufficient illumination upon the scene around her, for her to behold, that the place in which she stood was the burial vault of the convent, crowded with stone coffins placed in niches in the walls; and with monuments of mortality of a superior order, ranged along the centre.

She chilled at the sight; and despair of there being any outlet from this dismal receptacle of those whose cares were at an end seizing upon her mind, she almost entertained a wish that she herself were numbered with them. Her last resource was to retrace her way to her melancholy cell; but determined not to do so till she had ascertained that no possibility of effecting her escape remained, she moved on a few paces, and by a change of situation the light which pierced through the lofty casement, fell in such a direction as to discover to her some steps leading up to its base, in order to give those within an opportunity of looking out from it; which without this assistance its height from the ground rendered impossible; these she ascended, and on looking through the casement, a most dazzling scene met her sight—she beheld, what from those descriptions of the manners of the world which she had received from her father, she knew to be a camp by fire-light. Along the plain as far as her eye could stretch, she perceived ranges of tents, amidst which at equal distances, blazed circular fires, from whence the flames ascending in fantastic curls, appeared to paint the atmosphere with a refulgent glow; and the reflections of which falling upon the polished armour, and glittering pikes of the sentinels pacing their allotted portions of ground, added to the snowy whiteness of the tents, left scarcely a speck of shade visible for the space of nearly half a league; at which extremity the gloomy hue of the majestic forest, appeared to form a screen of security to the picture.

Christabelle stood, wrapt in admiration at the novelty of the sight, and filled with surprise at the appearance which she beheld, although conscious that her knowledge of the affairs of the world was too limited to justify her experiencing astonishment at whatever she might witness to be passing in it. For the moment she forgot herself and her own apprehensions, in contemplating the grandeur of the scene before her, and whilst she still stood before the window, a faint shriek at a short distance from her, caused her suddenly to turn round—near the foot of the steps which she had ascended, she beheld kneeling a nun of the order of St. Ursula, who was muttering a prayer, and extending towards her, the crucifix which was suspended from her neck; upon the ground by her side, stood a lanthorn, and almost immediately Christabelle recognised her to be the sister Corally.

The first idea which rushed into Christabelle's mind upon beholding her was, that her absence from her cell had been discovered, and that Corally was one of those sent in quest of her by the abbess; her mind was too much agitated to allow her to reflect that the attitude in which she saw the sister, was sufficient to confute this suspicion, and she exclaimed, "Oh save me! dear sister Corally, be my friend; do not betray me as the cruel Gunilda did?"

"Is it you, sister Christabelle!" returned Corally, "the blessed saints be praised!" and rising from her knees, she added, "I mistook you for the ghost of the late lady abbess, which is reported to wander here; and I had begun to address to you the prayer which is recommended to us, for our preservation from evil spirits."

Christabelle's education had given her no acquaintance with beings of a supernatural nature, and inattentive to Corally's explanation, she said, "You will not betray me, will you?"

"I have no intention of doing you any injury," replied the sister, "but how have you gained enlargement from your cell?"

"I found the door open a little while ago," answered Christabelle, "you could not have closed it last night when you brought me my supper;—did you close it after you?"

"I can't tell; I really do not know," returned Corally; "I was then so wretched, so miserable, so agitated in mind, that I know not what I did; and so I am now." The tears burst into her eyes, and she wrung her hands with emotions of the greatest grief.

"What are you doing here?" asked Christabelle, "is there any door hereabouts which will take us out of the convent? Are *you* attempting to make your escape?"

"Me!" exclaimed Corally, "Oh no, no, I am already a nun; I have pledged a vow to heaven of seclusion from the world, and I will not destroy my hopes of peace hereafter, though I break my heart in keeping that vow sacred."

"*I* have yet pronounced *no* vow," said Christabelle, "for mercy's sake then tell me how *I* may effect my escape."

"He will come hither presently," exclaimed Corally, wildly, "he sleeps tonight in the convent, and must pass this way to the camp; I shall see him once again, and I care not if the gratification be punished by penances of which the severity pulls me to the grave; I shall have all the satisfaction I desire in this world; that of telling him I was true to him, but torn from him by others."

"This way to the camp!" ejaculated Christabelle, "then there is a way out from hence.—Oh Corally, till death I will revere your memory, if you will but inform me where that outlet is."

"Oh my dear sister," replied Corally, "do not think of so rash an act as that of attempting to pass it; it is guarded by a number of soldiers; and their dispositions are rendered so idle, and irreligious by warfare that they would"——

"Surely they would not insult a female who represented herself to them as utterly helpless, and unprotected?" interrupted Christabelle.

"Oh yes, yes, they would; they deride our profession," returned Corally, "and seeing you about to quit the convent clandestinely, they would not hesitate to treat you with a freedom that would be more repugnant to your feelings than even the penance of your cell."

"Oh merciful Saviour of innocence," cried Christabelle, "I am either way in a strait that threatens me with wretchedness."

"Hush, is not that a footstep?" said Corally, "perhaps he is coming."

"Who is coming?—Whom do you mean?" asked Christabelle.

"The morning is rising, it will not be long now," rejoined Corally, with an increasing wildness both of voice and eye, "the army is to march at four and it is already near three."

"Whose army is it?" asked Christabelle.

"The army of prince John,"* she returned, "the youngest son of our king; terrible wars have broken out, and he is marching towards the coast to embark for France; the prince has lodged to-night in our convent, so have his principal followers, of whom, *he* is one, whom I am now awaiting to behold for the last time."*

"If one of the prince's followers is your friend," answered Christabelle, "would not he at your request vouchsafe to give a helpless female safe conduct through the encampment? O for the love of mercy, dear Corally, ask it of him! Will you not serve me by your intercession? Is not he a man of honour in whom I may place my faith?"

"Aye, that he is!" exclaimed Corally with the keenest emotion, "O heaven reward my Ranulph* for the constancy which he has shewn to me; a cruel father divided us; he discovered my Ranulph to be poor, in his catalogue of vices the most heinous; and without suffering me to bid the keeper of my heart farewell, he placed me here to sink a wretch into the grave. I had long since resigned every hope of consolation in this life; but one blessed ray of comfort shines at length upon me; I shall behold him once again; shall bid him farewell in this world, ere I meet him in a state to come—I bless the chance, and die resigned!"

"And will you, will you not save me from being a sufferer like yourself?" implored Christabelle.

The nun stood motionless with her hands clasped, and her eyes raised to heaven—"Wherever you go, dear sister Christabelle," she softly articulated after a pause, "pray for the repose of my mind, for I shall suffer dreadful struggles yet before I die!"

"I will, I will," replied Christabelle; "every morning and eve, I pledge myself to tell my beads for you, and for your Ranulph too."

"Will you pray for him I love?" ejaculated Corally; "will you pray for Ranulph? then short as will be the few moments I am permitted for the last time to behold him, I will dedicate some part of them to making known to him your petition—But remember you fail not to pray for Ranulph, as well as for me."

CHAP. XII.

——Let us hence from this detested place;
* * * * * * * * * * * *
* * * * * * * * * * * *
We'll fly, where love and virtue call;
Where happiness invites.

JONES.*

SCARCELY had the sister Corally ceased speaking ere the sounds of footsteps became audible, and Christabelle turning her eyes to the spot from whence they proceeded, beheld the flames of several torches issuing from a vaulted passage which she had not before observed; and Corally exclaiming, "Now indeed he comes," flew towards the lights.

In the next instant Christabelle beheld advancing a number of men in armour, whose polished coats of mail glittered beneath the refulgence of the torches; and scarcely had she time to observe the nun who had flown into the arms of a warrior upon whose helmet waved a knot of sable plumes, exclaiming, "Ranulph, it is your Corally, dear Ranulph!" ere her attention was diverted from the sister by the address of one of the strangers to herself. He was a youth of a tall and majestic figure, and his visor being raised, displayed a handsome, and manly countenance; which at the first moment of Christabelle's eye falling upon it, struck her as bearing some resemblance to that of Reginald de Brune, but as he approached nearer to her, the similarity faded away; the countenance of Reginald was comely, his complexion fair, and his hair of a bright auburn, whereas the expression of the stranger's countenance was of a more keen nature, his complexion dark, and his hair approaching to a black.

Moving up to Christabelle, he said, "By heaven fair virgin, your sister and yourself deserve immortality for your benevolence; ye are the only nuns I ever beheld with charitable feelings towards our sex. What are the meat, drink, and repose with which we have been entertained at this convent, compared with the smiles of its lovely inhabitants! Ranulph de Barthe is a happy man to be thus singled out by your companion; and if there be a Ranulph in your expectations too, I shall be tempted to curse my fates for leading me to this disappointment."

Utterly unaccustomed to the language of worldly men, and oppressed by the novelty of her situation, the poor Christabelle trembled with apprehensions unknown before, and was unable to reply, had she been resolved what to say.

"Why tremble thus?" continued the stranger, mistaking the cause of her emotion, "a soldier is only dreadful in war; his lion-mettle subsides into dove-like mildness in the service of the fair, which is ever his pride and inclination."

"Is it so?" exclaimed the innocent Christabelle, "blessings on the sound! it was my hope to find valour and compassion united."

The warrior's idea of his adventure was widely different from the fact; and pressing the hand of Christabelle which he held in both his to his breast, he turned to his followers, and said, "Proceed to the camp, and command the fires to be extinguished; I'll follow you presently."

"Oh no," said Christabelle, "pray go and suffer me to go with you."

"It would grant me the most unbounded happiness," replied the warrior, "and it is impossible for me to express how great a reflection I feel it upon my gallantry to be compelled to refuse an offer of so tempting a nature; but we are upon the point of embarking for an enemy's country, and none of your sex are allowed to accompany us."

"You do not comprehend me," replied Christabelle, "all I ask of you, is to lead me in safety to the neighbouring forest. I shall then be quite happy."

"Oh ho! *your* Ranulph lives in the forest then, does he?" said the warrior.

"You mistake me again," returned Christabelle, "I only desire to be placed in the road which will lead me to a holy father whom I wish to see; a pious, excellent old man."

"Nay, forbear, mercy on yourself," cried the stranger, "you are not of an age to seek comfort in an *old* man; such a declaration is an insult to your own charms;" and as he spoke these words, he placed one of his arms round her waist, and with a gentle earnestness pressed her towards him. Gathering her first cause of alarm from this action, Christabelle forcibly withdrew herself from him, and at the same moment raising her eyes, she perceived that she was now alone with the stranger, almost in total darkness. His torch bearers had obeyed his orders to depart; the fires in the camp were all dying out; and no light but the first streaks of the dawn now peeped through the lofty window—neither were Corally nor her Ranulph visible to her, nor could she hear any sounds that indicated them to be near.

With the most soothing accents of flattery, and passion flowing from his tongue, the young warrior still held her hand in his, and as she struggled to release it, she exclaimed, "Oh, why did you raise an expectation of your friendship within my breast only to crush it by the cruellest insult! is that the conduct corresponding with the character of a brave soldier?"

"A soldier is also a man," replied the stranger, "and I am acted upon as one by the impulse of your charms, which presents me with a heaven that I must be an atheist in love to fly from." Again his arm was twined round her waist; and a shriek for assistance burst from the lips of the astonished Christabelle.

"Hark! that is her voice; defend her innocence!" was instantly uttered in a tone which Christabelle recognised to be the sister Corally's; and in a few seconds appeared, rushing towards her, with a lamp in one of his hands, and a drawn sword in his other, the knight with the sable plumes in his helmet, whom Corally had a short time before hailed as her Ranulph. The moment he reached her side, and had fixed his eyes on her insulter, his weapon fell from his hand, and sinking on his knee, he exclaimed, "Pardon your vassal my gracious prince, he knew you not when he raised his sword against your person."

Corally was in an instant kneeling by his side, and joining her voice with his for pardon.

"Arise, arise, Sir Knight," replied the warrior, who still held the hand of Christabelle, and who was no other than Prince John himself, "your ignorance of my person, pleads your apology; but tell me, my friend, as you must know me to be one of your fellow soldiers, why were you so eager to prevent me from a participation in that happiness which you were yourself enjoying?"

"Your ideas of that happiness, my prince, are incorrectly formed," answered Ranulph de Barthe, "mine is of a much more sorrowful nature than you imagine. In this nun you behold my betrothed Corally, for whose loss you have oft heard me repeat that I wear these sable plumes upon my crest! that beloved Corally whom her cruel father tore from me and compelled to pronounce the vows of celibacy because the title which your gracious father conferred upon me on the plains before Verneuil, was my all. The accident of my having passed the night in this convent, of which I knew not till within this hour, that she was a member; has granted to us one more interview upon earth."

"Oh, Ranulph!" exclaimed Corally, "may the heart of that father who nipped the blossom of our peace, never ache as mine does now."

"Is it not a proof of the most spotless virtue," ejaculated Ranulph, "that now chance has once more led us to each other, she refuses to break her monastic vows, by flying hence with me?"

"But *I* have not pronounced those vows," cried Christabelle, addressing herself to Ranulph, "has not Corally told you so, and implored you"——

De Barthe interrupted her, "Set your gentle heart at rest," he said, "Corally has told me all; and whatever she demands, I hold it a religious duty to perform," then turning towards the prince, he in few words communicated to him the hopes and fears of Christabelle's mind.

When Ranulph had ceased speaking, the prince addressed Christabelle, from whom his eyes had not yet been averted, "Trust me, lovely flower of innocence," he said, "that had I known the spotless purity of your mind, you should not have had cause to dread me as an offender against the delicacy of your feelings; my error originated in beholding you upon this spot; whither it appeared likely that design only could have brought you at this hour; and the familiar address of your companion to Sir Ranulph, strengthened my mistaken suspicions—grant me forgiveness, fair maid, for my offence; and for my high raised hopes, grant me one kiss; when you have permitted me that chaste indulgence, I swear by heaven, I will myself conduct you through my camp; at the extremity of which, I will provide you with a protector in a confidential servant of my own, who shall accompany you to St. Michael's monastery; and moreover, I swear, that whatever request you may hereafter make of me, I will perform towards you, in remembrance of that one kiss."

These conditions were too flattering to Christabelle to be rejected by her, and Prince John impressed his lips upon her cheek; and although the action was marked with the fervency of delight, it was unaccompanied with that licentiousness which had before coloured his conduct.

"Now then, fair damsel," continued the prince, "place your arm within mine, and let us proceed; the grey morning which is already in the sky, warns us that you have no time to lose; the abbess may discover your absence from your cell, and your hopes be for ever cut off."

She suffered him to draw her arm through his, and they began to move towards a door, at the extremity of the vaults, which led out upon the plain where the prince's forces were incamped. Scarcely had they proceeded fifty paces away from Sir Ranulph and Corally, who had lingered behind, loath to pronounce the last farewell, ere their ears were assailed by the sound of hasty footsteps moving along various parts of the building, and these were almost immediately followed by the exclamations of "Christabelle! sister Christabelle! Where art thou Christabelle?"

"Oh heavens! they have discovered my absence, and are pursuing me," she exclaimed, "O for the love of mercy, quicken your steps!"

They instantly doubled their pace, but ere they had reached the wished-for door, the light of the torches began to glimmer along the arched roof of the cemetery, and a voice pronouncing, "Christabelle! whither art thou fled, dearest Christabelle?"—With a shriek of joy she exclaimed, "'Tis he! 'tis he! 'tis Reginald de Brune himself that calls upon me!"

"Is it then *he* to whom your heart is devoted?" inquired the prince in accents of surprise.

Ere she could reply, Reginald stood before her, "Almighty

powers!" he cried, "what is this I behold! my Christabelle in the act of flying from the convent with my brother!"

"Your brother!" echoed Christabelle, "are you the brother of a prince?"

Heedless of her question, Reginald advanced towards Prince John, and said, "Strong, and essential as is our alliance at this moment, if thou wert acquainted with my passions for that maid, and still hast by fraudulent arguments, or unjust persuasions, been endeavouring to win her to thyself; in this instant I forget thee for my brother, or my ally, and meet thee as the most determined foe that fate could face thee too."

The spirit of John was as fierce as that of his brother, and his passions as hasty. To be suspected of intending an injury where he was at the moment sustaining the character of a friend, was a reflection which fired his inflammatory temper, and rendered him too indignant to give the explanation which was demanded of him, and he replied, "Is it the nature of Richard to reward the services of his friends with these suspicions?" This answer although delivered in a tone at which he to whom it was addressed, would at any other moment have taken offence, was sufficient for him at the present one; of Christabelle were all his thoughts; and as it conveyed to him, that no attempt had been making to withdraw her affections from him, he was satisfied.

Christabelle, however, by no means secure that no ill effects were to be apprehended from the anger of the brothers, rushed between them, and after a few words of explanation besought them for her sake to forgive each other, "If you, either of you desire my happiness," she said, "you will become immediately reconciled, as you will else load my mind with the reflection of having been the cause of your dissension." She took a hand of each, and placed them in one another. "Do not Reginald," she said, "suffer the first hour of my introduction to your brother, to be one which I must be doomed to remember with regret."

The features of each softened at this appeal to their generous feelings; and Richard, for as such we must now know the pretended Reginald de Brune; who was indeed the immediate heir of England's crown, said, "But why my beloved Christabelle, by what motive could you be induced to leave your bed in the dead of night, to descend into this cold, and dismal spot? Some hidden cause must have prompted you to this action; I cannot believe that it was by chance that you did so, and that it was also by the direction of accident that you met my brother in this mournful receptacle of the dead. When I arrived here, not an hour ago, the abbess, whom I entreated to bring you to me, was alarmed, and astonished at not finding you in your chamber."

"Did the mother of St. Ursula express herself thus to you?" exclaimed Christabelle, "Oh! wicked falsehood! dear sister Corally, assist me to confute this shameless accusation; and you, treacherous woman!" she added, addressing the sister Gunilda whom she perceived in the midst of a crowd of personages who had attended Richard to the cemetery in search of her, "do you now advance, and by a confession of the truth, make me some amends for the unjust punishment you were the means of bringing upon me."

Richard looked round upon the different persons in amaze, his blood returning to the heat it had just fallen, "How!" he exclaimed, "have you suffered severity at the hands of the mother of this house?"

The voice of passion in which this demand was made, led the gentle Christabelle almost to wish that the truth had not escaped her lips, as she dreaded what might be the consequences of her confession, but it was now too late to retract; Sir Ranulph and Corally, in a few effective words corroborated the Prince's suspicions, and he exclaimed, "Lead me instantly to this disgrace to her sex and her profession; and happy had it been for her if death had spared her the meeting she has to encounter!

CHAP. XIII.

Madam, your majesty is much too sad:
You promised, when you parted with the king,
To lay aside life-harming heaviness,
And entertain a cheerful disposition.
———To please the King, I did; to please myself,
I cannot do it.

SHAKESPEARE.*

We must now for a while break off the thread of our narrative. It is necessary before we proceed in it, that we should take a retrospective view of the history of the times in which we have placed our scene of action, and of the principal characters then living. We have already said that the period of Reginald de Brune's temporary seclusion from the world took place in the thirty-fourth year of the reign of the second Henry; and as that monarch and his family will form no inconsiderable features in the subsequent pages, we must bring our readers to an acquaintance with them.*

Henry the second was a king, who as a monarch, merited, and obtained from his people that gratitude and love, which are naturally excited in the hearts of subjects by the acknowledged advantages which they derive from any sovereign under whom they are living.* Wisdom marked the formation of his laws; and a mildness attended their execution; he was beloved for his compassionate generosity to individuals; adored for the suavity and complacency of his manners; respected for the liberality with which he encouraged the exercise of the arts, and the cultivation of learning; forgetful of offences committed against himself; implacable in the revenging of insults or injuries offered to his country, yet so averse to the shedding of blood, that no private soldier fell unlamented by him.—He was at once the sovereign and father of his country.

Such was Henry as a king; as a man his conduct was by no means of the same excellent nature. To his queen, an open adulterer;—with his children, partial and tyrannical. He was an instance that the man who executes with fidelity a public trust reposed in his hands, may still be deficient in the duties of a husband, and a parent; it is undoubtedly difficult to conceive how the heart is actuated which displays its evil qualities only to those whom it ought to be the most tenderly linked in affection; but Henry is an incontestable proof that such instances do occur.

The partner of his throne was Eleanor of Acquitaine;* at a very early age, this princess had become the wife of Lewis the younger of France, who thirsting after her possessions of Guienne and Gascony, of which she was duchess, and of Poictou and Xaintonge, of which she was countess, pretended love for her, and obtained her hand in marriage.* The nuptials being consummated, Lewis proceeded to put into execution the principal motive by which he had been actuated in his alliance with the Duchess Eleanor, which was to have the power of raising contributions for the support of the holy wars, from the countries which she had brought him in dower; and having levied a heavy tax upon their inhabitants for that purpose, he set out for Palestine at the head of a numerous force; and according to the fashion of the times, his wife accompanied him on his expedition.

After having been for a considerable time absent from France, he returned filled with new projects, to the completion of which it is probable that he regarded his wife Eleanor as an impediment; accordingly at the national council of Boisgenci, he procured his union with her to be dissolved, founding his plea for the divorce upon scruples of conscience, which he pretended affected him, of their being too nearly related in blood.

Immediately after her repudiation, Eleanor was seen by Henry, then Duke of Normandy; she was at that time only in her twenty-second year; in her stature she was tall, elegant, and full of grace; in her person more interesting than beautiful, her countenance deriving its chief ornament from a dark and piercing eye, which was the exact transcript of her strong and intelligent mind; in her deportment she was majestic, and in her manners although bland, she displayed a certain reserve, which was by some construed into haughtiness, but which probably owed its being as much to a reflective mind, as to a proud one.

Henry, who had only a few months completed his eighteenth year, was materially guided in his conduct by the wary councils of his mother the Empress Maud.* At the divorce of Eleanor from his first husband Lewis, her possessions had been returned into her own hands; and the empress considering that the acquisition of those countries which acknowledged subjection to her, would prove to her son an advantage of the most important nature, as by adding them to this own dominions, he would become possessed of almost all the provinces of France situated between the Loire and the Pyrenees, most strenuously urged him to make an offer of his hand to the duchess.

Henry followed the advice of his mother, and without one sentiment of that nature, which *should* be the prompter to marriage, became the second husband of Eleanor; who, on her part, accompanied him to the altar, without any pleasing reflection but that of proving to Lewis, that she had very speedily been able to replace his loss.

Total indifference is frequently a safer passport to happiness than luke-warm affection; and under its influence, a considerable portion of time passed over the heads of Henry and his bride, without discord; but this placidity was not doomed to be lasting; Henry was in person remarkably handsome, and a general favourite with the female sex; and from beholding other women regard him, universally with admiration, and not unfrequently even with adoration, Eleanor felt the first buddings of passion open for him in her own heart; and habit, and intercourse, confirmed them into the most lively affection. But although she experienced delight at the tenderness of the sentiment with which she had become gradually inspired; she felt also that an opposite passion more than equal to it, in the disquietude of mind with which it afflicted her, had at the same moment taken root in her heart;—twined around the plant of love, as the nightshade robs the rose-bush of its health; jealousy had crept with its destructive poison into her breast.

In the fourth year of his marriage, Henry was called by the death of his uncle Stephen, to the English throne, and crowned with his queen at Westminster.* He was already the father of three children, William, Henry, and Maud. And in the course of the first year after this accession to the throne, his queen presented him with a second daughter, to whom was given her mother's name of Eleanor.

Having established himself upon the English throne, the first act of Henry's regal policy, was to endeavour to secure the same seat to his male descendants; he accordingly convened a council at Wallingford, in Berkshire, where the members swore allegiance to his two infant sons, William and Henry, as his eventual successors.

About a year after this time, which period had been employed by him in quelling various disturbances raised in different parts of the kingdom, by such noblemen as were dissatisfied with a proclamation which he had issued for the demolishing of castles, whose owners had gained from his predecessor Stephen almost a sovereign power; and which, with the exception of a few that were advantageously situated for the defence of the kingdom from a foreign enemy, he considered rather as nurseries of rebellion to the subject, than strong holds of safety to the prince; he turned his thoughts towards the conquest of Wales; and having for this purpose raised a considerable army, he marched at the head of it into Flintshire, against Owen Guynath, prince of North Wales, who lay encamped with his force at Besingwerk.*

The Welsh prince had made great preparations for repelling the invasion of the English; and information being brought to him, that the enemy was advancing through a forest known by the name of Coel Eulo, of which the intricacies were extremely great, and favourable to the Welsh, who were all well acquainted with those tracks which rendered it a labyrinth to their enemies; attacked the English van* with so great success, that many officers of distinction were slain, and the invading army driven for refuge into Cheshire; but this defeat was principally owing to an act of cowardice of the Earl of Essex, of which we shall hereafter have occasion to speak more largely.

But although disappointed in his first attempt, the King of England was not to be driven from his purpose. He did not quit the middle counties where he found it most easy to supply himself with recruits for his army; and having assembled a sufficient strength, as he believed, and as it proved, for effecting the conquest he desired, he renewed his attack upon Wales. But having already seen the danger of marching through unknown forests and fastnesses,* he now sent forward axe-men to open roads for his army; and to this precaution he added a second, of having the main body of his forces always preceded by detachments employed to reconnoitre the country.

By these means Henry arrived without any material impediment to his progress at Snowdon, where prince Guynath, convinced by his barons of the total inability of his army to resist the force of England, sued for a peace, and swore fealty to the king.

On Henry's return from this expedition to the palace of Beaumont, near Oxford, where he had left his consort and children, he found the number of his family the same but the members of it changed: his first born son William was dead, but in his stead the queen presented him with another boy, born during his absence.

However great had been the indifference with which Henry had regarded his wife, he had hitherto ever welcomed the entrance of his children into existence, particularly those of his own sex, with a pleasure which had imparted satisfaction to the heart of their mother: but in the present instance his blessing was bestowed much more coldly than it had ever been before; so much so, that the queen could not forbear inquiring from what cause he beheld this claim upon his affections with less parental extacy than he had done those which had preceded it into life? The king merely replied, "That he acted from his feelings; that he had no dislike to the child; but that it was impossible for him to account why he was not always in the same disposition upon similar occasions."

The queen had in many instances beheld the partiality of the king's disposition, and therefore concluded that what he had asserted, might be true; that it was possible that his elder born son to whom he had procured an oath of allegiance as his successor, might alone occupy his heart and leave in it no place for those of the same sex who had not enjoyed this mark of favour from the subjects of the realm; but still she felt inclined to suspect that there must be some concealed motive for this undisguised distinction made by a parent between his children.

The child was shortly after christened by the name of Richard.

Time did not wear out the queen's suspicions, but still she as yet found no one able, or at least willing, either to confute, or to confirm them. The king did not appear to bear himself more affectionately towards his youngest child, than he had done at the first moment of his beholding it; and the queen trembled when she found herself once more to become a mother, lest the child in her womb should be equally subject to the indifference of its father as her last born. Her fears were prophetic. Another son beheld the light of day under equally inauspicious fates as his brother Richard. This child received in baptism the name of Henry's brother Geoffrey; and a very short time after, the King was called into France by the death of that brother.

The queen's anxieties increased with the number of those children who appeared to be regarded by their father as intruders in his family, or at least as objects entitled by their later birth to a slenderer share of his parental love; and no sooner had Henry departed for France, than her attempts at prying into the secrets of her husband's conduct, which she guessed might furnish her with some explanation of his unjust partiality, were renewed.

In the court of Henry was a knight, named Sir Hugh Peverel, he had marched with Henry in his expedition against Wales, and an occurrence had there taken place, which had given him a private dislike to the king:—In the first attack which Henry had made upon the army of Guynath, and in which he had been defeated with loss, the Earl of Essex had committed the unpardonable crime of throwing the English standard from his hand, and at the same moment flying from the enemy, and increasing his error by exclaiming, "That the king was slain."

By this Sir Hugh Peverel, and another knight, Sir Simon de Montfort, the earl was immediately after the battle, accused of high treason;* and, according to the custom of the times, each was strenuous to be the person who should prove him guilty, by vanquishing him in single combat. To De Montfort, Henry permitted the encounter; and the Earl of Essex being confirmed a traitor, by being overcome by his arm, was shorn a monk, and confined to the monastery of Reading for life; and Sir Simon received many marks of honour for having been the instrument of his conviction. This preference shewn to De Montfort, Sir Hugh felt himself unable to forget; and although he did not withdraw himself from the service of the court, his heart had foregone its former attachment to the king.

Sir Hugh was a young man; and one of those whom the Prince Henry delighted to engage as a companion in his sports and exercises; and not unfrequently the queen herself would be an observer of them, in order to indulge her infant daughters with a sight of their brother's skill in throwing the ball, flinging the quoit,* and hitting a mark with the crossbow.

Sir Hugh was as well acquainted with the jealous disposition of the queen, as with many instances in the conduct of the king, which if known by her, could not fail to raise it to a higher pitch; and he panted for an opportunity of conveying to her knowledge, a tale which he wished to impart to her as an act of revenge upon the king, for the disappointment which he had suffered at his hands.

The queen on her part, perceived Sir Hugh to be one of those men who might be easily won to her interest by a little condescension, and upon this observation, she so conducted herself toward him, that in a very short time she drew from his lips a proof of her husband's infidelity. Of him she learnt that from the time of Henry's departure from Beaumont against the Welsh, his affections had been placed on a lady named Ruthinglenne, the wife of Sir Ralph Bloet, whose castle he had subdued in Flintshire, and who had already borne him a son.

"The illegitimate offspring of this shameful woman is, then," reflected Eleanor, "the rival of his affection for my unhappy sons! unhappy babes; regarded with indifference by your father from the moment of your birth, ye are entitled to a double portion of care and tenderness from your mother, and I pledge myself in the name of heaven, to extend it towards you!"

The soul of the queen was not of a nature to bear in patient suffering a discovered insult to her bed, her honour, and her affections; and considering it a duty which she owed not less to her children, than to herself, to prevent the king from future commerce with the mistress of his lawless love, she had already, heedless of the consequences which might ensue to herself from so rash a step, engaged agents to remove Ruthinglenne to some sequestered spot, where the king might never discover her seclusion; when intelligence reached her of the death of her rival, who had fallen a victim to a malignant fever, and had placed her son under the protection of the provost of Beverly, who was her distant relation, and a confidential friend of Henry's.

In her death the queen experienced a great relief to her tortured feelings. Henry himself had not been sufficiently attached to his Welsh mistress to lament her departure from life, although he had loved her whilst in existence; and Eleanor would have materially added to her own happiness, had she concealed from her husband her knowledge of such a connection ever having subsisted.

CHAP. XIV.

Oh! world, thy slippery turns.

SHAKESPEARE.*

THE nature of Henry was ambitious; and having by the demise of his brother Geoffrey become count of Nantes, by which he had gained a considerable increase of dominion in France; he resolved now to renew his wife's claim to the county of Thoulouse, which was founded in the right of her grandfather, the count of Poitiers, who had married the heiress of William the fourth, Count of Thoulouse.* To Raymond de Saint Gilles, who was the younger brother of William, these domains had been alienated, and the count of Poitiers afterwards for a considerable sum of money had confirmed the grant.

When Lewis the younger had become the husband of Eleanor, who was the sole child of the count of Poitiers, he asserted that the first alienation of the county to Raymond de Saint Gilles had been only a shameful juggle between the brothers, and that the unsuspicious count of Poitiers, had been imposed upon in the confirmation; that the entire business was a matter of non-effect; and that Eleanor had an undoubted right to inherit the possessions of her grandfather, upon repaying the sum of money which he had received for the confirmation of the invalid alienation.

Raymond the count of Thoulouse, in vain asserted his right of possession. The king of France declared his intention of settling the disagreement by force of arms; and after a considerable time spent in threats, the dispute was amicably adjusted by the marriage of count Raymond with one of the sisters of the French king.

From this time the count of Thoulouse, enjoyed his possessions in peace, till Henry conceived himself sufficiently strong in France, to renew the claim of Eleanor, who was now his queen. The count refused to comply with his demand, and Henry instantly raised a considerable force in France; and having summoned to his aid a large strength from England, he marched against Thoulouse, and began a blockade upon the capital, which he had no doubt of very soon compelling to surrender. But his hopes were not a little disconcerted by the arrival of Lewis with a division of his army to the relief of his brother-in-law. Henry had believed himself to be regarded as a friend by the French king, for they had lately entered into an alliance and had projected a marriage between Henry's eldest son, and Margaret the infant daughter of Lewis; but Lewis had conceived a private dislike to Henry, which he had not yet found an apt opportunity to display, on account of his having contracted a marriage with the wife whom he had repudiated; as he had wished her to be a sufferer, rather than a gainer, which he now believed her to be, by the divorce; and therefore proceeded to the succour of the Count of Thoulouse, not so much from motives of friendship for him, as of resentment against Henry.

No sooner had Lewis thrown himself into the city of Thoulouse than Henry considered it necessary to desist from waging hostilities against it; as it was deemed a breach of honour, and duty in a vassal, as Henry was to Lewis in France, to fight against his sovereign; accordingly quitting Thoulouse, he left in that county a sufficient force to maintain the ascendancy he had gained; and turned his route towards Paris, in the neighbourhood of which city, he caused several castles to surrender to him, in which he immediately placed garrisons, whence he made excursions for the purpose of ravaging the country; and giving a stab to commerce by cutting off all means of communication between that city, with Orleans and Etampes. At length Lewis and his forces were driven to straits which compelled him to sue for a truce, and this truce was followed by a treaty of peace.

Both monarchs were at this moment anxious that the peace should be lasting, and to this end, prince Henry of England, yet scarcely eight years old, was sent for into France, and affianced to Margaret, the daughter of Lewis, an infant not more than half the age of the prince.

The alliance which he formed for his son Henry, was not the only one which the king negotiated during his absence from England. At his first arrival in France after the death of his brother, he had found that Conan, count of Brittany had taken possession of Nantes; but at the demand of Henry, he yielded his title to it, notwithstanding it was an unquestionable one, because he dreaded to encounter the resentment which he was well aware the powerful king of England would not fail to assail him with in case of a refusal; Henry was however so well satisfied with his conduct; that he agreed upon an union between that nobleman's daughter Constance, and his third son Geoffrey, now an infant at the breast.

When he returned to England, his first moments after his arrival at his palace were spent in a communication of those occurrences which had taken place during his absence to his queen; and of which she had already received intelligence by messengers and by letters from him. Eleanor replied coolly. "And Richard, I perceive, has been entirely forgotten, in your contracts; or perhaps his interests have been sunk in those of your beloved Ruthinglenne's son."

This ill-judged disclosure of her acquaintance with those concerns of his heart, which it was his desire to have kept from her knowledge, raised a storm of wrath against her and her informers in the breast of the king. He immediately set on foot such inquiries as in a short time revealed to him through whose means she had gained a knowledge of his incontinency;* and Sir Hugh Peverel was compelled by him to enter a monastery of the most severe order, where it was well known that the abbot of the house inflicted on him, at the command of the king, penances of a most rigid nature, which, aided by the destructive force of disappointment, very shortly wore out his life.

To those who were to have been the queen's agents in removing Ruthinglenne from further intercourse with him, he was not less severe in awarding punishment; and to Eleanor herself he rigorously taught the difference between living subject to his neglect or his anger.

The severity which Henry had exercised towards Sir Hugh Peverel, and to all who had shewn themselves friends to the queen, had made so strong an impression on the mind of every member of the court, that Eleanor's well-wishers were entirely withheld by apprehensions for their personal safety, from communicating to her any instances of Henry's infidelity; and she had now only unconfirmed suspicions of various amours in which she had at times cause to believe him engaged, and which fed the torturing passion of her soul, by proving to her how many had the power of engaging that heart, over which she had so earnestly desired, but desired in vain, to possess some ascendancy.

Out of one evil generally grows another, and such was the case in the domestic concerns of the king of England; the particularity with which he bestowed his parental affections, rendered Eleanor partial in the bestowing of hers; but her partiality arose from the most amiable cause; whilst his originated solely in caprice. Her son Richard, being the child at whose birth his father had first expressed indifference, had excited for himself a proportionably strong interest in the breast of his mother over her other children; and although she struggled by every means in her power, to prevent this undue proportion of maternal tenderness from being seen; still through life she continued to love him most affectionately who had been the first of her children that had fallen under the neglect of his father.

Although well acquainted how low she stood in her husband's affections, Eleanor would not withdraw herself from his bed, resolute not to give him any cause for transferring his love from herself to other objects. Increase of time therefore produced to them two other children, the elder of whom, a son, was named John, and the younger, a daughter, was christened Jane.*

No event of importance to our history occurred till prince Henry had attained his seventeenth year.

The king had succeeded in quelling those tumults which at the beginning of his reign had broken out against him amongst the nobles who were dissatisfied with his edict for the demolition of their castles; but still he believed that there were many of them who were far from being true to his interests; and dreading that after his death they might revenge themselves upon his issue, by attempting to exclude them from succeeding to the throne, he resolved to have his favourite son Henry crowned, and to permit him to reign jointly with himself. It was true that he had procured him the oaths of allegiance as his successor, but aware that oaths for succession may be evaded, when oaths for present allegiance cannot; he published his purpose, and shortly after his son Henry was crowned king at Westminster, by the archbishop of York.*

The young Henry who was of a vain and subtle temper, was elevated by his new dignity, into a state of uncontrollable pride and extacy; and seized upon the first moment of his power for shewing his ingratitude to a father who had indulged him above all his other children. A most splendid festivity graced the day of coronation; and when the new King was seated at table, his father, in order to afford his subjects, in his own person, the example of obeying his son, set the first dish upon his table. "Behold, Sire," said the archbishop of York, who was by his side, "how great an honour is done you; your father condescends to serve you himself." "I perceive no condescension," replied the youth, "in my father, who is but the son of a duke, serving me, who am the son of a king."

The reply was made in the hearing of the old king, who almost at the very instant of his having made a division of his power, saw cause to repent that he had done so.

The queen triumphed in secret in the daily causes which the young Henry gave his father to repent his having admitted him to a participation of the regal power. "This punishment," she would say to her son Richard, "awaits on him for his unjust neglect of thee;" which arguments constantly repeated to the young prince, it can scarcely want to be said, were effective in sowing in his breast the seeds of jealousy against his brother, and of undutifulness to his father.

Although an alliance had taken place between their children, still Lewis of France could not forget the ancient grudge which he bore the king of England, and eagerly seized upon every occasion for bickering with him; accordingly no sooner was the younger Henry crowned king, than Lewis found a plea for complaint, that his daughter Margaret had not at the same time been crowned queen;* to which measure, Henry found himself obliged to accede, and the young princess being sent to England, was with her husband crowned at Winchester. After a short stay in England, the young king went over with his consort to the court of her father Lewis, where every compliment which could gratify his feelings was paid to him by the command of his father-in-law, who entertained him with the utmost festivity, and the greatest demonstrations of joy.

Lewis having succeeded in insinuating himself into the heart of his daughter's husband, no sooner found that he had done so, than he exerted all his subtilty to stir him up against the king, his father. —Now to this step we have already seen that he wanted very little incitement from the observation which he made on the day of his coronation; what little encouragement he did require to provoke him to an open revolt against his father, the French king gave him by constantly repeating to him, "That the title of a king without the authority, was a more horrible station than that of any common subject of his father's realm; for that an inanimate object might bear a title as he did, but that it required a man to be a subject; as such a one had a will of his own to exert, which he, a nominal king, had not."

Young Henry was now wound to such a pitch of pride and disobedience as to resolve to contend with his father for the supreme authority; and to this end he immediately opposed every step which the elder Henry attempted to take in the administration of his kingdom. The latter suspecting the king of France to have been instrumental in alienating his son from his obedience, sent ambassadors to the court of France, entreating Lewis to reason with his son-in-law, and endeavour to moderate his excesses.

"On whose part do you make this request?" asked Lewis of the ambassadors.

"On the part of our king Henry," they answered.

"I do not understand by what right you call him a king, who has assigned over his kingdom to his son," rejoined Lewis.

No other reply could the ambassadors obtain to their embassy; and they were obliged to return thus unsatisfactorily to England.

In the mean while, a party, perhaps not equally formidable to his power, but equally grating to his feelings, had been forming at home.

The queen had lately discovered the existence of a connexion between her husband, and a lady who was reported to be of most exquisite beauty, named Rosamond de Clifford, whom he had seduced from her husband, and whom he caused to be guarded with the utmost vigilance.* This fresh proof of his infidelity excited within the breast of Eleanor, full as warm a resentment against him on her own account, as she already experienced in the cause of her neglected sons; and summoning Richard and Geoffrey to her closet, she set before them in the strongest terms, the heinousness of the king's conduct, represented him as a most unlawful adulterer towards her, and a most unnatural father towards them; "To me," she continued to say, "he has never vouchsafed any part of that affection which is due to a wife; whilst on the profligate objects of his licentious desires, he has lavished that love, which I have in every instance of my life, made it my study to deserve, but have never yet been blessed with from him; to you, who are equal branches of himself with your younger brother Henry, he has not assigned a single rood of land as a present possession; nor has he appointed to you any inheritance in case of his demise. In our circumstances then, my sons, who are at this present moment fated to live under a king, in whom we unite a husband, and a father of this dreadful nature; is not a change of our monarch desirable? In the certainty that his successor cannot prove to us a greater enemy, than *he* has been. Pass over therefore into France, espouse the cause of your brother Henry; rank yourselves on his side, and trust to his gratitude to reward your endeavours in his behalf."

These arguments on the part of the queen sunk successfully into the hearts of the young princes. They eagerly agreed to her proposal; and having joined themselves with certain nobles, who already declared adherence to their brother, they passed over into France.

The younger Henry was not less surprised than delighted at beholding them; and emboldened by their presence, repeated his demands upon his father with increased insolence and audacity.

The king, chafed most violently by being caught in a toil, which he now when it was too late, perceived that he had spread for himself, denounced vengeance against his disobedient sons, and expended a considerable treasure in levying an army, which he trusted would prove of sufficient strength to subdue their intemperance. His animosity against his sons was not greater than against his queen, by whose interference the league against him had been strengthened; and previously to his quitting England, he doomed her to imprisonment for her practices against him.

The war was carried on upon the continent for nearly three years, during which time success leant alternately to either side; but at the expiration of that period the elder Henry began to gain infinitely the advantage over his foes; and in the course of a few months he was so successful in blocking up his son Richard in Poictou, of nearly the whole of which province he had gained possession, that he was driven by necessity to submit himself to his father.

Richard being thus humbled to his father, the King informed him, that it was his intention to send him in the quality of his ambassador to Lewis and his brother Henry, to negotiate a peace with them.

"I will go willingly," replied Richard, "provided my father will make me a grant of one request which I shall advance to him."

The King inquired what the request was, saying, "If it is aught in favour of my son Henry, you cannot expect that I shall accede to it after his late disobedience."

Richard declared "That it neither referred to his brother nor himself; that it would not cost him land or money, or loss of dignity or power."

"If such upon your honour you can affirm it," returned the King, "I can see no reason why I should not grant it, so name your demand."

Richard answered, "It is that the queen my mother, be enlarged from prison on our return to England."

The king had already half promised to grant the request of his son, and fearing lest he should refuse to become his ambassador to the opponent powers, upon the business of peace, of which he was now very desirous, he promised to comply with his petition; a promise which he performed on his return to England; and Eleanor became more attached than ever to her son Richard, on the knowledge of his having been the instrument of her restoration to her liberty and rights.

CHAP. XV.

———With a frown
Revenge impatient rose;
He threw his blood-stain'd sword in thunder down,
And with a withering look
The war denouncing trumpet took,
And blew a blast so loud and dread,
Were ne'er prophetic sounds so full of woe.

COLLINS.*

ACCORDING to the compact he had entered into with his father, Richard immediately proceeded to a meeting with the two kings. He found them weary of war, and an easy reconciliation consequently ensued between the powers; which was confirmed between Henry the elder and Lewis, by a younger daughter of the latter, named Adelais, being affianced to Richard as Earl of Acquitaine, of which county his father gave him the investiture.*

This princess was yet scarcely fifteen years of age; and being judged too young to take upon her the duties of marriage, she was committed to the care of king Henry the elder, who brought her with him to England, and placed her in the nunnery of Bordesley, there to remain till the proper period should arrive for her to become a wife.

The young Adelais was a female of extraordinary beauty; one who was universally admired as a prodigy, both in the just proportions of her shape, and in the fascinating composition of her features; and Richard considered himself as one of the happiest of men in being promised the possession of her charms.

In the nunnery of Bordesley, Adelais was recommended in a most strenuous manner by the king, to the care and protection of the abbess; none but the king, his son Richard, and the females of his family were permitted to visit her.

Four years passed on in tranquillity, at the expiration of which, king Lewis gave it as his opinion, that the proper period was arrived for the marriage of his daughter Adelais; and Prince Richard expressed a still greater impatience for the celebration of his nuptials. King Henry replied "That it was his intention to have the ceremony take place in the course of a few months, at which time his son would have completed his twenty-fifth year; but although Lewis appeared satisfied with this promise, the young Prince was not; for he had conceived an idea that his father had imbibed some recent objection to his marriage.

Ere these few months were concluded, the younger Henry was seized with a disorder which carried him rapidly to the grave; and his death was followed by that of Geoffrey, now Count of Brittany, in which title he had some years since succeeded the father of his wife Constance.

When a due period had been given to the memory of these princes, the king of France and Richard again applied to Henry for the solemnization of his son's marriage with Adelais; for which event Lewis was now the more eager, as Richard was become the immediate heir to his father's crown. Henry again attempted to create some delay, but Richard whose desires were sharpened by the procrastination of his wishes, declared his intention of enforcing an immediate attainment of his happiness, in terms which did not please his father, as they sounded predictive of a renewal of those hostilities which he had once already waged against his sons; he said, "If you will not accede to my proposal of delay, you will not doubtless refuse the princess this indulgence; and she has commissioned me to make it of you in her name."

Richard was an infidel to this assertion on the part of his father; and on the following day he proceeded to Bordesley in order to inquire of her in person, whether or not she had ever charged the king with such a petition to him.

On arriving at the nunnery, he was told that Adelais was not perfectly well, and begged to be excused from seeing him; at which information he was the more surprised, as she had always expressed pleasure at his visits, whether she had felt it or not. He inquired whether her indisposition were of a very severe nature; and being told that it was not, he desired her to be informed that he had a most particular reason for urging to see her, as he was the bearer of a message of importance to her from her father Lewis.

Still she refused him admittance. The fiery temper of the

prince was roused, and unable to bear tamely what he considered as a display of indifference on the part of one whom he so passionately loved, he broke heedlessly through the rules of the house, and rushed to her apartment; where to his utter astonishment and confusion, he found Adelais in the act of giving suck to an infant at her breast.

In fury of heart and agony of mind, the prince immediately quitted the nunnery, and sped to that mother from whom he regularly derived all his counsels. Eleanor was at this time at the palace of Beaumont, at Oxford;* the King was gone to Winchester.

With the tenderest sympathy the queen listened to her son's tale of horror, and of wonder; no sooner had he concluded his account, than she declared her intention of instantly proceeding to Bordesley, and making a personal investigation into the mystery; a short time was sufficient for her to prepare herself for putting her resolution into effect; and Richard remained during her absence a prey to the most torturing feelings at Beaumont. Every expedition was used by the queen on her journey, and she returned even earlier than the impatient Richard had expected her coming.

When they had retired together to a private apartment, "Well, my dearest mother," exclaimed the prince, "what has been the event of your visit to the convent; have you discovered who is the traitor, the seducer, whose blood my avenging sword must drink?"

Dreadful was the emotion expressed by the features of the queen, whilst she listened to his question. "My beloved son, my best beloved child," she returned, "the vengeance that you speak of must not be taken; vengeance inflicted by thy hand upon the head of the aggressor would render thee a criminal of the blackest die; thus could not thy mother endure to behold thee—her heart knows no joy but thine honour and prosperity; do not break it by attempting this revenge."

"Speak, speak, explain," cried Richard, "I will be guided by your counsel, only explain."

"Oh my son," returned the queen, "unparalleled is the situation in which we stand! Oh how doubly criminal is the guilty one whose name you ask;—Richard, can you divine nothing from my words?"

"Powers of mercy!" cried the prince, "preserve to me my reason, whilst I ask and hear, if it can be the king my father?"

A hysterical shriek burst from the lips of Eleanor, and she sunk upon the neck of her son; a few moments brought the relief of tears to her overburdened heart; and still clasping to her breast the wronged hope of her affections, a considerable period was passed by them both in the silence of painful and awful reflection.

At length a calm explanation took place.

The abbess of the convent, secure in the protection of a power superior to that of the queen, was less alarmed by her appearance than Eleanor had expected to find her; but Adelais, oppressed equally by conscious guilt, and the determined expression of the queen's features when she entered her presence, trembling under repentance of the past, and dread of the future, sunk upon her knees before Eleanor and confessed herself to have listened to the seductive voice of the enamoured king.

The wretched sensations which started into the breast of the ill-starred Eleanor, upon this confession, at the various appeals of wife, mother, and queen, may be easily imagined. "Miserable victim of temptation," she exclaimed, on quitting Adelais, "thou hast nought left thee but to pray for death, that thou mayest hide thy ignominy in the grave." To the mean and evil spirited mother of the house, who had sold herself a shame to her profession, for the indulgence of a voluptuous monarch and adulterous husband, she did not condescend verbally to express her contempt. On her features was legibly portrayed how great an object of abhorrence she regarded her.

The queen perceived that the attention which her son had given to her recital had been repeatedly broken by wild starts of despair; and considering him in the present distempered state of his mind, wholly unable to assist her with his judgment in those plans which she had during her return to Beaumont been arranging for the redress of his injuries she thus addressed him: "I am certain, my dear son, that you regard me as a mother most fondly attached; hear then my counsel, and let the entreaties of a mother's affection win upon your heart to pursue it; for the sake of your own future peace of mind, avoid a meeting with your father; remove yourself for a while to some spot of retirement from the world, where with solitude for your friend, you may regain that composure of mind, which cruel destiny has at this moment deprived you of."

"And must the crime of which my father has been guilty towards me, pass unpunished?" cried Richard.

"No, no, my son," returned the queen, "Henry shall not go unpunished. But from thy immediate hand must not proceed his chastisement; however culpable the eye of justice and of honour may behold him, he is still your father, although a criminal against the code of Christian duties."

Richard perceived the force of his mother's arguments; and she entreated him to pass over for a while into Cornwall, and request a temporary seclusion from the world, in the monastery of St. Michael, of its abbot, who had been one of the tutors of his junior years; promising that the instant he had quitted Beaumont, she would proceed with the utmost fervour in his cause towards putting into effect those plans which she had already formed for the redress of his wrongs; and also assuring him, that as soon as she had received from him intelligence of his safe arrival at St. Michael's, she would address to him by letter a full account of her proceedings in his favour.

The spirit-broken prince agreed to follow her advice; his father was expected to arrive at Beaumont that very night, and as he perceived the propriety of their not encountering each other, lest at the sight of the man from whose hands his happiness had received so severe a stab, he should forget the ties of blood by which they were connected, and be hurried by the violence of his feelings into an act which might cause him eternal remorse, he determined to quit the palace that very day and to take with him only one confidential friend.

Previously to his departure he informed the queen that in the present crisis of his fate, he could not endure the idea of being known upon the spot, and to the community into which he was going to retire, and that therefore he should assume the name of Reginald de Brune, and cause his friend to pass under the appellation of Arnold:—A parting of the most affectionate nature then took place between him and the queen; "Recollect dearest mother," he said, "that on your promise of redress, I rely; in your affection and favour I place my only hope.

"If I deceive thee, dearest and most injured son," replied Eleanor, "may I sink lower in thy esteem than the injurer of thy peace!"

Having uttered these words, she held him for some instants to her breast, whilst she pronounced on his head a silent, but fervent blessing; and Richard then with a heavy heart pursued his way towards St. Michael's monastery.

The ideas taken up by a man who is disappointed in the plan of happiness which he has marked out for himself, cannot be accounted for by any of the rules of reason; and the only negative species of felicity which presented itself to the imagination, of the Prince as he journeyed towards St. Michael's was that of passing his days in seclusion from the world, utterly unknown by such of its inhabitants as he was doomed to hold any intercourse with; and to this end one of his first actions on arriving at the monastery was, to dispatch a letter to his mother requesting her to send her packets of intelligence weekly to a village at the distance of about ten miles from St. Michael's, where he would commission his friend Arnold to receive them, as he dreaded lest any messenger to whom she might entrust them, if he were permitted to come to the monastery, should be induced to divulge the secret which his soul was bent upon retaining sacred.

The queen knew no happiness but that of her wronged and favourite son, and accordingly attended strictly to his request for the first five months after their separation; but on the first night of the sixth which it will be recollected followed the day on which Richard had received from the abbess of St. Ursula, a negative to his request for admittance into the nunnery for the purpose of beholding the fair Christabelle, a courier arrived at the monastery from his watchful mother in opposition to the instructions he had sent to her; but he came charged with a mandate to recal him to the assumption of his name and rank, and to an active share in the redress of his own injuries.

Already had Eleanor conveyed to her son intelligence of her having excited Lewis of France to avenge upon Henry, the violation of his daughter's honour, of the troops which were raising upon the continent for that purpose; and of those which the king of England was collecting to oppose them;—she now informed him, that Henry and his forces had actually sailed; that in the course of ten more days an army which she had by her own interest, and the adjunction of that of her private friends been drawing together in various parts of the kingdom would be ready to embark for France under the command of his brother John, who had, at her instigation, promised to join the cause of the French king; and that within the course of double that period, she doubted not being able to raise a second force of an equal nature, with which she wished him likewise to pass into France, and add fresh strength to the arms of Lewis.

These tidings were received with extacy by the prince; already was he become anxious to quit that seclusion from the world to which joint necessity, and inclination had led him; and proportionably pleasurable therefore was the hour of his recal. The charms of the innocent and virtuous Christabelle had proved efficacious in removing from his heart the impression under which it had once glowed for the now lost Adelais:—Christabelle Glencowell reigned the sovereign of his desires, and he panted with the utmost impatience for an opportunity of unbosoming his love to the queen, and asking her counsel relative to the means of securing his future happiness, by gaining him the honourable possession of the lovely object to whom the pitying hand of chance appeared to have led him as a reward for the unmerited disappointment which he had experienced.

With a light heart he accordingly prepared to quit the monastery, whose superior at parting once more repeated to him those admonitions which he had already frequently before urged him to attend to from his lips since his residence at St. Michael's. "My son," said the venerable abbot, "it is the voice of reason to which I ask you to listen when I implore you to summon resolution to your aid, and to banish from your heart those tender regards with which it is now filled towards the fair Christabelle; I am certain that you are possessed of too much virtue to tempt her to dishonour; equally am I convinced that she is too much in love with the delights of an unsullied conscience to listen to such accents, were you to breathe them into her ear; marriage therefore alone remains, as the sole means which can grant you the attainment of the bliss to which you aspire; and can you for an instant flatter yourself with the delusive hope, that it will ever be permitted to the immediate heir of England's crown, to share his throne with one whose origin is utterly unknown, and whose birth, if even it were possible to trace it, must be greatly inferior to his own? In the name of the esteem and friendship which I bear you, I therefore entreat you to triumph over your ill-placed passion!"

The prince thanked father Benedict for his counsel, but he entertained no idea of being guided by it; the treatment he had met with from the king his father in the instance of Adelais, induced him to believe that it was now become a justice which he owed to himself, to secure his happiness by any means which presented themselves to his acceptance. To Christabelle he had pledged his eternal faith, and he now breathed a secret vow, never to swerve from the sacredness of the promise which he had made to her.

At the village from which Arnold, who must now be known to us by his real name of Sir Philip Lucie, had been accustomed to fetch the queen's letters; the prince was met by a retinue becoming his rank; and his travelling was rendered as expeditious as possible, by relays of horses having been provided for him upon the road, at the command of his anxious mother.

Upon an extensive plain about six leagues on the south of Wallingford, Richard was surprised, as he pursued his journey, by beholding an encampment which rose gradually to his view, as he ascended a gentle acclivity in the road along which he was travelling. He inquired of his attendants whether they could give him any information concerning it, and found that it was conjectured to consist of a part of the forces with which his brother John was marching towards the southern coast, in order to embark for France.

Richard spurred his horse towards the tents, and on arriving at the lines, he perceived the standard of his brother flying in the centre; he accordingly directed the guards to announce to him his arrival, and proceeded with Sir Philip towards the tent of prince John; who on receiving the tidings of his approach, instantly came out to meet him; no sooner did Richard perceive him, than quickening his steps he advanced towards him, exclaiming, "Excellent brother, how kind are these exertions in my cause! how inadequate are words to thank you for ranking on the side of the oppressed and injured!"

"Am not I," replied John, "equally with yourself one of those unfortunate sons, who have seen our elder brother basking in the warmest sunshine of our father's favour, and ourselves subject only to his coldest neglect? In serving you, I am, as far as lies in my power, consoling a mother who is a sufferer from the same power as ourselves; and who merits from us every service in return for the affectionate anxiety with which she endeavours to repair to us a father's injustice."

Softened at the moment by a sense of their mutual wrongs, the princes rushed into one another's arms, and vowed to each other, eternal friendship and alliance.

Borne on the wings of impatience towards his mother, the stay of Richard at the camp of his brother was short; he learnt from John, that the spot where he found him encamped, had been appointed for the resort of such individuals from the middle counties, as were willing to join his standard, and that he was on the following morning to begin his march into Devonshire where a knight named Sir Ranulph de Barthe, who was his confidential friend, had been collecting those in the south, who had declared themselves ready to follow him to the field.

"Success smile on your arms, dear brother," ejaculated Richard, "my mother promises that I shall quickly follow you with an equal force; and I swear that not even the power of love, shall withhold me from participating in those toils of war, which generous friends like yourself are waging for my sake."

Once more their arms entwined each other in the bond of fraternal alliance, and they separated.

CHAP. XVI.

> It is the godlike attribute of kings,
> To raise the virtuous and protect the brave.
>
> JONES.*

RICHARD now pursued his way without interruption to Oxford, and on arriving at the palace of Beaumont, his mother received him in her closet; a short time only did the Prince allow to communicate upon the affairs of the state, ere he disclosed to his affectionate parent, the idol passion of his soul, and besought her counsel.

"My son," said Eleanor, "a virtuous passion like thine for

a virtuous object, it must ever reflect honour on the heart even of a prince like thyself, to entertain; fear not therefore openly to avow thine affection for the innocent maid:—lost to every sense of rectitude and honour must be the people who beholding in thee their future sovereign, will not glory in the sentiments of a king who shames the licentious conduct of his abandoned predecessor, by uniting himself in the bonds of religious constancy with an amiable and faithful partner of his throne—and for myself, I have breathed a vow to heaven, by every means which lie within the limits of my power, to repair to thee the injustice thou hast received at the hands of him to whom thou owest thy being; doubt not therefore, that her on whom thy choice has fallen, shall be equally with thyself the child of Eleanor—that in reparation of her loss, of whom thy father's criminality has deprived thee, thy mother will exert her every nerve, to place thee in possession of another bride, whose purity of soul renders her more worthy of thy affection."

Richard fell on his knees before his mother, and imprinted a kiss of gratitude upon her hand; in the course of the same evening he disclosed to her a full explanation of his first introduction to Christabelle, and every subsequent circumstance which had taken place since his departure from Beaumont; and he concluded by entreating her to take the object of his passion under her immediate protection.

The queen gave a ready assent to his request; and it was agreed that in the course of a few days, he should set out for the convent of St. Ursula, for the purpose of conducting Christabelle to Beaumont; and that the princess Jane, his sister, should accompany him, in order that Christabelle might not be compelled to travel without the society of a companion of her own sex.

Jane was at this time the only one of Richard's sisters either in England, or unmarried; Maud had many years been united to the duke of Saxony; and Eleanor had given her hand to Alphonso king of Castile.* Like himself one of the younger branches of his father's house, Jane was the sister whom Richard best loved, the amiability of her heart was not greater than the engaging gentleness of her manners, and he looked forward with delight to the moment of presenting her as a sister to his beloved Christabelle, who was herself not less pre-eminent in those insinuating graces of the mind.

Their journey was performed with all possible celerity, and the impatience of the prince once more to enter the presence of his Christabelle was so great, that as the close of their last day's travelling brought them within a few leagues of the convent of St. Ursula, he begged of his sister to allow them to proceed without giving any hours to repose, till they should reach the holy mansion, which was the period of their journey.

As they approached towards St. Ursula, Richard beheld the encampment which stretched itself along the plain, and was rendered observable by its fires; and doubting not that it contained the army of his brother John, halting for the night at the convent, (for it must be remembered, that convents were in those days, the houses which afforded entertainment and lodging to travellers) he felt some addition to his happiness in reflecting that chance had given him the opportunity of making his intended princess known to his brother before his departure for France; and of interesting his heart in her favour at a moment when the common claim in which they were embarked, would probably cause him to view her with a tenderer regard to her fate, than he might have done in an hour of cooler reflection; for aware that pride was the sovereign passion of John's heart, and conscious that it was his wish that both Richard and himself should unite themselves in marriage with females by their alliance with whom they might either enrich their coffers, or extend their dominions; he had felt some hesitation in declaring to him the purpose of his heart.

The surprise of the mother of St. Ursula, was by no means small, when an outrider from the train of Richard sounded the bugle before the gate of the convent at that early hour in the morning, and announced the approach of the prince and his sister; but dread and astonishment were weak terms for the feelings of her mind, when she beheld in the heir of England's crown, that Reginald de Brune to whom in his assumed character, she had refused admittance into her house: and heard him command Christabelle Glencowell to be instantly conducted into his presence.

Trembling with terror, the abbess knew not what course to pursue; she saw the eyes of the prince already flashing with indignation against her for a former offence; to what height would not his resentment rise, when he should discover the penance which she had inflicted on Christabelle; her only hope was to hasten to the cell of the suffering innocent; and trusting to the generosity of her feelings, implore her not to impart to the prince the severity with which she had been treated; a severity which she intended to assure her, she had exercised towards her for the eventual good of her soul; and that she would therefore be guilty of a heinous injustice, were she to be the cause of her falling under the anger of the prince for what she had done.

But the exercise of her hypocritical arguments was spared her, for on arriving at Christabelle's cell, to her utter consternation, she found the door open, and her captive fled. Upon this discovery her alarm increased; it would now, she dreaded, be impossible to conceal the truth from the prince;—what could she do? What steps could she pursue to shield herself from his vengeance? There was but one way, she considered, to save herself, and that was to make the attempt of throwing such obloquy upon the character of Christabelle, as should cause the prince and his sister to consider her unworthy of their countenance. Having found the iron grated door of the refectory, which formed the only communication from the main body of the mansion with the vaulted passage, in which was the cell of Christabelle's penance, locked on the inside; and being by this circumstance convinced that if she had made her escape from the nunnery, it must have been through the range of apartments beneath, which were set apart for such public purposes, as they were that night appropriated to, in lodging the officers of prince John's army; she resolved to return to Richard, and inform him, that Christabelle had that night deserted her chamber, and that her path had been traced down to the sleeping apartments of the soldiery.

With equal marks of fury and impatience Richard listened to her treacherous declaration, and not less convinced of the innocence of his Christabelle, than of some fraud lurking beneath the words of the abbess, he replied to her information, by throwing open the gate at which he had been admitted into the nunnery, and calling to his attendants to enter, and follow him through the house, in pursuit of Christabelle Glencowell.

Instant confusion prevailed within the walls of St. Ursula; the abbess wrung her hands, and pretended to bewail the intemperance of the young novice; some of the nuns ran from the approach of the prince's followers, and shut themselves within their cells; whilst the sister Gunilda, and a few others of the community whose dispositions were not unlike her own, joined in the search. How it terminated our readers are already acquainted, as likewise with the sudden pang which was communicated to the heart of the Prince, by beholding his Christabelle hanging upon the arm of his brother John; but an explanation quickly succeeded, which placed the innocence of Christabelle in the fairest point of view, and restored peace to the heart of him who lived only in admiring her virtues, and her charms. "I come dearest Christabelle," said Richard, "to remove thee hence to the protection of a mother and a queen, who has made her royal daughter the companion of my journey, as an earnest of the good will which she bears you."

"Gracious heaven!" exclaimed Christabelle, "a queen! your mother and a queen? And does she condescend to take interest in the fate of an insignificant being like myself? Oh surely you cannot have told her how humble my lot is!"

"I have told her of your virtues," replied Richard, "and she is anxious to witness and to protect them."

Christabelle stood silent, and lost in amaze; gazing successively on the countenances of those who surrounded her; and the smile which was struggling to grace her own, checked by the trepidation of her trembling heart.

Led by the hand of her brother, the princess Jane advanced towards her, "This," said Richard, "is the sister of whom I just now spoke to you; to you I give her as a sister also; receive her, Christabelle, to your heart."

The princess threw her arms around Christabelle, and clasped her to her bosom—the smile increased upon the lips of the astonished maid, and at the same moment the tears gushed into her eyes.

At the distance of a few paces stood prince John resting upon his spear; the eyes of Richard were turned towards him; in eloquent expression they inquired, "Does my brother approve my choice? Will not he follow the example of a mother, and a sister, to give his sanction to a brother's happiness?" The injuries which Richard had received at the hands of his father were such, that expressing himself of them, John had more than once said, "That he who would not willingly unite in the reparation of his brother's happiness, must be equally cruel with the father who had rendered such a reparation necessary to his wounded peace."—How then was it possible for him to resist the joint appeal made to his feelings by the recollection of his own words, and the supplicating eyes of Richard? He received Christabelle from the arms of his sister, and having pressed her to his breast, he said, "Mayest thou live to be a blessing to my brother, and to merit and enjoy his affection."

Christabelle now regained the power of utterance, "My ideas," she said, "are at this moment so bewildered that I know not in what words to express my sense of honours, great and unmerited, as those which are now falling upon me! or what it would become me to do to render myself deserving of such kindness! O, how great is the reverse between this moment, and the sufferings I have lately undergone!"

These words confirmed prince Richard in his suspicion of the abbess not having conducted herself with indulgence towards Christabelle, which he had drawn the moment of his entering the convent, from the confused and agitated manner with which she had received him; he looked sternly around him, and perceiving that she was not in the cemetery, (for on observing the failure of her plan, for her own security, in the joyful meeting of Christabelle and the prince, she had flown to her private chamber) he commanded instantly to be conducted to her.

Attuned to mercy was the soul of Christabelle, and catching hold of Richard's hand and arresting his steps, she entreated him to let his first act of favour to her in the character in which she now knew him, be to pardon the misguided woman at whose hands she had been a sufferer, "If she has any sense of what is just and commendable left within her heart, she will be induced by the lenity bestowed on herself, to exercise humanity toward those who may hereafter be placed in her power;" said Christabelle, "and for my own sake, I shall be infinitely more happy under the idea of having forgiven an injury, than in having resented it."

The prince could not reply; every sense was wrapt in admiration of the excellence of his adored Christabelle's heart.

Pressing his hand as she spoke, in the hope of strengthening her entreaty by the act, the fair maid continued to speak thus, "There is but one point in which I wish you to enforce your authority with her, which is that sister Corally, from whom I have experienced marks of friendship, and whose unfortunate lot creates my sincerest commiseration and sympathy, be doomed to undergo no penance for the interview which she has snatched with her Ranulph."

"Thou art an angel, Christabelle," exclaimed the prince, "the pleadings of thy voice are irresistible!"

Having said these words, he commanded the way to the superior's apartment to be shewn to them, and being arrived in it, he requested the implements for writing to be brought to him; he seated himself before a table on which they had been placed, and having passed some minutes in writing, he desired Corally to approach him, and attend to what he had written; she advanced to his side, and he then read aloud a scroll addressed to the bishop of Lincoln, in which he entreated of him in the most urgent terms the deposition of the present mother of St. Ursula from her seat, and the elevation of the sister Corally to her rank; and which arrangement he requested might be made with the greatest possible expedition.

Corally sunk upon her knee, and imprinting a kiss upon his glove in gratitude for the honour which he had conferred on her, she said, "In my actions shall appear my sense of the obligation under which you have graciously placed me; I am myself unhappy, and shall derive my only bliss from proving that I know how to feel for the woes of others."

Raising her from the ground, the prince said, "It is probable that some weeks must of necessity intervene before this change can be ratified by ecclesiastical authority; for your security therefore, and that of those who may be equally deserving as yourself within these walls, I command that the deposed mother be immediately conveyed to the cell which was lately the prison of my Christabelle, and confined there till the supreme authority of this house be adjudged to you: I do not wish her to be deprived of any of the necessaries, or even comforts of life, but I insist on her being restrained from the exercise of that authority which she may deem her own, until the voice of the church shall have debarred her of it."

Gunilda had long since, like her shameful superior, slunk away from observation, and Christabelle suffered her to depart with only contempt for her punishment.

Prince John and Sir Ranulph had accompanied Richard and his train to the apartment of the abbess, and scarcely had the latter issued his directions for the future rule of the house, ere a messenger entered to inform prince John, that the hour was arrived at which he had commanded his troops to be prepared to commence their march, and that they waited only his coming for proceeding on their way. This was the signal for Sir Ranulph to bid his Corally farewell; but the heaviness of heart with which they had before been about to part, when they had believed that their separation was doomed to be eternal, was infinitely lightened by the knowledge that in the station to which Corally was now raised, she would be at liberty sometimes to receive his visits.

"Good fortune guide your enterprise," exclaimed Richard addressing his brother, "once more accept my thanks for that active share of interest which you are about to take in redressing my wrongs; and once more hear me declare that whilst my friends are toiling for my rights, not even the charms of love shall detain me ignobly from participating in their labours; one only night shall pass over my head after I have placed my Christabelle under the protection of our mother, before I will bestir me in assembling the levy which has promised to rally round my standard, and join my strength to yours in France."

An affectionate parting then ensued; and prince John having placed himself at the head of his army, pursued his march towards the coast; whilst Richard escorted his sister and Christabelle to the neighbouring castle of a knight attached to his interests, whither he had already dispatched a courier to request that they might enjoy the refreshment of a few hours repose.

Great and unexpected sensations of delight are often as inimical to the balmy advances of sleep, as those of an adverse nature; a truth experienced by Christabelle, when she now reposed her head upon her pillow; her heart danced too wildly with joy and gratitude to be able to compose itself to rest; and the hours allotted to that purpose were passed by her in reflection.

The history of prince Richard and Adelais had been universally discussed throughout the kingdom, and was therefore not unknown to her; but she could scarcely induce herself to believe, that it was that very prince who had bestowed on her his heart; and who appeared to derive his only happiness from contemplating the superiority of her chaste mind, when compared with that of the woman on whom his first affections had so unfortunately been placed: with what exquisite kindness, attention, and love, did it become her to bear herself towards him, not only that she might confirm the opinion under which she had won his affections; but requite him for the honour of his condescending regards. The Princess Jane, too, how exquisitely tender, and fascinating was the manner in which she had conducted herself towards her; she had never yet known the name of sister, or the soothing attentions of any female friend, and to receive them now united from a princess! even to a mind of steadiness like that of Christabelle, there was something not less dazzling, than apparently incredible, in the idea; but how much more wonderful the truth that a prince had declared himself her devoted husband! a prince the immediate heir to the throne of his country! It might be possible that she might one day, reign the queen of that people from amongst whom she had on the preceding day, at that hour, been one of the most humble, and one of the most wretched! the reflection was one, which with the exclusion of every vain inclination, almost bewildered her faculties.

Of the number of those amidst whom she was so lately placed, by the wonder-working hand of fate, an adherent member, prince John appeared to her the only negative personage; she conceived that he had not seemed to express any heart-felt interest in her fate, although he had bestowed on her his salutary wishes; that in the character of the libertine under which he had first been introduced to her knowledge, he had shone more conspicuously than in that of the brother; she considered that his temper might perhaps be of a less fervid nature than that of either Richard or the princess Jane; that it was a species of ingratitude in her to indulge any idea which bordered upon dissatisfaction, when connected with any relative of him to whom she was about to be indebted for every blessing of her existence; and doubted not that if she were only permitted a farther acquaintance with the young prince, she should have cause to venerate him, as sincerely as she already did such other members of his family as were known to her.

Their journey towards Beaumont, was unmarked by any event, except an increase of affection on the part of the prince, and of gratitude on that of Christabelle—arrived at the palace, it was not without a considerable degree of awe that Christabelle entered the presence of the queen; but stern as appeared the countenance of Eleanor to almost every common observer, Christabelle beheld in it only one characteristic, which was that of benevolence; and when the queen extended her arms to clasp her to her bosom, the sensations produced by this condescension, entirely overpowered her, and she sunk fainting into the arms of the prince.

Christabelle had hitherto dreaded, lest, for her encouragement, or in order to flatter himself into a belief of what he wished, Richard might have drawn into glowing colours the friendly intentions of the queen towards her; that although for the happiness of her favourite son, she might be induced to give her sanction to his future alliance with one devoid of rank or dower, like herself, that still she might wear towards her a haughty air calculated to keep her in remembrance of the honour which she was permitted to enjoy;—but at the first moment of her beholding Eleanor, every apprehension of this nature was banished from her breast. Eleanor received her as her equal, and hailed her by the title of *daughter;* Christabelle would have knelt in return, and clasped her knees, but in the attempt all sense forsook her.

When she revived, "Tremble not at me, fair maid," said the queen, "thou hast possessed the power of restoring peace to the heart of my beloved son, and wilt therefore ever reign in mine with him."

"Yours and his, in duty and in gratitude, I shall ever be," replied Christabelle, "ye have made me what I am; of myself I was nothing—I therefore owe myself eternally unto you both."

Again the queen folded her to her breast, and breathed words of the most affectionate nature into her ear.

CHAP. XVII.

> This, this is life indeed! life worth preserving
> Thy virtue will excuse my passion for thee,
> And make the gods propitious to our love.
>
> ADDISON.*

How strangely different were the scenes of regal splendour which now met the eye of Christabelle at every turn, to those simple ones amidst which her days had hitherto been passed; even the inanimate objects of grandeur upon which her eyes fell, frequently appeared to her as reminding her of her own insignificance. These were ideas natural to the peculiarity of her situation, and which nothing could have tended so soon, and so forcibly to dispel, as those equalizing endearments which she received from her new friends.

Richard had promised his brother John to waste only one night at Beaumont before he hastened to show himself in person to troops which were to embark under his command for France; he had resolved not to transgress this promise; accordingly every moment of the swiftly-flying hours (those of course excepted which were dedicated to the renovation of nature's strength by repose) were passed by him in the presence of his Christabelle, to whom he again and again vowed eternal constancy of affection; whilst with a sigh of the bitterest regret he confessed the necessity of the period of their union depending upon the contingency of events; at least during the life time of his father.

As they wandered, accompanied by Eleanor and the princess Jane, through the flowery mazes of the gardens of the palace for the enjoyment of the cool breezes of the evening air which succeeded a sultry day, the prince took delight in reverting to his first sight of Christabelle, and entreated her to indulge him by repeating the song with which she had at that moment so forcibly charmed his senses.

At his direction accordingly her lute was brought to her into an arbour of the garden; the queen and the princess were far from expecting in Christabelle the melodist which they found in her; and the charm which her notes conveyed to their senses was so great, that again and again was she entreated to strike the chords of her instrument.

"Who was your instructor in the art of music?" the queen inquired of her.

"My father," replied Christabelle. "In whatever I know, I never had the benefit of anyone's instruction but his."

"He cannot have been a man of mean origin to have been thus qualified himself," returned the queen.

Christabelle could only repeat her total ignorance of every circumstance relating to his history.

"Did your father," asked the princess Jane, "himself write those songs which you have sung to us?"

"All but one, I believe," answered Christabelle.

"And whence did you procure that?" said the prince.

A blush spread itself over the cheeks of Christabelle, and as she did not immediately reply, he repeated his question.

"I ought not in justice, I believe, to have made the exception I did," she returned, "my father used to call it my song; but he lent me so much assistance in its composition, that indeed what little merit it may have belongs entirely to him."

"Is it *your* composition, my dearest Christabelle?" exclaimed Richard, "no wonder then it touched my heart;" and late as the hour was, he besought her once more to indulge him with a repetition of it, before they returned to the palace.

When she had complied with his request, he said, "It is the burden of this song which so particularly delights and affects me; these four lines,

'I've stray'd o'er the wold, and I've stray'd o'er the wild,
In hopes to find him whom my presence might save;
O ye saints lead me to him, O, tell him, I'm true!
And preserve him from sinking in youth to the grave.'

When they flow upon my ear in the silver tones of your voice, they possess a charm for my senses which will imprint them indelibly upon my memory:—when I lie at the dead of night, stretched upon my couch in my silent tent, pleased through the eye of fancy to behold thy image, and fearing to sleep, lest my dreams should not present to me the form which my waking imagination joys to dwell upon, should the gentle breeze murmur around me, I shall endeavour to believe its whispering, the echo of thy heavenly melody."

With the first dawn of the morning sounded the trumpet, which summoned prince Richard to head the troops that were destined to march under his command; early as the hour was Christabelle was arisen, once more to repeat to him those farewells which she had already so often spoken on the foregoing evening. The queen and princess were likewise present to witness his departure. Having bestowed on them the tender embrace of separation, received the blessing of his royal mother, and listened to her prayers for the success of his arms; he turned to Christabelle; a tear hung trembling in her downcast eye—"Farewell! and angels hover over the treasure of my soul!" he exclaimed.

"The merciful God of heaven protect thee in the battle's heat!" with difficulty pronounced the quivering lips of Christabelle, "should'st thou be doomed to fall!"—this idea checked all power of utterance, her tears burst forth unrestrained, and she sunk upon his neck.

"The talisman of thy love, my adored Christabelle, will protect me from every injury!" replied the prince as he pressed her for the last time to his breast. The queen received her from his arms, and as she encircled her in hers, she said, "Whatever be the fate of my son, Eleanor will never desert her whom he approved in life!"

"Merciful God protect him!" again breathed forth Christabelle, and raising her eyes, which had been cast, dimmed with tears, to the earth, she observed the prince already mounted on his proud charger, and placing himself at the head of his troops. Still his thoughts were with those whom he was in the act of quitting; again and again he waved to them his hand; again and again Christabelle returned the affectionate signal; at length the word for marching was given; the trumpet sounded a loud blast; various other instruments likewise poured forth their voices upon the air; and with these were mingled the trampling of the horses, and the shouts of the soldiery. The tumult of the scene for awhile suspended, as it were, the feelings of Christabelle; but when the sounds died away in the distance; when she could no longer descry the waving plumes of snow-white lustre nodding on the helmet of the prince; and the train in front of which he rode, was barely discernible, as one moving body, all her apprehensions for his destiny returned with double force to her heart; and she fled to her chamber to indulge in solitude in her tears.

CHAP. XVIII.

> Thy numbers, Jealousy! to nought were fixed;
> Sad proof of thy distressful state.
>
> COLLINS.*

THE soothing attentions of the queen and her amiable daughter proved a most lenient balm to the sorrowing soul of the fair Christabelle; in gratitude for the kind exertions of their friendship, she strove to appear cheerful in their presence; but the effort caused her many a painful struggle; the torturing whisperings of excessive anxiety communicated to her heart an unconquerable apprehension that she should never again behold him, on whom her affections were placed.

With each succeeding day Christabelle gained additional proofs of the highly-amiable disposition of the princess Jane; their hours were passed together in social intercourse of industry and amusement united; which they pursued with an unanimity which appeared rather as the result of a lengthened friendship, than as the effect of a recent acquaintance; so efficacious is gentleness of soul in linking together by the happiest ties, those whose breasts it inhabits.

The love which from excess of regard for her son the queen bore Christabelle, would alone have claimed for her in return the love of a grateful heart like hers. Had she experienced no other motive for bestowing on her the affection of a daughter; but to one who had not been placed in a situation to experience that tenderness from Eleanor which Christabelle had done; she appeared a character more calculated to excite respect or admiration than love; there was a certain dignity in her deportment from which she rarely relaxed, and a frown upon her brow which she as seldom unbent; these, to a common observer, seemed alone the effects of pride and conscious majesty; to those who had an opportunity of more intimately scrutinizing her disposition, it was evident that they owed their existence, at least equally, to a mind ill at ease within itself; and which, buried in its own reflections, was indifferent to the opinion of those by whom it was surrounded.

We have already had occasion to remark the wanton infidelity of the royal Henry to his marriage bed; and the pangs of jealousy with which a knowledge of his incontinency racked the sensitive heart of his queen. We have already seen in the case of lady Ruthinglenne Bloet to how impolitic a length a thirst of revenge spurred her on; already we have mentioned that she had discovered the existence of an illicit connection between the king, and a second favourite named Rosamond de Clifford; and we have now to add that she had resolved to use the period of his present absence from England, for placing an irremoveable bar to his ever again beholding her rival in his affections.

With this intention the bosom of the queen had long been agitated; but notwithstanding the royal authority of which she was possessed, she found this a point upon which it appeared a most difficult matter for her to engage the services of any of her subjects. The punishment which had been inflicted by the king on Sir Hugh Peverel, for his interference in the case of Ruthinglenne Bloet, was not yet, by any means forgotten; and those whose inclination it really was to serve Eleanor, were withheld from such an attempt, by their apprehensions of suffering under a similar fate.

The only progress which Eleanor had made in her plan was a recent discovery of the spot of her wanton rival's concealment; with not less indignation than astonishment, she had heard it to be situated at the distance of a few miles only from her own palace of Beaumont.

The name of this retreat of illicit love was Woodstock bower; it had been a favourite spot of retirement from the cares of state with Henry's predecessor, Stephen; and had devolved upon the present king with other lands annexed to the crown.*

In the early years of their marriage the queen had more than once visited Woodstock, and expressed herself much pleased with its local situation; the grounds with which it was surrounded being remarkably beautiful; and the gardens luxuriantly rich; but the mansion which they encircled, although denominated out of courtesy a palace, because Stephen had so frequently made it his residence, was too circumscribed for the accommodation of a princely retinue, such as it was always the pleasure of Henry to see himself, or any part of his family attended by; and accordingly it was no longer visited by them, but Beaumont selected as their most usual abode.

An inclination which the queen felt herself unable to subdue had led her to resolve to behold the woman whose personal charms were reported to be the magnet that had seduced Henry from his wedded affection; and having succeeded in discovering the spot, where, nursed in the bosom of luxury and bliss, the fair Rosamond enjoyed those smiles, which were by every law of justice and of honour hers; she conceived that it must be a matter of ease to present herself before the injurer of her peace.

But with mortification and surprise she heard that the attempt was not only of the most unpromising nature, but even regarded as utterly impracticable. Warned by the vengeance which his queen had meditated against Ruthinglenne, to preserve his still more tenderly beloved Rosamond from any inimical device which she might plan for her destruction; Henry had caused the gardens of Woodstock-bower to be converted into a labyrinth which it was impossible for any one to thread, who did not possess the secret of the clue, which acted as a guide to the concealed mansion that she inhabited.

A thousand various plans for accomplishing her desired end now occupied by turns the breast of the queen; and she ultimately decided upon engaging an armed force in her service; whatever might be the price of such an engagement; to commission them to surround the bower on every side; and to drag the victim of her jealousy to her feet.

But this plan was rendered abortive by a fact concerning the bower which had reached the knowledge of one of those friends who had been prevailed upon to espouse her cause, and second her designs.

In order to give the retreat of his beloved mistress every security which the art of man, or the purse of power could contribute to it, an entrance had been opened from the gardens to an immense range of subterraneous vaults, which were known to extend in various directions, and to considerable distances; by one of these therefore it was certain that Rosamond would fly from her enemies, in the case of such an attack upon the bower as the queen was meditating; and as the course of these passages beneath the surface of the earth, was known to but very few, and the spot where they terminated equally a matter of doubt, except to those who would not betray the knowledge of which they were possessed; this plan was obliged to be renounced.

Again Eleanor was thrown into a state of the greatest uncertainty in what manner to proceed with any hope of success; the difficulties which arose to combat the gratification of her soul's wish, instead of dispiriting her for the undertaking, did but serve to add keenness to her inclination.

She placed spies upon the bower to watch who had access to its mazes. Information was brought to her that none were seen either to quit, or enter the labyrinth, but servants whose attachment had already been so strongly proved to the king, that endeavouring to tamper with their fidelity to their trust, could only produce the event of placing them still more upon their guard, by acquainting them that some measures unfriendly to the interest with which they were allied, were in agitation.

The conduct of Rosamond's household was under the regulation of a gentleman, named Sir Eugene de Lancy, to whom the king was peculiarly attached on account of the ready disposition which he had on every occasion displayed to promote his pleasures; and whom he had on this account honoured with knighthood.

The disposition of the lost Rosamond was represented as one of the most mild, and engaging nature; which had acquired for her the love of all who enjoyed her friendship, or lived in her attendance. This excellence of temper had peculiarly attached to her Sir Eugene as a friend; and in the absence of her paramour he extended towards her many little assiduities and attentions which lightened to her those periods during which she reflected only on the moment of his return. The world, which authoritatively, but wrongly imagines, that a single instance of criminality cannot exist in any breast, accused Sir Eugene of being the rival of his monarch's bliss; but the accusation was false; Sir Eugene's heart was too strongly swayed by the principles of honour towards his prince; and Rosamond, although she had fallen into the snare of seduction with a king, could not have been bribed by the treasure of worlds, to have swerved from the fidelity which she had in her bosom sworn to him.

The depression of Rosamond's spirits had never been so great during any period of her Henry's absence as it was at the present one; various images of terror were constantly haunting her imagination; she dreaded that he might never return; that she might never behold him again; and by his death be cast a wanderer upon society; or, what filled her mind with still greater terrors, that she might, by being deprived of his countenance and protection, fall a victim to the resentment of his family, whose animosity she knew to be so justly awakened against her.

When these ideas did not occupy her mind, others equally gloomy never failed to glide before her eyes in the perspective of her waking visions; a knowledge of the frailty of the princess Adelais, had been conveyed to her; and lest she should supersede her in the favour of the king was often a subject of terror for her thoughts; and she would then declare her resolution of secluding herself for ever from the world, by taking the vows of some religious order before his return; during these fits of despondency it was, that Sir Eugene de Lancy possessed the peculiar and happy power of restoring her mind to tranquillity; he would draw to her attentive ear, in terms of energy, the joy which she would experience at the return of the monarch who lived but for her alone, and with whom her charms were a solace for all the cares which he experienced from an unquiet state, and an alienated family.

Then would the smile of joy dimple the cheek of the fair Rosamond; but it did not penetrate to her heart; for her love for Henry did not blind her to the injustice of which she was guilty towards the queen; and in Rosamond appeared a striking instance that the heart which is not perfectly innocent, can never be perfectly happy.

The chief, and almost only amusement of Rosamond's solitary hours was the voice of music; she loved to listen to the wild notes of the village minstrels, whom Sir Eugene frequently gratified her by introducing into the bower; and accidentally he would afford her a treat of a superior nature in the science which she loved, by inviting within its recesses those stray musicians who in their wanderings over the kingdom, in quest of bands of pilgrims whom they might accompany to the shrines of their favourite saints, were not unfrequently passing by the hallowed bower of bliss. Those who had been placed by the queen as spies upon the bower had observed the occasional admission of these minstrels; and according to the injunction they had received, to suffer no single transaction connected with the labyrinth to pass unrecorded, communicated to Eleanor the friendly reception of these musicians.

This information, which reached the queen about a month after the departure of her son for France, immediately inspired her with an idea which appeared to promise success to her wish of beholding the paramour of her faithless husband. She believed her person to be unknown to Sir Eugene; she was certain that it was so to Rosamond; were she therefore to disguise herself as one of a band of pilgrims, and to take with her any musician of superior skill, there appeared little doubt of her obtaining admission within the labyrinth.

She gave due deliberation to this idea, and her conviction of its promised efficacy increasing upon reflection, she resolved to hazard the attempt; should it fail, which was a contingency she did not apprehend, the avowal of her rank must inevitably preserve her from personal danger.

She was possessed of friends who would readily consent to become members of her fictitious pilgrimage; but her greatest difficulty rested on the choice of a minstrel whose superior musical excellence was such as to ensure them admission into Woodstock-bower. Whilst the queen was ruminating on this point, in the solitude of one of her private apartments in the palace; the silver tones of Christabelle's voice, warbling a plaintive and simple air, as she passed along in the garden under the casements of the queen's chamber, attracted her attention. Eleanor listened to her notes with pleasure, as she had frequently done before, and believed that she was of all other beings the most likely to give credit to an assumed profession, by the excellence of her talent, if she could be prevailed upon to undertake the office.

Without hesitation she accordingly resolved to propose to her the plan with which her mind was filled; and to this end immediately sought Christabelle in her chamber. The gentle maid attended with interest and with pity to the queen's detail of the injustice, the sufferings, and the indignities, to which herself and her children had been exposed on account of the dissolute attachment of the king to Rosamond de Clifford; and after this introduction, Eleanor proceeded to state to her the purpose which she had in view, by addressing her upon the subject; and informed her of the desire which she entertained of entering into the presence of the frail fair one; expressing herself, as if it were her wish to endeavour to release her husband from the trammels in which he was now bound to Rosamond by reclaiming her from her present incontinent life; and explaining to Christabelle, that through her alone she had hope of accomplishing her design.

Bound as Christabelle considered herself by a debt of gratitude to all those relatives of her beloved Richard, who were allied to him by the ties of friendship, as well as of consanguinity; in particular to the queen his mother who had bestowed on a friendless orphan, like herself, not only the name, but the affection of a parent; and perceiving in the plan which was agitated by Eleanor no step but what was natural to the cruel peculiarity of the situation in which she was placed; and likewise commendable to a mind of reason, generously seeking to produce the reform of one of its fellow beings; she gave a ready assent to the request which had been submitted to her.

With the greatest delight the queen received Christabelle's acquiescence; and having imprinted on her lips a kiss of thanks, in the name of her best beloved son, she quitted her, and calling a council of her confidential friends, proceeded to arrange a plan for visiting the bower of the unsuspecting Rosamond.

CHAP. XIX.

> Dar'st thou, presumptuous, to invade my rights!
> Restore him quickly to my longing arms,
> And with him give me back his broken vows,
> Or I will rend them from thy bleeding heart.
>
> LEE.*

AFTER much deliberation, an evening at a short distance of time was appointed for the execution of the queen's plan. By the two friends who had undertaken to accompany her on her expedition; the dress of a pilgrim, similar to the habits which they were themselves to wear, was provided for Eleanor; and the garb of a minstrel prepared for the disguise of Christabelle.

The appointed evening being arrived, the queen caused herself and Christabelle, to be conveyed to the house of a friend, at the distance of little more than a mile from the bower; from whence it had been resolved that she and her party should set out.

The evening was bright and clear; the moon rose with resplendent brilliancy; and the queen and her friends being equipped in their disguises, left the house, where they had prepared themselves for appearing before Rosamond; and entered the high road leading to the bower.

They pursued their way without interruption, till the dark shade, caused by the lofty beech and maple-trees, which formed the groves of the labyrinth, announced their near approach to the destined spot.

At the distance of scarcely half a furlong from the entrance into the bower, one of the queen's friends suddenly stopping, directed the attention of his companions to a knot of thick and stunted shrubs, which grew on the opposite side of the road to that on which the labyrinth was situated; and in the covert of which he affirmed that he could discern a number of men planted in ambush who had been discovered to him by the reflection of the beams of the moon, glancing upon the polished blades of pikes borne in their hands; and which denoted their profession to be war.

Casting her eyes with the coldness of indifference for an instant towards the spot to which her friend had pointed, Eleanor said, "If they are warriors, I trust there are none in this kingdom, who do not respect the person of their queen." And without having faltered in her pace, she continued to proceed.

In the course of a few more minutes they reached the entrance to the bower. According to the instructions which Christabelle had received, she seated herself on a bank of turf by the side of the gate, and drawing her lute from the folds of her garment, began to play a soft melody, which she accompanied by some words, which had been given her for the purpose; and which contained an exhortation to her companions, in their character of pilgrims, not to droop under the fatigue of their journey; but to trust to the charitable, and feeling to relieve their wants.

The queen's party had been careful to strew their sandals with dust; and to assume other marks of their having performed a long and tedious journey, the more readily to excite the compassion of whomsoever might reply to the entreaty which they had sounded for admission, by blowing the bugle at the gate.

A considerable time having elapsed and no one appearing to attend the summons; one of the queen's friends blew the bugle a second time, more loudly than before.

At length a person appeared behind the grate, and demanded their business?

"We are," replied the queen, "benighted pilgrims, who have travelled from the rising of the sun to this late hour, and who humbly request of the owner of this mansion to grant us a little hospitality."

"I am sorry for you," answered the servant, "your suit is hopeless; no strangers are ever admitted here."

"Cruel decision!" exclaimed Eleanor; "we must then pass the night upon this damp turf; our fainting limbs are unable to bear us farther.—Oh! that we were at this moment near to the abode of any friend of the royal Henry's; unlike his excellent sovereign would he be, if he suffered us to remain here, exposed to the inclement air of the night!"

At this instant a second person advanced towards the grate; it was Sir Eugene de Lancy; he had been surprised by the length of time that the person who had replied to the bugle had been detained at the gate; and ever watchful against danger, had come to investigate the cause of his stay.

"Who are these with whom you are parleying?" he demanded of the servant. The man repeated the words of Eleanor.

"As ye speak in terms so meritorious, and still so just of my sovereign," said Sir Eugene, addressing the strangers; "ye have doubtless the honour of being known to him?"

"Oh yes, yes we *are* known to him indeed," replied Eleanor; "were we now near to his palace at Beaumont we should not need to stray farther for a night's repose; will ye be sufficiently kind to inform us if it be situated within such a distance of this spot, as limbs already too weary even for penance, may hope to reach, ere strength entirely fail them?"

Sir Eugene listened attentively to the queen's words, and when she had ceased speaking, he requested to be informed of their names.

Pointing to one of her friends, "Sir Charles Blansay and his wife Constance," answered the queen, "are the suitors for your hospitality; we experienced the honour and satisfaction of entertaining our royal master on his pilgrimage to the tomb of Becket;* and on this account I pronounce with confidence, that he would not refuse us entertainment on a similar journey to our tutelar saint."

"I am certain that he would not," replied Sir Eugene, "nor as one honoured with his friendship would I display myself backward in such conduct as I know he would himself practise; were I not enjoined by a mandate from his own lips, not to suffer any one to enter here."

"A mandate from *his* lips!" ejaculated Eleanor; "is this then an abode of the King's?"

"Yes, it is," was the reply.

"We know that he is absent in France," rejoined Eleanor, "and cannot grant us his own permission to shelter ourselves within his royal walls; but surely his queen would not refuse the boon of destitute travellers like ourselves."

"This is no abode of the queen's;" returned Sir Eugene—then turning to the servant he commanded him to go and bring out refreshments of wine and fruit.

"Wine is not for our profession," said the queen, "your fruit I shall thankfully accept;" and as she spoke she leaned against the gate, appearing to be overcome with fatigue; whilst the fictitious Blansay lent her his arm.

"Who are your companions, lady?" asked Sir Eugene.

"One is an old servant of our household," replied Eleanor, "who attends our steps from fidelity to his master and myself—the other is a youth whom I entertain as my minstrel, a member likewise of my household; and my attachment to him is so great, that it once impelled me to the performance of an action, to which no other consideration could have induced me. It prompted me to refuse my honoured King a request which he condescended to ask of me."

The queen paused; and Sir Eugene inquired, "What that request had been?"

"To add some little grace to the humble entertainment which my board could afford a monarch," answered Eleanor, "I introduced to it this youth, and his lute; pleased with the honour of engaging the attention of a king, he played perhaps more skilfully, and sung more sweetly, than he might have done without such a spur to exertion. Be that as it may; the royal Henry professed himself charmed with his powers, and questioned me if I would part with him? The boy is an orphan, who has from his infancy enjoyed my protection; I am grown attached to him; and I could not therefore consent to his wish, without much pain to my own feelings; I expressed myself humbly, but fully to the king, and he displayed his gracious benevolence, in naming the subject to me no more. 'It was his desire,' he said, 'if I could have dispensed with the youth's services, to have placed him in attendance upon his favourite mistress, the Lady Rosamond de Clifford, who he informed me was passionately attached to music; and whose peculiar taste for the soft, and tender melody, he considered the talents of my poor boy to be exactly calculated to delight.'"

"Said the king so of your minstrel, lady!" exclaimed Sir Eugene, in an animated tone of voice.

"Yes indeed he did," replied the queen, "and I think he did not much over-rate poor Edwy's powers."

"And should you object, lady," continued Sir Eugene, "to suffer your minstrel to play before the lady Rosamond?"

"To what end do you ask that question, Sir?" returned the queen; "it is not likely that any chance should lead a simple boy like him into the presence of one who is reported to be sedulously concealed from the eye, even of every noble of the realm."

"Perhaps, lady," Sir Eugene rejoined, "that chance may be infinitely nearer than you imagine."

"I cannot think it," replied the queen, with a smile.

"What you have told me," answered Sir Eugene, "will render me more explicit with you than I should otherwise have been. Is it possible that you can live in England, and still be ignorant that this is Woodstock-bower, the abode of that Rosamond?"

"It would be more strange if I *had* been acquainted that it were," replied Eleanor, "as neither my husband, nor myself ever travelled this way before!—I now perceive the caution which withholds you from granting us admission; and I am glad the royal Henry has men of such fidelity in his employment."

The servant now returned with a basket of fruit and cakes, and was opening the grate to present them through it to Eleanor. Sir Eugene stopped him, and said, "Unlock the gate, lady Blansay will permit her minstrel to play before my fair charge, will you not, lady?" he added, addressing the queen.

"Sir," she replied, "I would willingly in any wise promote the amusement of those on whom it would gratify my king to know that I had conferred an obligation; but as my husband and myself cannot be admitted within the bower, we have no time to lose in seeking a lodging elsewhere; and how would Edwy ever be able to overtake us?"

"But," returned Sir Eugene, "were I to say, lady, that my scruples about admitting yourself, and Sir Charles Blansay within the labyrinth were removed; would you now accept from me that hospitality which I, a short time ago, considered myself bound to refuse to you?"

The queen appeared to hesitate, and one of her tutored friends said, "I pray you accept the invitation; you will sink with fatigue if you attempt to proceed farther ere you take repose."

"But will lady Rosamond receive us graciously?" demanded the queen addressing Sir Eugene; "will she not deem us intruders; and perhaps speak to the king in terms that may draw down upon us his displeasure?"

"Knew you the gentle soul of Rosamond, you would not express such a fear," replied Sir Eugene; and as he spoke he opened the gate, which had hitherto closed the entrance into the groves of Woodstock-bower; and invited them to pass freely.

The queen took the arm of the pretended Sir Charles Blansay, and as she entered the gate, turning to Christabelle, she said, "Come, my boy, let me not leave thee behind; thou art my introduction to hospitality on this spot; my heart was truly prophetic when it would not surrender thee to any other employer; but anticipated both advantage and pleasure, from retaining thee in its own service."

With a smile at the queen's remark, Sir Eugene led the way; Eleanor observed him attentively, and perceived the silken clue in his hand. By their side moved the domestic who bore a silver lamp, of which the flame was rendered almost unnecessary by the splendour of the moon, which had nearly filled her horns, and was floating through a peaceful sky, unspotted by a single cloud.

As they proceeded, the queen could not forbear remarking in silence the beauty of the spot over which she was treading; and which in cultivation, and elegance of plan, now far surpassed what the bower had been at the time of her first acquaintance with it. Here, were scattered knots of the luxuriant larch, around whose boles entwined themselves the sweet-scented woodbine, the musk-rose, and the jessamine; there clusters of the delicately-beautiful barberry, amidst whose white blossoms peeped forth the painted pea, and the odoriferous lavender.

Here, presented itself to her observation a pond for the preservation of fish, around whose margin a light net-work of brass added security to the amusement of ensnaring the subtile inhabitants of its waters. There, an aviary filled with the rarest of the feathered tribe met the wandering sight—whilst on every hand the jonquil, the violet, the primrose, and the hyacinth were casting incense upon the scene.

These observations were additional daggers to the heart of the queen;—"These," she reflected, "are the rewards of a deviation from the path of virtue, while the faithful and deserted wife, mourns her wrongs without a hand to exert itself for her redress. Thus too long has she mourned; but the period of her retribution is at hand." This idea communicated a sudden emotion of bliss to her heart, which she with difficulty restrained from mounting in an exclamation of delight to her lips; or from displaying itself by a flash of triumph in her eyes.

After wandering through repeated mazes, which truly constituted the spot a labyrinth; and of which the varying scene was ever beautiful; several lights attracted the attention of the queen, which on turning her eyes towards them, she perceived to proceed from the mansion, that was seated in the bosom of the bower; and which they were now rapidly approaching.

She had scarcely time to observe that it had undergone equal improvement with the grounds through which she had just been passing, ere she was invited by Sir Eugene to enter.

The strangers, with the exception of that one of the queen's friends, whom she had represented to De Lancy as an ancient servant of her household, were ushered into an apartment of the most fantastic and elegant kind; the walls were covered with a green silk drapery; which being drawn up at certain intervals by festoons of flowers displayed within recesses, figures of alabaster, which extended from their hands, silver lamps that cast a brilliant illumination over the scene. Couches of purple velvet, adorned with silver fringe were placed around. A carpet of goat's hair of the purest white hue, was spread upon the floor; and on tables of rosewood, polished to the brilliancy of a mirror, were set before the guests those refreshments which had first been offered to them through the grate.

Having seen them seated Sir Eugene retired, to prepare Rosamond, as he informed them, for encountering her unexpected guests; and for the pleasure which she was to derive from the musical skill of their minstrel.

Fearing even during his absence, to express her feelings in words, lest there should exist any possibility of their being overheard; the queen was compelled to display the disgust, the resentment, and the jealousy with which her bosom was swelled, alone by the eloquent turns of countenance which she glanced upon her companions.

At the expiration of nearly a quarter of an hour, the door of the apartment was opened, and Sir Eugene led Rosamond into it. Her figure was tall, justly proportioned, and graceful; her dress was of white silk, confined round her waist by a cestus* of pearls and amethysts, blended together with the most curious workmanship; by corresponding clasps her robe was united in front; and with bands of the same costly materials were the sleeves confined upon her wrists. Her golden tresses were seen depending in wanton luxuriance upon her shoulders, from beneath a veil of the richest lace, by which her countenance was shaded; and which was fastened upon her head by a single amethyst of an unusual size and lustre.

Rosamond expressed a welcome to her guests, and took her seat. The tones of her voice were gentle and persuasive in the extreme; upon the queen and Christabelle they produced effects of the most opposite nature. The jealous and exasperated queen, silently execrated them as the artful tones of a syren; and believed them to have been her principal charm in seducing the king from his wedded fidelity. Could Christabelle have disunited from her other ideas that of the criminality of Rosamond's present life; she would have regarded the melody of her voice as the soft eloquence of the most interesting virtue; even as it was, she could not divest herself of an unaccountable prepossession which the first sound of the pitiable frail one's voice had excited for her in her breast.

Rosamond reverted to the unpleasant situation from which Sir Eugene had relieved the strangers by admitting them into the bower; she commented on their pilgrimage, and asked them many questions concerning it; but the ready eloquence which the queen had displayed on the outside of the labyrinth, was silenced by her sight of Rosamond; with the lawless rival in her view, it required the exertion of superior fortitude to keep down the feelings with which her bosom was agitated; and which nothing would have tempted Eleanor, even for a while to subdue, but that the moment of her vengeance was not yet ripe.

Sir Eugene now spoke of the skill in music possessed by the minstrel, and mentioned the praise which the royal Henry had once bestowed on it. At the name of the king, the emotion of

Rosamond was evident; she wiped a tear from her eye; and in faint accents pronounced, "God preserve him!"

The agitation of the queen increased in proportion to that which she beheld produced in Rosamond, by the recollection of her royal paramour; Eleanor's friend perceived a deadly pallidness to overspread her cheek, as her rival pronounced her prayer for the king's safety; and dreading that an entire failure of her powers might follow, he requested Sir Eugene to produce a cup of the wine which he had before offered to their acceptance, and which he said the weak state to which she was reduced by excess of fatigue, would authorize her to taste, although engaged on a pilgrimage.

Having drunk the wine the queen's fortitude returned; and Rosamond seeing her guest restored, entreated the supposed minstrel to produce his lute, and to indulge her with a proof of his powers.

Christabelle acquiesced; and having for a few instants struck the chords of her instrument, preparatorily to commencing her song, she accompanied herself through some lines, with which she had been provided by the queen, calculated to set forth the superiority of a spotless countenance over every other blessing.

At first Rosamond listened attentively to the sweetness of Christabelle's voice; but as she proceeded, it was evident that all her thoughts were given to the subject of her song; and before it was concluded she was heard to sob violently; and the tears flowed so quickly down her cheeks, that she threw back her veil in order to apply her handkerchief to her eyes.

The view which the queen now obtained of Rosamond's beauty was a fresh poniard to her bleeding heart. She saw that it justified every report which she had heard of its perfectness; and as she dwelt upon her soft blue eyes; the exquisite and expressive arches by which they were surmounted; the blushing roses which adorned her cheeks; the fascinating dimple which gave eloquence to her vermillion lips; and the enamelled snow which composed her bosom; she found herself compelled to admire, even where the direst hatred set liberality of sentiment at defiance.

Having concluded her song, Christabelle bent her eyes to the point at which the queen's were directed; and no sooner did they rest upon the countenance of Rosamond, than she was surprised by observing in her features a familiarity with her memory, for which she could not account; again and again did she gaze upon them, and still recollection gave no assistance to her doubts. At the first minute of Christabelle's observing Rosamond since she had withdrawn her veil from before her face, her eyes had been cast upon the ground; she now suddenly directed them towards her, and with this action flashed upon the mind of Christabelle a conviction of the most unexpected, the most dreadful, the most torturing nature; for past all probability of error, in *that Rosamond* she beheld the countenance of the portrait which her deceased father had informed her represented—HER MOTHER.

CHAP. XX.

———The great King of kings,
Hath in the table of his law commanded,
That thou shalt do no murder.

SHAKESPEARE.*

INDESCRIBABLE were at this moment the emotions of Christabelle's soul! To behold a mother for the first time under circumstances of this afflicting, this peculiar nature! To be restrained by the vow which she had pronounced to her father, from acknowledging her as a parent, or confessing herself to her as a daughter! What event could the hand of chance have produced more distressing to the feelings, more agonizing to the senses!

The name of Rosamond de Clifford had been familiar to the ear of Christabelle ever since she had become a member of the royal household; and when she had alternately pitied the frail state into which she had sunk, and reprobated the criminal injustice of which she was guilty towards the queen; how far had she been from imagining that the being who was the subject of her thoughts was her mother! She had heard Rosamond spoken of as the wife of a knight, Sir Walter de Clifford, a man of the highest respectability and honour, from whom the king had seduced her; and who had been driven in despair from his country, by the domestic misfortune which had so unmeritedly fallen upon him.

Now was it explained to her that this unfortunate man had been her lamented father; now did she comprehend the fatal calamity which had exiled him from an intercourse with his fellow beings; now was it apparent to her by what apprehensions his mind had been impressed, when he had so earnestly prayed for her preservation from temptation! One only clause had the vow by which he had bound her not to acknowledge her mother, contained; "Never," he had said, "unless in the dying moments of repentance the hand of God should interfere to produce so unlooked-for a re-union." By this vow had she in the most solemn, the most earnest manner bound herself at the altar of her God; the sacredness of the act would not admit into a mind religious like hers, even the most distant idea of infringement. But had the liberty of addressing her mother been Christabelle's, as was the inclination, the power of so doing had fled from her; a sensation almost approaching to the fading away of existence had seized her, upon the discovery of the few last moments; she was sensible of life, but entirely bereft of the faculty of exerting any of its powers.

The emotion of Christabelle was unobserved by all present. Her task of singing was fortunately concluded; and it was not the purpose of the queen to call upon her for a second display of her powers. The period was arrived at which Eleanor hoped to produce an event of consequence to her future peace. She perceived Rosamond affected to her wish, by Christabelle's song; the tears were still trembling on the fair frail one's cheek; and still her bosom heaved with the half-smothered sigh.

Eleanor rose from the couch on which she had hitherto been reposing; and placed herself by the side of Rosamond. Upon this signal, the queen's friend, who represented Sir Charles Blansay, took occasion, according to the instructions which he had received from his royal mistress, to draw Sir Eugene de Lancy from the apartment. When they had left it, the queen thus addressed Rosamond:—"Am I deceived, fair lady, in believing you moved by the subject of my minstrel's song?

"Indeed you are not," Rosamond replied, "however I may have deviated from the path of virtue, I am still conscious of the blessings it can bestow!"

"How excellently then is your heart prepared for repentance," rejoined the queen, "and a return to the straight path from which it has erred."

Rosamond replied only with a deep sigh.

"Although this is the first time of my beholding you," continued Eleanor, "I feel an interest in your reformation—for your history is known to me, so was your family; and I have often sighed over the delusion which had captivated your senses. Alas! what is the favour of a king, compared with the approbation of your own heart? Is not the cell of a convent more inviting, if inhabited with peace of mind, than the luxuries of this bower, enjoyed with an unquiet conscience?"

"Oh, too truly do you speak," returned Rosamond, "each moment teaches me that even my Henry's undivided love, cannot grant my life substantial bliss!"

"And how will it affect your death?" demanded Eleanor; "will the knowledge of having enjoyed his love be able to shield you from the dreadful phantoms that will present themselves around your dying couch? the images of your Henry's much injured queen, and her neglected offspring! the visions of those relatives upon whom your conduct has brought disgrace! the shades of your heart-broken father, your distracted husband—however brilliant the sun of your present life, this scene *will* overcloud its splendour at the last!"

Rosamond clasped her hands in agony together—"Oh, preserve me pitying heaven, from miseries like these!" fell in faint accents from her quivering lips.

"The benignity of heaven *has* interposed to preserve thee from them," replied Eleanor, "in me behold its chosen instrument. Renounce henceforward the love thou bearest to man, for the adoration which thou owest to thy God! exchange thy present futile joys for the solid comforts of repentance, and of prayer. Oh fly ere it is yet too late from this witchery of tainted pleasure, to the peaceful seclusion of some holy edifice! There, be thy sole employment the preparation of thy soul for its flight into eternity. Act this praise-worthy part, and angels will accept thy orisons—even those whom thou hast most wronged on earth will count their beads for thy salvation; even the injured Eleanor will pardon thee!"

"Your arguments are just, are kind, are charitable, I feel their force, they sink into my heart," answered Rosamond; "I have often dwelt on these reflections before; there is only one fear which withholds me from pursuing your advice; and it awes me more than any other joy can charm my soul."

"What can that apprehension be?" asked Eleanor.

With hesitation, yet with energy, Rosamond pronounced, "It is, lest if I were to renounce my Henry, his forgiveness should never follow the act—such a knowledge would unfit me for repentance, or for heaven—It would break my heart!"

"What!" exclaimed Eleanor, "do you value the forgiveness of the king, more than the forgiveness of heaven?"

A fresh flood of tears burst from the eyes of Rosamond; on her countenance was visibly portrayed the anguish of a conflicting soul. She did not reply, and the queen repeated her question.

Rosamond now spoke; "Oh! do not urge me," she cried, "to a confession which will make me appear only more guilty in your eyes, than you already consider me; I cannot, I cannot renounce the king; he is now my *only* friend; he omits no kindness which may prevent me from feeling the loss of those whom I resigned for him; I never behold him that he does not repeat to me that I stand in the same relation to *him*—that I am *his* only happiness on earth; whatever therefore *my* doom may be, never, never will I voluntarily deprive *him* of one moment's bliss!"

"Sayest thou so? frail, and resolute minion!" exclaimed the queen. "Then force shall tear thee from thy adulterous paramour; since gentleness and persuasion have failed in the attempt! never shall thy deluded eyes behold *thy* Henry, as thou vainly namest him, more!"

"What mean these accents?" inquired the astonished Rosamond, "why do your eyes flash thus in anger on me? How has my conduct offended *you?* By what authority do you thus taunt and threaten me?"

"By an authority, which, lost and hardened even as thou art, will turn thy heart to marble, when thou hearest it named," replied the queen; "does no secret instinct whisper to thy conscience who it is that stands before thee? Does it not inform thine heart whom thou most hast cause to dread? and having rejected her mercy will it not cause thee to shrink within thyself at the approach of her just vengeance? She who stands before thee is Eleanor, England's queen, *thy* Henry's WIFE!"

Whilst speaking, the queen had arisen from her seat; and casting off her pilgrim's garb, now appeared adorned with those ensigns of royalty which struck conviction of her rank to the mind of the beholder.

Rosamond cast upon her a single glance and with a piercing shriek, sunk fainting on the couch on which she had been sitting.

The lips of Christabelle breathed a faint groan, but it escaped unheeded.

The sound of Rosamond's exclamation reached Sir Eugene de Lancy, and he rushed hastily into the apartment. At the sight of the change which had taken place in the dress of the supposed pilgrim, he gave an involuntary start. The queen stepped forward to meet him—"Doubt not whom it is that thou beholdest," she said, "*I am the queen!* Heaven has favoured my attempt of gaining access to the object of a husband's illicit love; I have offered her my mercy; she has rejected it, and it now alone remains for her to feel the weight of my resentment;—nor shalt thou, vile instrument of an adulterous monarch's guilt escape thy just reward!"

Excess of astonishment chained for the instant the faculties of Sir Eugene, and rendered him incapable of action.

The shriek uttered by Rosamond, had been heard by the domestics of the bower, and they now entered with anxious countenances, inquiring the cause. The queen, firm and majestic in every look and gesture, placed herself between them and a door of the apartment which opened in the gardens; she drew a dagger from her girdle, and grasping its hilt firmly in her hand, she said, "I trust that not even the slaves of a pander like De Lancy, have souls sufficiently hardy and rebellious, to dare to place a hand upon the person of their queen—if any such there be, their blood shall answer the attempt!"

Now first waking, as it appeared, from his stupor of surprise and turning to the domestics, Sir Eugene exclaimed, "Where are the guards? Summon them instantly to protect the lady Rosamond!" and he rushed towards the door by which he had entered, repeating his commands.

"Let your force be strong!" cried the queen with emphasis and irony united, "or mine will supersede it, I forewarn you." Throwing open the door which led into the gardens, and calling to her one of her two friends, she commanded him to discharge the pistol with which he was furnished; her order was immediately obeyed; and in the course of a few seconds it was replied to by a similar report at some distance. "Now, my friend," she cried, "you will soon learn who were the armed men that you remarked in ambush as we approached towards the bower—they are my soldiers!"

In a silver vase which was placed within a niche of the wall, close to the side of the door by which Eleanor was standing, and with one of its ends knotted to the vase, lay the silken clue. The queen snatched it up, and putting it into the hand of one of her friends, she added, "Fly to the gate; open it to my warriors; and use this to conduct them hither!"

He hastened to execute her commands, and the queen then turning her regards towards Rosamond, perceived some female attendants employed in attempts to restore her to life; and several men in the livery of the king's royal guard standing on either side of the couch on which she rested. Upon this observation the fire which was already raging within her breast flamed with additional fury; but her thoughts were immediately turned into another channel, by observing Sir Eugene de Lancy apply the flame of a lamp to the end of the clue, which was tied to the vase, and thus deprive it of its power of assisting her emissary in retracing his way to the house.

This action which she considered as a tacit mark of defiance to her power, the violence of her increasing passion scarcely granted her power of utterance to inveigh against. Sir Eugene replied; solely to her upbraidings, "I am faithful to the trust which the king has reposed in me," and approaching Rosamond, in whose opening eyes was announced her return to her recollection, he warned her of the impending danger; and besought her to suffer herself to be conveyed to the subterraneous vaults before the arrival of the queen's band.

Aware of his intention, for he had spoken it sufficiently loud to be overheard by the queen, she stepped forward; but ere she could address Rosamond, with a second shriek, she had again sunk into a state of insensibility; for the naked dagger which Eleanor bore in her hand, was regarded by her, as raised to strike the blow that was to separate her for ever from the king. The terrors of death in such a form were more awful than her spirits or fortitude could endure the idea of; and a cold, and death-like sensation now oppressed her.

"Remove her at your peril!" exclaimed the queen; but the mandate was unnecessary, for such a removal was at that minute rendered impossible by the wretched state into which terror and agony of mind had thrown the suffering sinner—and she added, "I design her no injury; but to convey her to a spot where her wiles can no longer be exercised to interrupt my peace."

Distant voices and footsteps were now heard approaching from different parts of the labyrinth. "They come! my soldiers come!" exclaimed the exulting queen.

"We must then prepare to meet them," replied Sir Eugene; and rallied his men before the entrance of the apartment.

In a few moments some straggling members of the queen's troops appeared bursting through various thickets of the labyrinth, and Rosamond's guards extended their pikes to oppose their approach.

The number of men in the service of the queen upon this enterprise was at least treble that of those of whom Sir Eugene had the command; and could they have entered the bower in a body, and burst united upon the mansion, there could not have existed the most slender doubt of their executing with ease their royal mistress's mandate of carrying off Rosamond to the palace of Beaumont; from whence it had been her determination to transport her to some nunnery, whose gates she would have taken effectual measures to have prevented her from every repassing. But the guiding clue, having proved, through the management of Sir Eugene, useless in the hand of that friend of the queen's with whom she had confided it for the purpose of conducting her soldiers to her presence; they were compelled to trust to chance for leading them to the mansion; and therefore arrived in such slender detachments, that by the guards who opposed them, and who had both the advantage of acting in union, and likewise the superiority of situation, they were vanquished with scarcely an exertion.

This strife of arms continued for a considerable time; the soul of the queen suffering upon the rack of torture, lest a total overthrow should attend her men:—and the silently sorrowing Christabelle, perhaps the most truly wretched member of the scene. Oh, how sincerely did she wish that it were permitted her to whisper into the ear of Rosamond a prayer for her to accept the mercy of the queen! how truly did she mourn the mad, disgraceful infatuation by which she had declared herself bound to her king! how greatly did she dread the event of the resolution which she had expressed!

The clangour produced by the uninterrupted clashing of arms, recalled Rosamond into sense. Wildly she cast around her eyes; terror met them on every side; she beheld her defenders and her enemies dealing around the blows of death, and the earth bedewed with blood, for the shedding of which her frailty was the first cause. A cold trembling oppressed her; her limbs were shivering with ague; whilst a painful fire was scorching her heart.

The queen was wandering about the apartment, awaiting with the most tremulous anxiety the event of the struggle; and with a determined fierceness depicted on her countenance, which bespoke her feelings to be wrought to such an acme that she would not scruple to revenge the defeat of her adherents, if a defeat should be their lot, by any effort however desperate of her own.

Rosamond closed her eyes and leaned her head upon the bosom of one of her female attendants; the relief of weeping was denied her; great was the agony of her brain, but it refused to distil itself into tears.

The effigy of silent despair sat Christabelle, she was neither addressed nor remembered; her lute had fallen down at her feet; clouds swam before her eyes; and sickness oppressed her heart.

At length an exclamation on the part of Sir Eugene's men, which appeared to denote a victory, arrested the steps of the queen; to the horror of her feelings it was repeated; and in the succeeding minute one of her friends rushed into the apartment; "Your soldiers," he said, "are vanquished, no hope remains of accomplishing your object."

"And thinkest thou," cried the queen, "because one of my plans has failed me, that I am so tamely-minded as to quit the injurer of my peace, unrevenged? that I will give her an opportunity of escaping for ever from that justice which I have it now in my power to inflict upon her, and thus grant her the means of eluding my vigilance, and preserving her existence to add new bliss to the life of the adulterous Henry? If I submit thus willingly, thus weakly, to my own disgrace, which I have too long already borne unrevenged, may those heavenly powers which I now believe to rank on the side of my injuries, and to yield me fortitude for their redress, eternally desert me!"

Darting towards the object of her hatred, she exclaimed, "Rosamond thou art at this instant in my power; wilt thou renounce Henry for ever?"

"Oh spare me! in mercy spare me!" replied the terrified victim of her resentment.

"Spare thee," ejaculated the queen, "to add new daggers to my peace? Spare thee minion! Unite together the love he bears thee, and sin most execrable, most unpardonable, and abjure them both unitedly as thou abjurest the punishment decreed against their cherishing; or this instant is thy last!"

The queen raised the hand which bore her dagger as she spoke, and the affrighted Rosamond exclaimed, "Sir Eugene! help! preserve me! save me!"

She attempted to rise, but the other hand of the queen confined her to her seat.

Sir Eugene heard her appeal, and was already rushing towards her.

The queen beheld his approach, "Once, and once only more I ask if thou wilt abjure his love?" she cried. Rosamond did not reply; and fatal was the silence which she maintained. The queen plunged her dagger to her heart!

The fountain of life gushed forth from the wound; a faint shriek issued from her lips; the quick of life was pierced beyond the art of man to heal.

The deed once done, the queen appeared to be struck with horror at the magnitude of her own daring. The dagger fell from her hand; the orbs of her eyes were fixed; and the quick heavings of her breast alone bespoke animation not to have forsaken her frame.

With faltering accents Rosamond spoke, "I die," she said, "the struggle of my life is almost past—Oh! may forgiveness be granted to me, as I repent the wrongs, of which I have been guilty towards others!"

"Should fate re-unite thee to thy mother in the dying moments of her repentance, thou hast THEN *and* THEN ONLY *my permission to acknowledge thyself her daughter!"* had pronounced Christabelle's father. Rosamond's tide of life *was* now at its last ebb, and she *did* confess herself repentant of her guilt. Christabelle heard the blessed sound, and flying towards her with all the swiftness of which her tottering limbs were capable; she sunk on her knees before her; and as she rested her head on her lap, she pressed her cold hand fervently to her lips, and said, "Oh, my mother! your eyes shall not be closed by strangers; heaven has graciously permitted your child to be near you for the performance of that sacred duty—*I am that child* now at your feet *my mother!"*

The sound of these words struck the heart of every one present with visible consternation.

"Thou my child!" faintly articulated Rosamond, "canst *thou* be the child of the wronged De Clifford?"

"Yes, yes I am now convinced that such was the real name of my father," replied Christabelle, "although I knew him only by that of Glencowell!"

"Oh! 'twas he, 'twas he!" shrieked forth Rosamond, and sunk back exhausted on the couch.

"And thou art *indeed* MY *mother!"* solemnly pronounced Christabelle.

"Thy mother," ejaculated the queen. "Thy mother!" she repeated; her tones were hoarse and sepulchral; agony was rending her soul, and its conflicts choked her utterance. "To what a scene of horror have *I* made thee witness!!"

The faintness of death now overpowered Rosamond; but with the assistance of her attendants she once more raised her head. Feebly she uttered, "Oh! my child, *if* such thou art, and nature credits the assertion; had I beheld thee before, I think thou hadst reclaimed me. Oh! why do we meet *thus in agony* to part, the moment of our meeting thus in"——

She shrieked aloud for the hand of death was inflicting a pang on her heart which announced the speedy dissolution of existence.

Once more she spoke—"Mourn not my loss, but pray for my

soul's repose! Oh! could I at this moment have beheld my Henry! could I have seen him shed a tear of regret over my fate!" She paused an instant; then again proceeded thus—"Should it be permitted *thee* to see my Henry, tell him that with her last breath Rosamond entreated the boon of his prayers; tell him that to him she owed her seduction from the path of virtue; and that on this account she implores *his* prayers for her forgiveness, before those of *all* other beings! tell him that although he destroyed her peace, his memory was dear to her in death. Oh! my spirit flies me. My heart-strings crack. Mercy! mercy God! My brain too. Henry! Henry! torments await me! Omnipotent heaven! pardon—preserve"——

Again the pause of a moment ensued.

"Henry! Henry!" she then whispered forth, "I have loved thee too well!" The accents were her last. Rosamond was no longer of this earth.

END OF VOL. I.

THE

FATAL VOW;

OR,

ST. MICHAEL'S MONASTERY,

A Romance,

IN TWO VOLUMES.

BY FRANCIS LATHOM.

AUTHOR OF THE MYSTERIOUS FREEBOOTER—MEN AND MANNERS—HUMAN BEINGS—MYSTERY—THE IMPENETRABLE SECRET—THE MIDNIGHT BELL, &C. &C.

VOL. II.

——————————The fatal vow
Has pass'd my lips! methought in those sad moments,
The tombs around, the saints, the darken'd altar,
And all the trembling shrines with horror shook.

THOMSON.

LONDON:
PRINTED FOR B. CROSBY AND CO. STATIONERS' COURT,
By C. Stover, Paternoster Row.
1807.

THE

FATAL VOW;

OR,

ST. MICHAEL'S MONASTERY.

CHAP. I.

————————Oh thou weed,
Who art so lovely fair, and smell'st so sweet,
That the senses ache at thee—Wou'd thou hadst ne'er been born!
I should make very forges of my cheeks,
That would to cinders burn up modesty,
Did I but speak thy deed!

SHAKESPEARE.*

BEFORE we proceed in our narrative, it will be necessary to give a more explicit account than we have hitherto done, of the events which had marked the early lives of Christabelle's parents.

Sir Walter de Clifford, by the death of his father, became, at the early age of nineteen, possessor of one of the most splendid mansions, and valuable domains in the kingdom, situated in the country of Herefordshire.* He was a man by no means calculated to waste the fortune he had inherited; the turn of his mind was studious, without being gloomy; in contemplating the laws of nature, and in forming acquaintance with such branches of literature as had, at that early period, been introduced to the knowledge of man, he found greater delight, than in those sports of the tournament, and of the chase, which constituted the chief amusement of men in his rank in life.

Upon the borders of the adjoining county, stood the castle of an eminent warrior, whose bravery had particularly signalized him under the standard of Henry the first in France;* he was distantly related to Sir Walter, and his name was also De Clifford.*

Robert the Brave, which was the title that this hardy veteran's courage had acquired him in the field, and which had ever since become his common appellation, had many years been a widower; and the only pledge of her affection which his deceased wife had left him, was a daughter named Rosamond.

Sir Walter was a constant visitor at the castle of Robert the Brave, and the daily intercourse which he enjoyed with the fair Rosamond, raising in his heart the flame of love, he asked her hand in marriage.

The character and rank of Sir Walter, were such as Robert the Brave approved, and, as was the usual custom of fathers in those days, he replied for his daughter, by destining her to espouse De Clifford.

Rosamond had not yet completed her eighteenth year, she had rarely been permitted to wander beyond the limits of her father's castle; their guests were few; and her heart gave assent to her parent's decision, without reflecting that the progress of time, and an increased acquaintance with society, might introduce her to the knowledge of some being, who might communicate an ardent passion to her feelings. Their nuptials were accordingly solemnized; Rosamond quitted the castle of her father for the mansion of her husband; and the expiration of a year brought them a daughter, whom they named Matilda.

Scarcely was Rosamond restored to convalescence, ere information was brought to Robert the Brave, that the King was setting out on a journey, into the middle counties, and that he intended to honour him, by residing a few days at his castle.

The idea of entertaining his king, animated with pride and joy the soul of the old warrior, and he commanded every preparation, calculated to do honour to so noble a guest, to be made for his reception. He immediately issued invitations to various nobles of both sexes, to make his castle their abode for the period of Henry's stay at it; and in the number were, of course, included Sir Walter de Clifford and his Rosamond.

The passionate love which Sir Walter bore his wife, was such as had rendered his conduct towards her, as a husband, of the most exemplary kind. He lived but in her sight; he delighted but in the gratification of her wishes; her safety was his health; her tear his agony. Nor had Rosamond ungratefully received these marks of his pure affection; she had ever returned him good humour and complacency for his smiles, and kindness for his anxieties. But her character was infinitely different from his; he acted from the firmest conviction, that he preferred her before all her sex; her actions were but such returns as she deemed necessary requitals for his assiduities.

The period was now quickly advancing which was to prove to Rosamond the nature of the regard which she bore to Sir Walter; and to nip eternally the bud of those rich joys, which the possession of her charms afforded him.

The visit which the royal Henry was about to pay to the castle of Robert the Brave, was purposely undertaken to procure him an opportunity of beholding his daughter.

The beauty of Rosamond was universally spoken of as the fairest and most enchanting that the kingdom could boast. In his conversation with his courtiers, this inviting representation had been frequently made to the king; and the warmth of his disposition had ultimately caused him to resolve that he would behold this superior being.

On the day of his appointment, the king and his train arrived at the castle; and, at a splendid repast, which was served up for him in the grand hall, he, for the first time, beheld the peerless charms of De Clifford's wife. Rosamond exceeded the expectations which he had formed of her beauty; the fire of love ran tingling through his veins; his eyes gazed till they almost lost the power of vision in their intenseness of observation; and his soul then almost sickened in the bliss of reflection.

The entertainments of the day were concluded by a dance, and the hand of Rosamond was instantly engaged by the king.

Her father and husband judged her thus honoured as a compliment due to the exertions of the former for his amusement; but already did the eyes, the actions, and the sighs of the royal guest began to impart to Rosamond, ideas of a more tender nature.

For two successive days, the attentions of the monarch continued, if possible, to increase towards the object of his passion; and already was the heart of Rosamond fluttering round the net, spread for her by her tempter, and ready to fall into the snare, which was so richly baited with the tinsel lures of ambition, and the seductive vows of love.

But we are already acquainted with the success of Henry's artifices; and will therefore draw a veil over the frailty of her concession; let it suffice to remark, that Rosamond, whose soul had hitherto been spotless; to whom even the name of impurity had scarcely been known; who would with indignation have rejected the same advances towards her heart, on the part of an equal; yielded to the alluring tongue of royalty, and sunk into the gulph of criminality, and shame.

Still, Rosamond! the voice of pity does not refuse to heave a sigh to thy fall. Had thy mind been stored with an early knowledge, that equally heinous is the sin which owes its existence to a monarch, as that which proceeds from the meanest of his subjects, thou hadst perhaps been preserved from ruin! But the garb of splendour cannot cloak immorality from the eye of an all-seeing Providence. Nor will the lures of the sovereign which have betrayed the peace of the innocent, escape that retribution, which eventually awaits the seducer of meaner rank.

The sixth morning of the king's abode at the castle had been appointed for the chace. Sir Walter rose with the sun, in order to superintend the preparations for the sport. The dogs were led out; the horses caparisoned; and the foresters ready stationed to drive the deer from their coverts; and the king's appearance was to be regarded as the signal for mounting.

The hour at which the king had himself appointed to meet the hunters on the borders of a forest, at a short distance from the castle, was long past, and still he came not; nearly another hour was worn out by Sir Walter and his companions in tedious expectation; and as Henry did not then arrive, they resolved to return to the castle, and inquire the cause which had prevented him from joining them.

But what were the emotions, the pangs of De Clifford's soul, when entering the castle; he was met by the father of Rosamond;

his countenance, the index of a breaking heart; the tears trembling in his manly eye; his words rendered almost inarticulate by the conflict of his feelings.—"Rosamond—shame—disgrace!—lost for ever!" were the only words which Sir Walter could comprehend; but they were more than sufficient to convey horror to his soul. "Shame, disgrace," coupled with the name of Rosamond! The tortures of hell could not communicate a severer pang to his heart: "Where—where is she?" He had alone power to utter—"Fled with the King!" pronounced her father, in a voice of phrenzy.

No sigh, no groan escaped the lips of De Clifford; he sunk senseless upon the ground.

Agony of soul had driven the power of reflection for a while from its seat; and to agony of soul he again revived.—Redress was unattainable; none but Rosamond could have preserved him from the excess of despair and misery, into which he was now sunk; and she had joined with the destroyer of his peace; rocked by ambition into a forgetfulness, that the same was the destroyer of her own peace likewise.

"Oh! Rosamond," he frantically exclaimed, "who wert to me the most peerless of gems, which the treasures of the earth could select to gratify my desiring soul! thou, in whom my love, my friendship, my adoration, and my life were centred! since thou hast made my return ingratitude, since thou art false; there cannot be truth in any breast, of faith in any tongue; and I will fly all intercourse with man *for ever!*"

This declaration was at first considered, by his friends, only as the wild ebullition of a despairing and agonized heart; but at the expiration of the second day after Rosamond's flight, he found the means of secretly quitting his mansion; and taking with him only his child, and an ancient female of his family, to whom the care of Matilda had been intrusted, from the moment of her birth; and proceeded with as great expedition, as his obscure mode of travelling would permit, towards the coast; intending to embark for France, and quit for ever the land which contained his faithless wife.

But the opening of our tale had already informed us of his change of plan; as likewise of the motives by which he was induced to remain in England. The assumed names of Glencowell and

Christabelle protected himself and his daughter from a suspicion of their real rank, on the part of those few individuals by whom they were known; and in the task of educating his daughter, in reflections of the most wretched nature on the solitary and stormy beach, and in unremitting acts of devotion, passed the hours of the ill-starred De Clifford.

The first observation made by the youthful mind of Matilda, for by that name we must henceforward know Christabelle, was, that her father would repeatedly, in the course of every day, draw from the pocket of his vest, a small black case, which he would open, and fixing his eyes upon the contents, remain gazing thus for hours together; whilst he appeared entirely lost outward objects; and the big tear would trickle down his pale, and furrowed cheek.

Often had she inquired what the case contained, but in vain; for the moment she advanced her question, he regularly closed it, and returned it into his pocket. At length, about the time of her attaining her fifteenth year, being one day more importunate than usual in her inquiries, De Clifford said, "It contains, my child, the portrait of your mother; when I judge you to be arrived at years of sufficient discretion, to comply sacredly with the terms upon which it is then my intention to suffer you to behold it, it shall be shewn to you; till that period arrives, importune me no more."

"My mother, I suppose, is dead, as I have never seen her," said Matilda.

"No, my child," replied De Clifford; "she lives."—

"Lives!"ejaculated Matilda.

"But not to us," returned her father, "nor ever *can* live to us;—more thou wilt never know of her;—thine ignorance is thy bliss; be thou sufficiently wise to credit the assertion of thy father, and to search no more into a knowledge which is forbidden thee, for thy good!"

Matilda obeyed, she saw the eyes of her father fixed, as usual, upon the portrait; but constrained herself to confine within the limits of her own breast, her ardent desire of being permitted to gaze upon it likewise.

Having completed her seventeenth year, the period at which De Clifford had resolved to permit the portrait of his lost Rosamond to be inspected by her daughter; he took Matilda one evening with him to the midnight devotions in the chapel of St. Michael's Monastery; and when the monks had left the holy spot, conducting her to the altar; she pronounced the oath which he dictated to her lips; and, for the first time, beheld the countenance of her who had given her birth.

From this moment she was frequently allowed to contemplate the portrait, together with her father; but to the hour of his death, he strictly adhered to his declaration of never making her acquainted with a single circumstance relative either to his own, or to her mother's life.

The few events which marked the days of Matilda, previously to her introduction to the protection of the queen, as the future wife of her best beloved son, have already been detailed; and almost as little chequered by circumstance were the days of Rosamond, after her desertion of her wronged husband, as those of her innocent daughter. There was only this difference in their lives:—in peace, tranquillity, and simplicity, glided on the days of Matilda. Whilst pomp and power gilded those of Rosamond; but seldom did she taste the tranquillity of mind which blessed the lowly cot of her daughter. At times a sense of the injustice of which she had been guilty towards her husband, her father, and her child, would rack her heart, and turn her downy couch into a bed of thorns; at others, an apprehension of being supplanted in the king's favour by some more fortunate rival, would cast a gloom even over the moments in which his attentions and caresses were showering upon her; and more dreadful than these reflections, were the terrors which occasionally assailed her mind, relative to her expectations in a future state.

Still without fortitude to fly the flattering but delusive ill, at the retribution due to the enjoyment of which, she wept, and trembled, it was the constant prayer of her latter years, that judgment might overtake her on earth. Presumptuous would it be to affirm that because she felt the victim of the queen's resentment, her prayer was heard; for Providence does not permit to man, a choice of punishment.

From the retribution however which had overtaken her on earth, those friends who shed a tear upon her corpse, drew a consolatory reflection, in reference to the reception of her soul in a future state.

CHAP. II.

These eyes that now are dimm'd with death's black veil,
Have been as piercing as the mid-day sun.
* * * * * * * * * * * * *
Lo! now my glory smear'd in dust and blood,
My parks, my walls, my manors that I had,
Ev'n now forsake me; of all my lands
Is nothing left me but my body's length.

SHAKESPEARE.*

WHEN the breath had fled from the earthly form of Rosamond, a solemn silence prevailed in the apartment where she had died; still grasping the hand of her mother, Matilda fell inanimate upon the corpse, and none present had resolution, or sufficient recollection of mind to raise her from it.

The first who spoke was the queen:—"The mercy of heaven be extended towards me!" she exclaimed, "I have turned the guilt of mine enemy upon myself—And thou, innocent girl!" she added, addressing Matilda, "thou! to whom I had promised myself to be a mother; has the first act of my professed tenderness been, to cut the thread of her life to whom thou owest thy existence!" The conflicts of an agonizing soul, were expressed on her countenance; she had liberated from herself from the torments of jealousy, at the price of pangs to which that jealousy had been an enviable bliss!

Matilda could not reply; she raised her eyes for an instant towards the queen, and again sunk weeping upon the body of her mother.

Eleanor advanced towards her, and took one of her hands; Matilda drew it hastily back, and a faint shriek accompanied the action: "Oh, God!" exclaimed the queen, "what have I done? to what excess has my revenge driven me? already do I feel myself reprobated by the just and innocent! *Thou* wilt not suffer thy hand to be contaminated with the touch of a murderer's!"

Tears now came to the relief of Matilda's over-burdened soul; horror had hitherto frozen them in their course. The power of instinct now prevailed in her heart; and, in the contemplation of the almost equal guilt of the queen, and Rosamond, she could not forbear inclining to the side of her mother. True it was that Rosamond had been criminal, greatly criminal; so much the greater had been her need of repentance; from the blessings of which, the rash and avenging hand of Eleanor had cut her off! From the touch of that guilty hand, the soul of Matilda now recoiled, as it would have done from a participation of the sin which had stained it. Even from the mother of her beloved Richard, she withdrew her hand!

Her feelings were explicitly understood by the queen; they swelled almost beyond endurance the agony with which her brain was already bursting. She cast upon her a sad, last look of mingled compassion, entreaty, and dread; "Oh, Christabelle! if thou hast mercy in thy soul, let not thy curses pursue me!" she exclaimed; and fled from the apartment.

Sir Eugene now approached Matilda, and with accents the most soothing and tender, raised her from the ground. The first burst of the hapless orphan's agony being, in some measure, abated, one of the queen's friends, who was, by her command, still remaining at the bower, stepped forward, and entreated Matilda to permit him to lead her away from the scene of horror.

"Oh, no, no!" she replied, "short and dreadful has been the period, during which I have had a knowledge of my mother; and till the earth receives her unfortunate remains, I cannot, I will not quit her." She paused, then continued thus; "You, Sir Eugene, have been the friend of my unhappy mother, will you not be the friend of her daughter likewise?"

The heart of Sir Eugene was sensibly affected by this appeal to his feelings; and he promised her every protection and act of friendship which it should be in his power to afford her.

At length a tranquillity, even more melancholy than the confusion which had before prevailed, was restored to the bower; and Sir Eugene then besought Matilda to retire, to repose in one of its chambers; but she could not be persuaded to quit a closet adjoining to the apartment, which contained the corpse of her mother; and here her sad and cheerless night was passed in prayers for the repose of that lamented parent's soul.

Equally without sleep crept on the heavy hours to De Lancy; the melancholy fate of Rosamond dwelt obtrusively before his eyes; and his apprehension of the King's wrath agitated and distressed his mind.

With mutual satisfaction, at the presence of each other, did Matilda and he meet in the morning; she was impatient to gather from his lips such particulars as she was yet unacquainted with concerning the history of her parents; and he was alike anxious to learn in what seclusion the daughter of Rosamond had passed her life; and by what miraculous chance fate had led her to that spot, to close the dying eyes of her frail parent.

This exchange of communication produced no intelligence, but what has already appeared on our page; except that from De Lancy, Matilda learnt that her grandfather, Robert the Brave, had died very shortly after his daughter's fall from virtue, broken-hearted.

When evening arrived, and she was again left to the solitude of her own reflections, gloomy and unpromising, were the views of her future life which presented themselves to her imagination. She now stood alone in the world; she was possessed of no relative upon whose tenderness she had claim; of no friend, whose services she could accept; without suffering the reproofs of her own conscience! Richard, her honoured, her beloved, her revered Richard, could now never be admitted by her to a nearer connection than that of friend. By the seductive tongue of one of his parents had her mother been enticed from the paths of honour; by the cruel hand of the other, had that mother been deprived of her existence! Could she then ever consent to bestow her hand on the son of two beings, to whom her mother owed such heavy wrongs?

Against such an union, religion, nature, every gentle and generous feeling of the heart, rebelled:—Richard therefore could never be hers; the only being who had awakened in her heart, the finer chords of sensibility, she must now for ever resign! "Cruel decree of fate," she exclaimed, "which thus extracts from the guilt of the parents the infelicity of their children!—Oh! may the benevolence of heaven grant to my prince, when those dreadful tidings, which are now prepared for his hearing, meet his ear, the forbearance of reason to encounter them with; Oh! may it extend towards him fortitude of mind, and teach him to bear with resignation to its will, the divorce of affection to which our hearts are mutually doomed. Oh, my Richard! with tears of silent anguish do I withdraw my heart from thy keeping; upon that heart the image of no other man, beloved as thou hast been by me, has ever been engraven; and although now no longer permitted to cherish thee there with the same fondness with which thou hast hitherto been nourished in it; I appeal to heaven to vouch for me, that no other being shall ever supplant thee in its recesses."

A night of anguish was Matilda's; dreadful was the struggle which accompanied the resolution of resigning Richard for ever! equally painful were her apprehensions for the sufferings which he would endure on becoming acquainted with the existence of such a necessity.

From this heart-rending subject her thoughts wandered to the choice of an asylum for her future days. In the wanderings of her imagination she remembered the sister Corally as one of the few beings from whom she had ever experienced any act of kindness; and blessed the recollection as it entered her thoughts: that Corally was now the abbess of St. Ursula, and its walls would not fail to afford her the most desirable refuge she could now find on earth. "Ah!" exclaimed Matilda, "how short-sighted are mortals when they murmur at events which are unfriendly to their present comforts or wishes, and are too impatient to await the consequence which is intended to result from them! Thus did I murmur at the dispensation of fate, when I was doomed to suffer under the unjust penance inflicted on me by the former abbess of St. Ursula; and is it not now a cause of happiness to me? Is it not to this circumstance that Corally owes her present situation; and possesses the authority of granting me a friendly reception within the bosom of her community?"

This reflection contributed a considerable degree of consolation to her feelings. "Might it not be possible," she thought, (for hope with the wretched ever stretches its pinions to the widest extent of possibility) "might it not be possible, that some consequence might, at a future period, arise out of the events which now weighed down her heart with agony and sorrow, to recompense her for her present sufferings?" Could the frown of anguish, which was collected on her brow, have relaxed into a smile, it would have done so at the wild imagery of her hurried fancy; with her tears she confessed the little faith that she placed in the realization of the hope which she had been drawing.

With the seventh day after the decease of the fair Rosamond, arrived the period appointed for the interment of her earthly substance. She had frequently expressed to Sir Eugene de Lancy her inclination to be buried in a particular spot, in the cloister of a nunnery at Godstow; and he accordingly commanded preparation to be made there for the reception of her corpse.

Painful, as Matilda was aware the exertion must prove to her, she had still resolved on performing towards her mother the last sad duty of attending her remains to the grave. The morning which was to witness this melancholy ceremony arose in clouds congenial to her feelings; the sympathizing sun appeared to refuse to visit the earth, lest his gaudy beams should seem to mock the heart of the sorrowing orphan.

Arrayed in weeds of the deepest sable, Matilda entered the chamber, where, in the midst of funeral pomp, stood the coffin, which only waited to be closed for ever, till she had taken her last gaze of the form that it contained. Even in the cold embrace of death, the roses had not fled the cheeks of Rosamond; nor had the cessation of life sullied the purity of her snow-white skin. "Whilst this heart continues to beat, I shall never forget thee!" said Matilda, "it is not, therefore, as a talisman of memory, but of love, that I receive this memorial of my mother!" she accompanied her words by taking from the coffin a lock of Rosamond's hair, which had, at her request, been placed there for her. She kissed it, and drawing from her bosom a similar one, which she had preserved of her deceased father, she entwined them together; "This union cannot offend your shade, my injured father!" she exclaimed; "and, Oh! may it be granted to your sainted spirits thus to re-unite in a state of bliss, where the influence of evil shall have no power to separate you more!" She placed them in her bosom, and, casting a last look upon her mother, fled with clasped hands from the chamber. The distance of Godstow from the bower was considerable; horses had accordingly been provided for the procession of mourners, which was headed by Matilda, by whose side rode Sir Eugene.

As they approached the nunnery, the solemn beat of the tolling bell struck to the heart of Matilda; and as they drew still nearer to the holy walls, its dismal tolls were joined by the chanting voices of a body of monks; who, preceded by several youths, bearing lighted tapers came out to meet the corpse.

Having reached the gates of the sacred mansion, they were received by the sisters of the order, who led the way to the chapel strewing flowers in their path. The coffin having been placed upon supporters, which had been prepared for it, within the rails of the altar, a service of the most impressive nature was performed, and some minutes of silence having then been suffered to prevail, in order that the admonitory scene, and the words which had fallen from the lips of the priest might sink into the minds of the beholders; the doors leading from the chapel into the cloisters were thrown open, and the narrow spot of earth which was to enclose all the greatness, and all the frailties of her who had for so long a period been the mingled theme of pity, praise, and envy, appeared in view.

Still the fortitude of Matilda did not utterly forsake her, and with trembling limbs she approached the grave; as the coffin descended into the earth, her heart began to sicken; but her last, her severest trial was still to come; when the dust fell upon its lid from the spade of the sacristan, and even that was no longer visible to her, she sunk senseless into the arms of De Lancy.

In the apartment of the abbess, into which she had been conveyed, every attention was paid to her with the tenderest concern; and at the expiration of little more than an hour, she declared herself sufficiently restored to commence her journey back to the bower. With tears, she bade farewell to the walls which inclosed the sacred grave of her parent; and when they disappeared from her view, she felt her mind relieved from some part of the burden which had before oppressed it; and as they proceeded, the partial beams of the sun, darting from beneath the retiring clouds, appeared in some measure, to dispel the gloom of her spirits, and to smile approbation on her for the act of filial piety which she had performed.

CHAP. III.

———————Nay, then farewell!
I've touch'd the highest point of all my greatness,
And from the full meridian of my glory
I haste now to my setting.

SHAKESPEARE.*

WHEN Matilda had reached the bower, one of the domestics presented her with a scroll, upon which she beheld the royal signet; and which, he informed her, had been brought for her during her absence by a messenger from the court at Beaumont.

From the queen alone Matilda could suppose it to be sent; and, on breaking the seal, she found her suspicion to be just. The contents were these:—"Eleanor of England greets Matilda de Clifford! and let it not increase the hatred with which her breast is now swelled against her, if she cannot forbear to address her as her dearest daughter. Till Matilda had performed the duties due to the memory of her parent, Eleanor has restrained herself from suffering *her* recollection to break in upon the sacredness of her retirement. She now bids farewell for ever! and intreats of her the forgiveness of a Christian soul for the rashness of an act with which she knew not her connexion, till the deed of horror was past recal!—Yes, Matilda, Eleanor bids thee and the world farewell for ever. *This day* she quits the world; and binds herself by the most solemn vows of religion, never to again emerge amidst its busy, torturing scenes. Were not her heart racked with pangs at the recollection of an offence, which the solitude of religious penance can alone hope to heal, the dread which she experiences of the king's fury, of her son's resentment, would drive her to ensure the certainty of never encountering them again!—Oh! it would rend her heart asunder to behold the eyes of her idolized, her best-beloved son turned upon her in the wrath which cannot fail to be excited against her in his breast, when he learns that she has raised her hand against the life of his Christabelle's mother!—raised her hand! Oh, dreadful reflection!—Eleanor is a murderer!

"The purpose of her writing is not yet explained;—she conjures Matilda to return to the palace, and to become the solace of the princess Jane; to wait there the arrival of the prince in England; and to bless his return by preparing to receive him with the same welcome of affection which she would have bestowed on him, if——Matilda cannot be ignorant what Eleanor would write, nor can Eleanor command her pen sufficiently to trace the characters of anguish, and of entreaty which fill her heart. Matilda cannot be so unjust as to consider her Richard guilty, on account of his mother's guilt. And Eleanor entreats for justice to her son, even in preference to the forgiveness of her own crime! If the prayers uttered by the voice of guilt are allowed to ascend to heaven, may it shower down unnumbered blessings on the head of Matilda! Oh! may every breath of affection which she heaves to promote bliss of him who lives but in her love, be repaid to her in the paradise of eternal felicity! And, Oh! if the unhappy and the guilty can claim a share in the thoughts of one so pure; may the beads of Matilda be sometimes told for the peace of Eleanor. Once more, farewell for ever! Would the blessings of Eleanor avail thee, thou should'st have them from her inmost heart; in their stead, may that Providence which knows thy sufferings and thy merits, extend them tenfold towards thee!"

The arguments contained in the queen's letter, Matilda considered natural to the mind from whence they proceeded, but they produced no change in her sentiments; for her resolution had been adopted on a conviction of the conduct which she had determined to pursue, being the right and commendable.

Matilda had communicated to Sir Eugene de Lancy her intention of making the convent of St. Ursula the asylum of her future life; and he had kindly promised to become himself her safe conduct to its walls. The morning succeeding that which had been marked by the event of the fair Rosamond's funeral, had been appointed for the commencement of their journey; but Matilda now resolved to defer her departure for a single day, and to use that day in visiting the princess Jane at Beaumont, to entreat her to explain to her brother, on his return, her motives for withdrawing herself from his future attentions; and to become her mediatrix with him in prevailing on him not to infringe on the tranquillity of a life which she was resolved to devote wholly to acts of religion, by attempts which must prove fruitless to re-draw her into the world.

It was her intention to inform the princess Jane, that the gratitude and friendship which she bore her brother, no situation, no circumstance could ever diminish; that she should cherish his memory with reverence and affection; but that the nature of the events which had taken place since his departure from England, would never allow her to become his wife.

The friendly Sir Eugene offered himself as Matilda's escort to the palace; and, attended by some of his domestics, they arrived at Beaumont. Matilda was immediately recognized by the pages, and ushered by them into an apartment. It was the very apartment in which she had listened to the vows of her Richard's promised constancy and love, on the evening previous to his departure for France; she sunk upon a chair, and some moments elapsed ere the conflict of contending feelings would permit her to express herself; she then requested to be shewn to the princess.

The reply was, "that the princess was gone to accompany the queen on her journey to the convent of grey penitents, in the neighbourhood of Beverly, where she had determined to pass the remainder of her years; and that they had set out on their journey on the preceding day, immediately after the queen had received intelligence of her scroll having reached the hands of Matilda."

Her plan of communication with the princess being thus rendered futile; she had no alternative, but to resolve to write to her on her arrival at St. Ursula, those sentiments which it had been her wish to have verbally expressed to her.

After a few minutes repose, she rose to depart; casting a sorrowing look of separation around, she took the offered arm of Sir Eugene to support her tottering frame, as she descended the steps which led from the entrance of the palace to the avenue where their horses were awaiting them. "Oh! Sir Eugene;" she exclaimed, "with how different feelings did I two short months ago enter these walls, to those with which I now quit them!"

Once more, accordingly, Matilda returned to Woodstock bower; and, after a night passed rather in the waking dreams of anticipation, than the solid refreshment of sleep, entered with the succeeding dawn, upon her journey towards the convent of St. Ursula.

No untoward obstacle obstructed their even progress; and at the expiration of some days travelling, they arrived towards the close of evening at the gates of the holy mansion.

One of their attendants having knocked at the gate; the summons was replied to by the appearance of the portress at the grate.

"Rachel!" said Matilda, addressing her, "do you not recollect me?" After a moment's pause, with an exclamation of surprise at seeing her, Rachel unbarred the gate.

Matilda alighted from her horse, and followed by Sir Eugene, entered the hall of the convent:—"Pray acquaint the mother of the house of my arrival," she said; and Rachel was hastening to obey her commands; but Matilda stopped her, by adding—"I hope I am not mistaken in supposing that sister Corally now holds that station?"

"Oh no, no; you are not," replied the portress, "thanks to the mercy of Providence, and the gracious interference of our worthy Prince, she now possesses the rule of the house! Our former cruel mother has quitted our community."

Whilst the sister Rachel had been speaking, Matilda had advanced a few paces towards the apartment appropriated to the use of the abbess; but suddenly she stopped for the voice of music met her ear, and she inquired of Rachel the cause.

"I was going to tell you," replied Rachel, "but you stepped on so quickly, that our new mother was only yesterday admitted to her dignity; and that, on this account, she to-day gives a treat to the house, and those amongst the members of it who are skilled in the knowledge of any instrument, are adding to the hilarity of the hour, by an exercise of their talents."

Matilda answered, that her spirits were at that time unequal to any effort of joy; and that as such was the case, she wished Corally to be requested to meet her in another apartment.

Her wish was obeyed; the mother of St. Ursula attended her in a private chamber; Matilda expressed to her in few words the distressing circumstances which had driven her from the world; and concluded her account, by explaining her wish to become a boarder of the house.

The generous conduct of Prince Richard towards Corally, had rendered her the ardent friend of Matilda, and from her heart she breathed a promise of ameliorating to her by every means in her power, the severity of her fate; with absolute firmness the mother refused to return to her guests, since Matilda could not be persuaded to join them likewise; and the evening was accordingly passed by her with Matilda, and Sir Eugene ,in a conversation of the most interesting nature.

With the morning, Sir Eugene departed; and Matilda having bade him a farewell, adequate to the kind and essential services which he had rendered her, bent her thoughts alone towards solitude and the preparation of her soul for heaven.

CHAP. IV.

——————May he live
Longer than I have time to tell his years!
Ever belov'd, and loving may his rule be!
And when old time shall lead him to his end,
Goodness and he fill up one monument!
SHAKESPEARE.*

LEAVING for awhile Matilda we must now inquire the success of Richard's arms in France.

No sooner were tidings of the landing of Prince John and his troops upon the continent carried to the French king, than he placed himself at the head of his forces, and marched to join him. This union being formed, they pushed boldly forward to those quarters in which Henry, who had now been already six weeks in the kingdom, had made his strong holds.

After many severe conflicts, in which fortune frowned universally upon the king of England; and during which period of ill success, he had been driven successively out of Montfort, Malestable, Balon, and various others of his possessions; he shut himself up with seven hundred of his knights, and his remaining forces, of which the number was comparatively small, in the city of Mans.*

Here Henry believed himself, for a while at least, safe; for a report had gone abroad that his enemies were proceeding towards

Tours; but he was suddenly disconcerted by the appearance of a hostile force advancing to an attack upon the city.

The first attempt made by the English to oppose the progress of the enemy, was to send out a body of men to break down a bridge in their road, across the Sarte; but the enemy, advancing by hasty steps, came upon them ere their task was performed; and flying back in disorder to the city, they were pursued by the French, and nearly all of them killed, wounded, or taken prisoners.

This misfortune, however, did not dispirit Henry from standing the siege; and for nearly three days the English bore the battering of the enemy with constancy and bravery; but towards the evening of the third, an additional force was seen to join the French army; and Henry, to his utter consternation, learnt that it was headed by his other son Richard. The knowledge of both his sons having risen in arms against him, was a severer trial than his spirit could bear with patience, and in the phrensy of an agonized soul, he exclaimed, "This is the city in which I was born; the only spot on earth I really value; and should God permit it to be taken from me, I shall never love his name again!" But the moment he had spoken these words, he repented of his blasphemy; and, being told by his generals, "that the siege could not be held out six hours longer;" he left the city privately; and fled with a small body of his men towards Frenelles.

After his flight the defence of Mans was supported for a very short time, by about thirty knights, and little more than twice that number of soldiers, who had stationed themselves on a high tower, for a last and desperate effort; but who were quickly obliged to surrender.

The vexation and torture of Henry's mind, threw him immediately into a violent fever; and with the utmost difficulty he was conveyed to Chinon, where he still possessed a castle:—and here, a victim to the destroying sensations of an unquiet heart, he breathed his last sigh. His soul had been rent by beholding his own issue turned into his deadliest foes; and by the repeated losses which he had sustained of his favourite possessions in France, added to which, the recollection of his past crimes arose to his mind to accelerate, and embitter the period of his death. Then it was that he remembered with anguish of heart, his unjust partiality to his children; his adulterous conduct to his queen; his seduction of the princess Adelais; the lures which he had spread for Ruthinglenne Bloet, and Rosamond de Clifford; the misery and disgrace which he had been the means of entailing on their unhappy relatives! and not least, the blasphemous exclamation of which he had lately been guilty at the city of Mans! These were all accusing records round his bed of death; and he sunk into the grave dissatisfied with his present existence; and in dread of encountering that state which was doomed to succeed it!

Information of the king's death being conveyed to his sons, they immediately repaired to Chinon, in order to pay the last offices of humanity to his corpse; and forgetting the injuries they had received at the hands of the father, in the respect which they considered due to the king, they commanded his funeral to be of the most sumptuous nature.

Accordingly, when placed in his coffin, Henry was attired in his royal robes; his crown upon his head; white gloves upon his hands; boots of gold upon his legs; gilt spurs at his heels; a ring of great value upon his finger; his sceptre in his hand; and by his side, a sword, of which the hilt was studded with many precious stones. Corresponding with the sumptuousness of the apparel, worn by the deceased, was every circumstance relating to the funeral of the king; and attended by a train, equally numerous as splendid, his remains were interred in the abbey of Fontrevault.

These ceremonials, which it is not improbable that the princes regarded as a peace-offering to the manes of a father, against whose authority they had rebelled, being concluded, they immediately returned to England, and Richard flew on the wings of love towards Beaumont;—but what language can describe the emotions of the prince's soul, when he beheld his sister Jane come forth alone, to welcome his return? when he learnt from her lips the direful events which had taken place since his departure? and received from her hand a scroll written by Matilda, wherein she resigned him forever?

Rage and astonishment by turns possessed his soul; and wound his passions to the fierceness almost of phrensy.

Alternately he raved against the adultery of his father, and execrated the mad revenge of his mother's jealousy; the joint effects of which had blasted the prospect of his fairest hopes! At one instant he resolved to exert the royal authority of which he was about to become possessed, for compelling Matilda to grant him her hand; at the next, he would declare his intention of resigning his pretensions to the crown, and retiring for life to the seclusion of a monastery.

Thus passed on no inconsiderable time; both the person and health of the prince being visible sufferers, from the agitation into which disappointment had thrown his mind. The day for his coronation was now quickly approaching; and Richard himself, the least joyful individual in his whole realm.

At length a determination entered his mind, which was no sooner taken than put into effect; it was to demand an interview of Matilda, and to receive from her own lips the decision of his fate. He imparted his design to the princess Jane, and having obtained her promise to accompany him on his visit to the convent of St. Ursula, they set out together without delay.

The prince and his sister arrived at the spot of their destination, at that hour in the afternoon at which the nuns were engaged in their chapel, in the performance of vespers. The portress however replied readily to their summons for admission at the gate; and the well-known countenance of Richard caused it to be instantly opened to them.

They entered the apartment of the abbess, by whom, at the conclusion of the evening service, they were directly joined; Matilda was not yet apprized of their arrival, and the prince requested his sister to seek her in her cell; and to urge to her his entreaty of beholding her.

With true pleasure Matilda met the unexpected embrace of the princess; but on being informed of the arrival of Richard and his request to see her, a trembling agitation seized her frame, and she said, "Oh why is he come to withdraw my thoughts from that tranquil seclusion to which it is my wish now solely to devote them?"

"But you will not refuse to see him, since he *is* come?" replied the princess.

"Alas! what can our meeting avail!" breathed forth Matilda.

"It will afford him the satisfaction of hearing from yourself those reasons which actuate you in renouncing the world," returned the princess; "and he conceives you would act unfriendly, and unjustly towards him, in refusing him this gratification."

"Does he think so?" exclaimed Matilda, "then I *will* see him, whatever pangs such an interview may occasion me. The noble, the generous Richard shall never have cause to believe me ungrateful to the memory of the unmerited kindness which I have received at his hands!"

Whilst uttering these words, a tear had started into her eye; she wiped the sacred drop of mingled gratitude and affection from her cheek; and suffered the princess to take her hand, and lead her to the apartment of the abbess; in which the prince was now alone, anxiously awaiting her coming.

With slow and faltering steps, Matilda entered his presence; she longed to cast her eyes upon him, yet she could not assume resolution to raise them from the ground.

The prince flew towards her, and sinking on his knee before her, he clasped one of her hands between his, and imprinted on it repeated kisses. Burning tears stood in his eyes; labouring sighs escaped from his bosom;—but the silence of the tongue remained unbroken.

At length the prince spoke, "Christabelle!" he said, "for that tender name, by which I first knew thee, I cannot resign for any other less attuned to the soft feelings of my heart! Christabelle! it cannot be that thou hast resolved to tear thyself from him, to whom existence is not life, unless blessed by the contemplation of thy charms; the participation of thy friendship; thy heart! Oh! possessor of my soul, contradict the fearful sentence, under the bare apprehension of which my senses tremble and my being fades!"

With eyes, flashing with agony and impatience, he now awaited her reply.

For the first time Matilda turned her regards towards him; the tears were trickling down her pallid cheeks; in faint and faltering accents, she pronounced, "My mother! Oh, my prince! recollect who was my mother!"

"I recollect also," replied Richard, with emphasis, "who is *my* mother; but can it be just that the criminality of which our parents may have been guilty, should interrupt the felicity of their innocent offspring? Oh, consider this! Oh, reflect that we loved each other long ere these circumstances had met our knowledge! and why are they to interrupt our future bliss? True love should never suffer itself to be swayed by any accident of fate; it should regard only the happiness of the being who excites the passion in its breast. Thus pure, thus fervent did I once believe the love of Christabelle for me; and can it be possible that she no longer loves me?"

"Oh, my prince! my Richard!" replied Matilda; "or if thou wouldst a tenderer epithet still, my Reginald! for by that name I first learnt to esteem thee. With equal purity and fervour of affection as Matilda ever loved thee, does she love thee still—ever will love thee, whilst the vital spark of life shall animate her bosom! Oh, could the means be granted her of proving to thee the strength of that affection which she boasts; with gratitude would she encounter any calamity of which her endurance could add a single moment of felicity to thy life! To render thee more blest, she would meet poverty, sickness, pain or death itself, in its most angry form, and hail their torments as the glad sensations of delight! but the sting of memory forbids her to unite her fate with thine!"

A groan of agony burst from the lips of the prince; he struck the palm of his hand with violence against his head; and throwing himself frantically upon the earth, he exclaimed, "Christabelle deserts me! she dooms me to misery! be this the resting place of my future days; they will be few, and wretched!"

Hanging over him in supplication, Matilda said, "Oh, my prince! by the love which you profess for me, I beseech you, as a proof of that love, not to suffer your fortitude of mind thus to desert you! Oh let the entreaty of Matilda prevail on you to call into action the exercise of that reason and sense which are the natural growth of your strong mind; and to prepare yourself to shine a bright example of royal dignity and benevolence to other monarchs in the exalted station which you are now called upon to fill! Oh do not commit towards your subjects the injustice of suffering any secondary cause to render you less active than they might otherwise find you in the promotion of their interests! Oh, my Richard! the love of an admiring people will repay to you every other loss!"

After a considerable pause the prince arose from the earth;

the expression of his countenance denoted a severe struggle to be passing in his heart. "Matilda!" he with difficulty pronounced; "Matilda! thou hast pointed out to me what conduct will render me estimable in thine eyes; I live but to obey thee; and accede to thy injunctions! But, Oh! remember it is in compliance with thy intreaty that I consent to wear the crown of England; and that I shall exist on the blessed hope of thy eventually sharing it with me."

"As my arguments have prevailed thus far with you," rejoined Matilda, "suffer my advice to prevail still a little farther; consent to seek a union suited to your virtues and your rank, amidst the courts of monarchs equal to yourself; and place upon your throne a partner of your honours, whose dower and whose alliance may do credit to your choice in the estimation of your subjects!"

"What!" exclaimed the prince, "bestow this hand on any other being than thyself! madness and torture lurk in the idea!" Falling on his knees before a crucifix, which stood in the apartment, and clasping his hands solemnly over his breast, he pronounced, "By this holy sign I swear, that the hand of Richard shall never be given to any other woman than his Matilda!" he kissed the cross, and added, "so may heaven extend its mercy or its vengeance towards me as I preserve my vow!"

Matilda uttered a faint shriek and sunk into the arms of the princess.

The composure of mind which had appeared in Matilda, before this act, on the part of the prince, was now transferred to him; and the wildness of dissatisfaction and pain expressed on her countenance. In vain was it that she implored Richard to procure absolution for his vow; he only replied to her entreaties by a smile of affection; and appeared to glory in having pronounced it.

The prince's presence was, at this time, urgently demanded in London. In visiting St. Ursula, he had trespassed on time, which he could hardly be permitted to call his own. It was therefore impossible for him to waste a moment more at the convent, than was important to the object of his visit; accordingly having bade a most affectionate farewell to his Matilda, at the hour of retiring to rest, and repeated to her his determination not to forsake his vow, the princess and himself quitted St. Ursula with the first dawn of the succeeding day.

CHAP. V.

Hope is a lover's staff; walk hence with that;
And manage it against despairing thoughts.
SHAKESPEARE.*

THE coronation of Richard was the most sumptuous which had ever yet graced the ascent of any monarch to the English throne. The soul of the new king was not free from a certain portion of pride, and he observed with a confessed exultation the complacency and homage with which his subjects beheld him invested with the sovereign authority. The only draw-back which his triumph experienced, was the absence of his Matilda.

For the first few weeks after Richard's accession to the throne, his hours were fully occupied with matters of importance to the public weal; with the first moment of leisure, which was granted him from the interests of the state, he addressed to his Matilda the most persuasive arguments which the eloquence of love was capable of dictating to his pen; once more entreating her to quit her voluntary seclusion from the world, and share his honours, as she already possessed his heart.

Still was the soul of Matilda inflexible. But the king was not to be discouraged from repeating his attempts to gain her assent, to his bliss for which his soul sickened, and for the period of twelve months, he was indefatigable in pouring out to her, in writing, the sentiments of his heart, and the prayers of his anxiety. At the expiration of this time, having been unable to work any change in her opinion, and considering life almost as a burden, unblest by her society, he hastily formed the determination of placing his kingdom under the regency of his brother John, of taking up the banners of the cross, and journeying himself to the Holy Land.

His plan being formed, he occupied himself immediately in raising all the force he was able to muster, and in collecting various subsidies with which to defray the expense of transporting an army to so great a distance.

The fashion of the times bestowed great honour on such females as displayed themselves sufficiently zealous in the cause of the Christian religion, to accompany their male relatives on those expeditions, which had gained the name of crusades. Actuated by this knowledge, and a desire of imitating the example of her mother, Eleanor, who had accompanied her first husband, Lewis the younger, of France, on a similar journey, the princess Jane resolved to become the companion of her brother's expedition; and that she might not be the only female, at least of some distinction, which would have been to her an unpleasant consideration, in a band of many thousand warriors, she engaged the wives and daughters of several knights to become her escort.

Every preparation for the king's departure being arranged, his last act, previously to quitting England, was to address a farewell epistle to his ever-adored Matilda. The scroll which she received from him contained these words;—"Richard of England greets the beloved possessor of his heart; the *present* is perhaps the last time of his addressing her! Ere she shall peruse these lines, the shores of England will have vanished from his sight; and uncertain, *very uncertain*, is the period of his return! It will be directed by the fate of war; and the same fate may forbid his ever beholding his native land again! Matilda, it is thou who hast impelled him to his present undertaking! Thou, who by refusing to bless his sovereignty with thy participation, hast driven him to seek relief for his desponding heart in the battle's savage heat! Oh, Matilda! should he be fated never to behold thee again; should it be his destiny to fall by the sword of the enemy; Oh! grant him the only consolation which he can now taste; grant him thy prayers for his safety! and if thou *dost* consent to offer up thine orisons to heaven for his preservation, which he cannot doubt thou wilt do, the reflection will cause him to endure life with comparative ease, during his absence from his native land, in the belief that thou wilt not, on his return to it, refuse to behold once again that being, for whom thou hast unremittingly prayed, whilst separated from thee! Now then, Oh, Matilda! fairest of earthly saints! most perfect of nature's works! farewell! a long farewell! Oh, should this fatal word have been pronounced by thy Richard, FOR EVER! Oh, may the God of mercy, to whom are known the pangs of his disappointment, the sincerity of his affection, reward his endurances on earth, by the union of his spirit with his Matilda's in eternity!"

The perusal of these lines greatly affected Matilda; she now almost wished that she had, by any concession, on her part, withheld him from encountering the battle's heat; still was she almost equally satisfied that she had adhered to the line of conduct which she had marked out to herself to pursue. Immaterial now however were her ideas upon this subject to the peace of Richard; her voice could no longer reach him; it could only breathe forth prayers for his happiness and safety; as it had never ceased to do, since her heart had first begun to feel for him the esteem of friendship, and the throbbings of affection.

Agonizing were the reflections which now not unfrequently occupied her mind; often would visions of horror assail her in the hours of sleep; then would she start from her restless couch, and traversing with the wild step of terror her chamber, doubt whether the subject of her dream might not be prophetic; whether the life of her Richard might not be opposed to the relentless arm of some unfeeling pagan, who, too merciless to grant him speedy death, might condemn him to chains, imprisonment! famine! "Should this dreadful probability be realized," she would then exclaim, "the love which he has hitherto borne me, must be turned to curses on his dying lips, for it was *I* who drove him to encounter these perils! Oh, dreadful idea! but how much more dreadful will my reflections be, to have occasioned the death of him to whom I owe *every thing!* Oh heaven! selfish is the prayer which I offer to thy throne for his preservation, since the peace of my own heart is entwined with it!" Thus would she for hours together suffer despondency to rack her brain, till a flood of tears restored calmness to her senses, and the wildness of grief became succeeded by a silent melancholy.

Richard, in the mean while, proceeded on his journey towards the Holy Land. Lewis of France was now succeeded on his throne by his son Philip, which prince having agreed to join the expedition of the king of England into Palestine, their first step was to convene a meeting for the purpose of arranging their future plans; which conference was appointed to be held at Vezelay.* Richard, accordingly, detaching himself from the main body of his army, passed over into France, attended only by such persons of distinction as had offered themselves the companions of his expedition; and such a number of servants and guards as it was always his custom to travel with; having directed his ships, which had on board his troops, when to sail, and meet him at Marseilles.

Being arrived in France, Richard received the scrip and staff, the insignia of his mission, from the archbishop of Tours; and, being thus invested, proceeded to his conference with Philip. An adjustment of the most amicable nature having taken place between the two kings, they commenced their march at the head of considerably more than one hundred thousand men, and entered Lyons; but having found the inconveniences of proceeding with so great a body almost insurmountable; they here agreed to pursue different roads; the king of France accordingly proceeded towards Genoa; and Richard directed his course to Marseilles.

Riding in this harbour, he had expected to find his navy, but he was disappointed in his hope; his fleet was detained by adverse winds, and after having waited several days in vain for its arrival, he hired a sufficient number of gallies to transport himself and his companions to Sicily. By stress of weather they were however compelled to land at Salerno; and here he resolved to remain till he should receive intelligence of his fleet having reached Messina. These tidings were shortly brought to him, and he then once more bent his course towards Sicily, whose shores he now reached without disaster. The voyage of the French troops had been infinitely more prosperous than that of the English; Philip and his army were already lodged in the city; and Richard, with his troops, took up their quarters in the four suburbs which surrounded it. But dissatisfied after a time with this accommodation, particularly as he intended to pass his winter in the island, he possessed himself of two castles of considerable strength, in one of which he resolved to keep his court, and to convert the other into a store-house, for his arms and ammunition.

The Messinese, predicting from these proceedings, that it was the intention of the king of England to attempt a conquest of their island, immediately sought a quarrel against him, and endeavoured to drive him from his quarters. Enmity being thus declared, continual acts of hostility were waged by both parties, with the greatest asperity, till the Messinese had been such considerable sufferers by the acts of plunder which the English soldiers had committed upon them that their king Tancred sued to Richard for an accommodation of their dispute, offering him his sister Olinda in marriage; and an immense sum of money towards defraying the expenses of the expedition in which he was engaged.*

Upon this offer Richard demanded three days to deliberate. He had pronounced a vow never to give his hand to any other woman than his Matilda; it was therefore impossible that he should make Olinda his queen. But Tancred's promise of a subsidy was a utility which he felt himself extremely loath to resign; and he wished to invent some accommodation which might be substituted for the first article of Tancred's proposed treaty, without destroying the latter.

Having duly weighed the matter in his own mind, he resolved to appoint a conference with the king of Sicily, to explain to him the bond by which he was with-held from marriage, and to propose to him to receive the hand of his sister Jane as an equivalent to his becoming the husband of Olinda.

The beautiful person and amiable qualities of the princess Jane, were such as could not fail to interest the feelings of a man whose heart was not glowing under any former impression of love; and the treaty was consequently signed to the mutual satisfaction of the parties who were engaged in it.

These arrangements being made, the remainder of the winter passed on in tranquillity; and with the ensuing spring, Richard, having witnessed the union of his sister with Tancred, again pursued his way towards Palestine; but his course was not fated to be smooth; some of his ships having been stranded on the island of Cyprus, and those on board, who survived the shipwreck, stripped, imprisoned, and otherwise cruelly treated by Isaac, who styled himself Emperor of the island; he turned out of his track, in order to revenge the insult which had been offered to him in this inhospitality to his knights and soldiers; he landed in Cyprus with a force, which, in less than two months, made him master of the island, and obliged Isaac to surrender to him on the humblest terms.*

At length, after various conflicts, Richard reached Palestine, where he was again joined by the king of France. Many successes crowned their progress; but the glory fell almost undivided on

Richard. His courage, his liberality, his expertness, and his magnificence were the universal theme of both armies; and Philip, whose heart was rent by hearing those praises bestowed on another, for which his own vanity caused him to languish, without possessing any merit for which he could claim them; began to complain of his health being a sufferer from the climate of Asia, and to speak of returning into France.

Richard heard him without a reply; and Philip still continued to advance with his troops. An exact division of the spoils, which they might capture from the infidels, had been agreed upon between the two kings; they were now approaching very near to the garrison of Acre; the wealth contained in this fortress was reputed to be immense; and doubting not that that the bravery and perseverance of the king of England would cause it to surrender; and unwilling to lose his share of the riches which would result from its fall, although little of the honour might be given to him, Philip resolved to wait the event of an attack upon this spot, ere he quitted the Holy Land.

On the arrival of Richard before Acre, terror and dismay were filling the hearts of the besieged; the English fleet had a few days before encountered and taken an immense vessel, which had been dispatched by Saladine for the relief of the garrison, with fifteen hundred of his best troops, and laden with warlike stores and provisions;* added to which disaster, the appearance of the united armies left them scarcely a hope of preservation.

The siege had lately been carrying on with the greatest languor, and the infidels had entertained the expectation of an eventual triumph. Now the threatening clouds of fate appeared to be again gathering in awful blackness over their heads.

On arriving before the walls of Acre, Richard found no force stationed there, except about four thousand men, headed by Leopold, duke of Austria.*

The presence of Richard added fresh vigour to the siege; he encouraged his men to bravery by dauntlessly exposing his own person to danger. Thus passed on a few weeks of unremitting acts of warfare; at the expiration of which, the besieged being driven to the utmost extremities, by the loss of these supplies which the English fleet had cut off from them by sea, and Saladine finding that the siege could not be raised, allowed them to surrender upon the best terms they could procure from the conquerors. The gates being opened to the victorious armies, duke Leopold, followed by a few of his knights, was amongst the first to rush through them, and having gained the interior, commanded his standard to be displayed upon the walls. This infringement on the laws of justice and honour was no sooner observed by Richard, than with severe animadversions upon the innocence of the duke, he directed the Austrian standard to be immediately torn from the walls, and his own colours mounted in its stead.

Chafed to the soul by this open mark of the king's contempt, Leopold looked around him for revenge, but in vain; his own forces, opposed to those of Richard, could but act as the buzzing of a knat matched against the prowess of an elephant. "Richard," he exclaimed, "although circumstances now restrain me from taking vengeance on thee, thy temerity shall not go unremembered by me!"

His words were reported to Richard, who, too much delighted by the success of his arms, to banish for an instant the smile of triumph from his lips, merely replied, "I am glad he finds consolation in the idea!"

CHAP. VI.

> ——————Tell us, soldier,
> Since thou hast shar'd the glory of this action,
> Tell us how it began.
>
> HUGHES.*

THE ransom of the besieged, who had capitulated for their lives, being paid, and the spoils of Acre divided between the two kings, Philip immediately withdrew his army from the cause of the cross, and turned back towards France. The duke of Austria likewise professing that the insult he had received from the king of England would not allow him to act in concert with him, returned into Germany.

Although bereft of his allies, Richard was not discouraged from maintaining the field; and for considerably more than another year he continued in Palestine, daily gaining fresh laurels by his sword.

At the expiration of this period, news of a most unpleasant nature reached him; his brother John was tempting his English subjects to revolt, upon the plea of the little interest which it was evident their king took in the welfare of his kingdom, by the length of time which he had been absent from it: and the perfidious king of France was endeavouring to create a similar dissatisfaction amidst his subjects in Normandy. This information caused him to resolve instantly to quit the Holy Land; and having gained the coast with all possible expedition, he set sail for Europe on board one of his own ships.

Not wishing to pass through France, as he was at present unprepared to punish the perfidy of its king; he bent his course towards Istria, from whence he intended to travel through Germany into England, in disguise.

This determination the king had made, because he judged it possible, were he to attempt to pass through Austria, in his real character, that the grudge which he doubted not that duke Leopold still bore him, on account of the siege of Acre, might induce him to interrupt his progress; in order therefore to obviate the occurrence of such an obstacle, he had adopted the plan of assuming an attire which should conceal his rank.

Impatience to reach England made every day appear to the king seven. At length, being arrived on the frontiers of Germany, Richard, and Sir Philip Lucie, whom he had made his sworn friend ever since their temporary residence together at the monastery of St. Michael, and whom he had now selected as the only companion of his present plan; having equipped themselves in the garb of peasants of a middle rank in life, and using every caution necessary to their concealment, pursued their way in the direction which was eventually to bring them to the coast.

Travelling sometimes on horseback, sometimes on foot, as convenience or security dictated, they had nearly passed through the Duchy of Austria, when their impatience to quit the territories of Leopold having one night detained them too late upon the road, the shades of evening were beginning to fall, and they still believed themselves at the distance of several leagues from any town or village. This was a situation of the most unpleasant nature to persons who were strangers to the country; and perceiving a light which shone from a house that stood encircled by some trees, at the distance of a few paces from the road, they resolved to go up to it, and request its inhabitants to grant them shelter for the night.

The moment Sir Philip had rapped at the door, it was opened by a man, who exclaimed, "Well, lads, how far are your companions behind?"

Surprised at this address, Richard replied, "We have no companions, friend; we are two poor travellers, who, having lost our way, fear to be benighted on the road, and implore your hospitality."

"I perceive you are strangers now," returned the man, "but at the first moment I mistook you for some of our hunters;"—he paused, and then added, "If the hospitality ye mean be a bed, I cannot promise you that, for our beds will all be full; but ye are welcome to enter, and sit by the kitchen fire."

Our travellers returned him thanks, and went into the house; as they passed along a passage which led to the kitchen, they perceived in an apartment, of which the door was open, a table which appeared to be spread for a company of fifteen or twenty persons.

"You seem to have a large family here," remarked Sir Philip.

"There is at present," answered the man, "no one in the house besides my old wife, and myself; but we shall have a large party arrive presently. This house is not mine, it belongs to a nobleman, who frequently makes it, for a few days, the residence of himself and some friends whom he brings with him, for the enjoyment of the chace, which is excellent hereabouts: we expect them home to supper in about an hour's time; and when I first opened the door I thought you had been two of the huntsmen come to announce their approach!"

They had now reached the kitchen, where a cheering wood fire was burning on the hearth; before which Herman placed a bench for their repose; whilst his wife Minna, spread on a table before them refreshments of meat and drink.

They had travelled from the morning without eating, and the viands prepared by Minna presented a most grateful invitation to their senses. They had not long enjoyed their repast, ere the cry of dogs and the trampling of horses announced the return of the hunters. Herman ran out to meet them. During his absence,

Minna said, "I am glad supper is ready, for I have one to provide for in the kitchen, who is more impatient of delay, and worse to please by half, when his mess *is* set before him, than his master."

"Indeed," replied Sir Philip, pretending to take interest in her communications, in return for the civility which she had shewn to the king and himself; "who is he?"

"Aye, who *is* he, *indeed?*" ejaculated Minna, smiling at her own jest; "that is what I often want to know when he gives himself airs to me! but I'll tell you the privilege upon which he does so; he is an old soldier, and so great a favourite with our duke, who has himself been a warrior that he may do as he pleases with impunity."

At the words, *duke* and *warrior*, the eyes of the king and his friend cast an expressive glance at each other. "Is it possible," it conveyed, "that our fate should have led us beneath the roof of the very man whom we are studying to avoid?"

"Prythee," said the king, "what duke is he of whom you speak?"

"Duke Leopold," she replied, "Duke Leopold of Austria, as he is called; you must be strangers indeed in these parts to ask that question."

Their worst apprehensions were now confirmed; but to fly would have been to have confessed fear, and excited suspicion; their most promising chance of safety rested in not suffering the discomposure of their minds to be seen. Several footsteps were now heard entering the house; and a gruff voice singing a martial air, approaching along the passage towards the kitchen.

"Here comes Adrian!" exclaimed Minna, "as noisy as usual!" then moving a step or two towards the travellers, she added, "this is the old soldier I told you of; Adrian Thelk is his name."

She had scarcely finishing speaking ere a tall, bony figure entered the kitchen, habited in the military uniform of the country; his swarthy visage striped with black whiskers, and one side of his body supported on a wooden leg.

With a slight inclination of his head to our travellers, he threw himself on a bench by their side, and grumbled, as Minna had predicted that he would do, till his mess was placed before him.

Our travellers remarked that Thelk had his repast served up to him on a small distinct table, stationed near the fire, at which he alone sat; whilst the huntsmen and other domestics, when they returned to the kitchen from having waited upon the duke and his guests, supped all together.

Thelk having concluded his meal, drew the bench on which he was seated nearer to the fire; and with a jug of liquor in one hand, and a horn cup in the other, the latter of which he filled from the former as he spoke, he said, "Come here's my usual toast after supper; and I hope these strangers will not refuse to join in it—Honour to the duke Leopold's bravery at the siege of Acre!"

The toast was drunk; and Richard wishing his conduct to appear as much disembarrassed as possible, began to enter into conversation with the old soldier; "You have been in the wars, my friend, yourself, I perceive," he said.

"Yes, I have, indeed!" replied Thelk, with a pompous smile; "you heard me this instant speak of the siege of Acre; and you have doubtless heard others speak of it as well as me!"

"Yes, I have, frequently," replied the king.

"Well, then," returned Thelk, "it was I, who, with this good right arm, placed upon its walls the first standard of victory that was erected on them:—the standard of our noble duke Leopold!"

It was now evident why Thelk was in so high favour with the duke; Richard observed his countenance well, but did not recollect a single lineament which composed it; and, trusting that Adrian might be equally ignorant of his, he still entertained little fear of being recognised.

"Yes," rejoined Thelk, "that was a glorious day; I performed my share of its labours creditably, although I say thus of myself; and my noble commander has not forgotten to reward me for my services! I have never since been separated from his person; where the duke is, there is Adrian Thelk likewise! the duke is himself a brave man, and esteems brave fellows!"

Adrian's liquor was now beginning to render him extremely loquacious, and he continued thus;—"No, no, the duke and I shall never part till death levels his crossbow at one of our lives; but let him point his arrow at us when he will, he cannot deprive us of our fame, by taking from us our existence; our laurels will still continue to bloom when we ourselves are withering!" He paused once more to fill and empty his horn, and again proceeded thus;—"Ye have all heard me relate that I lost my leg at a sally of the enemy, from the city of Ptolemais—Ye have"———

"Yes, yes, we *have* all heard it," interrupted one of the servants, "a thousand and a thousand times; and will not trouble you to tell it any more."

Darting upon the speaker a look of contempt, which he directed at each domestic in turn; for every countenance was dilated with a smile, which Richard and his friend understood to be the usual reception that the old soldier's battles, regularly fought over by him, in the chimney corner, once every evening, met with; Thelk said, "is every communication to be for *your* entertainment alone, dotards! Have these strangers heard my adventures, I would ask!—No! And shall not *they* be regaled with the interesting detail? I know that *you*, and Gilbert, and Martin, and Winceslaus, and Ranolf, and Herman, and all of you have heard them.—That *ye* have heard by what chance I got this scar on my hand; by what accident, I lost my limb; in what manner I erected the Austrian standard on the walls of Acre!"———

"Yes," replied Gilbert, again interrupting him, "and in what manner, Sir Philip Lucie, a knight of the king of England, pulled it down again, and mounted his sovereign's banner in its stead!"

"By the honour of war!" exclaimed Adrian, "thy insolence is great, but it does not affect me; the Austrian standard could not be pulled down till it had been erected; and I once more repeat that the glorious act was mine."

"Methinks," said Winceslaus, "as the king of England was our duke's ally at the siege of Acre, the matter should have been compromised between them, by letting both their standards fly from the walls together."

"And what imports it what thou thinkest?" returned Thelk, "thou! who hast never opposed thy spear to any other enemy than a boar; how dost thou venture to give thy opinion before one who has hewn down men in battle like blades of grass? If our duke and the king of England *were* allies, ought not every man to be rewarded in proportion to his labour and perseverance? The Austrian army had lain for nearly half a year round the walls of Acre, before Richard advanced towards it, and then forsooth, because the fortress was compelled to surrender a few weeks after his arrival, he takes all the honour of the conquest to himself! By the blood of the martyrs it was an arrogance not to be borne.—'Plant my standard on the walls,' exclaimed our noble duke, when we first rushed into the vanquished fortress of Acre. In a second his orders were obeyed: I, Adrian Thelk, obeyed them!—The duke honours me for my promptness and bravery, as much as he despises the English king for his injustice.—Oh! should he ever trap him in Austria, I had rather be hung up alive as a mark for our soldiers to practise at with their cross-bows, than stand in the shoes of that Richard! It is an adventure which to behold would make my blood circulate with the vigour of sixteen, the age when I first took up arms!"

"But Richard was accounted a brave man, was he not soldier?" asked Sir Philip.

"Why, yes, yes," replied Thelk, "although the noble duke and I have a quarrel against him, I must not belie him; good soldiers ever speak the truth; and I do not believe that Richard's honour was ever tarnished by a wound in his back."

"A wound in his back!" cried Gilbert, "now, prythee, Adrian, explain to us what thou meanest by that?"

"Ha! ha! ha!" exclaimed Thelk, "these are the questions which you ignorant fellows, who have never been in battle, ask; who know no more of the laws of war than I do of trimming a coif! Why, when a man receives a wound in his back, on the field of battle, it is termed an ignominious wound, because it appears natural to suppose that it overtook him when he was flying from the enemy; for the opposite reason, a wound in the front of the body is deemed creditable and glorious! dos't understand me now, valorous boar-fighter?"

Chance had placed Richard the very next person to the old soldier; and as he observed him attentive to his conversation, he kept his eyes almost constantly fixed upon him; a ceremony which alarmed the king, and caused him to wish, but in vain, to change his situation, as he dreaded lest Thelk might have seen him in the Holy Land, and ultimately recognise his person; this apprehension was however causeless, for Thelk's liquor was entirely incapacitating him for a close observation.

"Well," cried Gilbert, winking to his companions as he spoke, "and of what account is a wound in the side!"

"Why," replied Adrian, with a sneer, "it is like an idle, prattling fellow in the world, of no account at all!"

The laugh went round, and when it had subsided, Winceslaus said, "I have heard that your great commanders generally keep aloof in battle, and therefore are seldom wounded. Our duke, for instance, has not a wound about him to prove that he has ever been in fight, and, perhaps, Richard, although a brave man, was equally lucky."

"No, he was not," replied Thelk; "I have been as near to Richard as I am now to you; he is a light-haired man, rather above the middle size, and his eyes are light, but still there is a fire in his countenance which bespeaks him deserving of his title of Cœur de Lion. The very day I beheld him he was just recovered from a wound he had received a short while before, from an arrow shot at him by an infidel, on the walls of Acre. And the scar which the wound had left on his forehead was a very remarkable one; the arrow had passed obliquely through the skin, just above his left eye; and the scar was in the form of a barb, exactly like the point of the arrow. I should know him by it again, let me see him where I would."

Richard raised a silent thanksgiving to heaven that his fur-cap was at that time pulled over his forehead, down upon his eyes.

"Why, now," said Winceslaus, "I cannot for my life conceive how such a wound could be made without an injury to the eye; it may be all very clear to you who have seen it; I cannot understand," he added, pointing as he spoke to the forehead of one of his companions, "if the arrow went in here, as I may say, how"——

"But the arrow did *not* go in there, as you may choose to say," cried Thelk, contemptuously interrupting him; "the arrow—but you must have definitions, your senses are too dull for words to produce any effect upon them!" Turning to Richard, he said, "Give me leave, young man to describe the case to them on your forehead;" and, without waiting for the permission he had requested, he snatched off the king's cap.

What a moment of horror was this! Richard endeavoured, but in vain, to withdraw himself from Thelk's inspection. But Thelk placed both his hands on his arm, and pinned him down by it for a few seconds to the bench, whilst his eyes were fixed in astonishment and triumph on the scar in the shape of a barb, above the left eye of the king.

"By the holy cause of the cross!" Thelk burst forth; "if here is not the very scar of which I was speaking! It is! it must be the king of England himself! Light hair, light eyes, yet full of fire; yes, by my troth, and fiery enough they *do* look now. Hurra! victory! triumph!—Run all of you, and announce to the duke—no stay; —detain the prisoner till I go myself and acquaint the duke of his capture!"

Instant confusion ensued; half incredulous, half convinced, the servants all gathered round Richard; each pressing forward to gain a view of the scar; and offering their opinions upon the subject with the greatest freedom.

The proud soul of Richard was fired; he could have brooked any feeling sooner than the indignity of his present situation; and, bursting from Thelk, whilst he assumed an expression of countenance which struck conviction of his majesty to the hearts of all present, he exclaimed; "Banish your doubts! it *is* Richard who stands before you! Go then and report to your duke, that the king of England, unarmed and unattended, except by one single friend, is at this moment in his power; and let me behold what use his honour will teach him to make of such advantage!"

Thelk rushed forward to seek the duke; some of his companions following him, others remaining to guard the king.

"Oh, my sovereign! my best-beloved friend and master!" exclaimed Sir Philip Lucie, "why did I not exert the counsel of a friend to counteract the rash expedient which has led you into this toil. Oh! why did I suffer my king to bereave himself thus of protection?"

"Fear not for me, my friend," returned Richard, "I have committed no crimes to draw a veil between my injuries and the eye of heaven's protection!"

CHAP. VII.

————————Tho' fortune
Has stript me of the train and pomp of greatness,
That out-side of a king,—yet still my soul,
Fixt high, and of itself alone dependent,
Is ever free and royal.

Rowe.*

A considerable time having elapsed, not the duke, but Thelk, entered the apartment; his cap was now in his hand, and, with the humblest submission of voice, he requested the king in the name of Leopold to follow him.

In expectation of being conducted to the presence of the duke, Richard complied; his guide led him up a staircase, at the top of which was an area, which terminated in a stone arch; they passed through it and entered a chamber, in which stood a handsome bed. "As proof of the duke's hospitality," said Thelk, "he appropriates to your use this chamber; in the morning your majesty will be removed to a lodging better suited to your rank than the one you must this night be satisfied to repose in."

"Why am I not permitted to see the duke?" asked Richard.

"He did not explain to me his reason for not seeing you," replied Thelk.

"Then *I* will!" exclaimed the king: "It is because he has not courage to encounter the man to whom he intends to be unjust!"

Thelk did not reply; but, leaving the room, closed the door, and locked it.

From the duke's refusal to see him, Richard augured some event inauspicious to his wishes. He traversed the apartment in thought and restlessness; already he believed himself detained a prisoner; still the courteous language which Thelk had addressed to him, did not appear to announce any intentions of a cruel nature, with regard to his future fate, to have place in the breast of Leopold.

Presently a second door, which he had not noticed in the chamber, was thrown open, and he beheld through it an apartment brilliantly lighted, in which a table was spread; and to this, some domestics, immediately entering, invited him to sit down; their invitation would have been without effect, had he not perceived his friend Sir Philip conducted into the adjoining apartment, and upon this observation he went in.

At the present trying moment, it was some consolation to his feelings, to be allowed the society of his friend; but it was an inefficacious good; for of what advantage could the counsel of a friend be to him in his present situation? The night was passed by Sir Philip in the apartment contiguous to the king's chamber; sleepless were the hours to both, and the first dawn of day was hailed by Richard as a relief to his over-burdened feelings.

When the first streaks of the rising sun began to gild the heavens with their refulgence, Richard looked out from the casement of his chamber, and beheld that the house was surrounded with guards in the Austrian uniform.—"I am then a prisoner!" was the conclusion of his mind, and he endeavoured to bear the reflection as it became a hero; but Sir Philip beheld on his countenance a painful struggle, which communicated a severer pang to the heart of that friend, than it would have done to have witnessed the anguish of his soul distilled in tears from his manly and commanding eye; so much more forcible is the silence than the eloquence of grief.

In a short time a summons was brought to the king to descend from his chamber into a small court before the house; information being at the same period given him that he was about to be transported from thence to some other spot. In silence, but with the step of an undaunted mind, Richard moved forward. Arrived on the outside of the house, he found a detachment of guards, mounted on horseback; they were drawn up in a semicircle round the entrance, and in their centre were a couple of horses, which were led towards Sir Philip and himself; and on the saddles of which they were requested to place themselves.

As the king was in the act of mounting, Thelk stepped forward and addressed him; "I informed your majesty last night," he said, "that you would to-day be placed in a habitation better suited to your rank; by the hour of noon you will have reached the castle of Trivallis, one of the most magnificent in Austria."

Richard replied only by a look intended to awe Thelk into

silence. He knew not whether to believe him really humble, or civilly insolent; and the name of Trivallis led him to believe the latter. The castle of Trivallis was universally known over the world, as one from which it was reported that no prisoner had ever come out alive;* but the courage of Richard was not to be shaken by a covered threat, such as he regarded the duke to have intended the information, which he had doubtless charged Thelk to give him to convey; and he resolved to believe that he was to be transported to Trivallis only in the hope of drawing from him the better ransom.

The king and his friend having mounted their horses, the guards surrounded them, and a signal was given for their departure. As they moved out of the court-yard, the king, casting his eyes almost unconsciously towards one of the windows of the house, beheld at it a figure which, for an instant, arrested his attention; it was that of an extremely beautiful, and elegant woman, who appeared to be regarding him with a considerable degree of interest.

The female remained at the window till the cavalcade had proceeded to so great a distance from the house, that objects within it were no longer distinguishable to those who composed it.

By the side of the king rode a young man who had the command of the horse-guards; his deportment was of the most gentle and courteous kind; and many were the acts of civility which he extended to Richard in the course of their journey; and which were performed in a manner at once so engaging and unassuming, as rendered them acceptable, even from one of the emissaries of his determined enemy.

Notwithstanding the numerous and weighty cares which filled the mind of Richard, he could not entirely drive from his thoughts the recollection of the female whom he had that morning seen. And unaccountable to himself was the impression made by her on his senses; he felt for her neither love nor admiration, and yet he could not prevent her idea from recurring occasionally to his memory; and the only reason which he could suggest for its doing so was the grateful recollection that his heart entertained of the sympathy with which she had appeared to regard his fate.

For a while Richard received in silence the civilities of the young officer, at length entering with him gradually into a broken conversation, the king inquired "If the duke were married?"

The reply was in the negative, he was not a husband, nor had he ever been so.

After a pause, Richard asked, "Who then had been the lady whom he had seen at the window of the house which they had that morning quitted?"

His companion replied, "That she was the chosen favourite of the duke, an infidel of great beauty, whose father had perished in the holy wars; and whom Leopold had brought with him from Palestine."

As they proceeded, the country which had at the commencement of their journey, been cultivated and diversified by scenes of industry, became mountainous and barren; no screen interposing to cut the bleak winds which blew over its face, except accidental forests, the refuge of beasts of prey, against the savage attacks of which the king's guards unsheathed their weapons; and with which they were often obliged to expose themselves and their horses to a contest.

Between the tenth and eleventh hours of the morning, their course lying over a barren and sandy heath, where whirlwinds of dust inclosed them at intervals, in clouds of misty darkness; Richard descryed, upon the verge of the horizon, a range of lofty hills, on the most eminent of which appeared the outline of a stately edifice. The young officer perceived his attention directed towards it, and informed him that it was the castle of Trivallis which he beheld.

As they advanced, and the features of the place became more distinct, Richard perceived that it was of immense strength, surrounded by a deep moat, and accessible only over a bridge, enclosed in the bosom of massive fortifications.

Having ascended the acclivity on which the castle stood, the bridge was lowered, the port-cullis drawn up, and the gates opened for their reception. In the court-yard they were met by several domestics, who advanced with the most officious civility to offer their services to Richard, and when he had dismounted, they conducted him into the castle, and passing through the grand hall, they ascended a stair-case, at its extremity; from whence a stone gallery led them to a chamber, which composed the first of a noble suite of apartments, which Richard was informed were destined to the use of himself and his friend.

This intelligence was conveyed to him by the young officer, who had commanded the escort by which he had been conducted to the castle, and on whom the task now devolved of being answerable for his not escaping from his present imprisonment.

The accommodations which were offered to Richard, the repasts which were placed before him, the humble obeisance with which he was served, were evident marks that nothing was intended to be denied him but his liberty; and he constrained himself throughout the day to wear a countenance which might convey an idea of the utmost composure of mind to those who beheld him; but when left alone, at the approach of evening, with his friend, his oppressed soul could not forbear braking forth into a confession of its real feelings.

"Oh, my friend," exclaimed the captive monarch, "how are the vain expectations of man blighted by the hand of fate! The sovereign and the subject are alike exposed to the fate of its commanding voice; and their equality beyond the grave is pointed out to them on earth by the equal power which misfortune maintains over their feelings! Oh, why did I ever quit my native England!" A long pause succeeded this question; his heart replied to it, by reviving the memory of Matilda, and the many painful associations connected with her history. From these his thoughts wandered back to those days when his breast first glowed under the impression of her loveliness; when flattering fancy promised him more than mortal bliss in a union with her charms. A sensation almost approaching to distraction followed this idea:—"Where are ye now, ye many coloured bubbles of my ardent youth!" he again burst forth.—"The picture of connubial bliss which I had drawn, is fled! the dream of royalty is vanished! I am a prisoner—deserted!" The tear stole down his cheek, and he sat for some moments with his face buried in his hands. When he again raised his head, his eye encountered that of Sir Philip, who was standing over him, with the most vivid sympathy portrayed on his countenance; he snatched his hand, and pressing it earnestly; he said, "Forgive me, friend, I was ungrateful to thy services, when I pronounced myself deserted; whilst I am yet permitted the society of one whose constancy of affection has been tried towards me as thine has been! be the pangs of my soul the apology of words which I recal!"

In Sir Philip now shone forth that truly excellent spirit which his king had so justly extolled. The attentions which he extended towards his sovereign, and the many arts by which he attempted to lighten to him the burden of captivity, were performed with an earnestness which he had ever been careful to avoid, when the prosperity of Richard might have sanctioned a belief that he was actuated by views of an interested nature; now the adversity of his royal master bade defiance to such an opinion, he gloried in an opportunity of displaying the full benevolence of his heart.

Nearly a month passed on without any alteration taking place in the treatment shewn to the king; and without his having beheld Leopold, or received any tidings of him. He was surprised that no terms of ransom had been offered to his acceptance; and at length inquired of the young officer who had the command of the castle, if he were acquainted with the cause?

Anhalt, for such was the young man's name, declared himself utterly unacquainted with the duke's motives and proceedings, and said; "That he had not quitted his post since the king's arrival at the castle, nor received any intelligence from Leopold, except what concerned his military duty."

The weeks rolled on, and still the duke proposed no terms of enlargement to Richard; and Richard still continued too proud to sue for liberty.—"Surely!" he would repeat, "my insidious brother cannot have disaffected all my English subjects! Surely there are still some true and loyal hearts remaining amongst them, who will collect together, trace out the spot of their king's concealment, and release him from the indignity of a prison!" Thus would he express himself in the moments of hope;—When the dark clouds of despondency overcast his mind, of the same melancholy hue were the expressions which he poured from his labouring breast:—"Why should I continue to endure life?" he would then exclaim; "no heart desires my preservation; no voice is raised for my prosperity to heaven!—No one remembers me!—No one loves me! Matilda!—Yes; I cannot believe that Matilda has forgotten her Richard. Though it was her own act to separate herself from me, I cannot believe that she ceases to love me as she ever did. Perhaps, at this moment, *she* prays for my deliverance!—Live, Richard, live! 'Tis an idea to re-animate thy heart, and pour a balm on all thy sufferings."

The winter was now rapidly advancing; and the natural gloom of the season was infinitely deepened to the heart of Richard, by the approach of the only calamity which, in his present state of captivity, it was in the power of fate to level at his already shattered peace.

The constitution of Sir Philip Lucie had been a material sufferer from the climate of Asia; and every symptom predictive of a speedy termination of nature's powers was now apparent in him. Such medicines as were supposed to be efficacious in his peculiar case, were administered to him with regular attention in the castle, but they proved insufficient to stay his fleeting spirit; it evaporated in a prayer for the preservation of his beloved sovereign.

Now, indeed, *was* Richard a prisoner—deserted! a king! without one subject to lend the ear of pity to his sovereign's sighs of anguish!

CHAP. VIII.

————————By the roses of the spring,
—————by honour, truth, and every thing,
I love thee so, that maugre all thy pride,
Nor art, nor reason, can my passion hide.

SHAKESPEARE.*

SOLITUDE does not weaken a mind of reason and of sense; the reaction of such a mind upon itself, adds vigour to its natural fortitude, and prepares it for bold and honourable action. Thus Richard, by being bereft of his only companion, his only friend, did not sink nervelessly into the humiliation of unmanly despair; but, gaining prowess of heart from dwelling on the rank, the dignity, the honours of his former life, resolved rather to be a prisoner in Trivallis, than to suffer the pages of history to be stained with the record of a king of England having sued for his liberty to an Austrian duke!

Having determinately formed this resolution, the elevation of sentiment which accompanied it to his mind, imparted a greater degree of composure to his feelings, than they had yet experienced since he had been the prisoner of Leopold. The only idea which recalled the softness of affliction to his heart, was the memory of his adored Matilda. Yet hope, which never flies the breasts of mortals, united even her recollection with an assuasive balm. It was possible, he thought, that if he were ever restored to his throne, in remuneration of the miseries he had endured, during his absence from his kingdom; an absence to which her determination had impelled him; she might draw a veil in her memory over those occurrences which had actuated her conduct, and consent to bless him with her hand.

The genial breath of spring had already thawed the frozen brow of winter;—and still Richard was a solitary captive. The beams of summer suns had kissed the blooming rose, and still the king of England was duke Leopold's prisoner; and the golden tints of autumn were already adding richness to the landscape, ere any incident broke the sameness of his unchequered existence.

One evening, about this time, when the domestics, who had attended upon him during his evening repast, had placed the lamps for the night, and quitted his apartments, and the king was on the point of retiring to rest, he was surprized at hearing the door of the first apartment which composed the suite appropriated to his use, once more opened, when he did not expect to behold any one enter again till the morning.

The sound drew him to the spot from an adjoining chamber; and he beheld a figure which appeared to him by the dress that it wore, to be one of the Austrian guards, in the act of closing the door which he had heard open. Acquainted that one of these guards was constantly stationed as a sentinel on the outside of the door, his first idea was, that the man was charged with some message to him; and he immediately called to him, demanding his business.

The figure turned hastily round, and, placing a finger on its lips, enjoined the king to silence by the signal; then advancing hastily a few steps into the apartment, it said, "I am a friend."

"A friend!" echoed Richard. "Who and what art thou?"

"A woman; and in love!" replied the apparent guard.

This confession astonished Richard still more than he had already been. He did not immediately reply, and the stranger continued thus; "I have used a stratagem which has procured me to be placed a sentry at your door to-night, in order that I may have an opportunity of communicating to you a plan for your escape."

"To whom do I owe this kindness and humanity?" asked Richard.

"Have you," she returned, "no recollection of these features?" taking from her head as she spoke, the cap which formed a part of the dress which constituted her assumed character.

Richard gazed upon her countenance, his memory confessed some slender acquaintance with its lineaments, but he could not recollect where he had gained that knowledge, and requested her to inform him what was her name.

"It is Zulima," she answered, "but I do not think you have heard it before."*

The king replied in the negative.

"Do you not remember," rejoined Zulima, "that when the vanquished inhabitants of Acre were compelled by the victorious Christian armies to quit its walls, an ancient warrior, named Axalla, disabled with the wounds he had that day received, was brought forth on a litter, and expired ere yet he could be borne a prisoner to the camp?"

The countenance of Richard bespoke that the circumstance was not entirely obliterated from his recollection.

Zulima proceeded thus; "Axalla was my father, my only parent; when life had fled from him, I sunk upon the earth by his side, and pressed to my heart the insensible clay which his spirit had once animated; whilst I lay weeping thus, I heard a voice;—Oh 'twas the voice of more than mortal to *my* ear! exclaim, 'Poor fatherless girl, how I pity thee!' I raised my head to behold the sympathizer in my fate; I beheld one, whose features have, from that moment, been engraven on my heart; I beheld, Oh, royal Richard!—yourself!"

The king listened attentively, but did not interrupt her.

"From that moment," continued Zulima, "I saw you no more in Palestine; my prayers to behold you once again were not heard;

and urged by the fate of captivity, I accepted of the protection of the duke of Austria."

At these words, the light of recollection suddenly flashed upon the senses of Richard, and he exclaimed, "You are the female whom I beheld at the window of the house where I was recognised by the duke's old soldier, Thelk?"

"It was I," she replied, "whom you beheld witnessing your departure; and surely my countenance must have acquainted you with the interest my heart took in your fate! Oh what a moment of mingled sensation was to me that in which I heard of your arrest! I could have wept for the indignity you were suffering, whilst my heart bounded with extacy at the hope which presented itself to me of once more beholding you! I resolved to exert every nerve for entering your presence, and declaring to you the sentiments which animate my heart, I am in your presence; it *is* permitted me to confess myself devoted to you alone!—I am blest!"

"Do you not feel sensible," said Richard, "that, in the step you have taken, you are ungrateful to the duke for such favours, as you may have received at his hands?"

"Ere I knew the duke," returned Zulima, with energy, "my heart was devoted to you; the services of that heart I now devote to you likewise! The unwilling shackles by which an orphan state, and the desertion, or death of every natural friend, once compelled me to suffer Leopold to unite me to himself, I now shake off. Do *you* place others upon me in their stead! Whatever chains you will condescend to impose upon Zulima, she will experience pride and ecstasy in wearing! Oh, revered Richard! suffer me to effect your escape from this castle, which it is at this time in my ability to do; make me the companion of your voyage to England, and when you have reached your kingdom, let the reward of my exertions in your cause be, to share some portion of your tenderness and love, under whatever name it shall best please you to bestow it on me!"

After a short pause given to reflection, Richard spoke thus;—"I owe you, fair lady, my thanks for the preference which you profess yourself to feel for me; I owe you still more for your ardour in my cause—a candid explanation of my heart: I have bound myself by a vow of the most solemn nature never to become the husband of any woman, save one alone; and I am equally resolved never to debase the purity of affection which I bear that woman, by an illicit connexion with any other object, for which she could not fail to esteem me the less, if it were known to her."

"By the affection which I bear you," replied Zulima, "I swear that I would subscribe to any plan which you might devise for screening myself from her knowledge."

"But my falsehood would be known to myself," answered Richard, firmly.

"You are not even yet a husband," rejoined Zulima, playfully.

"I regard it as extremely doubtful whether I ever shall be one," replied the king.

"And are you thus constant upon a contingency?" cried Zulima. "Do you hesitate to accept your freedom at the hands of one woman, because there exists the possibility of your being ultimately united to another?"

"It is the *condition* connected with the offer of liberty which you make me, that I reject," said Richard.

"Oh, Richard! great and magnanimous king!" exclaimed Zulima, "thou wilt rive the fondest heart that ever loved thee, if thou refuse to let me become thy preserver! Oh, hero of my soul! hear me, and weigh my words within thy heart; would a smile of love bestowed on me, be too dear a price for thy restoration to the object of thy warmer affections?"

"Oh, shameless libertine!" answered the king, "thy flattery cannot tempt me to dishonour; I had rather never again enter the presence of her, in whom my soul alone lives, than present myself before her, conscious of my own unworthiness."

"Your contempt," replied Zulima, with a mixture of agitation and earnestness depicted on her countenance, "shall not turn me from the purpose which brought me hither; you must, you shall, listen to the imminent danger in which you stand; a knowledge of it may induce you to become more temperate in your zeal of love;—tell me, Oh, tell me, whose prisoner it is that you at this moment believe yourself?"

"Whose?" cried Richard, his curiosity, in some measure, excited by the question; "can there be a doubt that I am Leopold's captive?"

"But you have yet to learn," answered Zulima, "that you are equally the captive of the emperor of Germany!"

A start of surprise shook the frame of Richard, but he did not interrupt the fair infidel's explanation, who continued thus;—"That very evening in which you were discovered by Thelk to be the king of England in disguise, the emperor Henry was the guest of the duke; the intelligence of chance having led you beneath the roof of your enemy was accordingly heard by him when announced to Leopold—And Henry, urged by a mercenary spirit, offered to the duke his castle of Trivallis (for this castle *is* the emperor's) as your prison; on condition of receiving in return for the accommodation, half of the sum which should be paid for your ransom!—A refusal of any proposition of the emperor's, the duke was too well acquainted with his character not to be aware, would eventually lead to his own disadvantage; and he was consequently compelled to assent to his terms. You are doubtless surprised that no demand of ransom had been made of you; they are aware that the spot of your concealment is unknown to any one of your friends; and therefore, secure in their own opinion, that you cannot be rescued from their tyranny, it is their intention to weary out your fortitude by a lengthened captivity, which shall ultimately lead you to propose to them terms far superior to what they could, at this moment, expect from you!"

"But they will discover how great is their error!" replied the king, "for sooner than become the dupe of their artifices, or bend himself to their unfeeling minds, in supplication for his liberty, Richard will be content to *die* in Trivallis!"

"But Richard *shall not* die in Trivallis," exclaimed his new friend. "Zulima will release him from the horrors of his fate!—shall she not? Oh, noble Richard! declare, that she shall be the instrument of your preservation!"

"I have already explained to you, why I cannot become your debtor for this service," replied Richard.

"Oh, heavens!" exclaimed Zulima, "how little did I imagine that the tidings of joy, which I believed myself to be bringing you, would be replied to with these scruples."

"Are you still an infidel?" asked Richard, "or have you been converted to christianity since you have lived in Europe?"

"No," she answered, "the duke has never spoken to me upon the subject; and I have been debarred by him from intercourse with almost every one else."

"Your mind, fair maid," returned Richard, "is not then prepared to comprehend those scruples which you deride in me."

The king had moved a few steps towards the door; "Surely you are not going to bid me depart," said Zulima.

"For your own sake I recommend it to you," replied Richard; "it is near the hour at which the sentinel who guards this door is usually relieved; and you would doubtless lose the favour of the duke by being discovered here."

"I have quitted the duke for ever," returned Zulima. "I cannot longer submit to grant the possession of my person where my affection does not follow it; whilst there exists a being like yourself, to whom my heart is so tenderly, so ardently devoted!—Oh, admirable man! if you will not immediately accept my proposal, Oh promise me that you will reflect upon it; that you will sometimes admit me to your presence, and listen to the arguments which I shall use for inducing you to its acceptance?"

"Whilst you are thus safe from the duke's resentment, let me entreat you to quit these walls!" rejoined Richard.

"I shall not quit them," she answered, "whilst you remain inclosed within them;—I once more repeat to you, that I have left the duke *for ever*—till you agree to fly hence with me, I am a soldier, subject to all the labour of a soldier's duty! to all the hardships of his nightly watchings; to all the punishments which ignorance or disobedience may subject me to;—and this do I voluntarily, joyfully encounter for your sake! Shall I tell you how cunningly I managed to convert myself into my present form? A poor old woman who lives in a cottage near the palace where Leopold resides, had a son who was a member of the body of guards, stationed perpetually at this castle; being herself extremely old and infirm, it was her earnest wish that her son might be allowed to return home to her, in order that he might till a piece of land of which she was possessed, for their mutual support. She applied to the duke for his permission, and he replied to her petition, 'That her son's release could only be granted on the condition of her providing some other young man to serve in his stead;' instantly I resolved to become his substitute; I fled from the duke's palace; sought the old cottager; and, by the present of a piece of gold, bought her secrecy and consent, to my becoming the substitute of her son.

She provided me with a suit of youth's cloaths; and with Leopold's order in my pocket, for the release of him whose place I was to supply, I arrived here. The exchange was soon made, and I have now been five days one of the guards of Trivallis; but this hour is the first of my having been placed in a situation to make myself known to you without the danger of a discovery."

Richard listened with astonishment to her narrative; there was a peculiar energy of mind in the character of Zulima, which charmed him, although he could not approve the motive by which she was induced to call it forth;—as he continued silent, she exclaimed with some degree of alarm; "You will not surely betray me to Anhalt; if you do, he will discover my imposition to the duke and I am lost!"

"Indeed I will not, lovely pagan!" he replied; "I will do thee no injury, depend on me; if I could confer on thee any good, it would delight me to do so; Zulima, I should joy to teach thee that faith which would reclaim thy heart!"

"I would learn any thing from you," she answered.

"But still," rejoined the king, "the motive from which you would attend to my instructions, might destroy the merit of your diligence!"

A bell was at this moment sounded from one of the towers of the castle which announced the period of relieving the sentinels on their posts. "Hark!" cried Zulima, "I must away! rely on seeing me again the first moment that presents itself to me for visiting you with safety."

"My sentiments will not change!" replied Richard.

"Nor my ardour for your liberty diminish!" exclaimed Zulima.—Moving towards the door, she lingered an instant on her way.—"Will you refuse me your hand as a token of friendship at parting?" she said.

Richard did not reply; she ran back hastily towards him, snatched his hand, and would have carried it to her lips.

From this attempt Richard withheld it; "You asked to press my hand in friendship," he said, "a kiss would exceed the limits of your request.—Good night Zulima."

"Oh, Richard!" she exclaimed; and darted from the apartment.

CHAP. IX.

——'Tis the mind that makes the body rich;
And as the sun breaks through the darkest clouds,
So honour peereth in the meanest habit.
What is the jay more precious than the lark,
Because his feathers are more beautiful?
Or is the adder better than the eel,
Because his painted skin contents the eye?
————Oh no, neither art thou the worse
For this poor furniture and mean array.

Shakespeare.*

The visit of Zulima made a great impression on the mind of Richard. He could not forbear feeling a considerable degree of gratitude for the interest which she took in his fate, and of pity for the delusive sentiments of her unenlightened mind. Again and again he reflected on the terms upon which she had promised to effect his escape from prison; and upon every revisal of his conduct, he felt more satisfied with the manner in which he had acted. In the case of his father's love for the fair Rosamond he had seen sufficient of the miseries which result from the divided affections of a husband, to contemplate the erring conduct of Henry as a mark of caution to himself; and he considered himself as the husband of Matilda;—if their hands were not united, their sentiments, their souls were; and the purity of this mental union, he resolved that no act of his should sully.

The comparison likewise which he could not forbear drawing between the fair infidel and his Matilda, strengthened the opinion he had already adopted. For as he dwelt on the bliss which he had experienced in advancing by a slow and timid progress towards the heart of Matilda, awed by the virtuous modesty which had shone around her, like a circle of protecting glory; the free and undisguised confession which Zulima had made to him of her sentiments, appeared in a light more offensive to the feelings of delicacy, than it would perhaps have done, had it been opposed to the conduct of any woman less peerless than Matilda, in the retiring graces of a feminine soul!

Four days elapsed and Zulima returned no more; Richard knew not whether to believe that her absence was caused by her inability to gain access to his apartments; or that dissatisfied by the coldness with which he had treated her advances towards his heart, she had relinquished her project of procuring for him his enlargement. He felt sufficient interest in her fate to hope that the duke had not discovered her treachery.

On the fourth evening after Zulima's visit, about the hour of twilight, as the king was standing near an open casement in one of his apartments at which he could alone procure the benefit of air; for every window to which he had access was shut from a view of the country, either by the projecting parapet walls, or the interference of the high-raised bastions; his ear was struck with the sound of distant music, which appeared like the gentle tinkling of the strings of a lute.

Anhalt happened at this moment to enter the apartment, and Richard inquired of him, if he knew by whom the chords were struck? Anhalt replied that he was not acquainted with there being any individual within the castle walls skilled in the art of music; and expressing equal surprise at the sounds as the king had done, he went out to inquire the cause.

In little more than a quarter of an hour, Anhalt returned. "The musicians," he said, "whom your majesty heard, for there are two of them, are vagrant minstrels; an infirm, blind man, and his son, a youth of at most fifteen, who guides his parent over the country, in order to procure themselves subsistence by the exercise of their talents. When you heard the sound of their instruments, they were reposing at the foot of the drawbridge, and imploring hospitality from the inhabitants of the castle."

"Poor souls!" exclaimed Richard, "I hope their wants have been relieved?"

"They will be speedily," replied Anhalt; "some of my soldiers have obtained my permission to invite them to pass the night in the castle; and in return for this hospitality they are to entertain them with their ballads and romances."

"There was a period of my happier days," rejoined Richard, "when I myself used to consider an hour pleasantly spent in listening to these wandering musicians."

"Perhaps an hour thus passed might afford you the same amusement now," rejoined Anhalt.

"I have discovered in you an honourable and a benevolent heart," answered Richard; "to *you* therefore I do not scruple to confess that my feelings are little adapted to any enjoyment."

"But your majesty knows," returned Anhalt, "that music is allowed to possess the power of lulling the mind to peace."

A smile of incredulity stole over the features of Richard.

"There is a court beneath these windows," continued Anhalt, "into which I will willingly introduce the minstrels; if their notes offend instead of soothing your senses, I can but dismiss them from it again."

"Your intention," replied the king, "is extremely kind and grateful to my feelings."

"I sincerely wish that its event may prove the same," answered Anhalt; and retired to execute his intention.

"Oh my Matilda," burst forth Richard, when left by the departure of Anhalt to his solitary prison; "with what extacy do I still dwell on the charms of thy mellifluous voice! on the soul-inspiring tones drawn by thy fingers from the chords of harmony! Still do they vibrate on my heart; still does the recollection of their melody run thrilling through my veins. Oh Matilda! thy notes have perhaps been heard by me for the last time!"

From the train of thought into which these reflections had thrown him, Richard was roused by the sound of the minstrels tuning their instruments in the court-yard of which Anhalt had spoken.

The casement of Richard's apartment was so situated that it was impossible for him to behold either the court-yard or any one within it; he accordingly threw himself on a couch near it, to attend to the music.

After the minstrels had played many popular airs of the country, with considerable effect and execution; the voice of a man, which Richard concluded to be that of the blind father, sung a romance, which he accompanied on the strings of his instrument, entitled:

The Two Knights of Alsace.

I.

Through bogs and fens at dead of night,
A warrior urged his furious way;
To gain an old embattl'd tower,
Ere twilight ushered in the day.

II.

Arriv'd, his horse's thundering hoofs
Made the wide court-yard awful ring;
Whilst ravens croaking at the sound,
Wheel'd their dull flight on cowering wing.

III.

Three times the horn's sonorous voice
The vassals rous'd in wild affright;
Whilst gleaming on the casque of steel,
The moon revealed a warrior knight.

IV.

"Where is the lord of these domains?
To him a message I convey:
Arouse him from his dreams of bliss;
I must away, away, away!"

V.

Sir Ulric rose, and gazing, said,
"A brother knight methinks I see."
"I'm come," a voice sepulchral cried,
"To prove affinity to thee!"

VI.

"But neither this the place nor time,
My mystic message to proclaim,
The spot is mark'd with brakes and briars,
And a rough stone secures the same."

VII.

Sir Ulric, as by instinct urged,
Dar'd not his secret fear betray;
The clock struck twelve, the warrior cried,
"Let us away, away, away!"

VIII.

These sounds Sir Ulric's life-blood froze,
It curdled in each quivering vein;
His shivering limbs beneath their load,
Scarce could his trembling frame sustain.

IX.

Swift as the wind the warrior flew,
Nor fen, nor bog his haste impede;
Whilst drench'd with sweat, and white with foam,
Dash'd through the swamps his snorting steed.

X.

Fain would Sir Ulric back have turn'd
Yet dar'd he not the knight defy;
Who seem'd to guess his secret thoughts
And on him turned his piercing eye.

XI.

And now a lonely heath appear'd,
And sharp and shrill the cold wind blew;
Whilst owls just issuing from their haunts,
Scream'd clamorous on each blasted yew.

XII.

And harsh the murderer's gibbet creak'd
Whilst the wind wav'd its clanking chain;
As under it the warriors pass'd,
Sir Ulric held his aching brain.

XIII.

"And who is this," he frantic cried,
"Condemn'd to glut the birds of prey?"
"*A murderer!*" the knight replied,
"Let us away, away, away!"

XIV.

Onward they sped, o'er wild and waste,
Furious the horses dashed the ground;
Till fearful on Sir Ulric's ear,
A bell toll'd forth its sullen sound.

XV.

And now they gain'd a dreary dell,
Where nought but briars profusely grew;
Whilst here and there rude stones appear'd
And cast around a dusky hue.

XVI.
Now bright and clear the moon arose,
And on one spot conspicuous shone,
Where crusted with a brother's blood,
Crimson appear'd, a cold grave-stone!

XVII.
Sir Ulric shuddering, turn'd his head,
Full well the spot he knew again;
Where urged by ruthless avarice,
A brother he had vilely slain.

XVIII.
"This grave is mine," the warrior cried;
"Beneath this stone my ashes lie;
But fate now checks thy dark career,
And the vile fratricide must die!"

XIX.
His beaver rose with sudden haste,
And long and lank his visage hung,
And sapless were his bony limbs,
That once with sinewy strength were strung.

XX.
"Blood will have blood, 'tis so decreed;
Justice thou can'st not sure deny;
Down! Down! Upon a brother's grave
Long may thy worthless body lie!"

XXI.
Full in his heart, he drove his spear;
Groaning in death Sir Ulric lay:
"I am revenged!" the warrior cried,
"And must away, away, away!"

This romance gained considerable applause from the listeners, and was followed by several others of a similar nature; at length Richard heard the old man request his son to sing, and relieve him. The youth directly prepared to comply by striking the chords of his lute, and in a few seconds commenced his song. But what words can give an adequate idea of the sensations which burst upon the heart of Richard when he recognised not only the melody of the air, but the words of the song, to be those by which Matilda had first charmed his senses.

The very song which he had listened to from her lips with rapture on the coast of Cornwall was now repeating beneath the window of his prison in Austria! the voice too by which it was now singing, appeared to him not less similar to hers, than was the resemblance of the song itself.

He could scarcely believe that the effect at this moment produced on his senses owed its being to any other cause than that of magic! With breathless impatience he waited for the burden of the song. At length those words which had ever possessed so peculiar a charm for his feelings; and which were rendered still more dear to him, by being the last that he had ever heard Matilda sing, at the palace of Beaumont, on the evening previous to his departure for Normandy; those very words, rendered by every fascination touching to his soul, now stole on his ear.

> "I've strayed o'er the wold, and I've stray'd o'er the wild,
> In hopes to find him whom my presence might save;
> O, ye saints lead me to him, O, tell him I'm true!
> And preserve him from sinking in youth to the grave!"

Whilst these lines were singing his every sense appeared bound up. The moment they were concluded, clasping his hands together in the delirium of rapture, he exclaimed, "'Tis she! 'tis she! it is Matilda herself!"

For a few succeeding minutes his senses became bewildered, and he lost the power of analyzing ideas, or occurrences.

The first circumstance of which he was conscious, was that of being addressed by Anhalt, whom with a couple of domestics he beheld standing by his side; and who was anxiously inquiring, "Whether he had been suddenly taken ill?" his exclamation having been heard by them in the court-yard; but fortunately for the king, the words which had composed it, not understood; and therefore conjectured to have been an ejaculation caused either by sudden pain, or illness.

Richard answered that he had been seized with a sensation of a most unexpected nature, but that its violence was now abated. Anhalt brought him a refreshing beverage, and having persuaded him to drink it, endeavoured to induce him to retire to bed; but this advice the king resisted—and Anhalt after a time, observing in him no symptoms of illness, proceeded to superintend the locking of the castle gates for the night.

The moment he was gone, Richard flew to the open casement, in the hope of once more hearing that voice which every sympathizing feeling tempted him to believe could only have been that of Matilda herself! but uninterrupted silence now prevailed in the court-yard beneath; the minstrels and their entertainers had all retired, at the approach of night, into the castle.

As the fervour of a first impression became in some degree cooled, the king began to reflect whether it might not still be possible that his senses had deceived him; whether it had not been the resemblance, and not the reality of Matilda's voice which he had heard? But the palpitation of his labouring heart refuted this idea; Matilda had informed him that she had herself composed so great a portion of this song, that her father had called it *her* song. Her life had been passed remote from all intercourse with her fellow beings; a circumstance which rendered it extremely unlikely that this song should have been taught by her to any other person, from whose repetitions it should have become so commonly known to the world, as at last to be in the possession of a wandering minstrel! it *must* therefore have been Matilda herself by whom it had within that very hour been sung!

"And can it be, almighty powers!" he exclaimed, "that she has exposed her soft and tender frame to the sufferings of weary pilgrimage, for the purpose of tracing out my prison? Oh Matilda! thou, to whom every additional moment of thy existence gives fairer claims to excellence; is it thou of all my subjects who alone possesses an affection for thy prince, thy Richard, which has led thee to seek the spot of his concealment! Oh exquisite and unrivalled maid! more welcome to my soul is this testimony of thy unchanged love, than an invincible host in arms for my restoration to liberty!"

Tears, which the grip of misfortune had wrung singly and seldom from his heart, now burst unrestrained from his eyes; and it was a relief which had long been foreign to his over-burdened soul.

The night continued to advance and no circumstance occurred either to confute or to confirm the suspicions of Richard. He considered that if his Matilda were indeed a lodger within the walls of the castle, it was evident that she had some greater plan in view, than that of merely beholding him: Anhalt would doubtless have informed him of it, if she had made any attempt at seeing him; and hence he concluded, that as any inquiries which he might urge concerning the minstrels, might but awaken suspicion; when it might be of the utmost consequence to his future peace to keep it dormant; it must be his care not to mention them at all in any conversation which he might have with Anhalt; and he farther believed, that if it had indeed been Matilda herself, by whom the song had been sung, that she had chosen it as the most promising signal for informing him how near she was to him; and for preparing him by this knowledge, to second any measure which she might have in agitation.

CHAP. X.

Happily I have arrived at last
Unto the wished haven of my bliss.

SHAKESPEARE.*

To Matilda we must now for a while dedicate the page, and recount the events of her life since the departure of Richard from England, on his expedition into Palestine.

We have already described the anguish of heart with which Matilda was affected by the consideration that it was she who had driven Richard from his native land; and exposed him to encounter the spear of the ruthless Pagan! equally did she lament the cause from which her conduct had sprung, as she mourned in the privacy of her heart, the effect which had arisen out of it. Her days and nights were passed alike in weeping and in prayer; the only consolation of her sorrowing mind, the soothing attentions and friendship of the affectionate Corally; who having like herself been separated from the object of her love, was well acquainted how to feel for the pangs inflicted by a similar fate on the heart of another.

Although resolute in her own idea, never again to quit the convent of St. Ursula, still Matilda forbore to take the vows of the order; she experienced a melancholy inclination, for which she herself found it difficult to account, to have that awful moment of separation from the world, graced by the presence of her two best esteemed friends; the royal Richard, and his sister Jane; and to this end she deferred her assumption of the vows till their return.

The first intelligence of importance which reached her after the departure of the king, was, that of the nuptials of the princess Jane with Tancred of Sicily; and scarcely had her prayers been offered up to heaven for the happiness of the married state of that friend, whom it was now unlikely that she should ever behold again; ere she was called upon to tell her beads for the repose of the soul of queen Eleanor, who, worn down with disappointment and remorse, had sunk into the grave, the victim of her own criminal rashness.

With the most vivid anxiety Matilda awaited the arrival of every fresh news from Palestine; and when the victories of Richard were reported to her, she hailed the information with a tear of heart-felt joy; and breathed a fervent prayer that the pride of conquest might repair to him, the loss of happiness which he had sustained in England.

But alas! how quickly is the alloy of pain mixed with every cheering sensation of the human breast; the revolving year brought fresh misery to the heart of Matilda in the information which she gained that prince John was false to the trust which his unsuspecting brother had placed in his hands, and was endeavouring to convert the period of Richard's absence to his own lawless advantage; and even raising his ideas to the crown of England.

The intelligence which Matilda acquired upon these subjects, was principally collected from Sir Eugene de Lancy. The extraordinary circumstance of her first introduction to him had stamped an interest in her favour upon his heart; which being reciprocally felt by Matilda, to whom his kind and benevolent conduct at the melancholy period of her mother's death had rendered him estimable; led him frequently to visit her in her retirement from the world; and of him Matilda impatiently inquired "Whether a knowledge of his unjust brother's machinations had been conveyed to the king?"

Sir Eugene's reply was in the affirmative, some of the king's steady friends had sent over emissaries to him, charged with this very purpose.

"God speed his safe return!" exclaimed Matilda, "God forbid that in addition to the loss of his peace, I should be the means of losing his kingdom likewise!"

Time moved on leaden wings with Matilda; at length the English fleet returned from Palestine, and communicated the tidings of Richard having been, by a detached vessel, conveyed to Istria; from whence it was his intention to travel through Germany into England, attended only by his confidential friend, Sir Philip Lucie. At the expiration of another week arrived the vessel which had borne him to Italy; and according to probable conjectures, Richard was to land in his kingdom in the course of a fortnight.

With the most painful anxiety Matilda counted the days; but how were the agonizing sensations of her heart increased, when days, weeks, and even months rolled on without his appearance, or any intelligence being received concerning him. In her present distress of mind, she besought Sir Eugene not to desert her, and he was affectionately obedient to her entreaties; she charged him with the task of collecting for her every conjecture relative to the fate of the king, which was circulated in the kingdom; and she found the universal idea to be, that of his having fallen into the power of the duke of Austria.

"And has he no friends, no armies ready to march to the relief of their king?" exclaimed Matilda.

"He has friends, and strenuous ones," replied Sir Eugene, "but they are without power; his subtle brother has found the means of seducing over the force of the kingdom to his own interests."

"Merciful God!" cried Matilda, "of what dreadful events have I been made the instrument! Driven by me from his kingdom the noble Richard may languish out life in solitary prison!" she clasped her hands in agony, and for a considerable time sat motionless, and apparently without sense; then starting suddenly from her trance of thought, she said, "Sir Eugene, my friend, my almost only friend, you must accompany me to the monastery of St. Michael; I must see the holy abbot of that place."

Sir Eugene consented to be her companion, and instant preparations were made for their journey on the following day.

With the first hour of the morning they set out; their progress was silent; Sir Eugene observed that his attempts at offering consolation to the mind of Matilda, appeared only to disturb her from reflections in which she was busily wrapt; and therefore forbore to address her.

As they approached the walls of the monastery, their ears were struck with the chaunting voices of the monks—"What may these sounds import?" said Matilda, "this is not one of their hours of prayer, nor is this a holy day to demand any particular devotions."

"Who are ye?" was the reply to their request for admission, when they had blown the bugle at the gate.

"Tell father Benedict," answered Matilda, "that it is Christabelle Glencowell, who implores to see him."

"Till the devotions now performing in our chapel are concluded," replied the monk who appeared at the gate, "neither you, nor any one else can behold him; but you may enter, and await his leisure."

Having alighted from their horses, Matilda said, "Is it not an extraordinary service which is now performing?"

"Yes," replied the porter, "and heaven prosper the end for which it is instituted! We have now an additional service every morning and evening for the restoration of our beloved king."

"Is that the purport of these holy men's devotions?" exclaimed Matilda, "then I must join in them too," and with a feebleness of step which the porter was unable to stay, she rushed towards the chapel; unobserved by any of the members of the community, she gained the spot to which her father had been accustomed to lead her in order to join in the prayers of the monks; it was still encircled by the curtain which had at his particular request been placed around it, in order to screen it from observation;—upon this spot she had not knelt since his death;—with it returned to her mind a vivid, an agonizing recollection of him, and of all the events in which she had been involved since she had been deprived of his protection. The name of her Richard was at the same instant poured forth in supplication from the united voices of the monks;

the combination of ideas which burst forth upon her senses overpowered every faculty, and she sunk fainting upon the ground.

Sir Eugene had followed the steps of Matilda; the spot of prayer to which she had fled, was not concealed from the view of any one entering the door of the chapel, and at the moment De Lancy reached it, he saw her fall upon the pavement, and instantly hastened to her assistance. The monks happened at this period to be rising from their devotions, which were drawn to a close; and observing a stranger, some of them approached De Lancy to inquire his business.

The sight of Matilda who was recognised by more than one of the brethren; gave a turn to their ideas, and father Benedict approaching from the altar, with mingled exclamations of surprise and pity assisted Sir Eugene in leading his fair visitant to his own apartment.

When recollection returned to Matilda, and she beheld the abbot by her side, a smile of satisfaction stole over her pallid countenance, "Father, father!" she faintly uttered, and sinking on her knees before him, imprinted a kiss on his hand, which she at the same moment bedewed with her tears.

He raised her from the earth, pressed her for a moment to his bosom, and replaced her in a seat, accompanying the action with his blessing.

"Friend of my father! friend of Richard!" rejoined Matilda, "to thee I fly in the hour of my wretchedness, my agony"———

"My daughter," replied father Benedict, "if pious care can sooth thy feelings, from me thou shalt experience it in every tenderness."

"Heaven will repay to you in future blessings, the prayers which you offer up for your king"—She rejoined with fervour, "Oh how few friends like this community has the unhappy Richard now left him!—Father," she continued after a pause, "I come to implore of you to sanction with your blessing, and to further with your prayers, the endeavours which I am about to exert in the cause of him whom we both love."

"You cannot doubt that I shall feel both joy and duty in the performance of such an act as you require," replied the abbot.

"But holy father," rejoined Matilda with increased energy; "would you, if the spot of Richard's concealment could be discovered, would you, upon such a discovery being made to you, consent to quit for a while these walls of silent peace, and joining in the world's unquiet throng, endeavour by your eloquence to spur on his tardy subjects to rise in arms, and restore their lawful monarch to his rights?"

"Whatever my single voice could effect in Richard's cause," returned the abbot, "you need not, cannot doubt, my will to execute. But how can the spot of his concealment be traced out?—By whom?"

"By me" exclaimed Matilda.

"By you?" returned the father.

"Yes, by me," affirmed Matilda, "my heart and I shall never be at peace, till I have made this bold attempt at repairing to him those wrongs which have, through me, innocently 'tis true, but still through me, descended on him."

Father Benedict and Sir Eugene listened with astonishment to her declaration; they represented to her that the labours and danger of such an enterprise were too great for the strength of her sex. But no arguments could turn her back from her purpose; "She had resolved," she said, "to assume the male habit; and wandering over Austria in the disguise of a minstrel, to endeavour to find the prison of the king; should she fail in her attempt, she had determined never to return to England; should her endeavours prosper, it was her design to hasten back; and communicating the intelligence of her success to father Benedict, call upon him to disperse throughout the kingdom the blessed information; to invite Richard's friends to assemble in his cause; and to rally to a point from whence she would lead them on to his rescue.

The holy father and Sir Eugene perceived that they might as soon expect by their arguments to expel light from the heavens, as to turn Matilda from her determination; and they therefore only exerted their endeavours to persuade her to accept a companion and a protector in her undertaking; for which office Sir Eugene immediately proposed himself.

With some difficulty Matilda was prevailed on to consent to his proposition; and it was then agreed that they should not return to St. Ursula, but proceed without delay towards the coast, and engage a vessel to transport them to the first port of Germany.

On the following morning the blessing of the abbot having been poured forth on the head of Matilda, and his promise given her that his community should offer up daily prayers for her safety and success, she departed from the monastery accompanied only by Sir Eugene; and ere the shades of evening had fallen to the earth, the English shore was vanishing from their sight.

It would not increase the interest of our tale to describe the many difficulties encountered by Matilda, ere a smiling fate led her to the castle of Trivallis; suffice it to say, that on reaching the German empire, Sir Eugene and herself having assumed disguises, which they considered as the most likely to conceal their real characters, began their anxious peregrination over the duchy of Austria; stopping to ask charity and to exercise their musical talents at every edifice of which they judged it possible that the walls might enclose the object of their search; yet studiously avoiding to ask any questions which might draw upon them the slightest suspicion.

The invitation which they received from the soldiery at Trivallis to enter the castle, was joyfully accepted by them; and the heart of Matilda thrilled with hope and impatience, when they were requested to enter a court within its walls, from whence they were told that the sounds of their music were wished to ascend to an apartment above it, which was the abode of a prisoner of rank. A secret instinct whispered to the heart of Matilda, that this prisoner could be no other than her Richard, and she resolved to use the opportunity which was thus fortunately presented to her, for breathing in his ear those words and that melody, which he had ever affirmed to communicate rapture to his senses. If *he were* the prisoner, she could not doubt, that those sounds would inform him beyond all possibility of doubt, who was the musician, by whom they were executed: to that particular air she accordingly struck the chords of her instrument; and the exclamation which proceeded from the prisoner at the end of the first repetition of the burden, whilst it conveyed to his attendants only an idea of sudden illness or pain, was to her an undoubted conviction, that her voice had been recognised by him.

Now then would Matilda gladly again have quitted the walls of Trivallis, and hastened to England for the execution of her more important design; but the guards had offered De Lancy and herself the accommodation of pallets for the night in the castle; and without departing from their assumed characters, they could not do otherwise than accept the offer with apparent joy and gratitude; Matilda was now therefore that night fated to repose once more beneath the same roof with her Richard.

CHAP. XI.

An accident!
The luckiest accident presents itself!
SOUTHERN.*

BUT that night was destined to bring forth still more events of an unexpected nature than it had already done.

The sentinels were just placed for the night, and the different members of the castle about to retire to rest, when the shrill sounds of the bugle at the outer gate demanded admittance.

Anhalt went out; and found Adrian Thelk accompanied by two of the duke's guards on horseback; the drawbridge was lowered, and they entered.

Arrived within the walls, "What brings you hither at this late hour?" asked Anhalt, addressing Thelk.

"My duty," replied the old soldier, "a call, that no man ought to inquire the hour before he obeys."

Having reached Anhalt's apartment, Thelk closed the door, and said, "I bring you the duke's orders not to suffer any individual now within the castle, to leave it till after he has visited it to-morrow morning, which it is his intention to do."

"I shall obey," replied Anhalt, "but what is his grace's reason for issuing this command?"

"Reason enough, I'll promise thee by my conscience!" returned Thelk, "a most villanous piece of treachery I have been the means of discovering, and the duke comes hither to-morrow, to subject the traitress to the punishment she merits."

"A woman, and within these walls!" exclaimed Anhalt, "I was ignorant that they contained any other of her sex, besides old Caterina, our cook; surely she can have done nothing to offend."

"Pshaw! an old hag!" cried Thelk, "your old women create anxiety and contention only amongst their own sex; they are your young ones who stir them up in ours!"

"But I repeat," returned Anhalt, "that I did not know we had a young one within our walls."

"I did not much suppose you did know it," replied Thelk, "but it is true for all that; as I hope never to be disgraced in war it is! and I'll explain the matter to you; you must have heard of the beautiful Pagan, named Zulima, that our duke brought with him from Palestine?"

Anhalt replied in the affirmative.

"Very well," cried Thelk, "and you cannot help knowing that a youth who was until within a very few days one of the guards of this castle, was suffered to return home to his mother, and another lad provided by him to serve in his stead: and who think you that other lad was? I wonder you should not have had an eye keen enough to see into the deception—why it was the duke's mistress; Zulima's herself! Aye you may stare, but I'll swear to it, for I found out the whole affair myself. I have been accustomed to stratagem both in love and war, and I was keen witted enough to make the discovery."

"The new guard a woman!" said Anhalt. "I can't believe it possible."

"Why zounds,"* cried our soldier, "do you think that old Thelk does not know a man from a woman, if it puzzles you? In the first place, Zulima ran away from the duke on the very day before the return of the young man to his mother; is not that presumptive proof of what I have been telling you? and now I'll give you proof positive;—as the young man had been a bit of a soldier, and as I respect all who have borne arms, I invited him last night to take part of a flask with me; in our conversation we spoke of Zulima; for your true hearted soldiers ever jumble women and war together in their cups; and he, young fool! for his heart was open with liquor, and overflowed at his tongue, confessed to me that Zulima had bribed his mother to furnish her with a disguise, and to assist her plan for becoming his substitute, to which she had been induced by her love for the English king.—There now! And I, like an honest soldier, communicated all I had learnt to my commander; I pity the wench for what she will in all probability be made to suffer for her rashness and ingratitude to the duke; but my conscience would not let me permit my general to be choused* by a woman with impunity. You now see the motive of the commands which I have brought you."

As Thelk continued to converse with Anhalt, the latter inquired of him, what he supposed would be the punishment which the duke would inflict on his false mistress. Thelk replied, "that Leopold's resentment was extremely great; that the crime of which she had been guilty, was increased by the discovery of a passion for the man he most hated, having been her attraction to this step; and that he made no doubt that the insulted duke would condemn her either to a cruel death, or to a life of ignominious bondage."

Anhalt supplied him plentifully with his favourite liquor, inviting him to refresh himself with replenished draughts after the fatigue of his journey; and Thelk required very little pressing to accept these invitations, saying, "that he was inspired by the subject of his commander's wrongs which he had been discussing, and that a warm argument always made him very thirsty." At length entirely overpowered by the joint effects of the spirit which had issued from his lips, and the spirit which had entered them, he retired to bed, with every symptom of sleeping very soundly. This was exactly the state in which Anhalt desired to see him; his benevolent and humane heart had been touched with pity at the approaching fate of the Pagan Zulima, whose unlettered soul never having received the strength of reason from education, or from example, had led her to the pursuance of a conduct which would have been inexcusable in a Christian mind; but which in hers required commiseration, and lenity to be extended towards it; and he had resolved if possible to be the instrument of her preservation.

Thelk being asleep, Anhalt accordingly proceeded to seek the object of his pity; and having informed her of the knowledge which he had obtained of her sex and history, as likewise of the danger which was impending over her; he explained to her his motives for becoming her protector.

With the utmost gratitude she received his promise to this effect:—Of duke Leopold's resentful soul, she had already witnessed many examples in his tyranny over other unhappy objects of his dependence, who had been so unfortunate as to draw down upon themselves his displeasure. Her love for Richard was forgotten in her apprehensions of the duke's revenge; and with the weakness natural to an uneducated mind, she was now ready to declare future subservience to Anhalt in return for the benefit he was about to confer on her.

The plan which Anhalt had devised for her preservation he explained to her in these words, "You are acquainted that the soldiers entertain to-night two minstrels in the castle; they are extremely indigent; the young one is about your height and size, and would doubtless be overjoyed to become the guard which you personate; hold yourself ready therefore to transfer to him your military garb, I will provide you with another habit in its stead; and when you are equipped in it, conduct you to a spot of concealment which I hope will prove to you a place of security against your pursuer; as I doubt not when the guards have been inspected by the duke, and you are not found amongst them, that Thelk's story of your having become the substitute of the poor cottager's son, will be regarded as false."

Zulima was all gratitude, humility, and tears.

Anhalt left her, and went to make his proposal to the young minstrel.

Upon retiring to the chamber allotted to their use, Matilda and her friend had poured forth to each other the extacy of heart which they experienced at having made the discovery for which their pilgrimage had been undertaken;—at length Matilda had been prevailed on to throw herself upon one of the pallets, and Sir Eugene had promised to watch by her side. Scarcely had this arrangement been made, ere they were surprised by a rap at the door, which was followed by the voice of Anhalt demanding admittance. They trembled at the apprehension of their real characters having been discovered by him, and cast at each other a look of silent eloquence, inquiry, and dismay.

Anhalt repeated his rap, and Matilda motioning to Sir Eugene to draw down the bandage over his eyes, which he had raised since they had retired, to their private apartment, rose, and opened the door.

Anhalt entered and having closed the door after him, began to explain the reason of his appearing there.

"Alas," replied Matilda, "I would willingly serve the lady you speak of, if in my power, but I am utterly unacquainted with the duty of a soldier, and should only betray the imposition of my ignorance."

"You must be at least as well acquainted with it as she is," answered Anhalt, "and she has contrived to pass unsuspected by me for nearly nine days. The soldiers of this place have none of the labours of war; and very few military exercises; to guard different sentry posts in their allotted turns, is their hardest duty."

Matilda knew not how to reply; she perceived that Anhalt would not be easily diverted from his purpose; and felt all impatience herself to depart from Trivallis. "But if I were to turn soldier," she said, "what would become of my poor blind father; he is unable to guide himself about the country, and therefore must starve for want of my assistance?"

"But your pay in your new situation would be sufficient for you to provide him a comfortable maintenance out of it," returned Anhalt.

"But my son is my only relative, my only companion," said Sir Eugene, "and to be bereft of his society would render my latter days wretched."

"It would be contrary to our rules, to suffer you, old man, to live here also," rejoined Anhalt, "else I doubt not but you might pick up enough to live upon from the inhabitants of the place, in return for your entertaining them with your ballads and music."

"I have been so long accustomed to a wandering life," answered Sir Eugene, "that I fear the confinement would throw me into ill health, and perhaps eventually make me a burden on your hospitality."

"And should my father die!" exclaimed Matilda, "Oh, I cannot bear the idea of losing my only parent, my only protector! No, Sir, I cannot accept your offer; I thank you gratefully for having made it to me, but I must go with my father."

"Well," replied Anhalt, "I commend your filial piety; but you doubtless know that to be truly good we must not confine all our exertions to one object, but extend them wheresoever charity demands their performance; for the sake therefore of preserving this poor lady from the duke's resentment, you cannot with the heart of a Christian, refuse to remain at least a few days in this castle, in the character of one of its guards. When the duke's inspection is past, I shall find little difficulty in procuring some other young man to supply your place; and will remunerate you with a handsome reward, for having lent me your assistance in performing a humane action."

There now appeared no alternative to Matilda's complying with Anhalt's request, and she said, "I hope you will let us go at the latest, the day after tomorrow, as there is a fair in the neighbourhood, which my father and I should lose considerable advantage by not attending."

Anhalt promised not to detain them beyond that time; and requested Matilda to follow him immediately, to the apartment where he had left Zulima, in order to assume the habit which she had lately worn.

CHAP. XII.

What has been left untried that art could do?

ROWE.*

THE extraordinary sensations which were at this time passing in the mind of Matilda may be easily imagined; having however for sometime past been accustomed to the male habit, the change which she was about to make was on this account less repellent to her feelings, than it otherwise would have been.

When they entered the apartment where Anhalt had left Zulima, whilst he had come to see Matilda, they found her habited in her female attire; and those thanks of gratitude which she had before bestowed singly on Anhalt, she now divided between him and Matilda. Enjoining her to silence, Anhalt led her forth, and conducted her to a cell in the subterraneous parts of the castle, which had once been used for captives condemned to execution, but which had now for many years been in disuse; and where he felt almost certain that no search would be made for her; he provided her with refreshments sufficient for the day, placed her a lamp, and having promised to fetch her away as soon as her own security would permit; he closed upon her the door, and brought away with him the key.

On his return to Matilda, he found her dressed in her military garb. The morning was already beginning to break; and having given her a few short instructions for the regulation of her conduct during the ensuing day, and encouraged her to perform her allotted part without timidity; he directed her at what station to place herself, and await the call for the morning's muster.

"Oh Richard!" mentally exclaimed Matilda, "could'st thou behold the situation to which I am at this moment reduced in thy cause, thou would'st no longer doubt the strength of the affection which I bear thee!"

Sir Eugene could not do otherwise than keep himself retired from the busy parts of the castle, which his pretended loss of sight gave him no claim for approaching; and Matilda was therefore left solely to her own reflections.

The hour of noon was already past, when the lengthened blast of a shrill horn winding over the adjacent mountains, proclaimed the approach of Leopold and his train.

"Now then I shall behold the tyrant of my Richard's fate," considered Matilda, "and, Oh! how shall I support myself beneath the scrutiny of his inquiring eye, when he inspects the guards?"

At the drawbridge the duke was met by Anhalt, who conducted him into one of the most magnificent apartments of the castle, where a repast was already prepared for his reception. "You know my business here?" said Leopold when he had seated himself at the table.

"Your soldier Thelk has communicated it to me," replied Anhalt; "may I," he added, "take the liberty of inquiring of your grace, whether you owe the information which you may have received relative to the lady Zulima's being an inmate of this castle, solely to him?"

"Solely to him," answered the duke. "Why do you ask this question?—Has he deceived me?"

"He may have been deceived himself," returned Anhalt; "but there is doubtless an error in the report which affirms the lady Zulima to have fled hither."

A frown of disappointment gathered on the brow of Leopold, and he commanded Thelk to be sent to him. "Have you seen Zulima?" asked the duke when Thelk appeared before him.

"No, commander," replied Adrian, "I have been fighting in ambush; I thought if she saw me, it would give her a suspicion of your coming, and prepare her to encounter you; so, as I wished you to take her by surprise, I have purposely kept out of the way of all the guards."

"Are you certain you were not mistaken, in what you informed me of the old cottager's son had told you concerning her?" demanded Leopold.

"Positive, positive, by the honour of war," cried Thelk, "I was in liquor when he gave me the account."

The duke smiled—Anhalt looked, as he felt, surprised.

Thelk observed how he was affected, and turning towards him, he said, "You don't know my way; when I am in liquor, I am always awake, and hear all that is said to me—when I am sober, I am mostly asleep, and appear to be listening whilst I am only dreaming."

"If the resentment which the duke inflicts on those who offend him, be in proportion to the favour which he bestows on those who have won his partiality, I am more than ever satisfied with the step that I have taken for the protection of Zulima;" thought Anhalt.

Thelk was again dismissed; and when the duke had refreshed himself, he commanded the guards to be drawn out on the ramparts for his inspection. When information was brought to him that they were prepared for his appearance, he went out, and, with a mind divided between hope and doubt, walked several times backwards and forwards in front of the ranks; at length addressing Thelk who had followed close at his heels, he exclaimed, "She is not here!"

For some minutes Thelk did not reply, he then said, "Here are but a hundred and nineteen guards. The number is one more."

Anhalt stepped forward, "That one, so please your grace," he said, "is at this time a sentinel at the door of the royal prisoner's apartment; a post which I have received positive orders from you, never on any occasion to leave deserted."

"Depend upon it, that sentinel is she," cried Thelk exultingly,

"I would lay the honour of my wooden leg upon it;—I'll bring her instantly into your grace's presence." And as he ceased speaking, he began to move towards the castle gate.

"The sentinel will not quit his post without my orders to do so," said Anhalt. "I will go myself and fetch him to the duke."

"I will go with you, if I never set the five toes war has left me to the ground again," exclaimed Thelk, and they entered the castle together.

In the course of a few minutes, Thelk came hobbling out again upon the ramparts as fast as his wooden supporter would allow him, and exclaiming, "'Tis she! 'tis she! she's found! her head is tied up, forsooth to disguise her person, but I knew her by a glimpse I caught of her nose!"

The duke moved impatiently towards Anhalt who was now advancing with the sentinel whose face was nearly concealed by a cloth bandage.

"Tear off the covering from before her face," exclaimed the duke; and with all possible alacrity Thelk obeyed his commands; when instead of Zulima, appeared the withered face of a veteran soldier, whose nose, the feature by which Thelk had professed himself to have discovered Zulima, had been almost entirely carried away by a shot from a cross-bow. He was at this time unwell, and had been permitted to wear a bandage as a protection against the cold.

The rage of the duke upon this confirmation of the disappointment which he had dreaded, and which the smiles of the assembled guards tended not a little to increase, exceeded all bounds. Calling to Anhalt, he inquired of him, "If he were not acquainted with a dungeon amidst the subterraneous vaults of the castle, bisected across the centre by an iron grating?"

In one of the divisions of this dungeon, Anhalt had secreted Zulima, he therefore feared to reply in the affirmative, and yet dared not deny his knowledge lest any other person more unfriendly to the poor infidel, should be sent to seek it in his stead, "He was," he replied, "acquainted with its situation."

"Let Thelk," cried Leopold, "be instantly conducted to it; I condemn him to imprisonment there till the retreat of Zulima be discovered for the insult he has offered me."

By two of the guards Thelk was accordingly seized, and Anhalt by whose side moved the duke, led the way towards the subterraneous vaults; in the loudest accents Thelk besought for mercy; he protested that the information which he had given the duke relative to Zulima, he had received from the cottager's son; and reminded him of his valour in planting the Austrian standard on the walls of Acre; but in vain; the duke's passion was wound to a pitch beyond the reach of argument or entreaty. The heart of Anhalt beat with apprehensions, not less on his own account, than on that of Zulima; should the duke descend to the dungeon, and Zulima not have sufficient presence of mind to blow out the lamp which he had left her, on the sound of approaching footsteps; her doom and his own for having endeavoured to preserve her from the anger of the duke, were equally inevitable.

When they had reached the head of the last flight of stairs which led through one short passage to the dungeon, Anhalt stopped, and buttoned his vest up to his neck, which action he followed by tying a handkerchief round his throat; at the same time, telling the duke, that if he intended to descend lower, he advised him to suffer a cloak to be brought him, ere he did so, as the dampness of the vaults was extremely great, and that he would subject himself to receive injury from the violent transition from warmth to cold, which must assail him in them.

"I shall go no farther," replied the duke; "as I find you are acquainted with the place, I shall remain here till Thelk is lodged in the spot I have destined to him."

The feelings of Anhalt once more revived; and followed by the guards who led the prisoner, he began to descend the steps; Thelk still imploring aloud for pardon and mercy.

As they approached the dungeon, Anhalt perceived the reflection of Zulima's lamp gleaming on the wall; and felt mortified and disappointed, that she had not the precaution to extinguish it; as he concluded that she must have understood from the sounds which accompanied his approach, that he could not be alone, or advancing towards the dungeon for the purpose of conducting her away from it.

The strength of the flame cast out by the lamp which Anhalt was himself carrying, caused the pale reflection of Zulima's lamp not to be observed by Thelk or the guards; and Anhalt taking advantage of this circumstance, commanded the guards to remain at a little distance from the door of the dungeon; and drawing his sword, in order to enforce his mandate, directed Thelk to precede him towards it.

With mingled murmurs and threats Thelk obeyed; and having reached the spot, Anhalt thrust him into the opposite division of the dungeon to that occupied by Zulima. Thelk instantly turned his face towards the grating by which the cell was bisected, and to which as he entered it, the lamp on Zulima's side drew his attention; and no sooner had he beheld for whom it was burning, than in the wildest accents he exclaimed, "My gracious duke! my worthy commander! Zulima is within this castle; I behold her at this moment; she is now before my very eyes; she is here in this very dungeon; descend, I entreat you to descend!"

Upon these words, the duke half incredulous, half willing to hope what he wished, ran down the steps leading to the vaults; Anhalt heard his approach, and beckoning to the guards to follow him, hastened to meet Leopold, and prevent his farther progress.

"What's this he says?" cried the duke, "that Zulima is now before his eyes; can this be, or"———

"Oh, no, no," replied Anhalt, "so please your Highness the unexpected sentence you have pronounced on him, almost affects his senses."

And even now the duke would in all probability have re-ascended the steps, satisfied that Thelk's words had been only the effect of a raving mind, had not at this instant a piercing shriek uttered by a female voice struck his ear.

At the period of Anhalt's descent into the vaults with Thelk, Zulima, overpowered with fatigue and anxiety of mind had sunk to sleep; awakened by the exclamations of Thelk, she had for a considerable time been unable to collect her ideas, or to remember where she was; on recovering her recollection, starting forward from the seat on which she had been reposing she had flown insensibly towards the iron grating which bisected the dungeon, and had most unexpectedly encountered the visage of her enemy Thelk;—upon this observation, the shriek of which we have just spoken, burst from her lips; her voice was recognized by the duke;

and fired with the rage of a demon, he immediately flew down the remainder of the steps, in the centre of which he was standing at the moment it reached his senses. But his precipitancy was inimical to his design; he fell, and in his fall, dashed the lamp, borne by Anhalt, from his hand, and extinguished it.

Of the momentary insensibility of the duke, whom the guards were raising from the ground, Anhalt availed himself, for rushing towards the dungeon, and having unlocked the door which formed the entrance to Zulima's division of it, he said, "Fly, fly, your only hope and mine lies in your flight; pursue the path along the vaults which leads to the left, and fly instantly!"

Not daring to lose a moment in waiting to observe the effect of his advice, Anhalt returned to the assistance of the duke, whose temporary absence of recollection was past, and who now approached the dungeon to which the voice of Thelk was still calling him:—"Where, where is she?" exclaimed Leopold, "if visible to thee point her out instantly to me."

"She is fled, she is fled, within this instant fled from hence!" cried Thelk, "by the holy cross, I saw her here, and saw her fly!"

Anhalt endeavoured to turn Thelk's assertions into ridicule; but the duke was become grave upon the occurrences of the few last minutes, "Improbable as this story is," he said, "it is still a possibility which shall not escape me unscrutinized," and directing Anhalt and one of the guards to remain with him, and having lighted the extinguished lamp at one which had been left Thelk in his cell; he commanded the other guards to ascend into the castle, and summon the soldiery to attend him, in order that the vaults might undergo a thorough search.

CHAP. XIII.

> Nor in his orisons let him forget
> The hand of heav'n, whose providential care
> Has order'd all, the innocent to save,
> To right the injur'd, and reward the brave.
>
> CIBBER.*

WHEN the duke retired from the ramparts after the inspection of the guards; and Anhalt was called upon by him to lead the way to the dungeon; the command of the men devolved for the period of Anhalt's absence upon a serjeant, who acquainted Matilda that she must immediately prepare to mount guard.

She had no alternative but to obey, till the expiration of the time for which she had promised Anhalt her services; and accordingly followed the steps of the serjeant. They ascended the stone stair-case at the extremity of the great hall of the castle, which led to the apartments occupied by the king; and stationing her on a particular spot, the serjeant said, "There youngster, you'll have an honour to brag of, the first time of your standing sentry which does not fall to every man's share."

"What is that pray?" asked Matilda.

"Why that you are sentinel at the door of a king's chamber," replied the serjeant. "These are the apartments of our royal prisoner; mind you are steady to your trust!" and with these words he departed.

"And it is possible," mentally exclaimed Matilda, "that this door alone divides me from my king, my Richard? And will not the opportunity of conversing with him, of beholding him for an instant, be mine? Are there no means of informing him how near to him his Matilda is at this moment stationed?" She examined the door and found that it was locked, and bolted on the outside. Her heart panted with anxiety to turn the key: she heard a step within the apartment approaching towards the door, and conjectured it might be his; in gentle tones she sung a few strains of the melody by which he had the evening before recognised her voice.

"Matilda! Oh my Matilda! art thou again near me? blessed, blessed moment!" the well-known voice of Richard, interrupted her by exclaiming.

Ere she had summoned resolution to reply, various sounds of a tumultuous nature burst upon her ear. She listened and found that they proceeded from the voices of persons who were calling loudly to each other as they ran hastily along the lower parts of the castle; of what they said, she could clearly distinguish these words, "The duke's mistress is discovered in the subterraneous vaults, ye must all hasten thither and assist in the search."

"Indeed!" exclaimed others, "there will doubtless be a handsome reward for him who finds her, let us hasten!"

The tumult now died away, and universal silence prevailed. The first sound which broke the stillness of the scene, was a gently moving footstep; Matilda turned her eye towards the spot from whence it proceeded, and beheld cautiously advancing Sir Eugene de Lancy; he saw that she observed him, and raised his hand to enjoin her to silence. Having approached her, he said, "I have taken the advantage of the confusion which prevails to steal hither—I had inquired for you, and was acquainted with your station before this disorder arose. Can we at this moment do nothing for the king?"

"We may doubtless enter his apartment and cheer him with the hope of a speedy rescue," replied Matilda.

"Can we do nothing more?" asked De Lancy hesitatingly, and casting his eyes around with an expression which conveyed, "there is no one left in the castle to observe our actions, or to interrupt them."

Matilda caught the inspiring idea which was passing in his heart.

"Yes," she exclaimed, "we will enlarge him or perish in the attempt!"

"But every instant that we lose may frustrate our design," cried Sir Eugene.

"To action then!" rejoined Matilda, and her hand was laid upon the lock of the door.

"Not so, no so," whispered Sir Eugene, "fly, and seek your minstrel's garb which you this morning threw off; draw it over your present attire, and return hither with all the speed you are able to use—the king shall be prepared to meet you."

With a heart bursting between hope and fear, Matilda flew to execute his instructions.

Sir Eugene entered the apartment of the king—"Royal Sir," he cried, "you know me not; I come to repair to you an offence which I have committed against your peace; my name is De Lancy; I was the emissary of your father's love to the lady Rosamond; in remuneration of my past offence, I now appear before you to offer myself up to imprisonment in your stead—question me not, but hasten to change habits with me; the present moment is destined for your rescue; heaven has created this blessed opportunity for your flight—your Matilda waits to accompany you!"

Thrown into the utmost surprise by this address, the king hesitated either to reply or to act.

"For heaven's sake lose not an instant," cried De Lancy, "let the reflection that your Matilda may be lost for ever, if discovered in her attempt by your delay, impel you to comply."

Whilst speaking, Sir Eugene had pulled off his upper garments, and already forced his hat upon the head of Richard, and thrown over him his vest and mantle.

Matilda arrayed in her minstrel's garb now appeared at the door of the apartment. In the dewy eloquence of their eyes the conflicting sensations of her soul, and of her Richard's expressed themselves.

"Oh generous De Lancy," exclaimed Matilda, "is this thy noble purpose? Is it thus thy excellent heart repairs the injustice which it once aided to perform? But what will become of thee?"

"I shall be at peace with my own heart," cried De Lancy. "I shall be happy, I shall be blessed! What more can a loyal subject ask, than the glory which must await him for becoming the saviour of his king."

Richard would have spoken—Sir Eugene prevented him, "Not one word," he said, "as you value the happiness of a nation whom your return will restore to gladness and to peace!" and taking the bandage from his own eyes as he spoke, and tying it over those of the king, he forced Matilda and him out of the apartment—"The smile of heaven prosper you!" he exclaimed, and closed the door.

With trembling steps Matilda led the king down the stairs.—They entered the castle hall—all was silent—equally still and unfrequented were the courts.—In safety they gained the draw-bridge; but here the pulsations of Matilda's heart beat with a sickly and tremulous quickness; for at its foot appeared a sentinel pacing his allotted portion of ground. He advanced towards them, and addressed Matilda. "What!" he said, "will ye away? Nay, tarry, and let us have your music again tonight, I pray you."

"We cannot indeed, Sir," replied Matilda, "we must be at a neighbouring fair early to-morrow morning; but we will gladly come hither at the end of the week; if you are so charitable as to give us your leave. "

"Aye, that I do," answered the man, "and so will all my comrades I am certain; but will ye come in good truth now?"

"Can you doubt that persons so poor as my blind father and myself, should be glad of your hospitality?" returned Matilda.

"Why indeed, I think ye must be partly fools," returned the guard, "if in the exercise of a sorry trade like yours, ye were not glad to come back to such fare as we gave you last night; and you shall be regaled still better the next time you come, if ye will but bring some new romances with you—so pass on, and a good journey to you!"

"Heaven bless you, Sir!" cried Matilda, and the blessing proceeded from her heart—a heart overflowing with gratitude to that Omnipotent Power which had benignantly vouchsafed her the means of releasing her Richard from the walls of Trivallis.

To the enraptured hearts of Richard and his Matilda, the instinctive voice of danger whispered a caution not to waste their present moments in the soft interchange of affectionate, or congratulatory sentiments, but to exert every nerve for securing the king's escape.

In her wanderings towards the castle, Matilda had observed within a couple of furlongs of its moat, the curving arm of a river with several boats moored to its banks in the front of a cluster of humble cottages, which, from the nets suspended between the trees that grew around, she had conjectured to be the habitations of fishermen.

To this place accordingly it was the counsel of Matilda that they should immediately proceed. "It appeared probable to her," she said, "that this river might run into some other of greater consequence, which would eventually bring them to the coast; and she doubted not that some of the fishermen would easily be prevailed upon for an adequate reward, to transport them to some considerable distance from the spot of danger on which they now stood."

The grateful and enraptured Richard could think only through the senses of his Matilda; her plan was therefore pursued, and proved consonant to their ardent wishes; a poor fisherman to whom they applied, informed them that after passing through a variety of mazes the little river before his hut, mingled its waters with those of the Rhine; and on receiving this intelligence they entreated him to name his price for conveying them to the point of their confluence.

The man, not suspecting their rank to be above their habits, replied, "that if they would pass the night at his cot, he would take them part of the way for a very small reward in the morning, as his own affairs would call him up the river."

In departing immediately from the neighbourhood of Trivallis lay their only chance of security; and acting upon this knowledge, Matilda stated to him that they had an engagement to meet some pilgrims, on whom they were to attend in a distant part of the country; that any delay in pursuing their journey might prove a very great loss to them; and offered him a remuneration, far exceeding his expectations, to take them on board, and begin their little voyage without delay.

On condition of a considerable part of the promised reward being paid in advance, the fisherman agreed to accede to their request. His terms were joyfully accepted by the fugitives; they entered his bark; and in a few minutes its little sail was hoisted before a prosperous wind.

CHAP. XIV.

This is the state of man; to-day he puts forth
The tender leaves of hope, to-morrow blossoms,
And bears his blushing honours thick upon him;
The third day comes a frost, a killing frost;
And then he falls.

SHAKESPEARE.*

THE voyage of our travellers, it may naturally be supposed, was past in explanations, and inquiries: in the effusions of gratitude, and in the overflowings of an undisguised and pure affection—and we trust that our readers will not be dissatisfied with the omission; if, waving a minute detail of their progress through Germany, we merely state that fate smiled on their wishes, and they reached the coast in safety. Here, at a small and little frequented port, they engage a vessel to transport them to Cornwall; as it was on many accounts the desire of both Richard and his Matilda that the first roof which sheltered their heads after their arrival in England, should be that beneath which resided their ancient and valued friend, Father Benedict.

The streaks of the grey dawn were just beginning to pierce through the dusky veil of night, when the king and his fair deliverer landed on the wished-for coast; and another hour brought them to the gate of St. Michael's monastery.

The brethren were assembled at their morning repast, and the joyful intelligence of the king's arrival was instantly conveyed to the abbot in their presence. Trembling under the agitation of delight, the good old man hastened to meet his royal guest; "Heaven! heaven be praised for its mercy!" he uttered as he advanced towards him. Into the hand of Richard he put one of his; the other he gave to Matilda; and whilst he stood receiving from them the silent pressure of friendship, the tears ran trickling down his aged cheeks.

Having in some degree recovered from his surprise father Benedict led them to his own apartment; and after he had listened to a brief detail from their lips, of such occurrences as had befallen the king and Matilda, since the departure of the latter from England, he said, "Oh my king at what a moment are you returned to your native land! your subjects disaffected—your barons forsaking the cause of their monarch—your unnatural brother upon the point of procuring those oaths of allegiance which have in justice been made to you, to be unjustly broken through, and transferred to him! for so great is the strength which he has acquired during your absence, that but five days are wanting to the period at which he has called a council to assemble round him at Wallingford, in the presence of which it is his intention to propose himself as the future king of England."

For a few moments Richard maintained the silence of dismay, of disappointment, and of smothered rage. "But are there none," he then burst forth, "none of my formerly loyal subjects remaining, to whom my memory is still dear? To whose hearts my presence would communicate courage, and a desire to shake off the yoke imposed on them by an assuming brother? Oh yes, yes, I feel that I am not yet deserted; that if Richard do but shew himself once more on English ground, crowds will return to their allegiance, whom circumstances may now insidiously be enticing from it!"

"Oh I fear! I fear me much in your cause," replied the abbot; "what is the time you now possess for making the required attempt, and putting to the test the feelings of the realm? But five short days to counteract plans which your brother has maturely weighed, and carried into their effect with equal deliberation, and craft. Alas, alas! is this the recompence which awaits the toils that you have so piously encountered in the cause of the holy cross? But I murmur sinfully; the blessed saints forgive my momentary error! The reward, my son, of the warrior who has valiantly fought in the noble cause of christianity, as thou has done, is in heaven."

A considerable silence now ensued; mingled reflection and sorrow were settled on the brow of all. At length Matilda spoke, "Richard," she said, "thou dost not, I am certain, doubt the strenuous devotion of my heart to thy happiness; thou dost also, I am well aware, feel satisfied that *I* would of all other beings be the last to propose to thee in thy emergencies any plan for their redress, of which I did not augur happily—perhaps also the success which attended my pilgrimage into Austria may have given thee some little faith in an idea which I confess cheers my bosom, and inspires it with no small degree of resolution; I mean that heaven vouchsafes to me its smiles, when I present myself the willing instrument of thy welfare."

"Oh my Matilda," replied Richard, "the cheap return of words my gratitude shall never render your exalted services, if I can display it in my actions it will ever be my proudest boast, my chiefest pleasure, to acknowledge it. In my obedience to your advice I shall glory to adduce the first proof of my feelings, and whatever may be the plan which you may propose to me to pursue at the present important crisis of my fate, I pledge my sacred word, to exert every faculty of my mind to the fullest of its ability upon the execution of that plan!"

"Deem me not chimerical; deem me not rash," rejoined Matilda tenderly; "if, in compliance with the promise which you have this instant made to me, I entreat of you that you will consent to retain your arrival in England a secret till the time appointed for the meeting of the council, summoned by prince John to assemble at Wallingford, be passed."

"Be passed!" echoed Richard.

Matilda returned a placid, but serious affirmative to his question.

"What can Matilda mean?" exclaimed the king; "conceal my return to my kingdom! Shall neither myself, nor any friend on whose truth I can rely, be present to assert my rights in opposition to the lawless grip of an unnatural and avaricious brother?"

"Oh yes, yes!" replied Matilda, "such a friend *shall* be present at the council; such a friend, the best, the most ardent in your cause that now exists, shall be present to convert, with the assistance of heaven, the heart of your brother from its present purpose; and once more lead it back to a sense of brotherly affection!"

Father Benedict joined his entreaties to those of Richard to prevail, if possible, on Matilda, to explain to them the ideas which were passing in her mind; but they could not be collected from her; "Richard has promised to obey me," she several times repeated; "upon no other occasion is it my intention ever to call upon him to prove his obedience; and may the God of mercy prosper the plans which at this moment occupy my brain!"

In conversation of this nature passed on the hours till the approach of noon, when Matilda complaining of fatigue, requested permission of the abbot to retire to a private apartment. On quitting father Benedict and Richard, she addressed the latter in these words, "Remember Oh my king! my reverend friend! The promise which you have made to me; and for the five succeeding days consent to retain your arrival in England, secret!" She cast at him a look which would have resolved him to obedience, if it had not already been the settled purpose of his mind; and quitted his presence.

The king and his venerable friend passed the hours together, in a recapitulation of past events, and in surmises on the future. About the fall of twilight the abbot inquired for Matilda, and to his great surprise learnt that she had quitted the monastery several hours earlier attended by one of the lay-brothers—with equal astonishment was the heart of Richard filled by the receipt of this extraordinary intelligence; and it was by no means diminished when the porter of the house delivered into his hand a paper, which he had been commanded by Matilda to give him, as soon as he should discover her absence—it contained these words, *"Remember your promise; and pursue me not!"*

"Great God!" exclaimed Richard, on perusing the paper, "what can this mystery portend?"

"In what manner, my son," asked father Benedict, "is it your intention to act amidst these perplexing circumstances?"

"Obediently," returned Richard with energy. "Oh! my friend, hadst thou ever loved as I have done, thou would'st feel that there was no gratification on earth adequate to that of complying with the wishes of her who had inspired thee with so tender, so exalted a sensation!"

CHAP. XV.

> There's nothing in this world can make me joy;
> Life is as tedious as a twice-told tale,
> Vexing the dull ear of a drowsy man.
>
> SHAKESPEARE.*

WE must now once more pass over into the duchy of Austria, and inquire the fate of Zulima and her protector Anhalt. Nor must we omit to consider Sir Eugene de Lancy, whose disinterested loyalty had made him a hostage for his sovereign; with true delight he had beheld the departure of the king from bondage, and the door of his prison closed upon himself. Sir Eugene's was not a mind of a common kind; ever since his acquaintance had commenced with Matilda; and he had perceived the wretched events which had arisen out of the criminal connexion which had subsisted between Henry the second and the fair Rosamond; his heart had been stung with remorse at the reflection of his having been in any degree accessary to the facilitating of an intercourse so big with horror in its consequences to the innocent; and he had from that moment secretly resolved to seek the opportunity of repairing to the descendants of the guilty pair, as far as his ability might permit, his concurrence in the plans of their adulterous love.

Of the friendship which he exercised towards Matilda we have already had proof; and no sooner did he enter the castle of Trivallis than his heart was inspired with the generous idea of procuring, if possible, the release of the king, at the expense of his own liberty. The tumult which so unexpectedly arose in the castle favoured his design; he rushed to the execution of his purpose, and surprised even Matilda by the disclosure of his noble intention—he surprised her, for linked in the bonds of amity and mutual confidence as had been their souls since the commencement of their peregrinations, he had not imparted to her the latent design of his heart; as it was foreign to his nature to boast of an intention, which circumstance might never enable him to put into effect; and which might only lead her to consider him a vain braggart, and impel her to withdraw from him that esteem which she now felt for him, and which, he considered it his greatest happiness to possess. In the prison therefore of the king, Sir Eugene de Lancy was not only composed, but happy.

The wretched Zulima meanwhile, overpowered by a trepidation of soul which almost bereaved her of sense, pursued, with all the strength which her trembling limbs were able to exert, the advice of Anhalt and fled through the subterraneous passages which ran along the vaults; bending her steps carefully towards the left, according to the admonition which he had given her—now the shouts of her pursuers assailed her ears—now by a momentary effort she outstripped the sounds—again their voices became audible, and her beating heart almost forced its way through her bosom.

Still she pursued her way, till a door fastened on the inside obstructed her progress—she undrew the bolts, and opening the door, found herself upon a projecting mass of earth, beneath the ramparts of the castle, which was entirely surrounded by the moat: all hope of farther flight was now cut off—despair seized her; a groan of anguish escaped her lips; she stood the silent effigy of misery and dread.

In the course of a few seconds a loud voice struck her ear; it was that of the duke uttering threats of vengeance against her! No knowledge of religion had implanted in her breast a sense of the criminality of self-immolation, and dreading the agonies of death less than the fury of Leopold, she plunged into the waters of the moat.

With the utmost violence the duke commanded every effort to be made for preserving her life; offering a large reward to him who should be the first to draw her forth. Not actuated by the love which he now bore her, but by the desire of being enabled to inflict on her his vengeance. But the pitying hand of death had rescued her from his intended cruelty.

The exultations of Thelk, at the proof of which the duke had now received of his not having deceived him, in the information with which he had furnished him relative to Zulima, were vociferous and overbearing; but he was unheeded by Leopold whose breast was still too full of rage, for the admission of any other sensation; and with eyes darting the fiery anger of a demon, he was in the act of turning towards Anhalt, prepared to pronounce on him a sentence adequate to the crime of which he considered him to have been guilty, when the sound of a bugle blown loudly and shrilly without the walls of the castle, attracted the attention of all.

The projecting mass of earth from which Zulima had cast herself into the moat, was so situated, that the drawbridge was partially visible from it—Thelk was amongst the number of those who chanced to be so stationed as to be able to behold it; and raising his eyes at the sound of the bugle, he exclaimed, "By the holy cross! the emperor Henry!"

"What of him?" demanded Leopold.

"He is at this moment passing with his train over the drawbridge," replied Thelk.

This information gave an immediate turn to the thoughts of the duke; and he hastily quitted the vaults to receive the emperor, and inquire the cause of his visit.

The emperor had lately been seized with a religious inclination of sending assistance to the Christians in the Holy Land; to this end, he had been raising subsidies by every means which he could devise for that purpose; and had come to the resolution of offering terms of enlargement to the king of England, in order that he might throw his share of the ransom, which the duke had agreed equally to divide with him, into the scale of his collections.

Big with this idea he had on the preceding day visited the abode of Leopold, for the purpose of communicating to him his design, and communing with him upon the execution of it. When learning that he was absent from his palace and gone to Trivallis, he directly determined to follow him thither and in consequence of this resolution arrived there at the critical moment, of which a description had just been given.

Leopold having entered the presence of the emperor, an explanation quickly took the place of the motives by which they had each been actuated in visiting Trivallis; and they then proceeded to deliberate on the plan, which was agitating the breast of the latter.

After a communication of nearly three hours, having resolved what terms to offer the king, they sent to summon to them Anhalt, in order that they might charge him with the delivery of their proposals. Some time having past, and their messenger not returning, nor Anhalt appearing before them, the duke himself quitted the apartment to make inquiries into the cause of this neglect, and was informed that Anhalt was nowhere to be found.

Leopold was by no means surprised that Anhalt had availed himself of the opportunity of his conference with the Emperor for flying from his threatened vengeance; but Anhalt was quickly forgotten in the matter of greater import which was occupying their minds; and it was agreed that Leopold should himself become the bearer of the proposals for his enlargement to the king.

The surprise of the duke on entering the prison of Richard, and finding there a stranger, may be easily imagined; "Who art thou?" was the first question of his astonishment.

"An Englishman," replied de Lancy, "who glories in becoming the hostage of his sovereign!"

"What? has Richard then escaped?" exclaimed the duke.

"God grant he may!" ejaculated Sir Eugene.

The duke fled from the apartments, but having quitted them, he hesitated how to proceed. Had he not summoned the guards from their posts to pursue Zulima; it was probable that Richard would still have been a prisoner in Trivallis. However, judging that his error might not still be beyond repair; and being emboldened by the knowledge that his concern in the flight of the king, was at least equal to that of the emperor, he communicated the fact publicly throughout the castle.

A pursuit was immediately set on foot; but neither the king nor Anhalt, could be overtaken. The soul of the emperor was chafed by the disappointment which his high-raised expectations had experienced, and that of Leopold was humbled, by Henry regarding him in a suspicious point of view on account of the king's flight; and they were both compelled to content themselves with the resolution of more securely guarding his hostage; for whose enlargement they conceived it probable, that terms would be offered by the liberated monarch, not unworthy of their consideration.

CHAP. XVI.

What stronger breast-plate than a heart untainted?
Thrice is he arm'd, that hath his quarrel just;
And he but naked (though lock'd up in steel)
Whose conscience with injustice is corrupted.
SHAKESPEARE.*

AT length arrived the day appointed for the assemblage of the council which prince John had summoned to meet him at Wallingford.

The chosen spot was a plain on the outside of town, upon which lay encamped a considerable number of John's forces, by which he had never suffered himself to be unattended, since the ambitious views which he was now flattering himself with the idea of soon bringing to a crisis, had first entered his mind.

In the centre of the troops was stationed a spacious and magnificent tent, the drapery of which was drawn up in front, and on the sides; and left pendant only behind a seat which was erected on an eminence for the prince.

A vast concourse of spectators, differently interested, filled the plain; the soldiery stationed on guard around the tent, preserved a vacant space for the accommodation of the barons, and other characters of eminence who might attend the council: and the assemblage of men of rank was numerous; for the adherents of John did not fail to display themselves around him on this occasion; and the secret favourers of Richard were drawn to the same point; some from their desire of counteracting the bold attempt of the prince; others, apprehensive that if they did not appear, they might incur by their absence, the vengeance of the future monarch.

About the hour of noon the sound of warlike instruments announced the approach of the prince; surrounded by his guards he issued from a neighbouring tent, and took the seat prepared for his reception.

The heralds having thrice proclaimed silence; prince John rose, and doffing his beaver as he spoke, thus addressed the assembly.

"My much-esteemed and loyal fellow subjects, thanks for your attendance; it is a cause I trust of interest to your welfare that I have called upon you here to deliberate, and to give your judgments on.

To your opinions I submit myself; it is for your happiness alone, I wish in every instance of my life to act. I trust, that ye will all acknowledge, that ye have received conviction of the blessings of a well-regulated monarchy, in the reign of my deceased father Henry: with auspices not less promising, did my brother Richard commence his sovereignty; but he deserted his people. It is not ours to blame, but to lament, the religious zeal which drove him to neglect the duties of his royal station; and too severely, at least to a brother's feelings, has his misguided conduct been revenged upon him; for no doubt can remain that in a foreign land unfriended, unconsoled, he has fallen the victim of man's ruthless enemy—death." The prince here made a momentary pause, during which he appeared to be recovering his composure of mind, and then proceeded thus, "Of the calamitous broils, the discordant tumults which will arise to vex a state that has no head to regulate its movements, we have had sufficient experiences since the departure of my brother; were it not then, I ask, expedient to replace his loss with all celerity, and to restore our beloved country to its wonted peace?" Bowing to the assembly the prince ceased speaking, and resumed his seat.

The earl of Nottingham pressed forward, "Who with a heart to love his country, but approves the admonition of our worthy and generous prince?" he exclaimed. "Who that claims the title of an Englishman, but beholds in him our hereditary successor to the throne; likewise, the most eligible of human beings whom the hand of favouring chance could select to place upon it for a deserving people's happiness? Say then with me, you subjects of the English realm, Long live king John!"

Tumultuous repetitions of the exclamation issued from the lips of the prince's party; whilst despondency marked the features of those who still cherished in their hearts the memory of Richard; who still doubted his death without daring to avow their suspicions; and who cast their eyes anxiously upon one another; each desirous of hearing some one else assume resolution to express those sentiments with which his own heart was labouring.

Prince John again spoke, "Let my own claims to your favour, I pray you fellow subjects," he said, "be well weighed by you ere you pronounce on me this high dignity for my hereditary rights:—I shall be happier much to remain a subject, than to know myself a king if I do not live in the heart of every individual of my realm."

Once more the cry of "Long live king John," was loudly repeated.

Again John spoke, "Since unanimity of voice appears to force on me the most exalted of earthly honours, I can only reply to such unlooked for favour, that it shall be my constant and my firmest prayer to heaven, to be rendered worthy of the high trust reposed in me—in your king you shall behold the servant of your wishes and your welfare. I am not a man of words, or of vain boasts; what John of England has once promised, that he will religiously perform."

"I come to put thee to the test of that assertion!" exclaimed a voice; and at the same time appeared boldly approaching towards the front of the tent, a martial figure clad in a suit of complete steel, whose polished surface glittered beneath the dancing sun beams; upon his head he wore a barred helmet, on the top of which nodded a crest of fairest plumes; at his back flowed a mantle of cloth richly embroidered in gold; and in his hand he carried a silver-headed spear. Having gained the tent, he advanced a few paces towards the eminence on which the prince was standing, and fixing himself opposite to him, repeated the words which had just drawn upon him the attention of all present; "I come to put thee to the test of that assertion!"

"Who thou art I know not," replied the prince, recovering from his momentary surprise, "that thou concealest thy countenance does not bespeak thee to be fully conscious of the honour or innocence of thy purpose in coming hither. I however fear no man—explain therefore freely what promise it is that I have broken?"

"Not any that I am acquainted with," returned the warrior, "but you have made one which you have not yet fulfilled, and I am come to demand its accomplishment."

"You must explain yourself more clearly," said prince John.

"I wish to do so," replied the warrior. "You cannot but recollect that about six years from the present period, you reposed a night with your army on your way to France, at the convent of St. Ursula."

The prince made a gentle inclination of his head as an affirmative to the question.

The warrior continued thus, "Do you not also recollect, that to a young female whom you encountered within those walls, under circumstances of a most peculiar nature, and upon whose cheek your lips were for an instant imprest, you pronounced these words, 'I swear, that whatever request you may hereafter make of me, I will perform towards you in remembrance of that one kiss.'"

"The female of whom you speak," exclaimed prince John in a voice of agitation, "was Matilda."

"It was," replied the warrior.

"The intended bride of my lamented brother," said the prince.

"The same," answered the warrior.

"In consequence of events too well known, to require repetition from my lips, she has long since pronounced the vows of eternal seclusion from the world; is it not so?" asked prince John.

"No, she has *not* pronounced those vows," was the answer.

"Where then is she now?" the subsequent question.

"Before you," replied with energy the supposed warrior, who raising her visor as she spoke, displayed the countenance of Matilda herself.

"Why have you assumed this disguise to appear before me in?" demanded the prince.

"Because," replied Matilda, "I knew it to be a garb most likely to gain me a passage through the crowd which is surrounding you."

"And why did you wish at this particular moment to present yourself before me?" returned prince John.

"Because I wished our conference to be as public as possible," exclaimed Matilda.

A frown of displeasure gathered on the brow of the prince, and he said, "You must however be content to be heard at a more private opportunity; you interrupt the business of the state."

"The state is interested in my present business with you," returned Matilda, "only acknowledge the promise with which I charge you; and it will quickly conclude."

"I have no motive for denying it," replied prince John, "I did make such a promise; I confess it freely."

"Then I appeal to your honour for its fulfilment," exclaimed Matilda; "open your arms to receive your brother to your heart with the affection that the blood from which you both are sprung demands of you for each other; and be the first to cry, Long live the rightful king of England! Long live king Richard!"

The greatest astonishment and uneasiness of mind were depicted on the countenance of John, and he fixed his eyes in silence on Matilda; whilst the friends of Richard who had hitherto hung down their heads in despondency, were whispering anxiously together, and cheering each other with hopes of the most flattering and animated nature, drawn from the demand of Matilda.

After a pause, prince John said, "A power to which we all must bend has rendered your request abortive—could it be proved that Richard still lives"——he hesitated.

"How then?" asked Matilda.

"No matter," replied prince John, "that cannot be."

"It can!" exclaimed Matilda, "it shall—the hand of heaven has fought with Richard; it has liberated him from the dungeon's flinty walls, when not an English bow was bent for his deliverance; he treads again upon his mother soil! he invites his subjects back to their sworn allegiance, by the name of his children! he pants to throw himself amidst them, and to re-establish their felicity by his gentle rule!"

A shout of true loyalty and affection now burst forth from the lips of those who had before been silent; its strains were from the heart; they resounded through the skies in reverberations far exceeding those which had hailed the short-lived honours of the usurper; and a throng, which embraced a considerable majority of the barons crowded round Matilda, inquiring the retreat of their king, and imploring her to lead the way to them that they might march with their forces, and welcome his return.

Matilda's spirit now evaporated in joy; the tears flowed down her cheeks, "Oh Richard! Richard!" she exclaimed, "be praised ye powers of heaven; Richard is still the king of England!"

A tumultuous confusion instantly took place; prince John issued a command for Matilda's person to be seized; but the friends of

Richard rallied round her too formidably for the mandate to be put into effect: the prince's party chafed at the unexpected opposition which had arisen to the attempt of him through whom they were all looking forward to an increase of rank or wealth, rushed with the fury of lions upon those who had lately ventured to declare themselves their enemies; and a bloody conflict ensued; the adherents of Richard were however victorious; and Matilda was borne away by them in triumph from the field of danger.

CHAP. XVII.

> Once more we sit on England's royal throne,
> Re-purchas'd with the blood of enemies.
> What valiant foe-men, like to autumn's corn,
> Have we mow'd down, in top of all their pride?
> Thus have we swept suspicion from our seat,
> And made our footstool of security.
>
> SHAKESPEARE.*

PRINCE John retired to the bosom of his adherents not less astonished than dismayed at the transactions of the day; and still more spirit-broken did he become when he learnt from authority of an undoubted nature, the existence of his brother at the monastery of St. Michael; and the various powers throughout the kingdom which had declared themselves his supporters.

He passed his days in agony and dread; the owners of only three castles, offered themselves as the strenuous adherents of his cause, and these promised to live or die with their prince; the foremost of these was the earl of Nottingham; and to his castle accordingly prince John retired, although now disposed within his own heart rather to yield the contest than to uphold it.

Richard, in the mean while, in the seclusion of the monastery of St. Michael, awaited the event of the day, utterly ignorant what consequence he had to expect from the mysterious manner in which Matilda had left him; but what language can describe the emotion of his soul, when a messenger whose courser was wet with foam, arrived at the gates of the monastery, and announced to him, that two-thirds of his kingdom, were already in the act of taking up arms in his cause; and that his brother's defeat was undoubted. Eagerly he inquired the means by which this soul-inspiring change had been produced; and if his feelings were already animated by the knowledge of the simple fact, with what a tumult of glorying and grateful passions did they overflow, when he learnt, that again his Matilda had been the brilliant sun of light which had chased the lowering clouds from his perspective of life.

Sinking on his knees, he exclaimed, "Oh God of almighty mercy! if in thy store of bliss, thou hast a refinement of happiness yet untasted by mortals, distil it in the gentle dews of thy favour on the head of her who stands alone, a wondrous instance of perfectness in affection!"

The transports of his bliss and gratitude being in some measure abated, he read the scrolls which had been brought him by the courier from various barons in his interest, and without delay set out to join the forces, to the command of which they invited him.

The horrors of civil war now raged with considerable violence, but their existence was happily of short duration; the inimical castles were compelled to surrender; and prince John threw himself in supplication at the feet of his brother. The generous Richard immediately raised him to his heart, and said, "Do but thou forget the days which are past, and I will not remember them."

This lenity which he extended towards all who had been his enemies, gained him many more friends than a conduct of an opposite nature would have done; and he was conducted in triumph into London; where not a voice was heard, which did not hail his return; nor an eye seen which did not beam with complacency and satisfaction at the recollection of his generous, brave, and manly conduct.

Tranquillity being now once more restored to the kingdom, Richard applied himself indefatigably to the regulation of public affairs; which he found in a state of disorder that required his undivided attention.

Amongst the tumult of cares which occupied his mind, he did not forget the man who had exposed his life to peril for the deliverance of his king from imprisonment; and immediately dispatched emissaries to the emperor Henry, with unlimited offers of ransom, for the immediate liberation of Sir Eugene de Lancy; the terms of which were rendered very easy to be agreed upon by the emperor's present want of subsidies for the religious purpose which was agitating his mind.

Richard had not been more than one week at his palace when he was apprized that he had on a certain day to expect a visit from a deputation of the nobles of the realm; he could not guess for what purpose they were appointed to wait upon him; and with no small degree of curiosity expected their coming. With the utmost humility and respect they entered his presence; and the explanation of their mission filled him with sensations of an unpleasant nature, which he had not judged it possible for any event to communicate to his feelings at the moment of his present joy and triumph. In the name of his kingdom they came to implore of him to form an alliance of marriage; as his subjects were desirous of an immediate heir descending from him, who might succeed him on his throne.

What answer could he return? He had pronounced a vow of the most solemn nature, never to marry any other woman than Matilda. There was little hope he feared and conceived of turning her from her determination of never becoming his queen. After some deliberation with his own mind, he requested twenty days, in the course of which to return his reply; his request was granted to him, and the emissaries departed.

Richard had not beheld Matilda since the period of her quitting the monastery of St. Michael; from the council at Wallingford she had immediately retired to the convent of St. Ursula; thither he resolved without delay to repair; it was possible she might by this demand on the part of the realm, be induced to bestow on him her hand—she was now the fixed arbitress of his fate; and by her decision he resolved to reject, or to comply with the entreaty of his subjects.

CHAP. XVIII.

Oh why do wretched men so much desire
 To draw their days unto the utmost date,
And do not rather wish them soon expire
Knowing the misery of their estate,
And thousand perils which them still await.

SPENCER.*

WITH a heavy heart did Richard proceed towards the convent of St. Ursula. Every additional moment of reflection with his own mind, determined him more strongly than ever not to give his hand to any other woman whilst Matilda lived; "My vow," he exclaimed, "I will never forsake; if she refuses to become my queen I will sooner yield the throne of England to my brother, than retain my sceptre at the expense of my plighted faith!"

On reaching the holy mansion, and inquiring for her in whom his soul was wrapt, of the abbess who met him at the gate, his heart sunk within him at the downcast countenance, and the hesitation with which she replied to his question.

"What, what affects you?" he cried. "Oh explain to me these signs of horror! What dreadful intelligence is it that you linger thus in unfolding to me? Say, she is not dead; or if she be, then rest for ever mute; let not her adored name again resound on my distracted senses."

"Oh, no, no!" replied the abbess, "the ardour of your feelings leads you to entertain fears too sensitive—Matilda is ill, very ill; the violent exertions which she has lately undergone have been too much for her strength; a fever preys upon her, and"———

"Lead me instantly to her," exclaimed the king, "I alone must be her nurse; what she has undergone for me, requires as its recompence, the attendance of a slave, and I shall glory to become it."

The abbess withheld him from proceeding to Matilda's apartment, "You must not, indeed you must not go to her," she said, "it would afflict you to behold her; and render no consolation or service to her."

"What! would it not console her to behold her Richard?" he asked.

"She would not be sensible of your presence," replied Corally, "her brain is suffering under a temporary derangement, produced by the violence of her disorder."

"Oh Matilda! Matilda!" groaned forth the king, and clasping his hands in agony together, he sunk upon a chair, where he remained for some moments the silent effigy of sorrowing madness; suddenly starting up again, he cried, "It is her affection for me which has driven her to this calamitous state, and shall any power withhold me from visiting her sick couch?"

The efforts of the abbess were now unable to restrain his steps, and he flew to the chamber where Matilda lay.

He found the confessor of the house praying by her side; and several of the sisters watching over her;—a convulsive laugh was bursting from her lips, with which she mingled these words—"He is king again; I crowned him; they had shut him up in a prison, but I opened the door for him; Oh! joy! joy! joy!" Her laugh now increased to a painful violence; she then paused a few moments, and beckoning towards her one of the sisters, she said, "Do you know how I made him king again? I'll tell you; I sung thus to him,

'I've stray'd o'er the wold, and I've stray'd o'er the wild.'"

In notes of the sweetest kind she repeated the burden of her song; and when she had concluded it, she sunk back upon her pillow with a faint smile of satisfaction.

Richard could no longer restrain his feelings, he darted towards the bed, and leaning forward to observe her, he said, "Matilda! Matilda! dost thee not know me?"

She turned her eyes upon him—a shriek burst from her lips, "Oh yes," she said, "you are Eleanor; pray put up your dagger; I have not wronged you, though my mother did! Oh pray, pray take it away; the warm drops of Rosamond's blood trickle from the point upon my breast!"

This was a scene not to be borne by a heart animated with the feelings of Richard's, "Oh God!" he exclaimed, "why was this angel ever permitted to know me? for me, her delicate frame has undergone exertions which are now working her own destruction! Oh father! mother! Rosamond! what have ye to answer for? You have all lent your aid to pile sorrow upon the head of this innocent being! Great, Oh Matilda must be thy reward in heaven!"

Once more he addressed her; and in the hope of attracting her attention, and explaining to her who he was, he said, "Can Reginald do aught to serve thee, lovely maid?"

"Reginald!" she cried; "Reginald!" she repeated. "Oh my father, you need not distrust Reginald; he has a heart so noble, so brave, so generous, I could die for happiness!"

The tears gushed into the eyes of Richard, and with a hasty step, he quitted the chamber.

Unmarked by any change in the suffering Matilda, passed four days after the arrival of Richard at the convent; with the commencement of the fifth, the power of medicine assisted by the mercy of heaven, began to triumph over her disorder, and she was blessed by a gradual return to reason and apparent convalescence.

The soul of Richard was now the seat of boundless rapture; Matilda again recognized him, and received his attendance upon her with delight and gratitude. She possessed no recollection of the wanderings of her lately unsettled mind; but was only conscious that a severe illness had attacked her; and very unwilling to allow that it had been produced by the exertions to which her excessive affection for the king had prompted her in his cause.

About this time Sir Eugene de Lancy, liberated from Trivallis, by the ransom paid for his enlargement by the king, arrived in England, and immediately on his arrival came to the convent of St. Ursula; whither he was drawn, not less by a desire of beholding Matilda; the report of whose ill state of health gave him great concern; than by the respect which he considered it becoming in him to pay the king, by throwing himself at his feet, without delay.

Matilda felt extreme pleasure at his visit, and pressed his stay; and that he was respected by Matilda, would have been a sufficient motive for the king to have beheld him likewise with respect, had he not been indebted to him for the instance of disinterested loyalty which he had displayed to him on the continent.

But three days were now wanting to the period at which Richard had voluntarily promised to return his reply to the question, which had by the voice of his realm been submitted to his decision. He hoped that Matilda had now gained sufficient strength to be capable of enduring the agitation of mind which he was conscious that the subject on which he was doomed to address her, would not fail to excite in her; at the interesting moment of this disclosure, he considered that the presence of a friend might be of material service in sustaining her spirits; and knowing the friendship which she bore Sir Eugene, he engaged him to be a witness of their conversation.

Having made this arrangement, he reflected that the presence of one of Matilda's own sex would perhaps be more congenial to her feelings; the princess Jane was now beyond the reach of this friendly office; next to her in esteem he believed Matilda to hold the abbess Corally; to her accordingly he imparted the subject which filled his mind, and requested her attendance likewise.

Corally hung down her head despondingly, and said, "Is it not possible that you can for some time longer defer the reference of this perplexing point to Matilda's decision?"

"It cannot be," replied the king, "I have deferred it to the latest moment to which I could protract it; I shall now barely keep within the limits of the covenant which I have made with my subjects."

"It must then be done!"said Corally, "but Oh, as you value the health of your Matilda, use every gentleness in opening to her this subject; her strength is by no means restored; the roses which deck her cheeks are but the flushes of inward weakness; and the spirits which she possesses in your presence, are produced by exertions much too powerful for her debilitated frame; and owe their being to the excessive joy with which your attentions fill her heart."

Richard hoped, and believed that Corally's fears were too great; whilst he respected her more than ever, for the anxiety with which they expressed her to be watching over the recovery of his Matilda.

Accompanied accordingly by the abbess and Sir Eugene, he entered Matilda's apartment; it was the last hour of the afternoon; Matilda was just arisen from a short slumber with which she had been refreshing the weakness of nature; her dress was the emblem of the most innocent simplicity; and Richard conceived that he had never yet seen her so lovely: the effects of her illness had rendered even fairer than its usual hue, the complexion of her face and neck—a deceitful colour gave beauty to her cheeks, and animation to her eye; she smiled at the approach of the king; it was a smile which communicated joy to *his* heart only; to that of Corally, it conveyed an apprehension of a most painful nature; she could not forbear imagining that she saw in it, the ghastly omen of approaching dissolution.

At the desire of the king, Sir Eugene de Lancy explained the subject upon which they were met; with a considerable degree of agitation visible upon her countenance, Matilda listened to the demand which had been made of the king by his subjects; when De Lancy had ceased speaking, she clasped together her hands, and raising them towards heaven as she spoke, she said, "May the almighty God shower down his blessings on Richard's queen!!"

"Thy prayer be heard!" exclaimed the king, "thou knowest my choice—it is thyself; thou knowest my vow, *I cannot* wed any other woman than thyself; now hear once more the sentiments of my heart—*I will not* wed any other woman than thyself."

A crimson flush spread itself over the countenance of Matilda; suddenly it again died away; she made several efforts to speak, but in vain; she pressed the hand of Richard in hers; by a momentary effort of her little remaining strength, she sunk on her knees before him—"Richard," she said, "Matilda exhorts thee to wed."

The king raised her from the ground, and placed her in her seat; during this action, a faint but labouring sigh escaped her bosom—her head sunk upon the breast of the abbess, who had placed herself behind her couch—she raised her eyes for an instant to heaven, as if to implore that it would second the entreaty which she had made to Richard—a faint murmur passed her lips—she ceased to breathe.

The fears of the abbess were realized; Matilda had been too weak for the conflicting sensations produced in her mind by the decision submitted to her voice; her worn-down faculties had sunk under the exertion—and her spirit had fled before the tumult of her soul.

* * * * * *

For a considerable time the senses of Richard were incredulous of the dreadful, the heart-rending fact which his eyes beheld—with a deep and lengthened groan he then sunk to the earth, "I am the murderer of Matilda!" burst in low, but frantic accents from his lips—"curse me heaven; it is I who have murdered my preserver."

Having uttered these words, no other sound escaped from his tongue: he was conveyed to a couch in an adjoining apartment, where his breathings alone announced that animation had not fled from him likewise, as it had done from his Matilda. In this dreadful state of silence and inaction, from which his friends dreaded a worse event, than they would have done from an open violence of grief, were passed by Richard the whole of that night, and of the succeeding day; in the middle of the second night, he awoke as from a fevered dream; raving he called on the spirit of Matilda to descend from its present state of bliss, and upbraid him with her death; at the next instant he was distrustful of her not being still in existence, and intemperate in his rage against those who refused to lead him into her presence; and these efforts of violence were succeeded by floods of tears.

When the tolling bell sounded with mournful solemnity for the interment of the peerless maid, the delicacy of whose virtue had determined her to refuse the participation of a throne, Richard had not yet quitted the chamber to which he had been conveyed immediately after her death; he now sprung from his couch, and darted wildly away from his attendants; the chaunting voices of the nuns, drew his steps towards the cloisters of the convent, and as he entered them, he observed the first dust thrown upon the coffin of that being, supreme in earthly perfection, whose loss he was doomed for ever to mourn; but his grief did not gain violence from the affecting sight; in contemplating the last earthly office which was performing for her, he appeared to sink into a stupefaction of intellect—he gazed intently; but neither sigh escaped his lips, nor tear stole down his cheek.

The ceremony being concluded, and the king led back into the convent, he addressed Sir Eugene de Lancy, and such others of his friends as were present with him. "From this instant," he said in a voice of mingled solemnity and woe, "I discard every private affection from my breast, they are not comforts, they are deceptions to lead man on to madness; henceforth, one love alone shall animate my breast; that which as the father of my people, I am called upon by the voice of justice to bear to my children. Away, my friends, and announce to my realm, that I am ready to submit to its inclinations, whatever they may be; Richard lives only for his kingdom; and welcome will be the hand of death, when it releases him from the bondage of life!"

He was faithful to this promise made to his subjects; and after a few years passed in corroding grief, and silent agonies of mind, his earthly endurances were terminated by a shot from a bow in France, where he was defending one of his possessions from invasion; and where he died with the same magnanimity and heroism, which had in his lifetime acquired him the title of Cœur de Lion.

In the fate of Matilda and her Richard, may the seducer learn the uncounted miseries which flow from an infringement on the sacred honours of the marriage bed! may he believe that whilst there is an undoubted reward prepared in heaven for those who have innocently suffered, there cannot fail to be punishment in store for those who have been the criminal origin of their affections. There is no distinction in the grave; nor will there be any distinction of persons beyond it. A crime perpetrated by a monarch is not less a crime, than one of which the meanest of his subjects may have been guilty—not the rank of the person, but the virtues of the heart will be inquired into at the hour of universal retribution. The lesson before us applies therefore equally to the king and to the beggar; and happy will be the weak hand which has recorded it, if in either it check the first step toward the indulgence of a vicious inclination.

THE END.

NOTES

PAGE

3 Shakespeare, *Twelfth Night*, Act I, Scene I, ll. 1-7. The original reads: 'If music be the food of love, play on, | Give me excess of it; that surfeiting, | The appetite may sicken and so die. | That strain again, it had a dying fall; | O, it came o'er my ear like the sweet sound | That breathes upon a bank of violets, | Stealing and giving odor'. In common with many eighteenth-century and Romantic Gothic novelists, Lathom prefaces each chapter with dramatic or poetic passages that are designed to set the tone and theme of each chapter. Where the original differs substantially from Lathom's version I have quoted the original in the notes.

5 Henry II of England (1133-1189, reigned 1154-1189). The time at which the story is set would therefore be 1188.

8 Shakespeare, *Hamlet*, Act I, scene V, ll. 15-16.

8 Lathom possibly means an oriel window here, which is a small window that projects out in a semi-circle from a building, typical of the Gothic revival style.

9 The week referred to here is Passion Week, the fifth week of Lent which begins with Passion Sunday and ends with Palm Sunday.

11 *The Oxford Dictionary of National Biography* suggests that Samuel Taylor Coleridge named the eponymous heroine of his Gothic poem, 'Christabel', after reading *The Fatal Vow*. However, it is generally accepted that Coleridge was writing 'Christabel' in 1798, nine years *before* Lathom's novel was published, so this claim is unlikely. I have been unable to find any evidence that Coleridge had read Lathom's novel, although he read other Gothic novels such as Ann Radcliffe's work.

11 Shakespeare, *Antony and Cleopatra*, Act III, Scene XIII, ll.31-34.

15 A cottage.

19 Shakespeare, *The Tempest*, Act I, Scene II, ll.419-421.

19 An early morning church service.

22 A church service for evening prayers.

24 Lathom attributes this quotation to Walpole; however I am unable to find it in Walpole's Gothic drama, *The Mysterious Mother*. These lines do, however, appear on the title page of Ann Radcliffe's *The Italian* (1797) and are probably by Radcliffe herself.

28 Shakespeare, *The Tempest*, Act I, Scene II, ll.445-448.

33 Shakespeare, *King John*, Act III, Scene I, ll.29-30.

33 A league is approximately five kilometres or three miles.

36 Stained.

38 Shakespeare, *Romeo and Juliet*, Act II, Scene II, ll.126-128. Lathom misquotes the original: Juliet: 'What satisfaction canst thou have to-night?/ Romeo: 'Th'exchange of thy love's faithful vow for mine.'

41 William II (c.1060-1100), often called William Rufus because of his red face, was the third son of William the Conqueror and ruled as King of England from 1087-1100.

43 Shakespeare, *Romeo and Juliet*, Act II, Scene VI, ll. 32-34.

48 John Milton, *Comus*. The original reads: 'I under fair pretence of friendly ends, | And well-placed words of glozing courtesy | Baited with reasons not unplausible | Wind me into the easy-hearted man, | And hug him into snares' (ll.160-64). The supernatural power of Comus to assume another appearance (he describes himself as the son of the witch Circe) parallels the deceptiveness of Satan in *Paradise Lost*.

53 Alexander Pope, *Eloisa to Abelard*, ll.21-24.

54 A cloak made of woollen cloth.

60 Prince John, youngest son of Henry II (1166-1216). John became King in 1199 after Richard I (Richard Coeur de Lion) although he tried to wrest power from the throne while Richard was in Palestine on the Crusades. Prince John was known as John the Bad (reigned 1199-1216). Corally's earlier comment to Christabelle, that she may be at the mercy of the "irreligious" army camped near to the convent possibly refers to when John split with the Church of Rome, and closed down the churches. See note below.

60 Commonly known as 'Bad King John', John was the youngest of the five sons of Henry II and Eleanor of Aquitaine. He is best remembered, along with the Sheriff of Nottingham, for being the enemy of the now legendary Robin Hood, for establishing the Royal Navy at Portsmouth, and for agreeing (by force) to sign Magna Carta. The nephew of Richard I, Arthur of Brittany, joined forces with Philip II of France to fight against John's claim to the English throne when Richard died in 1199. The preparations for war that Corally is describing to Christabelle occur ten years later than the time in which the events of the novel take place. In 1188, Richard had not yet become King.

60 Corally's lover, Ranulph, may be named after Ranulf de Glanvil, Lord Chief Justice of Henry II who wrote one of the earliest treatises on English law and jurisprudence.

61 Henry Jones (1721-1770), *The Earl of Essex: A Tragedy* (1753), Act II. The

original lines are spoken by the Earl of Essex to Lady Rutland and read: 'Then let us hence from this detested Place; | My rescu'd Soul disclaims the House of Greatness, | Where humble Honesty can find no Shelter. | From hence we'll fly, where Love and Virtue call, | Where Happiness invites,—that Wish of all'.

68 Shakespeare, *Richard II*, Act II, Scene II, ll. 1-6.

68 I discuss the question of how Lathom's novel is situated in both the context of the historical novel and Romantic depictions of Richard the Lionheart in the introduction.

68 Henry II (1133-1189) was the first Plantagenet monarch, and the first ruler to use the title 'King of England'.

69 Lathom's spelling. Eleanor of Aquitaine (1122-1204), wife of Henry II. After Elizabeth I, one of the most powerful queens in English history, and one of the wealthiest women in Europe in the Middle Ages.

69 Lathom's spelling. Louis VII (1120-1180), King of France from 1137, the same year he married Eleanor.

70 Empress Matilda, or Maude (1102-1167). Although she was never crowned, Matilda was, effectively, the first female ruler of England for a brief period in 1141, when she seized power from her cousin, Stephen. However, standard histories list Stephen as ruler (1135-1154).

70 Stephen (1096-1154), predecessor to Henry II, is now remembered for 'The Anarchy', a period of civil war and unrest in his struggle with Matilda who claimed he had stolen the throne from her as rightful inheritor.

71 Prince Owen Gwynedd, (d.1169) ruled North Wales for thirty two years.

71 van: Vanguard.

71 fastnesses: A medievalism for vast.

73 Simon IV de Montfort (later the 5th Earl of Leicester) was a French nobleman in the court of Henry II and lived through Richard and John's reigns (1160-1218). Lathom's dating is troublesome here, as Henry II invaded Powys in Wales in 1165, which would make Montfort just five years old. Possibly Geoffrey de Mandeville (2nd Earl of Essex, d.1169), but Lathom is more likely to have in mind William de Mandeville (3rd Earl of Essex, d.1189). However, William de Mandeville was a loyal supporter of Henry II, and later, Richard I.

74 A quoit is a flat disc of stone or metal. A game of quoits refers to throwing quoits, with the aim of hitting the target of an iron peg fixed in the ground.

75 Shakespeare, *Coriolanus*, Act IV, Scene IV, l.12.

75 William IV, Count of Toulouse (c.1040-1094). William's daughter and heiress, Philippa, married William IX of Aquitaine (Eleanor's grandfather); it was through this bloodline that Eleanor claimed the region of Toulouse. When William IV fought in the Crusades, his brother, Raymond de Saint-Gilles governed in his absence. Raymond claimed the throne after William was killed abroad. Raymond's claim to the throne was contested by Philippa, and later, Eleanor.

77 In Middle English, this meant a lack of self-restraint regarding sexual matters.

78 Lathom is possibly referring to Joan of England (1165-1199), Henry and Eleanor's seventh child, and later Queen of Sicily (1177). She was the elder sister of John. There is no record of a child called Jane.

79 Henry was the second son of Henry II. He was made Henry the Young King in 1160 at Winchester and should not be confused with Henry III, who was his nephew.

79 Margaret of France (1157-1197), the eldest daughter of Louis VII, and married to Henry the Young King, at the age of five and two years old respectively.

81 Rosamond de Clifford (1150?-1176), the most famous mistress of Henry II. Speculation continues over whether or not Rosamond had a child by Henry. And fictional speculation that Eleanor arranged for Rosamond to be murdered continues to this day, for example most recently in Ariana Franklin's 2008 novel *The Death Maze* (in the United States, *The Serpent's Tale*).

83 William Collins, 'The Passions: An Ode for Music', ll. 39-45

83 Adelais is Lathom's name for Alys (Alice), Louis VII's second daughter. The betrothal took place in 1169. Bordesley Abbey, in Worcestershire, patronized by Empress Matilda (see above). The abbey was dissolved under Henry VIII.

85 Beaumont Palace, Oxford, built by Henry I around 1130.

91 Henry Jones, *The Earl of Essex. A Tragedy*, Act II, Scene I, ll. 99-101.

92 Maud (Matilda), Duchess of Saxony (1159-1189); Eleanor, Queen of Castile and Toledo (1164-1214) was married to Alfonso VIII of Castile. See note for Jane above.

101 Joseph Addison, *Cato*, Act IV, scene I. Lathom's conflates two speeches of Juba and Marcia.

104 William Collins, 'The Passions: An Ode for Music', ll.53-54.

105 The hunting lodge of Woodstock and its garden, "Rosamond's Bower", were demolished when Blenheim Palace was built on the site in the early eighteenth century.

111 Nathaniel Lee, *Alexander the Great, or, The Rival Queens*, Act V, Scene II, ll.16-19.

113 Thomas Beckett's tomb at Canterbury Cathedral.
118 A belt or a girdle.
120 Shakespeare, *Richard III*, Act IV, Scene I, ll.195-197. The original reads: 'Erroneous vassals! The great King of kings | Hath in the table of his law commanded | That thou shalt do no murther'.
133 Shakespeare, *Othello*, Act IV, Scene II. Lathom here condenses two speeches of Othello to Desdemona when he confronts her with his suspicions that she is having an affair with Cassio.
133 Walter de Clifford (1113-1190).
134 Henry I of France (1008-1060, reigned from 1031).
134 Rosamond's marriage to this distant cousin of her father's appears to be an invention on Lathom's part. Lathom may have been inspired by the figure of Robert de Clifford (known as Robert the Brave). However, Robert de Clifford was created the 1st Baron de Clifford in 1299, some hundred years later to the time of the novel.
140 Shakespeare, *Henry VI*, Part III, Act V, Scene II, ll.16-18 and 23-26.
146 Shakespeare, *Henry VIII*, Act III, Scene II, ll.222-225.
150 Shakespeare, *Henry VIII*, Act II, Scene I, ll.90-94.
150 Henry was defeated by the combined forces of Richard the Lionheart and Philip II of France (1165-1223) at Le Mans in 1189. He died at Chinon castle, in the Loire region of France.
157 Shakespeare, *Two Gentleman of Verona*, Act III, Scene I, ll.248-249.
159 Richard I, Philip II and Frederick I of Barbarossa went on the Third Crusade in 1189. Richard and Philip travelled together from Vezelay. They then went their separate ways at Lyons, reuniting at Messina in Sicily. Here their armies encamped for the winter before embarking for the Siege of Acre in Palestine, in 1190.
161 Tancred (1138-1194), 'Count of Lecce' and King of Sicily (1189-1194). Joan (Jane in the novel), Richard's sister, was married to William II of Sicily. After William died in 1189, Tancred seized the throne and imprisoned Joan. The presence of Richard and Philip's armies in Messina caused popular unrest and revolt, which Richard responded to by sacking Messina and forcing Tancred to agree to a treaty that released his sister Joan.
161 Isaac Komnenos, Emperor of Cyprus (c.1155-1196).
162 Saladin (1138-1193), 1st Sultan of Egypt and Syria. A Sunni, Saladin led the Muslim and Arabic opposition against the Crusades and was respected for his chivalry.
162 Leopold V, Duke of Austria (1157-1194) arrived in Acre in 1191. When Acre surrendered, Richard took down the standard of Leopold's army. Leopold also suspected Richard of murdering his cousin,

Conrad, who was made King of Jerusalem. Returning through Austria in disguise, Richard was spotted near Vienna and imprisoned in Dürnstein Castle, and was then removed into the custody of the Holy Roman Emperor, Henry VI, at Triefels Castle, a remote castle in Germany.

163 John Hughes, *The Siege of Damascus*, Act II, Scene I.

172 Nicholas Rowe, *Tamerlane*, Act II, Scene II, ll. 56-61. The first version of the play reads: '. . . and tho' Fortune | (Curse on that Changeling Deity of Fools) | Has stript me of the Train, and Pomp of Greatness, | That Outside of a King, yet still my Soul, | Fixt high, and of itself alone dependant, | Is ever free, and royal'. I am indebted to Michael Caines at King's College London for tracing this quotation.

174 Lathom spells Triefels castle as Trivallis. Triefels castle (literally 'three rocks') is in the Vosges mountain range and it stands on one of the three rocks, 500m above sea level, in a remote part of the Tyrol. A castle worthy of a Gothic novel.

178 Shakespeare, *Twelfth Night*, Act III, scene I, ll.146-150. The original reads: 'Cesario, by the roses of spring | By maidhood, honor, truth, and every thing, | I love thee so, that maugre all thy pride, | Nor wit nor reason can my passion hide'.

180 The character of Zulima is perhaps inspired by that of Selima, from Nicholas Rowe's *Tamerlane* (1702).

186 Shakespeare, *The Taming of the Shrew*, Act IV, scene III, ll.172-180.

194 Shakespeare, *The Taming of the Shrew,* Act V, scene I, ll.127-128.

201 Thomas Southern, *Oronooko*, Act III, scene IV.

202 An abbreviation for 'By God's wounds'; an expression commonly found in Shakespeare.

203 The *Shorter Oxford English Dictionary* lists 'choused' as a variant of the noun 'chiaus' 'after a Turk who received hospitality in England after claiming to be a messenger or ambassador of the Sultan'. Thelk uses the word in its sense of a person who is easily cheated, duped or tricked.

206 Nicholas Rowe, *Lady Jane Gray*, Act I, Scene I.

213 Colley Cibber, *Ximena; or, The Heroick Daughter* (1719), Act V, scene III.

218 Shakespeare, *Henry VIII*, Act III, Scene II, ll.352-358. The original reads: 'This is the state of man: to-day he puts forth | The tender leaves of hopes, to-morrow blossoms, | And bears his blushing honors thick upon him; |The third day comes a frost, a killing frost, And when he thinks, good easy man, full surely | His greatness is a-ripening, nips his root, | And then he falls as I do.'

222 Shakespeare, *King John*, Act III, scene IV, ll.107-109.

226 Shakespeare, *Henry VI* (Part 2), Act III, scene II, ll.232-235.
231 William Shakespeare, *Henry VI* (Part III), Act V, scene VII, ll. 1-4, and ll.15-16.
234 Edmund Spenser, *The Faerie Queene*, Book IV, Canto III, ll.1-6.

APPENDIX: CONTEMPORARY REVIEWS

Critical Review, 3rd series, 13 (Jan. 1808), p.105

This is by far the least interesting of any of the productions of this author. The story of Fair Rosamond, on which it is founded, is so threadbare and hacknied, that the reader, anticipating every incident, derives very little satisfaction from the denouement. The language is as usual very careless, and in many places, ungrammatical. The generous remark which Richard Cœur de Lion made when he pardoned his brother John, 'I wish I could as easily forget my brother's offence, as he will my pardon,' Mr. Lathom thus miserably alters, 'Do but thou forget the days which are past, and I will not remember them.'

Flowers of Literature (1807): pp. 52-53

In this department of literature [i.e. novels] we have had, as usual, a most abundant harvest, and we may justly say, that the crop is altogether more favourable than that of many a preceding season. We have always been of the opinion, that none but an author of *talents* can write a good novel; and however affected cynics, of the modern stamp, may pretend to *despise* such productions, we will contend, as we always have contended, that well-written novels and romances do more to improve the taste, and correct the aberrations of the heart, than all the other species of writing in congregation! If such impassioned females as *Rosa Matilda*, and such immoral and *delicately-obscene* scribblers as Messrs *Monk*-Lewis and *Anacreon*-Moore, have disgraced the English press by their *prosaic* and *poetical* masses of corruption, issued as they are year after year, shall it be said that they have affixed a stigma to *all works of fancy*? The genius of elegant literature forbids the prevalence of such an opinion; and while our country can produce such novels as Lathom's *Fatal Vow*, no reader, whether male or female, need be ashamed to place it in their library. Those novels in which history is judiciously blended with fiction, are of all others best calculated to please the mind of sensibility; and if in the one just mentioned, we have anything to object to, it is, that the quantity of historical matter is too great, and also too highly coloured to accord with facts. Nothing, however, can be more interesting than many of the scenes in this work, though it only consists of two volumes. The manner in which Christabelle discovers her mother, is a masterpiece of delineation, and when we consider the great versatility of this author's genius, we shall readily look over such anachronisms as the production of *pistols*, before the period at which they were invented!

***Monthly Review*, 2nd series, 58, (Feb 1809): pp. 216-217**

As this Romance is founded on historical facts, and embraces a period which includes part of the reign of Henry II and Richard I, the fate of Rosamond, the prowess of Richard in Palestine, and his subsequent imprisonment in his way home are therefore prominent features in the Tale. In the relation, however, as is always the case in these productions, the author does not hesitate to depart from historic truth, whenever it suits his purpose. And although he has made an amusing story, the pleasure derived in the perusal is considerably diminished. Even in works of this nature, the facts which are disputable, yet generally received, should not be altered on slight grounds. And those which have been handed down to us by respectable historians as undoubted truths should not by any means be perverted.

'Historical Romances,' Mr. Lathom says, 'are the taste of the times, and he thinks it a sufficient sanction for an author, whose remuneration is to arise from gratifying the public taste, to apply his pen to such subjects as interest the feelings of the majority'. It is surely the duty of an author rather to correct the taste of the times, than to regard it as a sufficient sanction for adopting a species of writing, of the propriety of which he has any doubt. And how can he avow himself an observer of morality, while at the same time he is violating truth?

Annual Review and History of Literature, 6 (Jan 1807), p. 666

The first twelve chapters of the Fatal Vow are singularly interesting and romantic: the discovery of her mother by Christabel, is pathetic; the character of Thelk is well-drawn. But there is too large an interval of historic matter, or rather of adventures ascribed to celebrated historical personages, which have no foundation in fact. Against this sort of narrative our protest shall be unrelenting. It tends to produce in the memory an inconvenient confusion of fiction and reality, and to level in the imagination the chronicles of antiquity with the fabliaux of romance. If, however, there be a period of our annals, as to which this license is tolerable, it is the reign of Henry the second. Fair Rosamond and Richard the Lionheart are already the property of the poet, and may be mingled, with little impropriety, in new scenes of invention. Yet a something of consistency with received fable is even here desirable: the desperate lion-hearted hero, the idol of an age of chivalry, was at not period of his life such a lover as Reginald de Brune. Nor is it without a disappointing effect to find a Matilda engrossing affections which conferred celebrity on Margaret of Hennegan.

The invention of this writer is admirable. Every year we have had new novels of his to announce. Yet their total dissimilarity of manner, incident, and personage render it difficult to indicate the favourite tendency of his mind. Few have composed so much and repeated themselves so little. There are some anachronisms in those stories, of which the scene is thrown far back into antiquity. In this relation, for instance, a pistol is fired, before pistols were in use. They came into vogue in the reign of Henry the Second of France, not in that of Henry the Second of England.

www.ingramcontent.com/pod-product-compliance
Lightning Source LLC
Chambersburg PA
CBHW030810310726
48980CB00006B/452/J

* 9 7 8 1 9 3 4 5 5 5 8 8 0 *